B P Walter was born an ✄ **W9-DDF-138** ...ng his childhood and teenage years reading compulsively, he worked in bookshops then went to the University of Southampton to study Film and English followed by an MA in Film & Cultural Management. He is an alumni of the Faber Academy and currently works in social media coordination for Waterstones in London.

Also by B P Walter

A Version of the Truth

Hold Your Breath

THE DINNER GUEST

B P WALTER

One More Chapter
a division of HarperCollins*Publishers*
1 London Bridge Street
London SE1 9GF
www.harpercollins.co.uk

HarperCollins*Publishers*
1st Floor, Watermarque Building, Ringsend Road
Dublin 4, Ireland

This paperback edition 2021
First published in Great Britain in ebook format
by HarperCollins*Publishers* 2021

10

A catalogue record of this book is available from the British Library

ISBN: 978-0-00-844608-6

This novel is entirely a work of fiction. The names, characters and
incidents portrayed in it are the work of the author's imagination. Any
resemblance to actual persons, living or dead, events or localities is
entirely coincidental.

Printed and Bound in the UK using
100% Renewable Electricity at CPI Group (UK) Ltd

For Rebecca and Tom

Here on my knee I vow to God above,
I'll never pause again, never stand still,
Till either death hath closed these eyes of mine
Or fortune given me measure of revenge.

— *Henry VI*, William Shakespeare

There's a storm coming, Mr Wayne. You and your friends
better batten down the hatches, because when it hits,
you're all going to wonder how you ever thought you
could live so large and leave so little for the rest of us.

— Selina Kyle in *The Dark Knight Rises* (2012), written by
Christopher Nolan and Jonathan Nolan

Prologue

The day of the murder

My husband Matthew died on an unseasonably chilly August day at dinner time. We had been together for just over ten years, married for five, and yes, we did love each other. But love changes over time, and in those final moments when I knew he was dying, well, I must confess that through the horror and the blood and the shock, the love I felt for him wasn't quite as profound as I would have expected. Even after everything that had happened. Back when we married, the thought of losing him would have sent a wave of devastation through me. It would have been barely comprehensible. And I thought it would always be so. It took the worst to actually happen for me to realise that things don't always play out like you think.

The moment that most stuck in my mind wasn't the knife going in, nor was it the terrible sound Matthew made as he realised what had happened. It was him struggling to speak that lingered the most. He had tried to say something, something he clearly really wanted to say. And I couldn't make out the words. He couldn't form them enough to convey any meaning. I couldn't even hazard a guess. The word 'after' might have been in there, although I couldn't be sure. But it was that not knowing, that sense of frustration, and ever since, the wondering and ruminating about what it was he wanted to tell me in his final moments.

Rachel was sitting calmly on one of the dining chairs, on the phone to 999, the knife in her hand. She wasn't even supposed to be there that evening. But I'd got used to Rachel's trademark: finding a way into places, situations, and events that would otherwise go on without her. Always the outsider. Not today, though. Today she was to take a starring role.

The police, when they arrived, placed her under arrest there and then. She confessed, after all. She sat there, holding the knife, the glint of a tear in her eye. 'I did it,' she said, in a small yet confident voice. 'I killed him.'

They were about to take her away, when one of the younger of the two officers asked her the question. The multimillion-dollar question, as they say. 'Why did you kill him, Rachel?' I suspect the older of the two would have wanted to keep this kind of thing for the interview room, but still turned to hear the answer. But Rachel kept her face almost impassive. Just a tiny tremor of emotion disturbed its calm surface for a fleeting second. Then she just shook her head, and lowered it to face the floor. 'I can't,' she said. Then she refused to say any more.

They took her away, into custody, and left another officer to take me and Titus to the station in a car with flashing lights. I had to coax Titus out of his room. He was on his bed, curled up amidst the blankets, headphones on, cancelling out the horror of the world around him. He had open in front of him an old scrapbook diary. He used to make one for every school holiday, back when he was a kid. It was something Matthew's sister had done, apparently. He'd told me that, once, when we'd watched the young Titus gluing in print-outs of holiday snaps. I couldn't quite work out if he was glad the boy was so involved in the activity or troubled by it. And the fact Titus had now reached for a volume filled with happy-family photos of us all just after the scene of violence in the kitchen was unnerving to me.

'We need to go,' I said to him gently. 'The police are here. We need to go to the station now, so they can talk to us.'

The officer behind me told me that we both needed to go downstairs now. He came and stood close, making it clear we didn't have a choice.

I saw the tears slip down Titus's face, and I wanted to pull him close, tell him everything was OK. But he drew away from me.

'Please, Titus. We need to go. They've already taken Rachel.'

He looked up at this, as I suspected he would.

'Rachel confessed. She told them she did it.'

The fringe of his light-blond hair fell over his face as he straightened up, mingling with his tears.

'But … *why*?'

He mouthed this last word, silently. I stared back at him, the real question swimming in the air, unanswered, between us. *Why would Rachel confess to a murder she did not commit?*

Chapter One

CHARLIE

Eleven months to go

We first met Rachel in a bookshop. Matthew and I had gone into town, leaving Titus at home baking cakes with my mother. When we'd decided to settle in Chelsea, it was one of my fears that my mother, based in neighbouring Belgravia, would try to micromanage our lives, but we generally muddled along just fine, with her popping in a couple of times a week.

It was my idea, that sunny Sunday morning, to go into Waterstones on the King's Road. I'd wanted to pick up a pretentious-sounding hardback I'd read about in one of the morning broadsheets, more to be seen reading it than because I would enjoy it. Matthew had always been critical of this. 'You treat books like *lifestyle accessories*.' He'd said the last two words with total contempt, a knowing smirk spreading across his handsome face. He was winding me up and I took the bait, telling him that what I decided to read and why was my own business.

When we got to Waterstones, he went straight to the fantasy section, probably to pick out a book so large it could pass for a fairly effective weapon, while I browsed the table of new hardbacks. I'd found the volume I'd wanted, and was just stretching out a hand to pick it up when another collided with mine. 'Oh, sorry,' she said, laughing, pulling her hand away. I looked up at her, at her wavy blonde hair, her bright blue eyes. There was something alive about her. Cheery. Carefree. Like she'd floated in on the breeze. I saw her looking me up and down too, the way women often did. I'd noticed it throughout my entire adult life. Longer, in fact. When I was a young lad, on the rugby field or at the clubs, there'd always be someone whistling at me, or a group of girls willing to talk to me. Then, as I journeyed into adulthood, through my late twenties and now, mid-thirties, the signs of attraction had become more subtle, but they were still there. I sometimes wondered if it had damaged me somehow, being the one in my group with all the looks. *Wonder boy*, my mate Archie used to tease me, nudging me playfully as girls instantly appeared by us as we walked into bars in our late teens. He used to love 'the moment', as he used to call it, when they'd come on to me, encourage me to buy them a drink, and I'd do my best apologetic smile and tell them that I'd happily buy them a drink but I was really sorry because I was into guys rather than girls. Usually, after a moment of disappointment (which, I admit a little painfully now, used to give my ego a boost), they would remain friendly but, more often than not, transfer their attentions to Archie, or one of the other guys with me. Or sometimes they'd just stay and chat. Either was cool.

It didn't quite get to that point with Rachel. Not that I knew she was called Rachel then. She was just the woman who went to pick up the same book as me. But as our hands drew back from each other, and our eyes met, I somehow *knew* she would end up becoming part of our lives. I just didn't know quite how much.

'I'm sorry, you first,' I said, grinning at her.

Another little laugh. 'No, you, honestly.'

I shook my head. 'I'm not even sure if I'm going to buy it. You seemed more certain.' This wasn't true. I knew I was going to buy it, but it was a habit of mine, coming out with chirpy little lines. Part of my constant need to put people at ease. After a few moments, we'd started talking about the review of the book in the *Observer* and how it had also been discussed on Radio 4's *Saturday Review* the night before. She was all nods and smiles and mentioned one of the author's other books, but I confessed I hadn't read any of them. 'My husband's the real reader,' I said, nodding over to where Matthew was, now browsing the buy-one-get-one-half-price paperback tables. 'Mostly fantasy stuff, but other books too.'

There it was. That very slight flicker in the eyes. I thought at the time it was the typical mild-to-moderate disappointment to hear I was married, coupled with the further surprise that I was married to a bloke. But of course, in retrospect, I know it was something more sinister than that. In that moment, however, it was another little boost to my ego. I'd once told Matthew about the double-no-chance disappointment theory and how I was sure I saw it in women's eyes every time. We'd been out with the guys, Archie and George next to us getting steadily drunk, and I'd expected them all to laugh, but Matthew hadn't. He'd just shaken his head and said, 'Please, please, please, my love, never presume to have an insight into how women think. It isn't endearing.' He'd laid a hand on my knee in semi-mock seriousness. 'Why not?' I'd asked, surprised by his comment. 'Because it sounds self-satisfied and patronising and maybe a little bit sexist.' And with that, he'd gone to fetch another round of pints, leaving me to look at the other two with confusion.

Because of all this, I hadn't planned to mention to Matthew the woman in Waterstones. We'd said our goodbyes and she'd gone off to purchase the large tome and I'd continued to browse, with the book under my arm. But then we'd bumped into each other again, just half an hour later, in the food section at Marks & Spencer's across the road. *What are the chances?* I'd thought to myself. She was balancing two packets of halloumi on top of a punnet of raspberries. 'Interesting combination,' I commented to her. That cool, breezy laugh came out again. And then, because it would have been strange and awkward not to, I'd introduced her to Matthew and she said hi and that was when I realised I didn't actually know her name, nor she mine. 'I'm Rachel,' she said. 'I've just moved to the area.'

'From the North?' I asked, then added, 'Sorry, I noticed the accent.'

There was a little falter in her response – maybe the

presumption had irritated her – but she still replied with a smile. 'Yes, Yorkshire.'

Matthew nodded. 'Very nice.'

Even I, the most personable, at-ease-with-himself guy you could ever hope to bump into, had started to wonder by this point how we were going to finish this without it seeming weird. Just because it was something to say, I bobbed my head towards her Waterstones carrier bag, slung under her arm, the corners of a hardback digging in a little to her bare arms. 'I see you got more than just our shared choice of interest.'

She peered down at the bag, as if she'd only just noticed it, and one of the halloumi packets went bouncing along the aisle. Once Matthew had caught it, after some awkward chuckling, she pulled out a few of her purchases. 'The guy at the counter said these were good.' I looked at the covers: traditional book-club-esque crime-fiction. More Matthew's sort of thing than mine.

'Oh, we've got this one coming up for our next reading group meeting,' he said, pointing at the blue one with a lighthouse and the silhouette profile of a woman on the cover.

'Oh, what a coincidence. I'm looking forward to starting it.'

'You should come,' he said enthusiastically. 'We're always looking for new members.'

What the fuck? There's friendly, and then there's weird. This random woman didn't need an invite to his book club. I cringed inwardly at the oddness of it, but to my surprise, she didn't shrink away, saying she'd got a lot on and it was a nice thought but she was OK thank you – none of that. She actually smiled and nodded, her eyes wide. 'That would be brilliant. If you don't mind me gate-crashing.'

'You wouldn't be gate-crashing at all,' he said, waving away her protests. 'It's just me and a few friends.'

'That sounds great,' she said, still nodding.

'They're a bit older than … well, than us, but we're all great fiction-lovers. You may have heard of one of them … Jerome Nightly? He's an actor. Was in a lot of those British romcoms back in the early noughties.'

Rachel had clearly heard of him. 'Oh yes, wow … I don't think of actors doing normal things like going to book clubs.'

'Turns out they're just human after all,' Matthew said, and they both laughed. And then it was settled. She got out her phone. He got out his phone. Numbers were swapped. And there was me, staring on, like a fucking nobody, while the two of them made their arrangements. 'It's at our house on Carlyle Square, the next meeting,' explained Matthew. 'Everyone normally arrives around 7pm. We take it in turns to host, but don't feel you have to.' He then gave her our home address – to a total stranger, the address where the two of us and our son lived and slept – and then it was time to say goodbye.

'Looking forward to it,' Rachel called after us. 'This has made my week.' She then vanished in the direction of the tills.

'Well, that was nice,' said Matthew, looking genuinely happy, apparently pleased to have made a new friend amidst the refrigerated food aisles. I give him a quick smile in return, and put a pack of gourmet burgers in our trolley.

'What?' Matthew asked. He knew I was a little pissed about the whole exchange; well, pissed was the wrong word, really. Bemused, maybe. Anyhow, I just found the whole thing a bit … fast. And there was something a little odd about the way she'd immediately leaped on the idea of joining a book club, to the point of arranging to come over to our house in two weeks' time.

'Nothing,' I said, with a little shake of my head. I saw him roll his eyes at this point, which riled me a little more.

We walked the shopping back to the house in near silence. The only words Matthew came out with were a comment that the Croftfield family across the same square as us had just got a new BMW hybrid. Inside, we found Titus had baked two cakes as well as a tray of cookies and my mother was already enjoying a slice of the lemon drizzle, settled on one of the breakfast-bar seats, with *Desert Island Discs* blasting out of the sound system in the lounge.

'Grandma did the icing,' Titus declared, pushing the stand holding the cake towards me as I came towards her. 'But I did the cakes of course.'

'It all looks delicious,' I said. 'Can we have a photo?'

I heard my mother sniff disapprovingly.

'You don't have to actually be *in* the photo,' I said, sighing a little. 'You can take it, if you prefer.'

She didn't reply to this, but instead tilted her head on one side towards the radio, as if she genuinely cared what the washed-up old pop star was saying to Lauren Laverne about his battle with alcoholism. She doesn't like the idea of

Instagram. She uses Facebook, but that's it, and that's only so she and the rest of her SW1 neighbours can moan about immigrant taxi drivers and the homeless from the safety of a private group – the new curtain twitching for the upper classes.

Instagram is a bit of a thing with us. It was just me, to start with. I thought I'd been late to the party when all my mates at the office started using it and telling me I was out of the loop. Archie and the rest of the lads from school were right on it. It actually gave me flashbacks to our school days, where one person was left out of a gang because of some trivial detail. Suddenly it was like we were back – I wasn't part of the 'cool gang' because I didn't have Instagram. I didn't take pictures of my French toast or eggs benedict on Sunday morning; I didn't get someone to snap my ripped torso on the beach as I casually stepped off a speed boat, glass of something bubbling in one hand and the other draped over whoever I was dating. And then, quite suddenly, that's exactly what I was doing. I downloaded it one Friday night when I had a cold and couldn't join the boys for a night of pills and pounding music. It was 2013, just before Matthew and I started dating. I was single and bored and I just downloaded the app to see what all the fuss was about. My first photo was of a massive burger I'd made out of hashbrowns, thick slices of cheddar, bacon, and a slice of fried chicken. Hashtag food porn. People liked it.

So I carried on in the weeks and months that followed. Got a bit of teasing from the guys about being a hypocrite. Then got some jealousy from them too because what I was posting was working. People were liking it. I admit it helped that I was good looking. That's what a lot of the comments were about. That and my physique. It wasn't long before people started to refer to me as 'Hot Charlie', send me messages to ask me out on dates, even tag me in posts where they'd profess to love me and want to have my babies. It does things to you, that sort of attention. Makes you not want to stop. And I carried on. Everything in my life became documented. Well, almost everything. A certain, very photogenic slice of my life. One that was prepped and colour-toned and filtered to fuck before being posted at the best time of day for 'my audience'.

I was a bit more daring in those early days. There were some mildly risqué shots, or me waking up looking oh-so-perfectly dishevelled in another guy's bed with hashtag morning-after-the-night-before as the caption. One or two shots of Archie and me with our arses out on top of a mountain somewhere on one of our holidays. But I cleaned it up completely when I started going out with Matthew. He just seemed so polished. So perfectly presented. It actually made me look at the photos on my feed with embarrassment, ashamed I had ever thought such childish silliness was attractive or likeable. I was suddenly entirely about presenting a very rose-tinted, picture-perfect portrayal of a young couple's life in London. Especially since Matthew came pre-loaded, so-to-speak, with little Titus, not quite nine at that point, and every bit as adorable as any child could be. I'd never really factored kids into my life-plan that much … until I saw Matthew with Titus. And I knew I needed that. Needed to be part of that. Needed to belong to a unit like that. And so I became Daddy, like he was Daddy, and before long, Titus had two perfect daddies and we were the cute same-sex kings of Instagram.

I wasn't naïve: I knew a lot of people loved us because we were gay parents, and may not have bothered to like our photos if we'd been a guy and a girl. And it came with the occasional bit of nastiness too – some comments, now and then, that bothered me at first but which now I greeted with an eyeroll and a shrug. But it was all just so easy. The photos of us having 'fun days out' took a bit of hard work. Some of them needed to be meticulously staged so as to look off-the-cuff natural. My followers lapped it up, liking pics of the single, adorable playboy-turned-family-man, with a family life so perfect it could have been designed in a lab.

Not perfect enough for my mother, though. She thought it empty and shallow, and as I took that photo of Titus grinning, holding up a slice of cake, Matthew leaning in opened-mouthed to take a bite out of it with mock-greed, I could see her give a little shake of her head. 'People like it, Mum,' I said, flicking through the resulting snaps, picking the ones with just the right amount of natural happiness in Titus's eyes. 'It's cute. It's sweet. It's funny.'

'If you say so,' Mum said, picking up my copy of the *Observer*, discarded on one of the sofas, to browse through its food monthly supplement. She never read the actual paper. She saw it as a left-wing rag. 'Did you have a good shop?' she said, whilst scanning an article on Nigel Slater's allotment tips.

I walked past her and sat on the opposite sofa, two

cookies on a plate in my hand. 'Yeah, just got the book I wanted and picked up some food for dinner.'

'And we made a new friend,' Matthew called out from the kitchen.

I shifted a little in the sofa, pulling out one of Matthew's jumpers from behind a cushion and draping it over the arm.

'A new friend?' she said, her interest piqued. 'You were only out just over an hour!' She peered over the top of her reading glasses to look back over at Matthew, coming in from the kitchen area, wiping icing sugar off his hands with a tea towel. I saw his eyes clock the fact I still had my shoes on – he was always keen to preserve the cream carpet – but he didn't nag me for it in front of my mum.

'Yes, a lovely young woman named Rachel. Practically collided with her in M&S, although Charlie had met her before. She's going to join my book club.'

I felt my brow crease a little at his words. The way he'd worded it sounded like Rachel and I were established friends. 'We'd only bumped into each other in Waterstones a few minutes earlier. I don't know her.' The last bit sounded slightly defensive and I think my mother noticed.

'Maybe you should join the book club, too,' she said to me. 'Give you something to do.'

This was the kind of comment from my mother that regularly irritated me. Just because I worked from home a couple of days a week, she often made out I was practically unemployed.

'I think I've already got enough to do,' I said, shortly. Matthew came over to me and sat down on the sofa, also holding a plate of food, although his one was loaded with

15

the large slice of cake Titus had used in the photo. His warm frame, the smell of his Ralph Lauren aftershave mingling with the scent of freshly baked cake, instantly made me feel less tense. He let an arm fall around me and said, 'Why don't you come to our next meeting? It would be nice for Rachel to see another face she knows.'

'Maybe,' I said, offering a vague nod, and extricated myself from Matthew's embrace, muttering about putting some washing on. Once we'd got off the subject of the book club, we continued our Sunday in our usual peaceful way – a walk in the park, dinner out in the evening – blissfully unaware that we had walked straight into a trap.

Chapter Two

RACHEL

Twelve months to go

It was better for everyone that I was leaving Yorkshire. The shit general-dogsbody job I had at a depressing garden centre wasn't exactly a dream come true, and I still hadn't decided what to do with my mum's inheritance. The idea of it sitting in a bank account, unused, while I rented a spare room above my manager's garage, made me feel ill. Squandered potential. A waste. Some would love to have a heap of cash sitting there, ready and waiting whenever they wanted it. Not me. Each pound and penny of it would be painted with the shitshow of the past. And using it would mean facing up to those demons. So I hadn't properly decided what to do with it, until the day I opened up Instagram to have a quick flick through during a quiet moment in between stacking up tubs of fertiliser. And on that day, my life changed for ever.

It was a hashtag. That's how I saw it. #WeekendBaking.

I'd clicked on it after seeing a photo of a delicious-looking banana and toffee cake come up on my feed, and fancied having a scroll through similar items. And there, suddenly, he was. The man from my dreams. My nightmares. My waking thoughts. He was older, of course. And age suited him. He was one of those lucky people that seem to wear their slight wrinkles in a comfortable way – a way that says to the world 'aren't I loveable and look at me enjoying life' rather than 'I'm approaching forty with the speed of a runaway train'. In the photo, he was standing with another man and a teenage boy, who must have been about fourteen or fifteen. He had his arm on his shoulder, and in front of them were about four different cakes, with different toppings. #SaturdayBaking. They looked so … perfect. The kitchen was clearly beautiful, with a shiny marble top, a sleek-looking American fridge-freezer behind them and one of those expensive standing-mixers to the side of the countertop. And the three of them dressed in those sorts of soft, pricy fabrics that beg to be touched. All these details made me fall to my knees, and then properly to the ground, so that I was sitting, like a strange child, awkwardly cross-legged next to the tubs of fertiliser, while the rain pattered loudly on the roof of the garden centre overhead.

'Are you quite all right?'

I looked up, bleary-eyed, to see a middle-aged woman staring down at me. She was clasping a small terracotta pot in one hand and a closed umbrella in the other, and appeared to be baffled to find me sitting there on the floor in the corner, phone out, my uniform making it clear I was a member of staff and should therefore be busy. I stared back up at her, quickly sussing out the type of customer she was – the sort of middle-aged middle-class visitor we often got at this time of the week. The type whose husband earned enough for them to float around garden centres in the middle of a working day, buying the odd geranium or accessory they didn't really need before meeting a friend for lunch in the connecting café.

'Hello? Can you hear me?'

The woman was still bending over me, and the look on her face – probably a reaction to the distant look I had on mine – suggested that she feared I was insane in some way. I saw one hand float subconsciously to her handbag, as if I might make a sudden grab for it and leg it out the door.

'I can hear you,' I said, not as politely as a member of staff should. But I couldn't focus on her right now. I just needed to get back to my phone. Make sure what I'd discovered was real rather than something I'd imagined. I felt the smooth surface of it clutched in my hand and brought it close to me as I stood up.

'Well, OK, I just wanted to check. In that case, I've got a question you could help with: a few weeks ago you were selling those little palm-tree ornaments that you could put tea lights in and I bought one and Otis, my labrador, had one of his tempers and sent the thing flying and I wanted to get another, only now I see the display has been taken down…'

I tried to stand still while she told me all this, even though I could feel myself swaying a little. 'Yes, well, that was a summer display. We're now putting in Christmas things, so…'

The woman's face remained blank. 'Christmas?'

I nodded. 'Yes, Christmas.' I looked down at my phone screen. Over an hour until I could go home. How I hated being tied into shift work like this. I longed to be a free spirit again. My own boss. Do what I wanted. Go where I wanted. Not clock in, clock out, remember to be deferential to a boss who I also paid rent to. I'd been feeling trapped for months, and now, this silly woman spoiling what should be an important life-changing moment, was causing it all to rush to the surface. All the frustration, all the anger, all the pain.

'I'm sorry, but it's still August,' she said, looking at me now like I was an alien. 'I really don't think we need to worry about Christmas just yet, do we?'

On another day I may have agreed with her, but on this day it was the wrong thing to say to me. I felt hot and a bit shaky, I glanced around, to see if I could pass her on to someone else, but the only other staff member I could see was Ruth at the other side of the building near the pet section helping an elderly man choose a dog lead.

'Hello?' the woman said. 'Am I boring you?'

That was the thing that made me snap. *Am I boring you?* I mean, she was kind of asking for it. 'Yes, you are boring me. In fact, all of *this* bores me.' I swept a hand around, gesturing at our surroundings. 'And if I'm being honest, not everyone can afford to get all their Christmas shopping in December with a few days to spare and load it into their Range Rover in one big haul. Some people have to spread it out because they're living paycheque to fucking paycheque with no hope of any lines of credit. So the next time you see some Christmas cards or chocolates or decorations for sale a little bit too early for you, just think, "Well, at least I'm lucky enough not to have to save up the pennies for a tub of Cadbury fucking Heroes."'

I finished my diatribe slightly out of breath. The woman looked stunned. Seconds passed that felt like lifetimes. The rain tap, tap, tapped on the glass ceiling above us. Then, at last, once the impact of my words had sunk in, she grabbed at the only line someone like her has to fall back on.

'I'd like to make a formal complaint.'

I kept very still, staring at her, trying to steady my breathing. After a few seconds, she continued.

'May I have your name? I'll need it for when I speak to your supervisor. Could you please send for him? I'd like to make my complaint straight away.'

The fact she presumed my supervisor was a man riled me even more. But before I could respond with a biting comeback, a voice behind me said, 'There's no need to send for me. I'm here.'

The normally kind voice of my manager, Allen, had a hard edge to it. More managerial than normal. 'Rachel, could you please wait for me in my office. I'll be with you in a moment.'

I didn't look at him. I couldn't. I was embarrassed and angry, with both the woman and myself. I left through the doors at the wall to my right and let myself into his little office. Only once I was sitting on one of the uncomfortable plastic chairs inside did I unlock my phone and stare down again at the photo that had started it all.

The photo of him.

And I knew nothing Allen could do – no reprimand, no disciplinary action, no firing – could match the earth-shattering power of seeing that photo. From that day on, everything else in my life became background noise. Noise to be turned off, so I could start from scratch and refocus my life with one clear goal in mind.

As soon as Allen walked in and lowered his overweight frame down behind the desk, I had made my decision. 'I'd like to hand in my notice. I'm resigning.'

His eyes widened a little. 'Rachel, I don't know what's going on, but whatever all this is about…'

'It's about nothing. I'd like to resign. And I'm going to move out of my room, too.'

He looked more and more puzzled. 'But … where are you going to go?'

I took a deep breath, then said with conviction, 'London. I'm moving to London.'

Chapter Three

RACHEL

Twelve months to go

I cleared my flat in under an hour. That's how long it took to scoop up my main possessions into my travel case and rucksack. The rest went in the recycling. I left a pile of food and an unopened bottle of skimmed milk at Allen's front door. He was more baffled than angry that I was going so quickly, and he was a good man really, so I thought he could have these.

I got a taxi to my dad's house – my old family home – and dragged the bags from the pavement to the door, desperate to get inside and start my research.

'Here, what on earth's going on?' he said, as soon as I got in the door.

'Hi Dad,' I said. 'I'm stopping here, just for a few nights while I find somewhere new to live. That OK?'

He stared at me with an open mouth as I started to haul the bags up the stairs.

'But … but I don't understand? I thought you said you were very comfortable in the flat above your manager's house?'

I sighed with the effort of the lifting, Dad still standing at the bottom of the stairs, too busy gawping at the situation to think of lending me a hand. 'It didn't work out. And anyway, *flat* is an overstatement, and it was above a garage, not a house. I'm better off out of there.'

He ended up wandering away, saying he was going out for some fish and chips for dinner and that he'd get me some. I shouted back my thanks and set about taking my laptop from my bag and plugging in the charger at the wall, then doing the same with my phone lead. I sat down at the same desk where I wrote my school essays twenty years previously and navigated to Instagram on the laptop's browser. I remembered the account handle with no problem – it was burned into my mind from when I first saw it. I went through, picture by picture, studying each frame, each colourful golden-hued square, every single one primed to show off the perfect life. *His* perfect life. *Their* perfect life. After twenty-five minutes, I heard the front door go; Dad was back from his fish-and-chip-shop run.

'Only me,' he called up.

Well who else would it be? I thought to myself. Everybody else is dead.

Five minutes later he called up to say the food was ready. I didn't mind. I'd found out what I needed to know. Everything was there to see.

I had a hurried meal with Dad in the dimly lit lounge. Dark, depressing, it irritated me he never switched the

24

lights on until he really had to. 'What's the plan, then?' he asked, eyeing me as if I were a strange, dangerous animal he'd only ever seen in films but never up close.

'The plan,' I said, crunching a bit of the batter from the huge fish he'd served me, 'is to move to London.'

His jaw literally dropped.

'*London?*'

'Yes,' I said, grabbing the salt. 'London. There's ... a photography course I'd like to do there. I was thinking of getting back into it. It's been over a year since I properly photographed anything.'

He seemed to be mulling this over. 'I suppose ... I suppose there's more of that sort of thing going on. In London.'

I nodded. 'Yes, there is.'

'But ... honestly, love, I've been and it really isn't all it's cracked up to be. There are these gangs of boys on bikes that stab people with knives. I've seen them on the news. And there are terrorist attacks almost every day now.'

'They're not every day,' I said, rolling my eyes. 'And we get stabbings here in Bradford.'

'Not that many, love. Not as much as *London*.' He said this whilst wagging a finger to me as if he was the only one who knew how the world works.

'I'm going, Dad. I've got that bit of money from Mum still put away. I'll use it to rent a flat there.'

He looked distressed at this. 'You always said you'd use that to start up another gallery of your own. Support local artists.'

I couldn't bear the thought of having this conversation

again. 'Because that worked out so fucking well last time, didn't it!' I put my knife and fork together and stood up.

'Here, don't go mouthing off at me. The recession wasn't my bloody fault.'

'I know that, Dad. I know. I'm sorry for snapping. I need to go back upstairs. I'm looking for flats and it may take a while. Don't wait up for me.'

I offered him a small, sad smile, then left him there, in the gloom, on his own.

Once I'd got back upstairs, I woke up my laptop and looked at the Word document I had open next to Instagram on my browser. On it, I'd written down all the key locations from the past few months of photographs that Charlie Allerton-Jones had posted. One thing was immediately clear: aside from a few daytrips and holidays, the family lived and spent the vast majority of their time in the Royal Borough of Kensington and Chelsea. If they weren't there, they were either in Belgravia, Pimlico, or other parts of Central London. They seemed almost never to venture to East London or very far south, or at least if they did, they didn't document their trips there for all the world to see. Charlie had been careful enough not to show their exact address, but a comment under one said, *'Tough life for the Carlyle Square Crew'* with a wink emoji under a photo of Charlie in a hammock in what was presumably their garden. From the interaction between Charlie and the user, it sounded like they were friends – and this friend had given away an important detail. I googled Carlyle Square, discovering it was indeed in Chelsea, SW3, just off the King's Road.

I set to work on my research on flat rental sites. The prices were horrendous. I'd known, of course, that London was expensive, but the rates people were expected to pay for a one-bedroom flat with a kitchen and bathroom shocked me. After half an hour, I was close to crying. I couldn't bear the thought of living in a flat share – the thought of being with a bunch of 'young professionals' in their twenties horrified me. They'd all be twenty-five, skipping off to work, full of the optimism of youth and all the things I'd thought I'd have when I opened my gallery and believed I could actually be a photographer and run a business and people would actually *care*. Maybe it was all a dream.

In the end, I had to stop looking for flats in Chelsea. There were some in the same borough, but I would be literally miles away, on the other side of Hyde Park, and I desperately didn't want that. In the end, I found a flat in Westminster I could just about afford, so long as I lived like an actual pauper, surviving on discounted ready meals and tins of soup. It was on the Churchill Gardens Estate in Pimlico. It would take me about half an hour to walk from the flat to Carlyle Square. It wasn't perfect, but it was certainly doable.

Could I really do it? I spent a few minutes debating this issue. Then I phoned up the agency listed on the flat details. After three rings a woman answered in a bored-sounding voice. 'Hi,' I said, trying to sound confident and committed to my decision, 'My name's Rachel and I'm interested in renting a flat on Churchill Gardens Road, Pimlico that you have advertised.'

Chapter Four

CHARLIE

The day of the murder

The police officer who comes to find Titus and me supervises the removal of our clothes, which are then placed in clear plastic bags. We're handed plastic tops and bottoms which crinkle and feel slightly uncomfortable against the skin. Then we're taken to Belgravia Police Station. And the questioning begins.

Titus and I are separated, although everyone is very kind and reassuring. I'm told by a kindly woman in uniform that this is all just procedure and how they just need to have a chat about what happened. 'Titus is only fifteen,' I tell them. 'I want to be with him.' I'm told this should be possible, and I'm shown into a room with sofas, with Titus sitting against the far wall alone. Another police officer follows me in and waits with us. Are they making sure we don't start getting our story straight? Strategising? Or is all this normal?

I'm on edge, and the true reality of the situation is settling in. I'm furious at myself for not talking to Titus properly before the police arrived, but my chance has now passed and before long a man of average height and build with brown hair and a flushed face comes in. 'Charles Allerton-Jones?' he asks, looking at me.

'Yes,' I reply.

'We need to get a formal statement from you about what's happened. I understand this must be very difficult and you must be shocked by this ordeal, but rest assured we're doing everything we can to get to the bottom of what's happened. The woman who placed the 999 call is now in custody and has confessed to killing your husband. However, as I'm sure you can appreciate, it's really important we get your side of the story, and your son's, as quickly as we can.'

His words hit me like little pins, each one jabbing somewhere sensitive in my brain. *Shocked. Confessed. Killing.* At last, I look up at him properly and say, 'I want to stay with Titus.'

DS Stimson looks over at the boy, who has his head down, staring at the floor.

'We would prefer to speak to you alone, Mr Allerton-Jones. Titus will not be questioned without you being present or at least aware of what's happening. Is there someone you can call to be with him?'

I nod. 'My mother ... but your colleague took my phone...'

'You can use a phone out here,' he says. He shows me

out to the corridor. I give Titus what I hope is a comforting smile as I leave, but his eyes stay on the carpet.

I phone my mother, then my father, but to my fury neither of them picks up. I phone my mother again and leave a message telling her to come to Belgravia Police Station and that something awful has happened. When I end the voicemail, I feel bad for not clarifying that Titus and I are safe and unharmed, but still, I'm incensed I can't get through to them straight away.

I'm then led into an interview room. Its aesthetic is drab and grey – more commonplace than the high-tech, space-age-style suites they show in TV dramas. DS Stimson varies his tone between firmly authoritative and compassionately sensitive. 'Please, just start at the beginning.'

I take a deep breath, then look at him, unwavering, my eyes meeting his, and then lie through my teeth. 'Rachel killed my husband. She interrupted our dinner, took a kitchen knife from the table, and stabbed him.'

Chapter Five

RACHEL

The day of the murder

My interview with the police doesn't last long. After going through the process of being arrested, cautioned, given clothes, my things being taken from me, and then being shown to a cell, I sit waiting for a few hours. Then Detective Sergeant Darren Stimson begins his grilling. Or tries, anyway.

The interview room is cold, the air conditioning blasting away. It seems those who manage the station haven't yet twigged that summer has taken a decidedly chilly turn. Even so, DS Stimson seems to be having something of a hot flush, with his jacket over his chair and the occasional loosening of his tie. Perhaps he has high blood pressure, or maybe a thyroid issue.

'Rachel, it really would help if you could give us a full picture. It may influence the outcome of how this plays out in court. If only we knew why you did what you say you did. Talk me through the evening, step by step.'

He's said this already. *Step by step.* I see no point in doing what he asks beyond what I've told them already. So I decide it's my turn to start repeating myself.

'As I've said, I murdered Matthew Allerton-Jones. I stabbed him. I don't want to talk about it anymore.'

That last bit's true at least. Because I really don't want to go into it all with them, not now.

'I think we'll take a break,' DS Stimson says, seeming eager to get out of the interview suite. Probably off to splash some cold water on his face.

Before I'm led out of my cell, I ask him when I'm likely to be charged. He gives me an odd look, like he can't quite work me out. 'That's to be decided,' he says eventually.

I curse myself as I sit down on the padded bench in my cell. *Too keen*, I think, leaning back against the wall, enjoying the clinking and thumping sounds of the police station around me. I need to be better at this. For this to work, I need to stay quiet and let the police do their jobs and see what they want to see. That's all I need them to do.

Chapter Six

RACHEL

Eleven months to go

Moving into my new rented London flat was an ordeal. I'd resisted buying any new suitcases or travel bags – I didn't have that much stuff, and would need all the money I could save. I regretted this decision when the zip on my old suitcase split open at the seams while I was lugging it into the lift to go up to the third floor. My clothes went everywhere, mixing with the dirty footprints and discarded junk mail.

'Oh, bad luck, dear. Here, I've got a few bags-for-life you can use.' The voice came from an older woman who was smiling down at me. I was so grateful, I could barely whisper my thanks as I threw jumpers and socks into the large Tesco bags she'd handed me.

'Are you moving in?' she said, looking at the other two rucksacks I'd dropped in my efforts to get the main suitcase into the lift.

'Yes,' I said, 'I'm trying to get to Number 32. I think it's on the third floor.'

She beamed a wide red-lipped smile. 'It is. That's right next to us.' She said 'us' as if there were someone else with her, so I presumed she must have a family or partner at least. I tried to guess her age, although it was hard underneath the make-up. There was something a little too strong in the colour of her red-brown hair, suggesting it was dyed, and looking closer I could see some substantial wrinkles around her eyes. She was probably well past fifty, maybe even in her sixties. 'I'm Amanda,' she said, warmly. I thought I detected a slight northern accent in her words, and I was tempted to ask where she was from, but worried it might sound rude. 'Come on,' she nodded at the lift, 'let's get your things upstairs.'

She helped me with my stuff all the way to the flat, and seemed happy to lug two of the bags inside once I'd unlocked the door. 'Oh, this is lovely,' she said as we walked in.

She was lying to be kind. It wasn't lovely. It was gloomy and small, with a scuffed carpet and a narrow corridor. At least the air smelled clean. I led the way down the corridor to the kitchen.

'Is this like your place next door?' I asked as I set the broken suitcase down on the countertop with a thud.

'Yes, well, ours is slightly bigger, I think, but generally the same. I live with my husband, Neil. We've been wondering who would take up the rent on this one. We've had...' she lowered her voice a little, 'we had a bit of a problem before. With the other tenant, I mean. He would play this terrible music at an astonishing volume. I don't know what it was; it sounded like a mix of bins being kicked over and livestock being slaughtered. We think he had a drug habit as well, but I don't think that's as unusual as we'd like to think it is.' She shook her head.

I nodded, not sure how I should respond to this, but Amanda seemed quite content to carry on without encouragement. 'And before him we had a young woman named Carly who,' her voice now dropped to barely a whisper, '*killed herself*.' She shuddered a little, as if the memory still bothered her. 'Poor young girl. She had deep, desperate problems, I think. Drugs too, probably. Never had much to do with her, though heard she'd come over from Clapham. We had a suspicion she may have worked as a … well, you know, a … *lady of the night*. A lot of gentlemen callers.'

Again, I had nothing to add to this, although it made me worry even more about what my neighbours might be like on the other side. Though this Amanda woman was gossipy and a bit full-on, at least she seemed relatively safe and normal. As if she could read my mind, she suddenly said, 'Oh, but I don't want to put you off, love. Pimlico's a lovely area, really. I know we're not exactly in the local beauty spot on the estate here, but there's so much history around these streets. All sorts of interesting people.' She gave me a big red-lipsticked smile. 'Well, I'd better leave you to get unpacked. If you ever need anything, don't hesitate to ask.'

I spent the rest of the day unpacking. It shouldn't have taken long, but I was starting to get a familiar anxious feeling – of being out of my natural habitat and surrounded by strangeness and uncertainty. Folding my clothes carefully and putting them in the white IKEA drawers provided in the pre-furnished flat helped calm me a little. After that, I needed to think about food. I was pleased to find the fridge nice and clean – it looked brand new – and there was a surprising amount of cupboard space for such a small kitchen. I put the keys in my pocket, put on my coat, and set off back down the stairs and out of the building.

My block was in the centre of the estate, and it was a bit of a maze to find my way out onto a main bit of road. I walked for a bit until I got to a street named Glasgow Terrace. I was about to get my phone out to access Google Maps, but a group of boys with their hoods up started coming towards me and I thought it best not to put temptation in their way. They passed me without comment, and I carried on walking purposefully in the opposite direction. I waited until I was alone again, then did a quick Web search of supermarkets near me. There were two Sainsbury's stores not far away, along with a massive superstore across the river in Nine Elms. It was a bit of a walk, but the sun had come out and although there was a slight chill of autumn in the breeze, it was still a nice enough evening. I decided a stroll in the fresh air was exactly what I needed. I zipped my hoody up to my chin and set off down the street, following the course set out by the Maps app until it opened out onto a large, busy road.

The rush of traffic – all beeping horns and growling engines – was a change from the relative quietness of inner Pimlico. I walked along the road towards the bridge and carried on until I was halfway across it. That's when I stopped and stared. Just stared. The sweeping surface of the Thames. The towering futuristic-looking apartment blocks of Vauxhall. The impressive sight of Battersea Power Station, surrounded by cranes. And, to the other side, a bit further down the river, the unmistakable shape of the London Eye.

I was here. In London. A place I had only visited twice previously in my thirty-two years. For a few minutes, I was entirely present in the moment, filled with optimism and hope and the thrill of the impressive change of scene I had brought upon myself. And then, as if a switch had been flicked, I remembered why I had done it. The purpose of the whole thing. *You're not here to have fun,* I told myself. I took a deep breath of the cool late-afternoon air, and carried on walking across the bridge into Vauxhall to get my shopping.

Chapter Seven

CHARLIE

Eleven months to go

Matthew had been asking me to be a member of his book club for *years*. It was practically the first thing he asked me when we went on our first official date.

We'd gone for dinner at the Mango Tree as it was relatively close to the flat I was living in at that point in Eccleston Square. It was a dull little place, and my parents had been going on at me to buy something better, but a little place suited me just fine while my career in marketing started to take off. I'd arrived late (couldn't find my shoes) and Matthew had been sitting there at the table, reading a book. That in itself was a major red flag for me. Who brings a book to a restaurant? On a date? I knew Matthew was quite quiet and bookish when we'd been at school together, but this was at a level I hadn't prepared for. When I'd sat down opposite him, he did at least have the grace to appear a little sheepish, setting the book to the side before greeting me with his lovely, warm smile. I'd known then and there that we were on to something special. I knew I'd been right to take our mutual friend Archie's advice and meet up with Matthew after all this time. This wasn't going to be just some casual one-night stand with a vague past acquaintance. This was something more concrete. More real. When we'd started talking about books, Matthew had said, 'You should come to my book club. There's a bit of an odd group of us. But your godmother, Meryl, is always there, so you'd know her.'

I think I pulled a face at that. 'Yes, she's mentioned it a few times. I did think it was a bit unusual for a woman of her age to be spending the evening in the company of a bunch of young men discussing naughty novels.'

Matthew grinned. 'Who says our novels are naughty? We have an eclectic range. And anyway, it isn't just us and Meryl. There's also Jerome; he and Meryl must both be in their sixties. And there's Anita, too.'

'Jerome?' I asked, raising an eyebrow. 'Not Jerome Nightly?'

He nodded with a smile. 'The one and only. Doesn't act as much these days. Just a few cameos in the odd romantic comedy. He and Meryl go back a long way.'

'And Anita? I don't think I know her.'

Matthew took a sip of wine and looked a little pained. 'She's a bit of a downer, I'm afraid. Jerome's daughter-in-law, although we think she and his son have now split. It would have been more normal for her to distance herself from her father-in-law a bit when she left his son, but for some reason she still turns up. Has a bit too much wine.

Moans a lot about whatever book we've read. Makes digs at Jerome.'

'Is she our age?'

Matthew laughed. 'Good Lord, no. About fifty. Only twelve years younger than her father-in-law; that's what made her marriage to his son Harry a bit strange. A nine-year age gap between them, I think.'

I helped myself to more wine. 'That's not such a bad age gap. I've seen worse.'

Matthew had a knowing glint in his eye. 'Are you referring to you and your aristocratic ex?'

I leaned back, laughing a little. I liked that he was teasing me so early on. 'There was little more than a decade between me and my aristocratic ex, as you call him. And that's the largest age gap I'd ever consider workable.'

Matthew was still smiling. 'Well, only one year between us.'

I felt a prickle of something along my arms. A buzz of anticipation. A trembling of destiny, someone a bit kookier than myself might say. The feeling of the tectonic plates of one's life shifting towards a new future.

'Indeed,' I said.

I went home with Matthew that night. We became an item almost immediately. That vague, 'seeing each other' period never really happened to us. I was introduced to Titus the following week, who was an angelic child and seemed devoted to Matthew. I started to spend more time with the two of them in their apartment near Marble Arch within the month. Moved my stuff over bit by bit. Matthew got used to my habit of leaving half-drunk mugs of tea, odd socks, and old newspapers about the place. I tried to get used to his neatness. And very quickly, after I sold my Eccleston Square flat, our two separate lives became stitched together into one. Everything fitted wonderfully. But still, I never joined his book club. It just seemed odd, a bunch of people – such different people at various points in their lives – meeting to discuss a book they've probably only skim-read. Or worse, studied word for word so they could have really in-depth discussions about a character's *motivation* and *emotional journey*. I mean, I love Meryl, and she's always seemed very fond of me, but the thought of her debating the latest Rushdie with an ageing film star and his bitter daughter-in-law … well, the whole thing seemed too bonkers to comprehend. So I resisted Matthew's charming efforts to make me join, and the years went by and I just never caved in.

Until, of course, Rachel came into our lives.

'I just don't understand why now? Don't get me wrong, you're very welcome to join. It's just never seemed like your sort of thing before. I thought that was why you've always arranged to be out when the meeting's here.' Matthew said all this as he stepped out of the shower, slipping a little as he hopped over the mat and back into the bedroom. He started drying himself with the towel, beads of water flicking onto me as I sat on the bed, only half listening. I didn't know why, but I had a strange underlying sense of anxiety about the evening. Matthew seemed to suspect exactly why though.

'Is it because of her? Rachel? Is that why you're coming?'

I looked up at him and shrugged. I'd been filtering an image on a photography app. It didn't really need any more work on it, but I felt oddly restless and needed something to focus my mind.

'Charrrrlie? Hello?'

There was something about the way he sometimes said my name, extending the Rs a little and making it kind of sing-song-y, that had always irritated me a little.

'It isn't because of Rachel. Why would it be because of her?' I didn't look at him properly as I said this, just glanced up quickly, then carried on with colour, contrast, and shadow reach.

Out of the corner of my eye I saw him pause, then heard the sound of him towelling his hair. It's strange how quickly things can change. There was once a time when I wouldn't have been able to sit still with him standing naked so close to me. I'd have been pulling him close to me, the scent of his shower-gel-scrubbed skin sending ripples of attraction through me, a desperation to get him onto the bed and have his long strong legs wrap around me almost impossible to ignore. But, like a string of Christmas lights that have lost their vibrant once-new glow, here the feeling of arousal fluttered briefly and dully through my body, then faded as quickly as it had arisen.

Christ, I thought to myself as Matthew finally moved away from me to pull on a pair of boxers from the chest of drawers, *have we really reached this stage already? A sense of disinterest and indifference around each other's bodies?* We were only in our mid-thirties, for fuck's sake. Was this really when things started wilting and dying?

'I'm not coming because of Rachel.' It was a lie, and I think he knew it. If I ever lied to him, whether it was about my whereabouts ('I'm just working at the moment,' a.k.a. watching Netflix on my iPad in the study) or sorting out the clothes to take to the dry cleaner's ('Sure, all done,' a.k.a. I'll get around to it soon), I'd feel this strange ripple of electricity in the air, which remained present even when we weren't in the same room. It was like my mind punishing me for stepping over some of my most closely held values: loyalty and honesty.

'And you've read the book?'

I sighed a little in frustration. 'Yes, I told you. When we were on holiday. Look, I think I even Instagrammed it. Hang on.' I switched over to the app on my phone and began scrolling back.

'I don't need photographic evidence…'

'Well you're getting it, whether you like it or not.' I did a sort of mock-annoyed voice to show I wasn't really pissed. Was I pissed? I wasn't really sure how I felt. I had this weird, slightly vertigo-inducing sense that we were on the verge of something not exactly pleasant. A feeling of foreboding I hadn't felt as strongly as this before.

Titus was doing his schoolwork in his room while we got the house ready before the book club members descended.

'What are you working on?' Matthew asked when the boy made an appearance to steal a slice of cake.

'Wars of the Roses,' he replied, dangling on the door frame, stretching his arms. He'd grown tall recently and was in that stage some teenage lads go through when they're a long tangle of limbs, not used to their own height, or the fast-paced changes their bodies are going through. I was the same at Titus's age. I'd been so ravenously *hungry*. Every second of every day. And always felt as if I could run a mile or four, even at 11pm after a long day of school and rugby. Titus wasn't quite like that though. His appetite didn't seem to have changed that much, and he was never one for exercise outside of his school sports. In fact, thinking about the amount of physical education his school put upon him, maybe that wasn't very surprising.

'I'm going to head back up. Have a nice time with your book friends,' he said, sloping off.

'Don't go to bed too late!' Matthew called back up after him.

'Can't hear you, Fathers!' came the predictable reply.

He always liked to call us that collectively: 'The Fathers'. Matthew sometimes complained it made us sound like people of the church. Titus had leaped on this, occasionally referring to us as Father Matthew and Father Charlie with mock deference, sometimes with a hint of an Irish lilt to his voice. The rest of the time, he called Matthew 'Dad' and used 'Dad' and 'Charlie' interchangeably with me – usually if he needed to make specific reference to one of us. Matthew had naturally been 'Daddy' all the way through Titus's early years, since he was the only father figure the

47

child properly knew. When I came along, I was just 'Charlie' for a time to the sweet little five-year-old who always greeted me with such joy when I came round to visit his dad. And then, quite suddenly, and seemingly without prompting, he'd started to call me 'Daddy Charlie'.

The day he first did this was etched onto my memory. It was the weekend I was properly moving into Charlie's Marble Arch flat. It was a Friday evening and I was driving the last remaining bits of my stuff over from Eccleston Square. It wasn't long after Matthew's mother had died in a car accident in the Highlands. He'd been back and forth between Scotland and England and it had been a difficult time for him, coping with all that and having a child to bring up, especially since his mother was the only close family he had left. That day, he was cooking a romantic dinner for the two of us and I was fantasising about the herbed cod and salad he'd promised, along with something to drink – something *ice* cold, since the hot Friday air was unforgivably stifling and the traffic around Victoria gridlocked. To make matters worse, the air-con had broken in my car.

When I'd finally got to the apartment block and was in the lift, the concierge on the desk having helped me with my bags, I was hot and irritable and annoyed that I was nearly half an hour late. But when I stepped into Matthew's air-conditioned apartment, a sense of calm came across me. The place was cool, warming and comforting and just so *right*. And there he was, sitting on the sofa with Titus on his lap, reading a picture book, my godmother, Meryl, sitting next to him, laughing along as Matthew did the voice of a monkey or something in a high-pitched voice. He'd always been the more playful one of us. The more naturally paternal. I can make adults feel at ease without much effort, but it took me longer to get used to being a parent. Charm doesn't get you very far when a stroppy nine-year-old feels his bedtime should be moved later. He looked up and saw me, and his smile filled his face in the beautiful way it always did. 'Look who's here,' he'd said to Titus, and the child had looked round and beamed, and shuffled off Matthew's lap and shouted 'Daddy Charlie's here!'

I have to admit that the thought of that moment years later would still cause me to choke up. Meryl had taken Titus off our hands that evening for a night of Disney movies at her house, but to be honest, I would have been cool with him staying. Because that joyful exclamation of 'Daddy Charlie' made me realise how special this whole thing was: this was the start of a new part of our lives. All three of us, together.

Anita arrived first for the book club. The one member I had the least wish to talk to turned up a good forty minutes too early. Sometimes she arrived with Jerome, her father-in-law, if he asked his driver to stop off at her Pimlico home on the way from Mayfair, but it meant a bit of a detour for him and sometimes she decided to walk. Her reconciliation with his son Harry five years ago, after their four-year estrangement, had forced Jerome to treat her more like family again rather than a distant acquaintance he wished he could be rid of.

Harry, meanwhile, refused point blank to join the book club and apparently saw it as the perfect opportunity to go drinking with his fellow TV-producer chums in oh-so-trendy bars in Soho.

'Charlie, darling, what are you doing here?' Anita asked when I opened the door. She looked at me as if a trained leopard had just greeted her on the doorstep. 'Lovely to see you too, Anita,' I said, smiling at her. She gave me a suspicious look, stepping past me with purpose and then handing me the coat she had over her arm. 'I walked,' she said, as if this explained her early arrival. 'Now, where's Matthew? What's going on? Why are you here?' She marched onwards towards the kitchen, no doubt homing in on the warm lights and smell of baking.

'Good evening, Anita,' Matthew said, looking up from adding a touch of icing sugar to one of the cakes he and Titus had baked earlier. 'You're early.'

'Yes, I know, I walked,' she said again. 'Tell me, why is your husband here? I thought he *hated* books?'

I made a sound whichI hoped conveyed polite disagreement. 'I don't *hate* books. I'm not a monster.'

She gave me another glance of distrust, then turned back to Matthew. 'I think there's enough sugar on that now, or we'll all have type 2 diabetes by the end of the night. Now, is anyone going to answer my question?'

I held my hands up in surrender. 'I just thought it was time for me to join.' I smiled at her, but Anita didn't smile back.

'You thought it was time? After all these years?' She looked back in disbelief.

I laughed a little. 'How welcome you make me feel, Anita.'

Matthew started talking before she could respond. 'He's not the only new addition. Did Jerome mention to you about our friend Rachel joining?'

Anita approached the island counter, rounding on Matthew in a way I'd have found intimidating if I were him. 'No, he did not. What do you mean, your friend Rachel? What Rachel? Not Rachel Evergreen? The one who had an affair with Sir Kenneth Lawford then sold her story to the *Mail on Sunday*?'

'No, not Rachel Evergreen,' Matthew said patiently, pouring Anita a glass of wine and handing it to her. He lifted a glass to me and shook it in question, and I nodded. 'This Rachel is a new friend of ours.'

'Friend,' I said, taking my wine, 'is an overstatement.'

'So who is she?' Anita asked, her head going back and forth between the two of us.

'She's someone we bumped into while out shopping. We ended up inviting her to our little gathering.'

Anita lowered her glass. She looked at Matthew as though he'd just produced a gun. 'Are you fucking serious? You've invited some *random woman* to join us at *our* book club? Someone you picked up whilst *shopping*?'

I couldn't help but smile at her consternation. 'That's about it in a nutshell,' I said.

She gaped at us both. 'Well, I'm stunned. Where was this?'

'On the King's Road,' Matthew said, patiently. 'In

Waterstones, appropriately. She's new to the area, is a keen reader, and wants to make some friends.'

I watched Anita chew on these details for a few seconds. 'I suppose that's not as bad as it could be. I was afraid you were going to say it was in Primark on the Archway Road.'

Matthew scoffed. 'There isn't a Primark on the Archway Road.'

'I wouldn't know,' she said, downing the last of her wine. 'I don't shop there.'

'We've been saying for ages we should increase our numbers,' Matthew said. I could tell he was trying to keep his impatience out of his voice. 'Ever since Douglas and George married and dropped out, we've been a bit light on numbers.'

Anita looked like she'd swallowed a wasp. 'I cannot *believe* you thought inviting a random stranger was the right way to go about this. There are loads of more suitable candidates I could have thought of in an instant. I could have made a shortlist. We could have *interviewed*. We could have *planned*. We could have *strategised*.'

'It's … er … a book club,' I said, quietly. 'Not a by-election.'

'Eileen Moran, for example,' Anita continued, as if I hadn't spoken. 'She's got lots of time on her hands since her upholstery business had to fold due to tax evasion. Then there's Louise Kellman, poor dear. If there was anyone who needed a distraction from the ills of this world, it's her. Or Timmy! Darling Timmy Braythorne. He's got nobody now his wife left him for her yoga instructor, and then his rabbits all died of myxomatosis. You *know* how devoted he was to those rabbits.'

'Unless I'm very much mistaken, Timothy Braythorne still lives in South Riding,' said Matthew. 'Rather a long way to travel for a book club.' He'd finished with the cakes by this point and surveyed them with all the pride of Paul Hollywood.

Anita rounded on me. 'So why are you joining us? You haven't said.'

I'd had years to get used to Anita's direct approach, but I still found myself wanting to shrink from her gaze. I explained to her that I'd read this month's novel on holiday recently and thought it might be fun to contribute to the discussion.

'*Fun?*' she said, the word apparently new to her.

'Yes, fun,' I replied, smiling.

'It hasn't got anything to do with your *Instagram* has it?'

'Oh, of course,' I said, partly wanting to mess with her. 'I'll be able to get a photo with you, won't I?'

She looked revolted. 'Certainly not. I don't know what sort of unsavoury types haunt your social media, but I certainly don't want to be gawped at or slut-shamed or whatever they call it.'

I could see Matthew trying desperately hard not to laugh at this, and I coughed a little to hide my own mirth. Anita was helping herself to more wine. She'd be sozzled by the time the second guest arrived, I was sure of it.

Twenty minutes later, Jerome hopped across the threshold, happy and energetic, then suddenly appeared to morph into a tired and world-weary old man the moment he saw his daughter-in-law leaning up against the kitchen counter. 'I see Anita's here,' he said in a tone mixed with boredom and resignation.

'Been here for quite a while,' I murmured, giving him a knowing glance that I hoped silently communicated *and she's already tipsy.*' Jerome nodded, understanding me instantly. 'She walked, apparently.'

I saw him raise an eyebrow. 'That's brave of her. Ever since a recent stabbing in the area, she's told me she won't walk the streets after 6pm.'

'Well, she got here in one piece at least.'

He turned away from his view of Anita in the kitchen and looked at me properly. 'It's nice to see you, Charlie,' he put his hand out and tapped me on the shoulder. 'Although, don't take this the wrong way, dear chap, but why are you here? You're never here when we have our meet-ups.'

'I just fancied joining in this time,' I said, giving a little shrug. 'And there's a new member joining. Rachel. Bit of an odd situation with that, really. Matthew invited her.'

Jerome nodded, 'Yes, he mentioned this to me. It will be nice to get some fresh blood in the mix. Might stop Anita holding court so prominently.' He rolled his eyes a little, gave me a smile, and then walked through into the kitchen.

Meryl arrived shortly after Jerome, prompting us to move into the lounge so we could sit down properly. Matthew was being the conscientious host, filling up everyone's wine glasses and offering more cake than anyone could handle.

'My goodness, Matthew, it's like you're going into the catering industry,' Meryl said, her smooth American accent instantly transporting me back to my childhood. My parents had known Meryl long before they had me. My father had some business association with her late husband's company and they all became firm friends. When they had me, they instantly made her godmother, and I'd grown up spending summers running around the large country house she and her husband had owned in Kent. She sold it upon his death fifteen years ago, preferring to live in Central London so as to have a better eye on her own business – a beauty cosmetics company called Streamline. She has a more distant, hands-free relationship with the company now, the day-to-day management carried out by a group of industry high-fliers she appointed. Although still only in her sixties, it felt sometimes like she'd aged rather quickly within the last few years.

'I'm looking forward to meeting our new member,' Meryl said, cutting into her slice of carrot cake with a small fork. 'I understand she's a young person, like the two of you.' She nodded at Matthew and me. 'Will be nice to have some more young voices.'

Anita's lip twisted at the thought of being lumped in the old club with Meryl and Jerome.

'She's a little late, it seems,' I said, checking the time on my phone.

'She hasn't messaged to say she's running late, but she confirmed yesterday she was still up for coming,' Matthew said, looking down at his phone.

The doorbell rang at that moment. Everyone looked

around at each other, apart from Anita who craned her neck to see if she could see whoever was on the doorstep, apparently keen for a first glimpse of our mysterious new guest. It suddenly felt like I was in a play and a pivotal character was about to enter stage right.

'That must be her now,' Matthew said, and disappeared out to the hallway. Everyone sat in an awkward silence while we heard him saying hello and being all welcoming and doing the host thing. Then he came back into the room, bringing with him the tallish, blonde, nervously smiling woman.

'This is Rachel, everyone. The new member we've all been waiting for.'

I saw Rachel's face fall. 'Oh gosh, I'm so sorry I'm late. I'm so embarrassed. I got the street muddled up with another…'

Matthew, realising how his phrasing may have been interpreted, cut in, 'No, no, sorry, I didn't mean waiting for in that way – just that we're all so excited to have a new member of the group.'

I saw Anita raise a mean-spirited eyebrow at this. Jerome, on the other hand, leapt up and clasped Rachel's hands in his. 'Delighted you could join us,' he said earnestly. She smiled and said a slightly breathless thankyou and Matthew guided her to the chair next to Meryl.

'Splendid to meet you, my dear,' Meryl said, nodding at Rachel. 'I'm Meryl, and this is Anita.' Rachel smiled and gave a little wave to them both, taking her seat and putting her handbag on the floor, before bending down to retrieve something from it – a copy of the book, it turned out – getting slightly flustered when a pack of tissues dropped out.

'Have you come far?' Meryl asked as Matthew poured her some wine. I saw his eyes meet mine then flick to the cake. I took his prompt and offered Rachel a slice, but she declined.

'From Pimlico. I decided to walk but got a bit lost somewhere just up from Sloane Square. Ended up walking in the wrong direction for a bit.'

I saw Anita's attention prick up. 'Oh, I live in Pimlico. We probably passed each other on the way.'

Well you wouldn't have, I thought to myself, *because you've been here for about nine hours.*

'Whereabouts are you?' Anita continued in her usual abrupt, borderline rude way.

'Oh, nowhere very grand,' Rachel said.

A normal person would have taken this as an indication to move on; Anita was many things but not, sadly, a normal person, so pressed on. 'Which street?'

'Oh, um, just off Johnson's Place.'

Anita's eyebrows rose so high up her head it was almost comical. 'That's on the Churchill Gardens Estate, isn't it?' From her tone, anyone would think Rachel had confessed to bedding down with a pack of wolves every night.

'That's right,' Rachel said, with a smile. 'I rent a little flat there.'

Anita's eyes widened even further. 'Is that so? Goodness. Well. What's it like?'

Rachel gave a slight shrug, 'It's fine. I mean, it could be

better. Not as lovely as round here. But I haven't been murdered by a gang just yet, so things could be worse.'

Jerome laughed. 'You must excuse my daughter-in-law. She lives in fear of anyone who doesn't get their avocados from Waitrose.'

Anita looked mortified. 'I don't eat avocados, Jerome. And you're painting me as some kind of snob, which is more than a little audacious while you sit on your throne in your Mayfair apartment…'

'Shall we perhaps,' Meryl said, her soft voice doing what it did best – cutting through a room as if she'd shouted – 'turn our attentions to our book this month?'

Anita moodily snatched up her bag from wherever she'd tossed it earlier, took out a pristine paperback, and said, 'Fine.' Jerome smiled at her, as if he were an indulgent uncle and she a sulking child. I saw Rachel's eyes meet Matthew's opposite. He offered her a little flick of the eyebrows and a grin, and then he started to talk about what he 'took away from' the novel.

Looking back now, I can't be sure how long Rachel was gone. I think I vaguely remember her asking Matthew the direction of the loo, and I thought she'd gone off in the right direction. But then Titus texted me and asked if I could bring up a book he needed from the pile of schoolwork he'd left downstairs, so I hopped up to get it. Carrying the weighty tome under my arm, I extracted myself from the group – I think Jerome had just insinuated that Anita was racist and was being treated to an irate response from her – and went to climb the stairs. It was as I was approaching the landing that a flicker of movement caught my eye – not from Titus's end of the landing, but from the main bedroom. Mine and Matthew's bedroom. I walked down the landing slowly, wondering if we were being stealthily burgled or if Titus had gone looking for something (the fact Rachel was absent from the room downstairs still hadn't properly registered). When I reached the doorway, I tilted forward a little to peer in without going properly through into the room. Rachel was there, standing at the side of our bed that leads into the en suite. She was peering to look at the photos we had lined along the top of the chest of drawers.

I was momentarily stunned – completely stunned – by this sight. Then my senses kicked in. I coughed and moved forward into the room properly. 'Er … hi,' I said, in a friendly but slightly questioning voice.

She turned around as if someone had fired a gun. 'Oh, God, I'm so sorry. I was looking for the bathroom and found my way in here, and then saw the bathroom but realised it was an en suite so thought I should go and find the proper one…'

She trailed off with a mixture of hand gesticulations and head movements to indicate *aren't I such a fool, getting the wrong bathroom.* I wasn't sure if it was the way I saw her staring at the photos – photos of me and Matthew and Titus when he was a little boy – or if it was the fact she'd gone somewhere so private – a space generally reserved for just us, away from guests, with sports clothes on the floor and a wrapper from a packet of shaving razors poking out of the waste-paper basket. It felt like an intimate invasion. And she must have known it, because she went bright red at my silence and said, 'I'd better go back downstairs.'

I think I said something daft like 'Sure' or 'Great', but I didn't know what else I should say other than *what the fuck are you doing in my bedroom?* And my overall need for politeness and lack of confrontation stopped me saying that. So she left, walked straight past me and back out to the landing. I just stood there. I felt uneasy, like something major and important had occurred, and I needed time to compute it. But of course, what really *had* happened? A guest had got the wrong room, or a guest had been a bit rude and nosy and been caught out. Nothing more. Then why was I feeling so ... *strange*? I shook myself a little to bring my mind back to the moment, and went to go back downstairs, but paused as I neared Titus's room. His door was closed. After my knock, he called for me to come in, so I pushed the door open gently and found him sprawled out on his bed, textbooks and sheets of paper arranged around him, some falling onto the floor. Titus didn't just *do* homework. He *immersed* himself in it.

'How's it going?' I asked, offering him a smile. 'Do you want me to bring you up some more cake?'

He grinned. 'Fine. And no, it's OK, I shouldn't have more sugar this close to bed.'

Christ, I thought to myself, *the boy's more of an adult than his parents.* I nodded, and told him I'd leave him to it. Then he said, 'Not enjoying the book club?'

I paused. 'Er ... well, it is what it is.' He gave a short

laugh at that and so did I. 'Why do you ask? Do I look grumpy?'

He shook his head. 'No, I just thought I heard you come up a while ago. Seeking sanctuary, or something.'

I considered telling him about Rachel. How weird it had been, finding her in the bedroom. But the thought of her overhearing the conversation – me bitching about her to my son – even if the chances were remote, made me stop. 'I was just directing Rachel to the bathroom,' I said. It was the truth, to some extent.

He nodded and his eyes went back to his work. I let him be and then went back downstairs, half expecting to find Rachel going through the pockets of the coats in the hallway. Of course she wasn't; she was in the lounge with everyone, accepting some more cake and laughing at something Jerome had said. Matthew caught my eye and raised his eyebrows, his silent way of asking *everything OK?* He smiled and gave a tiny nod, and carried on his conversation with Meryl. I went in to join them, slipping past Rachel's chair, noticing as I did so her eyes dart up to me, filled for a split second with something like trepidation, or fear. Like an animal, sensing danger.

Once they had all gone and we had peace at last, I helped Matthew tidy away the plates and wine glasses. Because I'm a terrible human being, I routinely left things like this out on the countertop for our housekeeper, Jane, to do the next morning. Matthew, however, frequently told me this was rude and we should do it ourselves, and whenever I reminded him that Jane was paid *actual money* to tidy things away, he always went temporarily deaf.

He was putting plates into the dishwasher when he said to me, 'Rachel was a success, don't you think?'

I paused. That was my big mistake. I paused, and it was enough for him to jump in and say, 'God, I *knew* you'd have some sort of problem with her. Tell me, then. What was it? Please don't tell me she doesn't fit in or something like that. That kind of snobbery is beneath you.'

I looked at him in outrage. 'I wasn't going to say anything of the kind. In fact, it's something quite different, if you'd let me speak.'

He closed the dishwasher and turned it on, putting his hands on his hips, 'Go on then.'

I took a breath, chose my words carefully, then said, 'I found her in our bedroom. She was … looking around.'

Matthew looked puzzled. 'What do you mean, looking around?'

'Just that,' I said, getting frustrated. 'She was … I don't know … snooping.'

'*Snooping*,' he said, looking at me like I was insane. 'She probably just got the wrong room when looking for the loo.'

I was about to respond, then stopped and bit my lip.

'Oh,' Matthew said, catching on. 'So she was just looking for the loo, then?'

'Well, that was her explanation, but it wasn't the truth. I could tell she was lying. She was looking at our stuff… It was … strange. Invasive.'

'*Invasive?*'

'Can you please stop repeating key words in that disbelieving tone? I know what I saw.'

He sighed and came around to my side of the kitchen island. 'I'm sorry. I believe you. But I honestly don't think she was doing anything sinister. Everyone's curious about other people's houses. I'm sure we've all snooped about on occasion. And she probably hasn't ever been in a house like this before.' He came close to me and wrapped his arms around my middle.

'Wow. Now who's the snob?' I'd intended it to be a snarky comeback, but with his hands now moving up to my shoulders and his body pressing into me, it ended up sounding weirdly flirtatious.

'Shall we go upstairs?' Matthew said into my ear, leaning in so I could smell his Boss aftershave.

'Let's.' I pulled him close to me and hugged him tight, feeling his warmth and the comforting familiarity of his embrace. And then we drew apart, and went upstairs together.

It was just as I was drifting off to sleep when the memory of finding Rachel in the bedroom – the very room I was in at that moment – fell into my head. I saw it again, and I remembered: it wasn't the act of finding her in the room that had startled me; it was the look on her face. A strange, faraway look, filled with something, some emotion that I couldn't quite place. I got out of bed and went over to the chest of drawers so as to stand exactly where she had been standing an hour earlier. In the dim room, the light from the streetlamps outside providing minimal luminance, I saw the outline of the three photo frames. One featured Titus as a little boy – probably seven years old, his face screwed up in a completely joyous smile, holding a school certificate in his hand. The other smaller frame was of Matthew and his sister Collette, taken a few years before her death. My memory wasn't completely clear on when and why, but it was probably shot at her university town of Durham while she was a student there when Matthew went up to visit her from Oxford. And then, in the centre, in the largest frame, there was a photo of me and Matthew and Titus taken at our wedding. Titus was only just ten and looked so smart and happy in his suit. We all looked smart and happy. Maybe it was this she had been staring at. Marvelling at our happy life. How we'd made it work, year after year. Or maybe she just had something else on her mind when she was looking at the photographs. I don't know how long I had been standing there looking at them when Matthew spoke to me from the bed.

'What are you doing?' His voice was slurred with sleep and I heard him shift a little to get a better look at me.

I turned and went back to the bed. 'Just looking at our wedding day,' I said as I got in.

'Nice day,' he murmured. Then his breathing became steady again and I could tell he'd drifted back off to sleep. And a few moments later, I was asleep too.

Chapter Eight

CHARLIE

The day of the murder

Titus and I wait on the steps of the police station. We are both unable to speak. Eventually, I step closer to him and put an arm over his shoulder. I feel him almost collapse into me, his firm form pressing into my side, and I feel his steady, rasping breaths. 'It's OK,' I say softly, although my words are probably lost to him amidst the noise of all the cars and pedestrians bustling past.

He doesn't say anything while we wait there for my mother to arrive, and although my mind is racing, throwing up question after question in my head, I don't have the mental bandwidth to form them into coherent sentences at this point. Mum parks around the back of the building, on Ebury Square, and we walk around to see her sitting in the front of the dark-red Bentley Bentayga. Even in the darkness and dull lamplight, I can tell she looks pale with shock. She motions from the window to get in quickly. We do as instructed, Titus getting in the back while I walk round to the spare front seat.

'Are you all right?' she says immediately as we climb in. 'I've been so worried.'

'We're … we're fine,' I say, though I know it isn't the truth – and so does she. She looks pale and tense, but her driving is smooth and controlled as we glide along the empty residential streets. I partly expect her to ask exactly what's happened, but she keeps silent for the rest of the journey. Biding her time. I presume she wants to question me away from Titus.

When we pull up outside the house, a few beats of silence pass, then she says, 'I understand all of this must be a shock for you, and I can't imagine you'll want to go through it all now. I'm just … just very thankful you're both safe. It's all a terrible tragedy, and we've undoubtedly got some difficult days ahead of us. So let's all get some rest, and tomorrow we can face the day with stronger and clearer minds.'

It's sort of like a hybrid between a speech a coach does before a sports game and a priest at a funeral. I'm not in the right state to match it, or reply in any way at all, so I just nod then turn around to Titus. A single tear is falling down along the bridge of his nose. When he sees me looking he wipes it and then opens the door. Both Mum and I follow his lead and we all walk into the house.

'I phoned your father,' Mum says as soon as the door has closed. 'He's flying back from New York as soon as he can.'

I nod. 'Will he be coming here or going to his house?'

My mother and father have a relationship I once considered unusual, but as the years have gone by, I've realised it isn't as uncommon as one might think. They're just more no-nonsense about it than most. After marrying in their late twenties, having me and then steadily growing apart, they opted for a compromise rather than a divorce: they have their own houses but they still do things as a couple. They go to dinners, to the theatre and opera, even holidays, but most of the year they live separated, albeit geographically close to each other. When he's in London, my father resides in a house on St George's Square, Pimlico, where I spent most of my time growing up, in between school and our country home, Braddon Manor. My mother's house in Wilton Crescent was purchased during termtime when I was thirteen years old. I just visited home one day to find a removal firm carrying out boxes, with my mother supervising. She turned to me and said, 'I'm moving house, darling. Join me in the car on the drive there and I'll tell you all about it.' And from that day on, my life was fragmented. Of course, I'm well aware that my broken home isn't, in the grand scheme of things, anything to complain about compared to what some children go through. My parents never had shrieking rows, never threw plates, were never nasty or cruel to me or to each other. They just decided the best way to manage the latter part of their marriage was to do it separately. And because of the wealth my family is lucky enough to have, they can do it from the comfort of two townhouses in Central London.

'Why don't you both go and get some of your own clothes on,' Mum says, noticing me looking down at the tracksuits the police have given us. 'Or your pyjamas,' she says this more to Titus than to me. 'I'm sure you'll feel more comfortable.'

Titus nods and mutters, 'I want to have a bath.'

I know how he feels. It's like we've somehow been infected with the horror of what's happened – like the invisible residue of the shock and the brutality of it still clings to our skin.

'Of course, dear,' Mum says. 'Would you like me to run it for you?'

He shakes his head. 'I'll be fine.' He then disappears upstairs, leaving Mum and me standing in the hallway in the spot where he'd just been seconds before. I can feel the air alive with tension. With all the things she wants to ask, all the things I want to say and not to say. But again, my mother surprises me once again by saying, 'You should go up with Titus. Keep an eye on him. You understand me?'

I meet her eyes. Then nod. 'Of course.' I start to go up the stairs, then turn back to her. 'Mum,' I say. She shakes her head, and walks away from me towards the kitchen. I pause on the stairs for a moment, then go back down the two I had climbed and follow her.

'I would have thought … you'd have wanted to talk.'

She pours herself a glass of water and is eyeing me over the gleaming countertop. 'I told you to go upstairs and keep an eye on Titus. There'll be plenty of time to talk later when your father's home. I doubt you'd like to go through the whole business more than once, so I suggest you go and get some rest.'

I look at her, uncertainty and concern bubbling somewhere within me.

'Please, Charles. I do have questions I want answered, particularly about Rachel and Titus. But now isn't the time. Please go and check on your son. I really don't think I should have to say it again.'

Our eyes remain locked for another few seconds. Then I relent and leave the kitchen, taking the stairs two at a time.

Titus shouts at me when I enter the bathroom without knocking. He pulls his legs up close and looks at me with outrage on his face.

'I'm sorry. I just wanted … to make sure you were OK.'

His head turns away from me, his eyes resting on the still gushing tap. There's something strangely comforting about the sound of the running water, and I feel crushingly exhausted all of a sudden. I sit down on the closed loo seat and put my head in my hands. 'I think we should talk,' I say to the floor.

I hear the water stop, leaving an odd ringing silence between us. Then: 'I don't want to talk about it.' He says it in the small voice of a boy years younger than him. It reminds me of the rare times when he's got into trouble at school, or lost his homework, or done something wrong at home. Matthew always accused me of rushing to reassure him too quickly, to tell him whatever it is doesn't matter, and he doesn't need to be upset about it. 'Some things do matter, some things are worth being upset about,' Matthew said to me one time when I'd hugged Titus before the boy had properly explained what was wrong. 'If you tell him it doesn't matter, he won't bother trying.' I objected to this. Although Matthew wasn't one of those harsh, tough-love sorts of parents, I didn't like his occasionally negative outlook on life and its woes. I understand why; he encountered more grief and regret in his teens and twenties than some do in a whole lifetime.

I focus my gaze on Titus, choose my words carefully, then speak: 'I think … I think it would be useful, for us going forward, to be clear on what each of us says to the police.'

He won't meet my eyes at first. 'Why?' he says, still staring at the taps. 'There's not much to say, is there? Rachel came into the house while we were having dinner. She killed Dad. She phoned the police.' His eyes flick up to meet mine, now, and although the bathroom is warm with steam, I suddenly feel a chill run down me.

'That's it, right?' he says, unblinking.

I stare at him, not wanting to move. My body is tense, frozen almost, the intensity between us growing. Eventually I say, 'Yes. That's it. That's what I said, too. Aren't you … I just thought you'd be wondering why. Why she confessed. Because I…'

A shake of his head stops me mid-sentence. 'I *don't* want to talk about it. Not now.'

I consider pressing on, ignoring his protestations, but something in his cold, hard gaze – at odds with the scared little boy he had sounded like moments before – keeps me silent. 'OK,' I say. He carries on looking at me for a few seconds more. Perhaps he's expecting me to leave, but I stay where I am. Then he leans back and stretches out his body and submerges himself under the water, bubbles rising as he lets his breath out. While he's out of sight, hidden under the rippling water, I let my eyes scan the shelves above the sink. I know Dad still likes to shave with a cut-throat razor, but there is no sign of it here, suggesting he rarely sleeps in my mother's house these days. Reassured, I get up just as Titus comes up for air.

'I'll leave you to get dressed,' I say, heading for the door.

'There's nothing to get dressed *in*. I don't have any clothes here, apart from that,' he says, jabbing a dripping hand towards the discarded tracksuit on the floor.

'The family liaison officer will be with us tomorrow. She'll bring some clothes for us from the ... from the house.'

The sentence snags in my mind as I say it. Because it isn't just our house any longer. It is a crime scene. The site of a murder. Forever to be tainted as such in the minds of whoever knows what's happened there. Especially us.

'Fine,' he says simply. I pick up one of the folded towels from the ledge to the left, and leave it by the side of the bath for him. 'Try to get some sleep. And come and see me if you need to talk.'

He nods and reaches for the towel. I leave him to dry himself in private, my heart thumping in my chest, a thousand thoughts scrabbling for attention as I walk towards the guest bedroom Matthew and I always stay in. As soon as I'm in the room, I collapse onto the bed. My head is pounding. Pulling myself up, I reach into the bedside cabinet and scrabble around, sure there is a box of paracetamol or ibuprofen somewhere inside. I find a box and don't stop to check what the tablets are or if they are within date; I just down two of them dry, the bitter, chemical taste coating my mouth.

I close my eyes and try to focus on the sweet smell of the fabric softener and the slightly rasping sound the duvet makes as I brush my face along its cool surface, trying to stop my mind dragging me back to the house. Our house. Our dining room. And what happened there. The blood. The noise Matthew made after the stabbing. Him trying to form words while the life dwindled from his eyes. I press my hands into my face, trying to clear the horror from my mind. I don't succeed. I end up back there, again and again. It's inevitable. I know by this point in my life that the more you try not to think about something, the more it feasts on every part of your mind. But, in spite of this – or maybe because of it – I still manage to drift off to sleep. A half-sleep. In and out. I swim between dream and memory, thought and fragmented image. I feel hot and cold all at the same time. It's as if I have flu – really bad, signed-off-work-for-a-week flu. I feel myself starting to shiver, my temperature rising in my head, pressure pounding against my temple. I shed my clothes like some deranged, desperate animal ripping off an old skin; there is something primal and strangely reptilian in the way the ugly grey tracksuit falls from me and I crawl across the bed, naked and new, relishing the sheets for both their coolness and warmth. I pull the duvet round me and clutch onto it like a life-raft. I lie there for hours, but it could have been minutes, or it could have been years. Time has stopped functioning for me. Then, dully, I become aware that someone has entered the room and is trying to talk to me.

'Charles. Can you hear me?'

There's a strong dose of urgency in the voice. Mum's voice. I look up, blinking at the brightness of the light above her head.

'Yeah … what?' I say, barely comprehensible.

She leans forward to pick something off the bed. 'Charles, how many of these have you taken? The ibuprofen and codeine. There's a whole sheet empty in here. How many tablets did you take?' I realise she has the box of tablets in her hands and is pulling out the blister pack.

'What?' I say again, only vaguely understanding the cause of her panic. 'No. I mean, I haven't taken too many. Just … two.'

'Are you sure?' she asks firmly, and I nod.

She lets out a sigh of relief. 'Sorry. I just … I was worried.'

'I know. It's OK.' I try to sit up. 'I wouldn't do that.'

She nods. 'I didn't think you would. But I just got a bit of a fright, seeing you there with the box. Never mind.'

I rub at my eyes. 'I don't feel too well,' I say.

'It's the shock,' she replies. She puts a hand onto my shoulder. I think she's about to say words of comfort, but instead she says, 'I'm not stupid. I know what happened. As I said earlier, I don't want to go through it all until your father gets home. But I promise that we'll do everything we can to make sure Titus is protected.' Her voice is low, quiet, and, typically for her, calm and controlled. 'Your father has already contacted our solicitor. Titus will never see prison, stand trial, or even be arrested by the police. Not if we can help it.'

Chapter Nine

RACHEL

Eleven months to go

Getting caught by Charlie in the bedroom was foolish, but I just had to see for myself. To see where *he* lived. How he lived. And where his adopted son lived...

I was disappointed, when I reached the landing, to see one of the doors shut, with music playing from inside. Some sort of opera music, from what I could hear. If only he'd been out, and his room left empty, his door open and inviting. Thankfully, however, the door to the master bedroom was open, its contents there for all the world to see. It was a dangerous thing to do, knowing there was someone else upstairs, but throwing caution to the wind, I stepped forward and walked the length of the landing over to the doorway.

The air smelled of men's perfume, plus another note, something fresher. Perhaps they had an air scent plugged into the wall – or would posh people find those vulgar?

Before I could notice anything else, I heard movement behind me and I ducked inside the room, crouching down on the soft carpet like a child caught with their hand in the sweet jar.

But whoever it was hadn't come for me. Very slowly, I leaned my head out so I could see the landing and, sure enough, the figure of Titus emerged presumably coming from the bathroom and returning to his room. I was surprised he didn't have an en suite to himself, but maybe only the main bedroom has one; I wouldn't know. I'd never been in one of these big townhouses before.

The pull towards him was so strong, I could feel my heart beating, pushing me forward; it was like a harsh pain within me, but one I never wanted to go away. It took all my effort not to run right then from the room over to his bedroom. Of course, I didn't do that. Instead I stood very still and, in order to calm myself down, I turned and faced the top of the chest of drawers I was leaning against. On its surface was an iPad in a smart dark leather case. I could tell from the small logo in the corner it was Louis Vuitton. It probably cost the same as my whole month's wages at the garden centre. Next to it was a Jo Malone candle, which explained the scent in the room. And next to that was a framed photo. It wasn't dissimilar to the one I saw on Instagram, just weeks previously, although the boy's face in it was a lot younger. It was of Charlie, Matthew, and Titus, with the latter probably around seven or eight, in school uniform, holding up a certificate of some kind. I reached out and touched the photo, then pulled my hand back quickly, worried I'd leave a mark.

There was another frame next to it, smaller than the other, this one a photograph of a teenage girl, laughing at the camera, a Christmas tree behind her. I didn't linger on this one. Instead, I turned my attention back to the photo of the happy, smiling family. And that's when I heard the voice from the doorway.

'Er … hi.'

I tried to iron out the awkwardness as best I could. I tried to be embarrassed and apologetic, saying I'd gone into the wrong room. But I saw a frown crease Charlie's brow that worried me. And it continued to worry me, all the way through the last part of the evening, and on my way home to my dark, lonely flat.

Patience, I tried to tell myself. *Keep things slow. Choose your moment. Everything will work out in the end.*

Chapter Ten

CHARLIE

Ten months before

Looking back at when I had my initial reservations about Rachel, it's hard to admit that some of them – if not all of them – were based on snobbery. But they were. Not because she wasn't as financially comfortable as we were, or had a different accent or any of that. It was because she just wasn't part of our club. Our little network, where everyone seems to know everybody, or acts as if they do. Of course, we meet new people all the time, but not in the aisles of supermarkets. And you certainly don't expect a seemingly chance encounter like that to play such a big part in one's life.

I was having a tedious day in the office one unusually sunny October afternoon when things stepped up a gear with Rachel. A simple phone call was all it took to turn the day on its head.

'Hi, it's me,' Titus said at the end of the line, even

though I'd seen it was him from the caller ID. 'So … this is a bit weird, but I'm at the police station. Something's happened.'

I dropped both the project folder and iPad I was holding. Crouching down to pick them up, as Juliette turned back to look at me and asked, 'You all right?', I nestled the phone against my neck. 'What's happened? What police station?'

'Kensington. I … I was sort-of mugged. A gang of boys. It happened near the Albert Hall.'

'Christ,' I said, ignoring Juliette's panicked look and walking away from the printers and into my office. I closed the door and reached for my jacket. 'I'll come right away. Is your dad already en route?'

'I couldn't get hold of him. I phoned but it rang and rang, so I left him a voicemail. And I've sent him a WhatsApp, but he's not read it.'

This was odd. Matthew was sometimes off on work trips to see professors and historians who often lived in secluded parts of the country, and of course sometimes that came with a lack of signal, but as far as I knew, today was just a general office day.

'Right. Not a problem. I'm on my way.'

He said, 'OK' then hung up. I stuffed my folder and iPad into my bag, then headed out of the building via the lifts. I tried Matthew's phone but just got his voicemail. As I walked towards the underground garage, I felt a strong sense of irritation towards him. The very time when there was an emergency and Titus needed us both, he was impossible to reach. I got into my car and punched out a blunt message:

Titus at Kensington Police Station. He's been attacked. Getting him now. Please call me.

I started the engine and drove out of the car park. The streets were jam-packed as ever, and it took me nearly ten minutes to get out of Fitzrovia alone. Images of Titus being held against a wall and punched by a gang of hoodies, all of them cheering as blood splattered across his face and his possessions were snatched from his person, flashed across my mind. I felt the frustration I'd aimed towards Matthew now twist into a fiery rage at Titus's attackers. How dare they mess with our boy?

I arrived at Kensington Police Station just under half an hour later. I marched through the doors and instantly saw Titus on some seats in the corner away from the counter, sitting next to a blonde woman. I went over and, without saying anything, embraced him, pulling him close into my arms. 'I'm fine, it's OK,' he said. 'They didn't really hurt me.'

I nodded, feeling tears rising behind my eyes, relief flooding my mind and body. As I let him out of my arms and looked at him, my eyes took in the blonde-haired woman next to us.

'Rachel?' I said, confused, wondering if there was something I was missing. 'Why … why are you here?'

'She was amazing,' Titus said before Rachel had a

chance to speak. She stood up and offered me a slightly shy smile.

'Hi,' she said. 'I'm glad you're here. You must have been so worried. But he was so brave.'

'I don't think I was brave; *you* were the brave one,' he said, looking over at her, then back at me. 'Dad, Rachel saved me. She really did.'

Rachel waved her hand in an it-was-nothing gesture. 'It wasn't that impressive. The lads who were bothering Titus were cowards anyway. I'm just so glad I was passing and could give them a piece of my mind.'

I tried to compute all this. 'Wait… You saw the mugging? And, what, stepped in?'

She nodded. 'Yeah, I was just out on a stroll, saw this group of lads trying to take this boy's phone and so I just … just told them to sod off, basically. And it turned out the boy was your Titus, here.'

I looked back at Titus who was now grinning. I could see a slight graze on his cheek and noticed his school uniform was all scruffy. It was a more reassuring sight than the visions of blood and bruises I'd imagined, but still… I hated the thought of someone being rough with him.

'I think the police will need to speak to you. I'm surprised they haven't already come over. They've been really good, though.' She nodded at me, as if trying to make me feel better, but I felt a slight jab of annoyance about the way she said it. As if *she* were the responsible parent, here at my son's side, and I was still playing catch-up, late to the game, secondary to the event. Which, in some ways, I was.

'Sure,' I said, 'I'll speak to them now.' I turned back to Titus. 'Have you got through to Dad yet?'

He shook his head. 'Haven't you?'

'No,' I said, glancing at my phone. 'He still hasn't replied.'

'Must be a busy day at work,' Rachel said in a jollier voice than I thought appropriate for the situation.

I gave a vague nod, then put my phone back in my pocket and went to speak to the police officer on the desk.

I hadn't really wanted to give Rachel a lift; I found her presence in this worrying ordeal more than a little awkward, similar to when I had found her nosing about upstairs. It was like she'd been helicoptered into the personal side of our lives. More than just friends, within the space of a month or so. She was being woven into the fabric of our family, and this little event seemed to make those threads tighter and more resolute.

We drove in silence for a little while, then, in lieu of anything else to say, I asked, 'So, how are you finding London?' I had a suspicion either I or someone else had asked Rachel the same question at our book-club meeting, but I didn't really care. After all, maybe her opinion on the place had changed since moving here.

'Oh, I love it,' she said. 'It's … it's so big. Of course, Yorkshire is vast, but in a different way.' She gave a little laugh after this, probably aware she was stating the obvious.

'Have you had time to explore anywhere nearby?' I asked, turning the car onto the Chelsea Embankment, bringing the Thames into view, glittering in the dying evening sun.

'Yes, I have. It's all I do, really. Walk about and listen to books as I go. I really need to find a job but I can't seem to find anything I'm very employable for.'

There was something strange about her whole story that didn't quite ring true. Who moves from the North of England down to London, rents a place in one of the most expensive postcodes in the country, and doesn't have any urgency to find employment? Of course, I know people who do just that – but they're living in townhouses and have assets, like sprawling country estates, and live off their inherited wealth. But Rachel's choice of a flat in a council estate with a history of gang violence and street crime suggested she didn't have a bottomless well of money. Maybe she just liked a simpler existence, but all the same, there was something a bit odd about her situation. Something she was choosing not to divulge.

This was the first time I'd driven deep into the Churchill Gardens Estate. Even though I had lived in Pimlico for years, practically just around the corner in St George's Square, I was shocked at how different everything could become by just turning down a few streets. Three hooded boys, one on a bike, the two others leaning up against a wall, watched us as I parked the car in front of the entrance of her block. They were smoking, and when Rachel opened the passenger door I could hear the tinny beat of music pulsing from their general direction – probably from their pocketed phones.

'Thank you so much for the lift,' she said as she went to get out of the car.

'Thanks for everything,' Titus said, turning round in his seat. It was the first time he'd properly spoken since we left the police station.

'Yes, thank you,' I said.

'I'd invite you both in but it's all a bit of a mess, and the size of a cupboard.' She laughed, again a little awkwardly.

I eyed the boys by the door, still overtly watching us (or the BMW X6 we'd arrived in). 'Are you OK to, er…' I felt compelled to ask if she was OK walking in alone, whilst being painfully aware this could sound both judgemental towards the boys and patronising towards her. I think she understood both my concern and dilemma, and smiled. 'I'll be fine. Well, I'll see you at the next book-club meeting. Matthew messaged me the details the other day.'

He did, did he? I wasn't sure why, but the fact he hadn't mentioned this to me felt slightly hurtful. Secretive, almost, as if he knew I had a 'bit of a thing' about Rachel being part of our lives and had chosen to keep the subject at arm's length, all the while sending friendly little messages to her on WhatsApp. I stopped myself continuing down this rather silly mental avenue in time to smile back at Rachel and wish her goodnight as she walked the short distance towards the entrance to her block of flats. The boys watched her go in, but didn't react or move.

'Are we going?' Titus asked when we'd been sitting stationary for a little while, my mind whirring.

'Oh, sorry. Miles away.'

I took off the handbrake and drove through the tight roads of the estate and out onto the main road. The rest of the drive home was filled with me questioning Titus about exactly what had happened. He remained frustratingly silent for the most part – not grumpy or surly exactly, just reliant on one-word answers and seemed more interested in staring out of the window. I tried not to be offended that he'd apparently seemed perfectly fine to talk to Rachel about the incident at the police station, but seemed to want to clam up now it was just him and me. She had been there though, I thought to myself. She was more than a kind ear during his moment of distress; she was a vital part of it. His saviour.

When we got in, I turned my attention to another pressing concern: my missing husband. Jane, who should really have gone home an hour ago, was just carrying a basket of laundry up the stairs when we walked in. She greeted us warmly, then said no, Matthew wasn't at home and she hadn't heard any messages come through to the answerphone. I checked it, regardless, even though neither of us ever used it these days, relying almost entirely on our smartphones. Just as I was starting to feel panic unfurl within me again, the buzz of an incoming call caused my pocket to vibrate.

'What's happened? Is he OK?' Matthew immediately started talking very fast as soon as I'd accepted the call.

'Where *are* you?' I replied, rather than answering this question. It was probably bad of me, but I was pissed off that in an hour of stress and concern he had vanished into thin air.

'I've been stuck in traffic. I had to go and see this

professor in Margate. There was a nasty accident on the way home and I was stuck in the jam it caused. Is Titus OK? Is he in hospital?'

I let out a breath of relief, then almost laughed at the thought of Titus being in hospital when in fact he was now lying on the sofa, pointedly perusing the Domino's menu. I'm not sure what it was – the light-headedness that comes with knowing things are all OK, or a natural high that follows a tense couple of hours of anxiety – but I suddenly felt happy and free. 'He's fine. He's completely fine. He's sitting here now. We're at home. Do you want to speak to him?'

I gave Titus the phone and he took it.

'Dad, I'm fine,' he said, rolling his eyes a little.

I took the Domino's menu he was holding and pointed at the American Hot on one of the pictures, and he grinned and nodded. I went through to the kitchen while I ordered the pizza from the app on my phone, all the while aware I was listening out for a keyword. And before long, I heard it.

'Yeah, Rachel. She was there. She was amazing.'

Chapter Eleven

CHARLIE

Ten months to go

When Matthew arrived home, almost at the same time as the pizza, we went through a proper post-mortem of what happened to Titus.

'I can't believe they just tried to take your phone. In broad daylight. In *Kensington*.' Matthew was both baffled and angry. I couldn't help feeling, if I had said the 'in Kensington' line in another context, he'd have taken the piss out of me. He shook his head, then chewed thoughtfully on a slice of pizza crust. 'I suppose they won't ever catch the boys.'

'Well, I don't know,' I said. 'There's a lot of CCTV around the Albert Hall area. They might be able to track them down.'

'And Rachel was there?' Matthew continued, looking at Titus questioningly.

He nodded. 'She was just walking by. It was really nice of her to help out. It was all … well, horrible, really.'

'I'm sure it was,' Matthew said, rubbing Titus's arm. 'Thank goodness Rachel was passing by.'

'Bit odd, isn't it,' I interjected, 'how she was just there, at the right place and the right time?'

A frown creased Matthew's forehead. 'What do you mean? I'd say it was jolly good luck.'

I chose my words carefully as I closed up the pizza box in front of me. 'I just mean that, out of all the thousands of people walking the streets of London, Rachel is in that very street at the very moment when Titus is in need.'

I could see Titus watching me now too, and I suddenly felt a tad rattled by their sceptical expressions. 'Oh, come on, I just mean … what are the chances?'

'Well, coincidences happen,' Matthew said with a little shrug. Then he turned to Titus.

'What were you doing in Kensington, anyway?'

The look of sheepishness was as plain as day on the boy's face. 'Oh, well … I was … just out for a walk.'

'A walk?' I repeated. 'With all your school things? Why didn't you drop them back home first?'

Titus was looking at his plate now. His lips twitched a little, like he was filtering his response, trying to think how to compose it. 'I was … visiting a friend.'

Matthew smiled. 'Well, why the secrecy? Is this a friend from school? What's his name?'

Titus shifted in his chair, as if he couldn't get comfortable. 'I … it's … she's a she. Not a he.'

I could see Matthew computing this and then come to

the same result at the same time as me: Westminster School doesn't have girl students in the lower years.

'So, if she's a she,' he said slowly, 'and a friend from school, she must therefore be…'

'A sixth former,' Titus replied, his eyes in the direction of the table.

A few moments of silence greeted this. 'Right,' Matthew said. 'Well, that's nice.'

'What's her name?' I asked.

'Melanie.'

'Since your school only allows girls in the sixth form, I presume Melanie goes to a different school?' Matthew said.

I saw a flash of indignation ignite Titus's face, but he didn't dodge the question this time. 'She's … she doesn't… She's eighteen.'

Silence. Matthew and I looked at each other. He decided to go first. 'Um … don't you think … that's a bit of an age gap?'

Titus met his gaze with defiance in his eyes. 'There are nearly three years between you two. Why's this so different? And anyway, why have you suddenly presumed that we're fucking? I didn't say we were.'

The shock at hearing him say 'fucking' hit me hard, almost like a physical force. Titus had sworn within our hearing before, but always in a comic way, or to deliberately wind us up. The use of the word in this context made it sound adult and serious, as if he'd joined a more mature and severe world without us realising it.

'It's different,' Matthew replied, 'because you're fourteen years old, and we're both in our thirties. And regarding the fucking, if we're apparently using such language at the dinner table now, I'm sure you realise that wouldn't just be a question of age-gap disapproval. That would be a crime.'

Titus let out a low laugh. 'Oh, come on. I'm not like a victim of grooming or anything. I thought you guys would be casual about it.'

'Well you clearly didn't think that,' Matthew snapped back, 'otherwise you'd have told us about her sooner, rather than us having to wait for you to be mugged outside her flat before we found out.'

Titus got up abruptly. 'I'm going to bed.'

Matthew stood up too. 'We need to get to the bottom of this. Are the two of you an item? Were her parents home? Who even *are* her parents? Would we know them?'

Titus tucked his chair in under the table with a slam. 'No, we're not an item. She just fucks me occasionally when we both have some spare time. I'm sorry I nearly got beaten up and ruined your evening. Goodnight.' He stormed out of the room and thumped up the stairs. We heard his door slam. Then Matthew put his head in his hands and rested his elbows on the table.

'Christ,' he said, 'this is awful.'

I moved round the table to the chair next to him and laid an arm over his shoulder. 'It'll be OK,' I said. 'We'll talk to him.'

'Do you think we should involve the school?' He took his head away from his hands and looked at me.

'I … I don't know. Perhaps it would be best to handle it

privately. We don't want to, well, overreact...' I said, treading carefully.

Matthew moved his jaw a little from side to side, something he does occasionally when he's thinking. 'We would, you know ... if Titus were a girl, and the eighteen-year-old was a boy. We would tell the school. So is this any different?'

I let out a sigh. After the evening I'd had, racing across London, talking to police, getting incident numbers, not being able to get through to Matthew throughout it all ... I really didn't need another slab of drama to go with the rest of it. 'Are you saying we'd be sexist if we didn't?'

It was his turn to sigh now. 'God, I don't know. I just feel like ... like I'm failing. That he's become a victim in two different ways, and I didn't know. Both from that gang who could have hurt him far worse than they actually did, and now he's being ... I don't know what ... seduced by this woman.'

'I think "woman" might be pushing it,' I said. 'She's still a schoolgirl. She probably doesn't think she's doing any harm.'

I felt Matthew tense and move away from me. 'Again, I don't think you'd be saying that if the genders were reversed.'

This annoyed me. 'Well what do you want me to say? That we should call the police and report her? I don't mean to sound like some sex-offender apologist, but it really doesn't sound like he's been coerced or forced into anything. And anyway, how old were you when you had your first experience?'

He frowned. 'I was fifteen.'

I raised my eyebrows at him. 'And the other ... er ... participant?'

He didn't meet my eye when he answered. 'Seventeen, I think. I'm sure I told you about it ages ago.'

'Well,' I said, 'I'm of course not saying this doesn't need sorting out, I just think we might need to pause and consider our best steps before we go crashing into the situation and potentially ruin people's lives.'

He continued to look back at me for a few seconds, then nodded. 'OK. You're right. I just don't like it. That sound of ... dismissive behaviour. Easy come, easy go. It reminds me of his...' He stopped speaking for a moment and I finished his sentence for him.

'His father. I know.' I let my arm fall down onto his and gave it a small squeeze of support. 'Come on, we should probably get an early night and talk to Titus about it in the morning when we're not all het up.'

He gave me a small nod. 'That sounds like a good plan.'

I was sitting in bed when Matthew said it. To be honest, if it hadn't been for the confusion about where he was and the distraction of learning Titus, aged fourteen, was no longer a virgin, I'd have expected the conversation to reach the topic of Rachel sooner.

'We should have her over to dinner. Rachel, that is.'

I pulled my eyes away from our upcoming book-club choice, and looked over at him, adopting an I'm-just-processing-the-question look. I'd heard him clearly enough – my whirring brain hadn't taken in any of the words on the page since I'd opened the book five minutes before – but I wanted to buy time. I had the feeling our discussion had the potential to descend into a row, and by that point in the evening, my stamina just wasn't up to it.

'Why? Because of her helping Titus?' I asked.

He stared at me like I was a dimwit. 'Of course because of her helping Titus.'

I said nothing for a bit whilst he pulled off his clothes and got into bed. Then, at last, I voiced the thing that had been most on my mind ever since seeing her there, in the police station. 'I'm puzzled why you don't think the whole thing's a bit odd. Surely this is too much of a coincidence? Her being there, ready to be the hero.'

'I'm puzzled why you're not already ordering her flowers as a thank-you. She saved our son from *potential death*.' He emphasised the words, his eyes wide and, stupidly, I laughed.

'Potential death? Oh, come on.'

'Do you know how many people have been stabbed in London this year alone? Most of them are boys and young men, too. Just because we live in our cosy little cotton-wool world, doesn't mean things like that can't knock on our door.'

I tried to slam my book shut in protest at his condescending tone, but it didn't really have the desired effect, since it was an old and flimsy paperback. 'Of course I know that. I read the news.'

'Then you'll know,' he continued, 'that things like that

can go tragically wrong. So many people would have just carried on past him. Many probably did when they saw those boys rounding on him. But Rachel chose not to. And that makes her more than just a good friend. It makes her amazingly brave, and worthy of thanks. I think a nice evening of food and wine at a restaurant or here, if you prefer, is a small price to pay as a thank-you, even if you are prejudiced against her.'

I grimaced. 'I'm not *prejudiced*. I'm just … I don't know. It just all seems too perfect.'

Matthew made a noise of disbelief as he reached over to turn off the light. 'What do you think she's doing? Following Titus around the streets of London, hoping for a chance to save him from some thugs? That would be a bit of a strange thing to do, wouldn't it?'

Chapter Twelve

RACHEL

Ten months to go

Deciding to follow Titus as he made his way from Westminster to Kensington had been a good decision. It had been one of those pivotal moments from which you can see all future events spin off as a result. It was dangerous, definitely ill-advised, but in the end, brilliantly effective.

I knew from my conversations with Matthew at the book club that Titus went to Westminster School as a day student. And being in Westminster, I figured I couldn't be far from him. Maybe I could just be passing, I thought, or taking a look at a touristy landmark and offer to walk him home, or watch to see if he got on a bus or tube back to Chelsea and then 'happen' to be in the same carriage as him. I felt the blood start pumping within me, and before any firm plan had properly crystallised in my head, I found myself walking along Grosvenor Road and towards his school.

It took me just over twenty minutes, due to me taking a wrong turning somewhere, but I got back on track, and by the time I got to the school there were indeed students walking about, laughing and chatting. I was struck by how … well, how ordinary they all looked. They didn't look like posh kids. They were dressed in the same sort of blazer and tie students at my old state comprehensive wore in Bradford. I looked at them carefully, watching out for his light-blond hair, smooth, clear skin, and straight back. But no luck. The students were starting to thin out now, and I was left watching the stragglers, standing by the ancient stone buildings as the sound of traffic filling the nearby roads hummed along in the background.

The whole thing had been a stupid idea anyway, I thought. The chances I'd have seen him would have been slim, and even if I had, would he have wanted to speak to me? We'd barely spoken when I saw him in his home. He probably wouldn't have even recognised me.

I walked up the unusually narrow road away from the school in a bit of a daze, hoping I was walking in the general direction of my home. I started to become aware of two people walking slowly in front of me, so I went to go round and pass them. Then I felt my heart leap. It was him. He was here, right here, in the street in front of me. Two teenagers, a boy and a girl, engrossed in conversation. I carried on walking past them, so as not to draw attention to myself, crossed the road, then stopped for a bit, stooping to look at my phone and holding a tissue to my nose. I don't think they even glanced in my direction. I waited for a bit, then stuffed my tissue and phone back into my pocket and started to follow them.

The hand-holding began on the underground at Westminster station and continued most of the way to South Kensington. From my seat, opposite and four to the right, I could see her moving their clasped hands slowly, teasingly, up his thigh. And he grinned at her, as if wanting her to continue. How dare she? They were on the District line, not in the back row at the cinema. And, although I couldn't be sure, I suspected the girl was a little older than him. They were around the same height and she carried herself with confidence, clearly leading the way, making the decisions, guiding him. She was attractive, I'd give her that, with deep-brown hair and a tall, slim figure. But there was something in the way she looked at Titus that I didn't like. As if she had a little pet plaything that amused her. His face was happy and excited, clearly thrilled to be in her company, wherever it may lead.

At South Kensington, they both stood up at once, and it took me a few seconds of panic to scramble out of the packed tube and get out onto the platform in time to see them disappearing up the steps. I walked a good few yards behind them as they came out onto a little pedestrianised space, with a Paul bakery and Five Guys restaurant opposite. My journey following them took me past Imperial College London and the Science Museum, and part of me was even grateful for accidentally getting to see a new side of London – places I'd heard of but never visited. I turned off the main street and onto Kensington Gore, all the while keeping my distance, terrified they'd both suddenly turn around and say, 'Why are you following us, freak?' But they didn't do that. And as the road curved round, the view of the Royal Albert Hall came into view. I think I even stopped and stared for a bit, then had to hurry along, fearing I'd lose the two teenagers within the crowd of people walking towards the Hall. When I'd reached the pavement near the houses, Titus and the girl were nowhere to be seen. I'd lost them. Then, as I looked around, furious with myself, I saw them. They weren't on the pavement anymore; they were going up to a building – a house – and the girl was letting herself in with a key. She lived here, it seemed. Right here, on Kensington Gore, with the Royal Albert Hall within spitting distance. And Titus was following her inside.

I thought that was it, then. I thought everything was over. What had I hoped for, anyway? That he'd leave the girl at some point in his journey and go off for a walk on his own? It was clear from the start they were some sort of couple, and this made it blatantly obvious what was going on. My stomach turned, thinking about what might be happening up there in one of the rooms of that big terraced house – itself probably worth more than half a street of houses in Bradford. Then I checked myself. It could all be very innocent. They may be up there watching Netflix, an oven-cooked pizza shared between them, her teasing him about liking *Gilmore Girls*, him trying to pluck up the courage to take her hand. The image of them both together on the underground, her hand over his, came into my mind.

Whatever they were getting up to, they seemed to have got past the hand-holding stage. I found out later, of course, at the police station, that he and the girl had been having sex. He was careful not to tell the police this. But he told me. Our first little secret.

At this point, though, with me on the street, getting in the way of pedestrians, I could only torture myself with my own imagination. I decided to walk away from the house, leave the whole sorry business behind me, and go and have a look at the Albert Hall. The whole thing was so huge and impressive that it was an enjoyable distraction, to a point, and I took some photographs on my phone, playing with the light exposure in a way I'd once done with my own professional cameras. Back when such things mattered. But I ended up back on the street outside the house. That was when I saw the boys. They passed me, kicking a can down the street, laughing to themselves, and I caught a few charming sentences of their conversation. 'She was fuckin' wasted … yeah, course I smacked her one … that fucking slag.'

If I'd been alone, I'd have been worried for my safety, but there were some other passers-by, either going to or from the concert hall, and even the sight of the building in the corner of my eye was comforting. It didn't seem likely anything sinister could happen anywhere so famous and beautiful. Then Titus came out of the door in front of me, and all worry about the boys vanished. I quickly crossed the road, walked up the street a little way, then crossed again so I could follow behind him at a safe distance. The girl was with him, in an expensive-looking cream dressing gown – I imagine it made her feel all grown up, pressed against her naked skin. They didn't kiss or embrace, but Titus raised a hand in a little wave and walked down the few steps away from the house to the street as she closed the door.

Instead of walking back out towards the main road, Titus turned and walked up a dimly lit side street. He seemed to want to be able to do something on his phone out of the way, and stood against the wall of a building, looking down at the screen. Him being stationary made it difficult for me to watch him without being discovered. I was thinking about maybe passing him, going on ahead, and hoping he'd continue up the road, at some point allowing me to cross the road and double back, but he seemed engrossed in whatever he was doing – texting, messaging, browsing.

'Oi, mate, mate!' It was a loud, brash voice. The same voice that had talked about 'that fucking slag' earlier. He and his two mates emerged from behind one of the parked Range Rovers and bowled over with a confidence and swagger clearly meant to intimidate. Titus, who had glanced up at the 'Oi mate' froze, then quickly put his phone away.

'Mate, do us a favour,' the ringleader said as he approached, his baggy white T-shirt swaying around his muscled frame as he reached Titus. 'Lend us your phone for a sec. Need to call my girl. Mine's dead, and if I don't call her she'll give me a fuckin' earful, know what I mean?'

Titus immediately shook his head. 'Sorry, I'm … I'm in a hurry.' He turned to go but the main boy grabbed his shoulder.

'Hey, hey, what's the fuckin' rush, eh? I just need to use your phone. I just need a bit of help, mate, you know what I mean? Nothing dodgy, mate, nothing bad.' As he said this, the two other boys laughed.

Titus gave another vague shake of his head and again said, 'Sorry,' followed by, 'I need to go.'

That was when the boy seized him forcefully, throwing him against the wall, shouting in his face, 'Eh, what you being like that for? I was being polite, you know. I was being nice to you, just wanted you to help a mate out, know what I mean? Just wanted you to be a fuckin' good Samaritan, you fuckin' posh cunt.' He said the last two words with such anger and hatred that it sent a chill right through me. Then he slapped Titus hard across the face. The other boys laughed loudly, then, without needing any prompts from their vocal leader, they roughly twisted Titus around so his face was pressed hard into the concrete and started to search his blazer and trouser pockets, apparently looking for his phone.

'Leave him alone!' The words left my mouth in a bark-like shout with such force that for a second I thought someone else had spoken. I felt my knees tremble as I walked over to them. 'Let go of him.' It was now quickly dawning on me how dangerous a situation I'd placed myself in. Any of the boys could have had a knife. And any of them could choose to use it – in panic, fear, anger – at any second.

They did let go of Titus, letting the boy stumble and fall down to the pavement. He picked himself up immediately, brushing the grit off his knees and wiping blood from his face.

'What makes you so fucking bold, little lady?' the ringleader said. 'Need fucking sorting, you do.' He bared his teeth and then licked his lips, his tongue startlingly pink next to his vampire-pale skin. He then grabbed his crotch and gave it a squeeze. The others let out more laughs, although not quite as jubilant as before. All this clearly wasn't going according to plan.

'Not today, thanks,' I said, keeping my tone polite and business-like, as if I were the type of person who regularly had to deal with the likes of him. 'Right, Titus, you got all your things?'

The boy gaped at me, then gave a little nod.

'Good. Let's be off then. Lovely to meet you all.' I then took Titus by the shoulder and led him across the street and away from the boys, back in the direction of the Royal Albert Hall. 'Keep walking,' I murmured into his ear. I didn't stop until we got to the entrance of the concert hall. 'OK, I think we're safe now,' I said. 'Let me see your face.'

He raised his chin and let me look at him. 'Only cuts and grazes. You'll be OK.'

I took my phone out and started to dial.

'What are you doing?' he asked in a small voice.

'Reporting this to the police.'

He stared back in shock. 'What…? I mean, do we…?'

'Of course we have to,' I said in response. 'This needs to be reported. If they're still in the area, the boys could still be arrested. This is a crime, an attack – and they may do it to someone else if we don't.'

He listened, his eyes swimming with tears. They fell down his cheek as he nodded. I wrapped my arms around him and pulled him into a hug.

'Thank you,' he said, sobbing quietly into my shoulder. 'I ... I was scared.'

'I know,' I said. 'But it's over now.'

Chapter Thirteen

CHARLIE

Ten months to go

The morning after our row with Titus was tense and …
well, it was weird.

Usually – in fact, on every single occasion previous to
this one – any rows we'd had with him over the years had
dissipated, as if by magic, by the next morning, and we all
got to start again afresh. A new day, a new world,
everything good. This time it was different. Titus was
different. Usually, on a Saturday morning, Titus would go
down to the kitchen at around 7.30 or 8am, already fully
showered and dressed, and do an hour of studying. 'Start
the day as you mean to go on,' was a motto Matthew had
instilled in him. I'd spent most of our married life thinking
how clever this all was – making sure Titus's first go-to task
on a Saturday involved keeping himself occupied
downstairs alone, giving us time to have a lazy lie in,
enjoying not having to rush out of bed for work. Then, at

9ish, we would wander downstairs to find him laying the table for breakfast, which he would cook for us – not as some put-upon child, forced to make his parents meals. No, not one bit; he *enjoyed* doing it. His hazelnut chocolate loaf would put most artisan bakeries to shame. Then we would all talk about our plans for the weekend, whether they involved us all going somewhere as a family, or splitting up to do separate things. We weren't dictatorial and regimented, but that routine on Saturdays was *our thing*. Something that laid the foundations for a good weekend. Put us in a good mood. Kept us all happy as a family. On the morning after the whole fuss with the attempted mugging of Titus, followed by the revelation that he was apparently happily banging an older fellow student, all of this went out the window.

When I woke at 8.45am, with Matthew reading a book next to me, there was no smell of baked muffins or warm bread. The house was completely silent.

'Something's odd,' I said straightaway, leaning up.

'Good morning to you too,' Matthew replied, closing his book and laying it on the bedside table. 'Shall we go down to breakfast?'

'It's … it's late. I've slept in.' I rubbed my head. I felt wrecked, as if I'd had a night out with the boys. 'We should go down and see Titus,' I muttered, getting out of bed and pulling on some tracksuit bottoms.

Matthew didn't say anything at first, just opened the door, poked his head round, then said, 'I don't think he's up yet. His door's closed.'

This was not a good sign. Usually it would signal a bad

bout of flu or something equally debilitating. The two of us went down the stairs and looked around. Sure enough, no Titus, no cooking. Nothing laid out for breakfast. Our housekeeper Jane had weekends off, so the plates and glasses and pizza boxes from the night before were all still out.

Matthew wandered over to the coffee machine, and I poured myself a large tumbler of water. 'He's definitely here?' I said, slightly worried the boy had absconded to meet his illegal lover off in the depths of Kensington Gore. As if on cue, a thudding down the stairs heralded Titus's arrival. Although it wasn't the perfectly turned-out, sunny, happy Titus we were normally used to on Saturday mornings. He was wearing only a pair of white Ralph Lauren boxer-briefs, his hair was all messed up, and his grazed jaw gave him a devil-may-care look. He'd obviously just arisen from his bed. It was like a completely different person had arrived in our kitchen.

'Oh, hi,' he said, in a low monotone, and moved past me in order to get to the fridge. He pulled a can of Coke Zero from it – another bizarre change, since Titus usually only drank mineral water or a small glass of orange juice in the mornings – and then turned to leave.

'Good morning,' Matthew said to him, making him pause on his way out of the kitchen. 'It would be good if we could talk.'

He turned around, his face impassive, then he gave a lazy shrug. 'Maybe later. Going to go back to bed for a bit.'

He then turned his back on us and walked out of the

kitchen. Further thuds from the stairs then the slam of a door suggested this was exactly what he was doing.

'What the hell was that?' I said, turning to Matthew.

Matthew was staring into the distance. He looked worried and deep in thought. Even without him, I could answer my own question. That was Titus showing he gave zero fucks about our normal happy-families Saturday-morning routine. At least, on this morning he did.

'I think,' Matthew said slowly, 'we should probably leave him to work through this himself today.'

I looked at him. This was rather a reversal of roles from last night, when I'd been trying to calm him down at the thought of his son being seduced by a predatory older student. He still looked deep in thought as he turned back to the coffee machine and poured us both a cup. 'It looks like we're fending for ourselves for breakfast,' he said, opening up the cupboards. 'So … muesli or cornflakes?'

Things later in the day didn't get much better with Titus. In fact, they got worse before they got better. Matthew had been reading up on the balcony garden and I was doing some research online for a new car when the sound of raised voices disturbed me. I left my iPad on the sofa and went out into the hallway to find Titus coming down the stairs, Matthew closely following, both of them in the middle of a clearly tense conversation.

'You're not going; this isn't negotiable.'

'What are you going to do?' Titus shrugged. 'Imprison me in my room all day?'

'If we have to. But I really hope it won't come to that.'

Titus bent down by the door to pull on his shoes. He had an overnight bag with him – the sort of thing he'd take if he was going to stay with my parents or we went up to Scotland to visit Matthew's mother.

'What's going on?' I asked.

'I'm going to stay at Melanie's.'

'You are *not*,' Matthew said forcefully. 'You are fourteen years old. You're not ready for … for whatever it is you think you're ready for.'

Titus scoffed and began to lace up his shoes furiously. I bent down so I was on his level and said, in a calm voice, 'Maybe you could just come through to the lounge. Let's just sit down and have a chat. After that, if you still want to go, we won't stop you.'

I heard Matthew take a strong intake of breath through his nose as an unspoken way of saying, *We'll see about that*, but he didn't interrupt. And, to my surprise, Titus looked up at me and his expression softened. 'OK.'

He led the way into the lounge and sat down with a thump on one of the sofas. Matthew and I took the two-seater opposite him and I started to speak before the argument had time to restart.

'Titus, as I'm sure you can understand, we have some … well, concerns. Concerns about the age difference between you and…'

'Melanie.'

'Yes, Melanie. The fact remains that you are fourteen

years old, and although you *think* you know how you feel about … intimate things and relationships and love and the like, the truth is you're still so young. And it's easy to get things wrong or confused when you're young.'

He stared back at me, his eyes becoming stern and cold once more. 'I think all that could apply to adults too. I think adults can get things wrong. Do stupid things. I don't think it's just to do with age.'

I nodded. 'Yes, of course. But can you at least see where we're coming from? Even if we thought you were old enough to know your own mind on … things of this nature…'

'You can say "sex", you know. I'm not a child.'

'Well, that's kind of the point. You are. And, as I was saying, even if *you* feel ready to …'

'Fuck someone.'

Matthew took a sharp intake of breath at this and cracked his knuckles – something he does when he's stressed. I laid a hand on his knee, silently asking him not to start raging.

'… be *intimate* with someone,' I said firmly, still finding his use of strong language more than a little unsettling, 'the law doesn't agree. You know the age of consent is sixteen.'

'There's only three and a half years between us.'

I shook my head. 'It doesn't matter. She's an adult. You're not. What you're both doing is still illegal.'

He made another noise of disbelief. 'I don't think any judge or jury is going to fling me in jail for getting a blowjob after school.'

Another crack of Matthew's knuckles cut through the air.

'No, I'm sure you wouldn't be punished. But she might. In the eyes of the law, she's having sex with a child.'

'Oh, come on. There are things called Romeo and Juliet laws, aren't there? I'm fairly sure I've read about them.'

I winced at this. It was one of the few instances of Titus doing his research poorly. He's usually keen on getting facts right. It's what makes him such a good student. But here, he'd got things very wrong.

'I actually did some reading on this earlier this morning,' I replied, trying to keep up my calm, measured tone of voice. 'The laws you refer to are controversial laws in the United States, sometimes known as a "close in age exemption". In the UK, there is no "close in age exemption". While there would be no rush to prosecute two underage sixteen-year-olds, the law isn't cast aside for people over the age of sixteen having sex with someone below the age of consent. Even if the other was just a couple of years older.' While I was reasonably sure this was true, I hadn't found out how frequent such cases were – or if they even happened at all. All of this was uncharted territory for both Matthew and me. I knew at some point we'd have to deal with teenage crushes and broken hearts and discuss things like sex and relationships with our boy, but I didn't ever imagine the topic would manifest itself in a form as thorny and difficult as this.

'Titus, we just want you to be safe,' I said less firmly, laying my hands open in front of me. 'We want you to be happy, and of course we know you'll be … well, experimenting and trying things like this during your teen years. But really, I think what your dad and I are saying is, there's no rush. You're still so young. So, maybe you could just think about that and, perhaps, if this girl Melanie hasn't quite thought through the difficult situation she's putting both of you in, maybe she isn't the right girl for you. At least, not at this moment in time.'

I watched as he computed this. I was worried that criticising Melanie, even though I'd tried to sound as kind and diplomatic as possible, would prove a bad move. But to my surprise, he diverted his gaze to his hands which were bunched in his lap, spent a few more seconds deliberating, then eventually gave a short nod. 'Yes. You're right. I'm sorry.'

I felt the tension in Matthew ease, heard the rush of his breath being let out, as if he'd been holding it ever since we'd been sitting down. Progress had been made, and suddenly the air around us was less tight, less likely to develop into a thunderstorm.

'It's OK. You don't have to be sorry,' Matthew said now, getting up and going to sit next to Titus. He put his arm around the boy's shoulder. 'I'm sorry for flipping off a little about the whole thing. This is all a bit new to us. I just don't want to fail you. And … and I don't want to fail your mum.'

This rare reference to Matthew's sister made me start a little. I examined Matthew's face for any warning signs. He was prone to get tearful on the occasions he did discuss Colette. He was biting his lip a little, but seemed to have a handle on himself. Titus, meanwhile, gave another little nod and allowed himself to be hugged. 'I'm sorry,' he said again.

I saw his hand rise and scratch the cut on his chin, which seemed to have a bruise developing underneath it. He was probably still shaken up about the whole experience, and part of his acting out this morning was no doubt a symptom of that.

'We were thinking of asking Rachel to dinner,' Matthew said to Titus. 'Perhaps next weekend. Just to say thank you for being such a help yesterday.'

I saw him smile at this. 'Yes,' he said. 'I really like her. She was just … well, she was brilliant.'

I felt a flicker of irritation at hearing Rachel described as 'brilliant', making me feel bad that neither me nor Matthew were first on the scene after Titus's attack. But I said nothing. The truth was, she *had* been amazing.

Looking back now, this whole thing with Titus should have been a warning sign. I didn't spot the clues, didn't take heed of some things that seem plain now, with hindsight. Things about Matthew. Things about Titus. And the way Rachel managed to find her way into our lives.

Chapter Fourteen

CHARLIE

Ten months to go

It was decided the following weekend would be a good one for Rachel to come over. Matthew and Titus would cook and I ... well, I would spend the first part of the day playing tennis with my friend Archie. When Matthew said he was going out shopping to get food (unnecessary, in my view – the larder and fridge were more than well stocked, but apparently there was a 'certain kind of pasta' he and Titus really felt would go with the sauce they were putting together), I made a few oh-should-I-cancel-tennis-and-help remarks that I didn't really mean, but Matthew seemed to think it was better I was out of their way. And besides, I thought it would be good for him and Titus to spend some time together. Maybe they could talk about the state of Titus's illegal love life, which was, as far as we could gather, on a tentative hiatus.

At the tennis court, Archie spent so much time in the

changing rooms showing me pictures of his two new cars, I was half tempted to suggest we ditch the tennis game altogether and just head out for lunch. 'Goes like a fucking dream, mate,' Archie said to me, swiping through photos that alternated between showroom-glossy exterior shots of the bright green Lamborghini Huracán Evo Spyder and interiors that looked like something from *Star Trek*. I went through a phase of these types of cars when I was in my twenties, but a decade later I can't help but think they just look a bit childish. Impractical for the clogged-up roads of Central London and they have a show-off value that wears off the more people you show them to. Still, I thought to myself as I nodded and tried to look interested, if it made him happy to see a futuristic-looking slab of metal parked outside his house, who was I to argue?

After tennis, once we were settled at a table at The Roseberry in Knightsbridge, we started chatting about how things were going with work, at home, the usual stuff. Archie moaned a bit about one of his friends Dominic, who I only knew vaguely, who was apparently cheating on his wife with two mums from his children's school. 'He's becoming a bit of a prick, to be honest,' Archie said. 'Plus, he tried to convince me a ball was within the line when we grabbed a quick tennis game the other day when it clearly wasn't. You're a much better player than him, I must say. I should have treated him to your old tactics and knocked his teeth into the shower walls afterwards.'

I rolled my eyes, attempting to make light of his words. He was referring to an incident when I was fifteen and furious with another boy at school, Jasper King, when we were playing cricket. He'd stepped out of position, put me off my game, and then lied about it to everyone else after, making out I was the one at fault. I was rather hurt, to be honest, since I'd always regarded him as a friend. Our scuffle in the changing rooms later put an end to that though, and he walked away with a bleeding lip and me with a strict telling off and a call home to my parents, where phrases like 'zero-tolerance policy' and 'never happen again' were used.

Once off the subject of my past misdemeanours, Archie did his best to convince me to accompany him to some ghastly art exhibition launch in the evening. I took a sip of my 'Gorgeous Greens' smoothie and shook my head. 'Can't, I'm sorry. We've got a friend coming round.'

Archie rolled his eyes. 'Oh, is it one of those book-club affairs Matthew's finally dragged you into?'

I gave a half laugh to this. 'No, no. Well, actually, sort of. It's this Rachel woman Matthew's become rather taken with. I'm probably being unfair, as she did come to Titus's assistance during an attempted mugging…'

Archie's eyes widened. 'An attempted mugging? What did she do, fight them off?'

'Well, something like that. Told them to fuck off and leave the boy alone. And it worked, according to Titus. They left. So I suppose we do owe her a dinner at least. Matthew and Titus are home preparing it now.'

Another eyeroll from Archie. 'It's only just gone twelve. Surely they don't need, what, seven hours?'

I waited a moment, nudging a bit of flaxseed out of my

teeth before I responded. 'Matthew seems to be a bit ... I don't know, a bit taken with her.'

Archie noticed the pause, and the way my voice had got a little quieter and more serious. 'You're not suggesting...'

I batted his unfinished question away with my hand. 'No, no. I know he never would. It's her I'm worried about. I think he's always super-friendly and keen to make friends and she's taking advantage of that. I'm just not thrilled with the idea of her coming over for supper ... dinner ... whatever.'

This earned another odd look from Archie.

'Matthew doesn't like the word "supper",' I explained. 'Thinks it makes us sound too upper class.'

Archie nodded with understanding. 'Delia can't abide what she calls "poshisms". Did you know she grew up partly on a council estate in Rainham? Her father was from, in her words, a "traditional East London working-class family". It was her mother who turned her into one of us. She was in a different circle. Probably why she ended up divorcing Delia's father, hence the Rainham flat. When she stayed with him, it was in some ghastly high-rise on some estate built in the 60s to hold Dagenham Ford workers – the Mardyke Estate or something.'

Something Archie said reminded me of our impending dinner guest. 'Rachel lives on the Churchill Gardens Estate.'

'That's Westminster, isn't it? I think I remember hearing about it getting some lottery grant or something similar.'

'Yes, it's in Pimlico,' I said. 'I grew up right near it; it's practically next to St George's Square. I dare say it has its fair share of troubles, but I never had any issue, although

Mother never liked me walking through there. Rachel's just moved in. I think that's why Matthew wanted to take her under his wing.'

Archie raised one eyebrow, then took a sip of his drink.

'What?' I said.

'It's nothing,' Archie said, turning a bit red. 'Sorry, I wasn't trying to say anything…'

I leaned in. 'Oh, come on, I saw that weird expression. What were you thinking?'

Archie looked pained all of a sudden, and I was struck how old he was getting – how old we both were getting. Still only thirty-six, but it was a long way from the sixteen-year-old boys we used to be, happily playing rugby and moaning about our schoolwork.

'Well,' he said, slowly, 'I … I've never known whether to mention this… I'm probably speaking out of turn, here…'

'Now I'm terrified,' I said. 'Please, spit it out.'

He let out a heavy sigh. 'This isn't my place to say, but you know Jeremy was at St Andrews when Matthew was there?'

I vaguely knew Matthew had known Archie's brother Jeremy at university, but they weren't very close, so it rarely came up.

'Well, Matthew … um, according to Jeremy, in his final year of his Master's, Matthew had sex with his housemate.'

I shrugged. 'So?'

'His housemate *Megan*.'

A small bud of foreboding started to bloom within me. Matthew had slept with a woman at university. This fact itself shouldn't really have concerned me. Of course, it's normal for gay men to have dabbled with the opposite sex in the past, the same way it's not uncommon for heterosexual guys to experiment with other boys. I wouldn't have minded a jot if I'd known about it before. But this was the type of thing Matthew would normally have told me. We'd chatted about past relationships, past dates gone wrong, past screw-ups and successes. Never once had he mentioned sleeping with a girl when he was at St Andrews. When he was twenty-two. That was relatively old – not an experimental fling when you're a teenager. He was a man. An adult. And, learning it now, from Archie rather than from Matthew himself was – there was no other word for it – hurtful. The secrecy, the borderline lying-by-omission … it hurt me.

'I knew I shouldn't have said anything.' Archie was looking pained, then leant back so the waiter could serve us our food. I wasn't a bit hungry anymore. I just wanted to leave.

'It's … it's fine,' I said, trying to pretend I couldn't hear the pounding of my own heart in my ear. 'I … well, I guess we've all got our wild pasts.'

He laughed and nodded. 'You can say that again. But honestly, mate, I didn't mean to imply Matthew was, I don't know, having it off with this book-club woman of yours just because he bedded a girl over a decade ago. As I said, it was foolish of me to bring it up.'

Archie did his best to change the subject for the rest of the meal, telling me about how he and Delia planned to holiday in Alaska over Christmas, but it didn't help alter my mood. None of it worked. My mind was still on my husband.

Back at home, I tried to show some enthusiasm for the food Matthew and Titus were in the middle of preparing. The sight of Titus baking a cake – one of his frequent weekend activities – cheered me somewhat. At least he was no longer giving a grunting monotone impression of a moody teenager anymore. Matthew too was in his element, going between sorting out vegetables to making sure the dining room was tidy (a pointless task; thanks to Jane, it was always immaculate).

I made myself look busy by adding their paper Wholefoods bags to the recycling and taking a disproportionately long time choosing what music we should have playing gently in the background. I instinctively selected some Max Richter from Spotify, but Matthew shouted out in protest from the kitchen ('We'll all be in need of Prozac by the end of the first course!'). In the end, I went with *The Best of Lang Lang*; some of the tracks weren't that much cheerier, but at least there was a bit more variety in tone.

Rachel arrived on time at 7pm. I'd been in the lounge, scrolling through our Sky planner, fantasising about all the things we could be watching instead of hosting this weird little dinner, but grudgingly turned the TV off and went through to greet her.

'Evening, Rachel,' I said. 'I hope you are well.'

I saw a flicker in Matthew's eyes, probably a micro-wince at my clunky, way-too-formal politeness – the opposite to the normal, laid-back, king-of-small-talk air that I liked to cultivate.

'Come through to the lounge,' Matthew said. 'Titus is just getting changed; he'll be down in a moment.'

'Oh, he's not getting dressed up for dinner, is he?' Rachel said, casting a self-conscious glance down at her perfectly lovely light-blue casual dress. Part of me found it amusing that she thought there was a chance we all wore dinner jackets of an evening, like characters from *Downton Abbey*.

Matthew was quick to reassure her. 'No, no, we were making a cake and he got flour all over his jeans. Shall we go through into the lounge? I'll get you a drink.'

The evening continued surprisingly smoothly and, before long, I started to relax in her company. I even began to enjoy myself and in spite of my initial reservations, I got a sense of why both Matthew and Titus liked her. She seemed to have a strength, a backbone, an internal core that helped her hold her own in social situations. I'd seen it at book club but hadn't been able to articulate it to myself. It wasn't a bluntness or boldness, quite the opposite. More simply a confidence in what she was doing that allowed her not to get too phased by people, surroundings and, if we're being frank, a social stratum she wasn't used to. Just as we were sitting down at the table in the dining room, the sound of the doorbell rang through the air, followed by the crunch of a key in the lock. This could only be one person: my mother, who always rang before letting herself in. She once explained this as 'the politest thing to do when letting yourself in to someone else's house'.

'Only me,' I heard her call out from the hall, and I got up to go and greet her.

'Mum, sorry, were we expecting—?'

'No, no,' she said, putting her bag down on the side table, 'I just wanted to pop round to give Titus these books on Anne Boleyn I had gathering dust on the shelves.'

The idea of a single speck of dust gathering on my mother's perfect bookshelves was so unlikely it was laughable. I took the books from her and looked down at their dreary covers. 'Both are out of print,' she continued, 'and he mentioned they'd be helpful for his coursework.'

I nodded, then looked up and said, 'We have a guest.'

She looked surprised. 'A guest? On a Sunday? Is this one of Matthew's book-club things?'

Matthew appeared at my side suddenly, as if conjured by the sound of his name. 'Sort of,' he said, smiling warmly. 'Our book-club member Rachel has come over. The one who helped Titus. You should come through and meet her, Cassandra.'

My mother has always been a little nosy, although she'd object to such a suggestion.

'Oh, well, if it wouldn't interrupt,' she said, allowing Matthew to take her coat.

We went through into the dining room where Matthew was talking to Titus. My mother greeted her warmly, saying how impressed she was to hear about her stepping in to help Titus the other week.

'Oh, honestly, it was nothing. I just did what anyone

would have done,' Rachel said, looking embarrassed by all the praise.

'I don't think they would,' my mother said as Matthew brought round the food – apparently he'd cooked more than enough for an extra guest. 'I was at the checkout at the Waitrose near me recently when I dropped the contents of my purse all over the floor, and not one person in the queue helped me pick them up. They were all on their phones, no doubt scrolling through Instagram and the like, oblivious to the rest of the world.' She emphasised the word Instagram slightly, her way of making a little dig towards me and my social media presence.

'I think people would have avoided intervening in a violent confrontation because of fear, not because they're on their phones,' I said.

She gave a little tilt of her head. 'Well, I'm not so sure. People aren't nearly as observant these days as they used to be.'

Rachel nodded. 'I completely agree,' she said. 'A young lad on the estate where I live literally collided with me the other day. He was swaying to music on his headphones, his eyes almost closed. Didn't seem to care about anyone around him.'

My mother nodded enthusiastically. 'Yes, exactly, I—'

Then she stopped. We all looked over to her, wondering why she had her fork paused in the air, her head slightly to the side, her eyes fixed on Rachel.

'Er … Mum?' I said, both a little embarrassed and worried. Was this the sign of a seizure or a stroke? Or the onset of Alzheimer's?

Her face then relaxed a little. 'Sorry,' she said, glancing at me, then turning her gaze back to Rachel. 'I just … do you know, my dear, it's the strangest thing, but I feel like we've met before.'

I saw a flash of something flicker across Rachel's face. Then she smiled and gave a little laugh. 'Oh, I don't think so. I must just have one of those faces. The type that just looks like everyone. I get mistaken for people in shops sometimes. For someone's sister or cousin and the like.' She picked up another scoop of pasta with her fork and started to eat.

My mother was still staring at her. 'Yes … yes, well. That must be it.'

I met Matthew's eyes across the table, and I gave him a minute shrug to say, *Not sure what that's all about*. He was quick to move the conversation on, telling Titus that his gran had dropped him round some of the Anne Boleyn biographies he'd been after. The subject then slid into a discussion about studying history and coursework and how Rachel was never a fan of it when she was at school, and things started to ease a bit.

But I couldn't help notice, all through the rest of dinner, my mother's eyes occasionally wander over to Rachel and linger on her face. As if she were pondering an unusual painting in a gallery that she couldn't quite grasp the meaning of. And her words continued to echo round in my head for the rest of the evening. *It's the strangest thing, but I feel like we've met before.*

Chapter Fifteen

CHARLIE

The day after the murder

After my strange, flu-like sleep the night before, I wake up feeling surprisingly well, though a little dazed. I sit on my bed, waiting for the nausea, the crushing grief, the panicky breathing, but none of it arrives. I go and pee and then shower in the guest room en suite. My room here in Wilton Crescent always feels like one of the guest rooms. Never quite 'my room', even though I've slept in the same one whenever I've stayed since my mother moved here nearly twenty years ago. My childhood bedroom in the house in St George's Square where my father resides still feels like 'my room', although I can't remember the last time I slept there. It may well be over a decade.

The steam and heat from the shower does little to shift the odd, numbing dreamlike state I'm in. When I'm back in the bedroom, I sit still in the chair by the window for a few seconds more, trying to find some clarity in my clouded brain. The feeling of waking up without my husband near me, without him passing some comment on the day ahead, some reason to look forward to an evening together or event we're going to, some light bickering about something stupid, something trivial … all of it has been part of my mornings for so long, I feel like I've been untethered, waking up here in my mother's house knowing that previous life has for ever been lost.

I go to the drawers at the other end of the room. They're filled with clothes, all perfectly ironed and folded, although some of them date back to my teenage years. I pull on some boxers and jeans I don't think I've worn since I was twenty, along with a light-pink shirt that's slightly tight across the chest (I had a sharp, skinny frame until I discovered resistance training in my twenties). I then go downstairs, the hallway carpet soft against my bare feet, the creak of the floor announcing my arrival to my mother.

'I'm in the kitchen,' she calls out.

I go inside to find her taking out a tray of croissants from the oven. 'Palomar nipped out to Waitrose to get us some supplies, but I sent her home afterwards,' she says by way of explaining why she is preparing breakfast herself, instead of allowing her housekeeper to do it. 'We can handle cooking and light laundry by ourselves, and then when your father gets home, we'll go to Braddon.'

I nod. 'I'm sure we'll survive cooking for ourselves.' It is obvious Palomar has been given an impromptu holiday because Mum wants to be able to talk freely without risk of being overheard. There is always the chance the police will want to interview her at some point, especially when they clock that she's in a prime position to eavesdrop on us all while we're gathered under one roof. 'Where's Titus? And Dad? When is his flight?'

I see a tightness pinch my mother's face. She's choosing how much to tell me. 'Titus is still asleep, and your father is on his way. He's just getting some work done beforehand.'

I stare at her. '*Some work done?* The murder of his son-in-law isn't enough of an emergency for him?'

My mother's eyes continue to bore into mine. 'Yes. Important work. Important people.'

I sit down on one of the tall chairs at the breakfast bar. I haven't got the energy to question her further on this, and my mother turns back to the sink. The gleaming modern kitchen is very different from the old design my father has in the St George's Square property. Mum's style and appreciation of the new-yet-homely feel to houses is something I've always shared with her. My father, meanwhile, is a strong believer in keeping the old character of a place alive. If my mother had remained in the house I grew up in, I'm sure she would have enforced a renovation upon it by now, as she has with a number of the rooms at Braddon Manor, much to my father's barely contained annoyance.

A croissant is placed on a plate and slid towards me. It's warm and has just the right level of crispiness and it's only when I'm biting into it I realise how hungry I am. I let a few seconds pass while I digest her words. Then she begins talking again and her sentence drives any thoughts of my father from my mind.

'This isn't what you'll want to hear, amidst your grief

and what you're no doubt going through, but you have to understand that Titus's position in all this is, shall we say, a little rocky...'

I get up off the seat. 'I can't talk about this,' I say, taking the croissant with me. I'd started to feel shaky as soon as she mentioned the word 'grief' – a word I'm not ready to accept or let into my world at present.

'Oh, darling, I understand this must be ... difficult.' She too gets off her chair and comes around to where I'm standing, laying a hand on my shoulder. 'Your father's plane will land this evening. We'll need to go through it all then, you realise? We won't be able to avoid it.'

I grit my teeth and try to breathe slowly. 'Don't you think it would be better for everyone – better for you both, at least – if you didn't know everything? The less you know, the easier it will be when...'

She grips me firmly with both hands now. 'No. We're going to talk it through; your dad has already contacted Oliver Harrington. We'll all talk it through first, then decide what's the best thing to do for Titus.'

I find myself wince at another mention of Titus's name, the thought of him upstairs asleep, about to wake into one of the most difficult days of his life – one of a series of them – paining me greatly.

As if reading my thoughts, my mother then says, 'If you wanted, I could talk to him beforehand. Tell him we're all going to...'

'No,' I say, firmly. 'I think ... I think we should leave things be for now. Leave *him* be. I tried to talk to him last night, but he clammed up.'

I see the anxiety in my mother's eyes. 'I'm just concerned that there's so much we don't yet know – so much none of us understands. And the police will be able to tell if we're not telling the truth if we don't first get a handle on what we want our version of the truth to be. Do you understand me? At the moment, Rachel holds all the cards. We can discuss for hours why that might be or what she might be up to, but it's important that, if she changes her story, we're able to fall back on firm foundations – not weak guesses and suggestions.'

All I can do is nod and say, 'I know.' I'm finding it hard to look at her now. Everything she's saying is unleashing the wave of anxiety I've had walled up within me since waking, and it's threatening to rush through my entire being. I leave the kitchen without saying another word, walk back upstairs, and within minutes I'm throwing up into the sink in the bathroom. As I'm letting the gush of the taps wash away my vomit, I jump to see Titus reflected in the mirror. He looks like he's just got out of bed, his hair all messy and ruffled.

'Sorry,' I say, giving the sink a cursory wipe with my hand, unsure why I'm apologising.

'It's OK,' he says, his face drained and pale. 'I've been sick too.'

Chapter Sixteen

RACHEL

Ten months to go

The dinner at the Allerton-Joneses' had been going well before Charlie's mother turned up. Cassandra Allerton seemed to be one of those very polite but chilly women – not quite over-posh and haughty, but not quite warm and friendly. There was something a bit Maggie Thatcher about her, although her dress sense was a bit more subtly stylish and modern. Anyway, our nice little dinner was interrupted by her barging in as if she owned the place (maybe she did, for all I knew) and sitting down to eat with us. That was when the odd moment happened. She was in the middle of talking when she suddenly stopped midsentence and looked at me as if I were a particularly confusing ghost. I could see her mind whirring, trying to work out what it was that had startled her about me. And I had a terrible feeling all this was a symptom of déjà vu.

Sure enough, when she finally spoke, her words made that crystal clear.

'Sorry,' she said, 'I just … do you know, my dear, it's the strangest thing, but I feel like we've met before.'

I tried to play it well. Make out I just had 'one of those faces'. But it did make me worry that my efforts to befriend the Allerton-Joneses would be destabilised so quickly. I wracked my brains as to how she could have recognised me, tried to think if she and I had ever come into contact before. Perhaps she'd seen a photo somewhere. I couldn't be sure. Or maybe, just maybe, it was a pure coincidence – that she once knew someone who looked like me, and I was reading too much into it.

Whatever it was, it meant I walked home later that evening feeling a lot more uneasy than I'd hoped, worried I was playing a far more dangerous game than I'd first realised. By the time I reached my flat, I was properly crying. Not sobbing, exactly – passers-by probably wouldn't even have noticed – but the tears were flowing freely down my face, causing my skin to smart as the cold wind hit me. I knew what I was going to do, as soon as I got in. I felt the need so desperately within me, had felt it all throughout dinner, with Titus opposite me and Matthew to my left. That familiar ache, that companionable pain, the feeling that would never go away as long as I lived. Or at least, not until I finished what I'd come to do.

At the door of my block, I could see someone holding the door for me and I ran to catch it. It was the busybody next door, Amanda, carrying Peter Jones carrier bags. 'Oh goodness, are you OK?' she said when she saw my tears.

'Yes, I'm fine. Sorry, it's the cold. It makes my eyes stream.'

If she didn't believe me, she decided not to mention it. 'Oh, it has got chilly, hasn't it! Part of me wishes I'd got the bus back.'

I looked at the bags she was carrying, feeling I should make some effort of conversation as we made our way over to the lift. 'Early Christmas shopping?' I asked.

'Oh, sort of,' she replied. 'My sister has a whole gaggle of children; couldn't stop breeding, bless her. The oldest is now in his forties, the youngest is now twenty-three, and some of them have kids of their own, too. It's a marvel I don't go bankrupt every year, what with all the birthdays.'

I nodded, even though the idea of a wide extended family was completely foreign to me. 'Do you have children of your own?' I asked, then immediately wished I hadn't, as I saw a shadow fall over her face, and her lips tighten.

'No,' she said, 'sadly that never quite worked out for me.'

The lift juddered to a stop and I felt a sense of desperation to get out of this awkward conversation and into the solitary safety of my little flat. 'I'm so sorry, I shouldn't…'

'Oh, it's fine,' she said, shaking her head. 'I've got a step-daughter, from my husband's first marriage but, well, we're not exactly close.' I stood back to let her leave first and followed as we walked the length of the corridor to our respective doors. 'She's a bit of a bitch, actually,' Amanda continued, a slight bitter note creeping into her voice. 'Very self-centred. It's all about *her* drama, *her* problems. Probably comes from being an only child.'

At her front door she stopped and flicked a look at me. 'Oh gosh, I'm sorry, are you an only child?'

I'd been rummaging in my bag for my keys and the question unsettled me so much, I dropped them on the floor, then ended up tipping the whole contents of my bag out as I leaned down to get them. 'God, I'm so clumsy today,' I said as Amanda put down her shopping bags and helped me scoop up my things. Though annoyed at myself, I was grateful the commotion gave me a reason not to answer Amanda's question. I managed to sound almost normal as I said goodbye and let myself in.

Although the food had been excellent at the Allerton-Joneses', I was suddenly starving, and scrabbled around in the freezer for something easy I could throw in the oven. I settled for a cheap, heavily processed pizza I'd picked up at the reduced counter in Sainsbury's a week earlier.

While it was cooking, I went into the bedroom and felt under the bed for the photo album. I nestled there, on my bed, pulling the covers around me, and looked at picture after picture of his smiling face. His bright blue eyes. So kind-looking, so happy with life. In the midst of sobs, curled up in my duvet, I ended up drifting into a half-sleep, thoughts and fears and memories circling my mind. I only woke when the smoke alarm cut through my dreams, alerting me to the charcoal-like state of the pizza in the oven.

Chapter Seventeen

CHARLIE

Eight months to go

When I was a child, one of things I loved most about Christmas was term finishing at Eaton Square School and, on that very night, my parents driving us down to Tolleshunt D'Arcy in Essex to spend the Christmas holidays at Braddon Manor. I probably over-romanticised it in my head over the years, but I still have vivid memories of the car winding up the drive past all the big trees glowing with warm-white lights. Inside the manor, nearly every room would have a Christmas tree, adorned with whatever theme my mother had negotiated with the decorators.

Although no longer eight years old, there was still a certain magic about arriving at Braddon at Christmas time. Of course, although I didn't know it then, that Christmas would be the last we'd all spend together as a family. It's a shame I would come to look upon that week over the festive season that year with hatred – both of myself and the situation I found myself in. For my inability to spot what was happening, almost in plain sight.

Matthew and I arrived separately that year – me in the BMW, him in his Tesla, me in the afternoon of the 22nd, him the next morning on the 23rd. We were supposed to all be going down together, but he said he had a dinner with some old school friends over in Ealing that night and it made sense to him to go back to the house in Chelsea then follow on the next morning. 'We'll wait for you,' I'd said, but he told me to go. He looked pained. 'You'll miss your mother's annual dinner,' he said. 'I'm just so sorry I'll have to miss it.'

My mother's annual dinner was less of an event than he made it sound. She would just end up inviting a select cluster of friends of the family, usually their close friends Lord and Lady Ashton, a handful of my mother's old friends she'd known from school and who'd become more-or-less aunts to me throughout my childhood, along with some rather dull people my father was working with at that point in time – usually from the world of politics. Occasionally she'd add in a surprise, left-field choice. It's amazing who my mother knows, or has connections to through her many networks of friends and acquaintances. One year she rustled up two minor royals and a celebrated film director.

This year the Ashtons had a prior engagement, to the disappointment of my parents. 'It just won't be the same,' my mother sighed.

'Who have you asked instead?' I'd enquired back in the autumn when she was planning the whole thing.

'Oh, just a few others – nice people, I'm sure you'll get on with them.'

These 'nice people', it turned out, were a former Prime Minister and his wife – something I wish my mother had warned me about, if only to avoid me freezing in surprise as they walked into the drawing room. I whispered this to my mother once they'd gone into the drawing room for pre-dinner drinks. 'Well, it was either them or the Kellmans or the Knights, and what with one of the Kellmans now being sort of … out of the picture, and one of the Knights … well…'

'Dead,' I said.

'Yes, well, quite. So I just thought they'd make up the numbers nicely. I did, in the end, ask Louise Kellman but she's rather withdrawn from view, as you can imagine, now married to a convict.'

The rest of the evening passed relatively pleasantly, with Titus clearly enjoying talking to our former PM, politely but firmly letting him know which parts of his policies he approved of and which, with respect, he felt were misguided. At dinner I was stuck next to one of my mother's friends, Baroness Vanessa Woodford, a sixty-year-old widow who simply loved the fact she had a close connection to a married gay couple (with an adopted child to complete the picture) and would regularly give me updates she believed I would find interesting ('Did I mention my window cleaner is gay?'). She considered herself very active on Twitter, although her timeline was mostly filled with retweeting anything posted by Stonewall, the Terrence Higgins trust, or me. In short, she generally considered herself to be a self-elected ambassador for the 'LGBTQ+ community' (I got the impression she loved the ever-lengthening nature of this acronym and spent most of her days hoping they'd hurry up and add a few more letters). On this night, over the pistachio ice-cream dessert, she told me that she had 'added her gender pronouns' to her Twitter bio, something she clearly expected me to congratulate her on. 'And where is dearest Matthew tonight?' she asked, looking terribly let down. 'It's simply *ages* since I've seen him.'

'He's got a work thing,' I replied, trying not to show my disapproval. 'He couldn't get out of it. You know what academics are like. Odd bunch. He's got to keep them happy.'

I have no idea really what academics are like, outside the forgettable lecturers I had at university, and I cringed inwardly at my attempts to make out as if they were like high-flying city-traders.

'Oh, completely understandable,' Baroness Vanessa said, patting my arm, almost knocking the glass of wine out of my hand.

'Yes,' I nodded, 'completely understandable.'

Matthew arrived the next day, and we all generally had a fun time going on long walks through the grounds, eating a lot and watching films by the fire while my mother wandered around, checking the staff had sorted out the right food for the coming week.

It was on Christmas Day that things turned odd.

We had, as is tradition, unwrapped our presents after Christmas lunch, then sat and watched the Queen's speech. Afterwards, Titus requested we watch some Dickensian drama thing involving lots of snow and poverty, and I was trying my best to look interested in it. My father had just asked Matthew if he'd like a brandy – only to find Matthew wasn't in the seat he'd been in moments before.

Puzzled, I presumed he'd nipped off to the loo. When he didn't return for another five minutes, I went exploring to see if he'd gone to get some of the leftovers from the kitchen.

He wasn't in the kitchen, but through the thin windows I could hear him; he was talking on the phone, outside.

'I'm sorry. You're right, I should have called earlier…'

My attempts to move closer to the window resulted in me knocking an iron tray into the sink. Matthew then stopped talking abruptly, finishing his call with 'I've got to go.'

I waited for him to come back into the kitchen, but instead he took the long way round, taking a right so he looped around the back of the house on the outside to enter through another side door. Frustrated, I stomped through, out of the kitchen, down the corridor, and almost collided with him as he came through.

'Christ, you made me jump,' he said, jumping back.

I had the feeling he'd thought he'd been able to sneak back in undetected. Before I could ask who he'd been talking to, he volunteered the information.

'Sorry, I was just talking to Ali.'

I looked blank, so he continued. 'My colleague, remember? There's been a flood at one of the co-publishers we're working with in Ireland. We're probably going to have to push back some of our projects. Bit of a nightmare.'

I couldn't help raising my eyebrows at this. 'And Ali called you on Christmas Day about this?'

Matthew laughed – a strange, tight laugh, somewhat unlike him. 'He's a Muslim, so he doesn't celebrate it, and it was me that phoned him. I didn't respond to his emails about it yesterday and he was getting in a bit of a flap. And it's an important book we're working on, about how the current economic policies in the west are deliberately rigged to disadvantage the poor.'

I could see his face become animated and eager, stimulated by his enthusiasm for the subject. Part of me wanted to roll my eyes in response, but I stopped myself. Matthew and I have avoided discussing politics and social issues too much in recent years. I never noticed the differences in our views so much in the early days, and if I ever did I'd just joke he was one of the 'trendy left' or a 'champagne socialist'. Now, his earnestness about the perceived injustices of the world had started to grate on me more than ever. 'Well, I hope it all sorts itself out,' I said. I turned to lead the way back to the lounge, but he spoke again behind me.

'Do you know, I think I might go for a drive. I've got a bit of a headache. I need to clear my mind.'

I turned round again to look at him. 'Are you sure everything's OK?' I asked, taking a step closer, peering at him. He wouldn't quite meet my eye, his gaze resting around my neck.

'Yes, I'm sure. I'll just drive about a bit, take advantage of the empty streets.'

I continued to stare at him, 'Do you want me to come with you?'

He shook his head and laid a hand on my shoulder. 'No, no, I'll be fine. You go back to the lounge. Tell me what happens at the end of *Bleak House* or whatever it is we've been watching.'

My mother looked puzzled at Matthew's decision to go out for a drive to clear his head. 'Surely a paracetamol or something would be better than getting behind the wheel?' she said, peering over the selection guide for a very chic-looking selection of Belgian truffles.

'Sounds like a jolly sensible thing to do, in my opinion,' my father said. 'I've always found a good drive around the countryside does me wonders.'

'Providing he doesn't feel too unwell,' my mother replied.

'He's not ill,' I said, sitting back down. 'It's just something to do with work.'

'Oh, I see,' my mother said, returning to her chocolates. 'Why's he worrying about work on Christmas Day?'

I shrugged a little and turned to look at Titus. He was engrossed in the drama unfolding on the screen, and had only vaguely looked in our direction, not properly taking in what we were saying.

'Do you know, I think these are even better than Pierre Marcolini's Grand Cru,' my mother said, offering the tray of chocolates out to the room in general.

When the clock reached 9.30pm, I began to get worried. I'd started clock-watching about an hour after Matthew had departed. This marked two hours and I could tell my parents were starting to get a bit puzzled too. 'Hasn't he messaged or anything?' my mother asked, going over to the living room windows to see if there was any sign of car lights on the driveway.

'He hasn't,' I said, lighting up my phone for what must be the hundredth time that hour.

'He wouldn't have gone back to London?' my father asked, pouring himself another drink. It always astonished me how much alcohol he managed to put away without it having any visible effect on him.

I shook my head. 'Not without telling me. And there's no reason why he should. His offices are closed until the New Year.'

It reached 9.50pm before, finally, the sound of the front door made everyone look up. I left the lounge immediately and walked into the hallway and towards the front door.

'Where on earth have you been?' I called out to him.

'I'm sorry,' he said, shaking his head. 'Fucking car died on me.'

'What?' I walked towards him as he hung up his coat and took his shoes off.

'I know. Just died on me halfway along a narrow

country lane. Somewhere near Goldhanger, I think. Was terrified another car would bomb round the corner and career into me. I had to walk across ditches and a field to get anywhere with a bloody signal. Called the breakdown people. Took them an age, then the car just started again.'

I was rather at a loss with all this information. 'How … what…? So you drove it home?'

Matthew nodded. 'Yeah, it's outside. But they said I should have a full check done on it. I told them it could wait until we get back to London.' He smiled at me and put his hands on my shoulders.

'It's *fine*, I'm fine. I'm just sorry to worry you.'

I smiled, relieved he was back and in one piece, not lying bleeding in an upturned motor on some dark, deserted back road.

Titus was, of course, relieved his dad had been found, but after a while he opted to go to bed with one of the large books he'd been given for Christmas. My parents had settled into a late showing of a James Bond film, so Matthew and I decided to get an early night. I still felt over-full from lunch, and struggled to get to sleep, so after a couple of hours I sat up properly and looked over at my still, peaceful husband next to me. Was I going mad? Was this just jealousy, or my tendency to control things? Or was there something strange going on here?

I didn't like these thoughts. I didn't like feeling unsure about someone I'd loved as strongly and passionately as was humanly possible. It made me feel dirty, or tainted, as if sprayed with that invisible dye that banks and cash vaults use to deter thieves. I watched Matthew's chest rise and fall for a few more seconds, then stepped out of bed and pulled on some pants and a T-shirt.

I could hear the television from the landing rumbling away from the living room. That was the problem with big, old houses – everything echoed. I padded quietly down the stairs, considering going to find something to snack on, when the door to the lounge opened and my father came out. 'Charles, I thought you'd gone to bed?'

I stood still, as if I were a teenager caught sneaking in late. 'Yes. I … couldn't sleep.'

'There's lots of food, darling, if you're hungry,' my mother called out from inside the living room, the sound of Daniel Craig's tones getting quieter as she turned the volume down.

'I'm fine,' I called back.

My father looked at me, as if trying to work something out. I've always found his gaze somewhat penetrating, ever since I was a child, and now it was as if he could tell there was something wrong and, crucially, I wasn't getting very far in working out what it was.

'Sleep well,' he said, finally, and went back into the lounge.

I was about to go back upstairs, try to read or do something until sleep overtook me, when something caught my eye.

Matthew's shoes.

They were by the door where he'd taken them off. The shoes of someone who had traipsed, according to him, through ditches and fields in order to get a signal to call for help. A call to a breakdown service, but not to me, his husband, or his son. And somehow he had managed to do this without getting a speck of mud on the main body of the shoes or the laces or, as I saw as I turned them over in my hands, on the soles. They had a few bits of grit and dirt on them. But that was it. No sign anyone had trampled through damp undergrowth. Through puddles. Through a muddy field.

I put the shoes back down, then went silently back upstairs, through the doors to our bedroom, then into the bed and under the covers. And all the while, I was desperately trying to stop my imagination running away with itself.

Chapter Eighteen

RACHEL

Eight months to go

I started to find it very difficult, turning up to the book-club meetings, appearing all happy and friendly, even though everything around me seemed pointless and impossible. I tried to get work in a garden centre in Hampstead, but they clearly wanted a plant specialist, not someone to stick 'reduced' stamps on the leftover Halloween decorations. A café in Battersea didn't want me, since I'd never had any other jobs waiting tables or handling food. They said they had twenty-two candidates answer the job advertisement and some of them had 'extensive experience in the food services sector'. This was for a minimum-wage position in a basic café. The whole thing made me want to cry.

It was Meryl who came to my aid. At the end of the November book-club meeting, she offered me a lift home on her way back home. I told her it wasn't on her way home at all – it would mean her veering off in a different direction – but she just waved her hand and said her driver Kenneth was used to her taking detours. In the car, Meryl asked me some direct, probing questions. Was I happy? What sort of work was I looking for? What could be done to improve my current situation?

It turned out she had the answer.

'I can put you forward for a job, my dear. It would be no bother.'

I blinked at her as the car crawled along in the slow-moving late-evening traffic. 'You mean … at Streamline?'

I was familiar with the brand – who wasn't? – but it had always been well out of my price range and the thought of entering their offices in my normal clothes filled me with horror. I've always thought I dress as well as I can on a budget, but thinking of setting foot in the corridors of a major beauty company … I'd feel like a fish out of water.

'Yes, at Streamline. I still flatter myself to think I have at least some sway with what goes on there, even if I have taken a bit of a back seat in the running of the business in recent years.' She must have seen how worried I looked because she smiled and reached across to lay a hand on my arm. 'Don't look so worried, my dear. It wouldn't be anything too high-powered or stressful. Just office work. I'm sure they can find you an admin role of some sort. It may not be the most intellectually stimulating job in the world, but I imagine it will be better than fighting for shifts in some dodgy café.'

I laughed. 'Yes, I expect it would.'

'Excellent,' she said, giving my hand a tap. 'I'll talk to

Sophia; she heads up PR and publicity and is also on the board. She'll settle everything in HR for you.'

Everything was settled, just as easily as Meryl had made it sound. The next day I had a call from Ms Sophia Nero-Booth at Streamline to ask me to come in for an interview at the end of the week. By the following Monday, I had a job. The interview itself, though held in the inevitably swish head offices on Buckingham Palace Road, was far more relaxed than I ever could have hoped. Indeed, Sophia greeted me like an old friend, even though I doubted she'd have looked twice at me if Meryl hadn't more-or-less instructed her to find me employment.

Those first few weeks at the start of December were, to my surprise, almost fun. I was good at organisational tasks and quickly got to grips with my daily responsibilities. By the end of the third week, however, I was starting to feel low again. The novelty of the job had worn off, and because I had a number of hours of down time each day (which I filled by reading novels in the ladies' loos) and not enough work to keep me mentally stimulated, I ended up ruminating. About the past. The present. And how things were going to turn out in the future. I hadn't really given myself a time limit in London, and suddenly the months were slipping away without me doing what I had properly come here to do. Perhaps it would have made more sense to keep a low profile, never to have sought out the Allerton-Joneses, to have avoided the long game for a quick moment of shock and adrenalin, and it would all have been over.

But that's too kind, a voice said in my head. *Much better to make him suffer.*

So I kept myself together. Just. I decided to carry on biding my time, exploiting the connections I now had, and waiting to see what the New Year would bring.

On December 20th, Sophia came up to me at the coffee machine in the staff canteen. 'Rachel, I'm so sorry, but I forgot to ask you if you'd like Christmas off? Do tell me if we've already spoken about this; my mind's like a sinkhole at the moment.'

She always did this – making herself out to be scatty and hopeless, whilst also giving the impression of having everything under control in a smooth and seamless way. There was an art to it that I couldn't help admire.

'Would it be OK to take some days off? I might go and visit my father in the North.'

'Of course, no problem at all. I'll book you off until January 2nd, if that works with you?'

I nodded, grateful to be handed such generous annual leave after only just starting the job. Allen at the garden centre would have had an aneurism if I'd tried to take that many days off in December. 'Thank you so much. Only if that's not a problem…?'

Sophia waved her hands. 'Not one bit. I'm going off to Denmark for two weeks with my husband, anyway, followed by an outdoors Twelfth Night ball on the ice in Sweden – I'd better pack my furs or I'll freeze to death!'

Even though I didn't think the idea of going to a ball

held out of doors in arctic conditions sounded very fun, nothing about my Christmas plans could compete with this, so I didn't bother to try. Instead, I just told her it sounded enchanting and thanked her again.

As it would turn out, I ended up enviously fantasising about Sophia enjoying an icy sparkling romantic holiday with her husband followed by a shimmering, exclusive ball on a frozen lake under the Northern Lights. Anything to escape the dull, drab, dreary and disappointingly snow-free Christmas I experienced. It was just me and my dad in his small terraced house, watching film after film on television, shovelling a Lidl roast dinner into our mouths without saying much to each other. At one point, he said to me, 'Don't you want to spend some time with your young friends? I saw that Kevin of yours up walking on the hills a few weeks back. Maybe give him a call? Do something nice and festive with him.'

I told him that calling my ex-partner out of the blue on Christmas Day – a man who is now married to a property-rich yoga instructor named Demelza and currently expecting their second child – would be the opposite of 'nice and festive'.

It was later that evening, when the grey skies outside gave in to rain, that I had my moment of weakness. Dad had fallen asleep in front of *Paddington 2* and I snuck upstairs, very quietly, trying not to wake him. I pulled the ladder down to the loft with the precision of a surgeon and trod carefully on each step, holding my breath as I hauled myself into the dusty darkness. Inside, I used the torch on my phone to light my way and crawled to the end where two boxes of photo albums were housed, providing refuge – as I discovered to my temporary fright – to two spiders the size of mice. Once I'd batted them away, I reached inside one of the boxes and pulled out a photo album.

I saw what I was looking for immediately. The photos Mum would routinely hide away, desperate to forget, then, when she couldn't bear it any more, frantically scrabble around for them again in a panic, convinced the pain would go away if she looked at them one last time.

The pain didn't go away when I looked at them. It burned even brighter. And, even though it made the tears fall from my eyes, it was worth it. Worth every painful second.

Chapter Nineteen

CHARLIE

The day after the murder

My father is here. I hear his car, no doubt driven by his almost comically obedient Scottish chauffeur, Malcolm, purr into its space outside the house followed by the unmistakable bold, purposeful tap of his shoes on the pavement.

My father's the type of man who you don't want to be caught out by. He's never been cruel or unkind to me, but he can be sharp and makes it clear he doesn't suffer fools gladly. He can command a room with a steely charisma – something I've been lucky enough to inherit to a degree when it comes to pitch meetings with clients, but haven't perfected as well in a social setting.

His work has always made me somewhat … awkward. I'm aware some people have a problem with it. Others just accept it as the way of the world. He owns a small consultancy business, working alongside two other partners, with a small staff working beneath them. They have offices in Millbank. Their work is very slow, complicated, and boring. That is the official version, anyway. The unofficial version is this: they are the men you go to when you need something to be *done*. When you need a certain member of the opposition party to be removed from their seat. Or if a member of the cabinet needs a conviction for drink driving to just conveniently … go away. But it gets darker than that.

Earlier this year, the CEO of a large supermarket chain was accused of improper behaviour towards a female colleague when visiting one of his stores. According to the newspapers, he touched her in a lift. Within a week, the accusations were dropped. I discovered my father's involvement via a newspaper article. Just one line. *The accused had sought the advice of Allerton & Quinn Consultancy services of Westminster, London.* Around the same time, I saw a reference to my father as 'a shadowy Thomas Cromwell figure for the Brexit era'. I quickly clicked off the article.

Last year, I was particularly haunted by something I saw when we were all watching TV in the lounge at Easter. There was a BBC News report about Operation Sundown, an investigation – triggered by an episode of the current affairs programme *Insight* – into prominent politicians' and businessmen's alleged involvement in an abusive sex ring. This was a complex case that seemed to be connected to an instance of historic sexual assault towards a young woman at Oxford University in the 1990s. Her accusations helped trigger the discovery of the sex ring, and led to a wave of arrests, some of which didn't hold and resulted in cases collapsing. Others had held firmer, with a concerted effort by the CPS to bring them to court. That whole situation had been very awkward for us, since we were family friends with at least two of the accused men and were acquainted with the others. During the news report, it was announced that four of the five men would each receive fourteen years in prison. The fifth man, arguably the most high-profile, was handed just three years – sentence suspended. The evidence showing the extent of his involvement was, apparently, mislaid.

I saw across the room, as my father sat watching the news, a slight smile nudging the corners of his mouth when this information was read out in the calm, neutral voice of the BBC journalist. And that was when I knew that it was him. He had been behind the disproportionate difference in the sentences. He had woven his magic and, I'm sure, would be amply rewarded for it. Back then, I'm not sure I ever felt guilty, knowing where a portion of our income came from. I'm not sure. You see, when you're brought up being told certain things are the way of the world, it becomes very hard to question them when you've just accepted them for so long. And I'm not sure it bothers me much now, as my father strides in, the picture of confidence and quiet power, his white-blond hair swept back neatly, his coat and suit fitting perfectly around his tall, thin frame. In fact, his appearance makes me feel relieved. He's the type of man who doesn't falter in a crisis.

'I think we should go to St George's Square,' he says in a level, authoritative voice. He's looking around the hallway of my mother's house as if someone has tipped him off that the walls might be bugged. Perhaps they have been. My mother, for once, doesn't ask questions, just nods and takes down her coat and starts to pull it on. I, however, have some major concerns.

'I don't think we should. The police…'

'Have requested that you don't leave the country. Is that correct?'

I nod.

'They shouldn't have a problem then with you travelling into Pimlico. You're not leaving London; you're not even leaving the City of Westminster.'

'But … Titus,' I say, lowering my voice, flicking my eyes up to the ceiling above. Titus had shut himself in his room and, according to my mother, was sleeping.

'He'll be fine,' my mother says. 'I put a sleeping pill in the cocoa I took up to him.'

My eyes flash with outrage. 'You did *what*?'

'It was the kindest thing, under the circumstances,' my mother says firmly, as if drugging children is something she does on a daily basis. 'He'll wake up as normal in the morning, then we're all going to Braddon. Be good to get out of London.'

I frown. There's something about this I really don't like. It's like cogs are turning around me in a machine too vast and intimidating to understand.

'Please can we discuss this in the car? I don't want to keep my guests waiting.'

I turn around to look at my father properly. 'Guests? What guests?'

'You'll see,' he replies, opening the front door and stepping out into the street.

My father has Malcolm drive us the short journey to his house, delayed only by a police cordon around a section of Warwick Square. 'Do you think it's a stabbing?' my mother remarks to the car in general, only sounding mildly interested. Seconds later she clearly realises what she has just said, and flashes me a horrified look. 'Oh my goodness, Charles, I'm so sorry, I didn't … I didn't think.' I don't bother telling her it's fine, I just shake my head vaguely, and before long we are outside the house I grew up in – a sizable Thomas Cubitt-designed townhouse near one of the entrances to the square's large publicly accessible garden. It feels menacing and strange, and the light on in its front-room window, curtains drawn, feels like a warning to keep away rather than a comfortable welcome home. My father doesn't tell me who's in there, and I don't ask again. I've learned that it isn't wise to press my father. He has his own order of things. His own method.

The secret of who is inside is revealed moments later when my father leads us into the house and directly to the sitting room. Sitting around the fire, though it is not lit, are two middle-aged men. One of them, the slightly older of the two, I recognise instantly.

'Charles, you of course know Jacob already,' my father

says, gesturing to the older of the two, our family lawyer, who gets up to shake my hand.

'I am so very sorry for your loss,' Jacob says, holding my hands together. 'Very sorry.'

I continue to nod, vaguely, unsure what's going on. It's the second man who's captured my attention. He has a small, thin, insect-like frame. A pair of glasses resting on his nose. Thick, red hair, still holding its colour when he must be in his late forties.

'And this is Peter Catton,' my father continues, 'who I'm sure you are familiar with by name.'

I can place him now. And I've realised why we're all here together. I don't like it. But at the same time, I can understand why it's happening.

We all shake hands and sit down while my father goes out into the corridor to tell his housekeeper, Mrs Flint, that she may go home. Once we are all settled and in private, he starts to explain properly.

'First, I need to make some things clear to my wife and Charles before we go any further.' His eyes fix onto me like lasers. 'Charles, I don't think I need to tell you how astonishingly foolish it was to allow the police to interview you without a solicitor present. Jacob is here to go through with you the correct way to approach instances like this if and when they occur in the future, but I think he will agree with me when I say this: when in doubt, call him. If the police arrive at the door and request a word with you or Titus, call him. If they require you or Titus to go to the station for whatever reason, call him. Understood?'

I offer a small nod, if only to put an end to the icy gaze

he has fixed upon me. 'Good. Now, Peter is here in, er, shall we say, a sensitive capacity.'

I sense my mother shifting uncomfortably in her chair. It seems she disapproves of Mr Catton. And I don't blame her.

'Peter was accused earlier this year of a crime. He has maintained his innocence ever since, and, through some careful engineering, his case did not go to court. Meanwhile, a number of other people – some of whom you know in person – did end up going to prison. The difference here is that Peter was wise enough to contact me to see what could be done. He, along with another key individual who shall remain nameless, saw the bigger picture. He knew things did not need to be black and white, good and evil, all that weak watery stuff the justice system feeds the public. And thankfully, some of the connections he has, and some of the people I know, will potentially prove very useful when helping us sort out your, um, little difficulty.'

Peter nods in response to my father's monologue and offers me a smile. It makes him look like a vampire. 'Your father is right. If the two of us combine our resources – and mark my words, our resources are considerable, we're pretty confident all of this will go exactly the way … well, the way we'd like it to go.'

I frown at him, slightly confused. 'I take it my father has told you what has happened? Rachel, our … for want of a better word, *friend* has been arrested for killing my husband. She has confessed. It's likely she'll be charged imminently then go to prison.' I now turn my gaze towards my father. 'I'm rather puzzled as to why all this is necessary?'

To my surprise, my father directs a nod to my mother, who gives a polite cough. 'That would be down to me,' she says.

It's my turn to stare at her now. 'What do you mean?'

She sighs, then purses her lips, clearly deciding how to word her reply. Eventually she says, 'I telephoned your father before he boarded his flight. About … about something I was concerned about.'

'Concerned about what?' I ask, looking from my mother, then back to my father, intensely aware of the presence of the two outsiders, watching this very personal, very private family situation unfold.

'This is, in a way, the heart of the matter, and why we're all here,' my father says. 'And we'll get to it. But first, it is important you tell us everything that happened, everything you did on that day, everything Titus did on that day, and how it came about that your husband ended up on the floor with a knife in his chest.'

The last few words of his sentence shock me a little and I feel a touch of the dizziness, the disconcerting corruption of my sense of balance, return for a few seconds. When I open my mouth to speak, I struggle to get the words out. 'I … er … well … I just told you how it happened. Our friend from our book club, Rachel, stabbed Matthew at the dinner table. She just randomly came over. Said she needed to talk to us about something. It was all quite surreal, really.'

My father's brow creases, his eyes drilling into me. 'And her motive for this?'

I make a sort of half shrug. 'I think … I think she might

have been in love with Matthew. There were a few times recently, particularly during our holiday in The Hamptons, when she did things that … well, I got the feeling she wanted to start an affair with him, and he rejected her advances.'

Silence greets this for a good few seconds, then my father says, 'And Titus?'

I feel something plummet within me. 'What about him?' I ask, trying to keep my voice level and convincing.

'Where does he fit into all this?'

I think about this question. Think about the many ways I could answer it. Then I say, with all the confidence I can muster, 'He doesn't. He has nothing to do with it.'

My father's frown strengthens, and when he speaks, his voice is even lower and quieter than before. 'I think that may be the first time since you were a child that you've told me an outright lie.'

It's as if he's shot me. I turn to look at my mother, who has her eyes trained on the carpet in front of her, then look over at Jacob and Peter. Both look grave and, in the case of the former, a little embarrassed. Unable to stand it any longer – whatever this weird little intervention may be – I stand up. 'I can't do this,' I say, knowing my voice sounds weak, like an emotional teenager. 'I'm leaving.'

'Sit down,' my father says sternly.

Peter stands up opposite me and puts a hand on my shoulder. 'Charles, my dear, please take a seat so we can discuss how we can *help* you. We're not stupid. We know something happened the other night that you're not telling us, that you're trying to hide from the police. The point your father and I are trying to make is that we can get one step ahead and work out a plan of action.'

I move back in order to get his hand off my shoulder. Being touched by someone I hardly know – someone like him – sickens me. 'Get off me,' I say, suddenly angry. 'You may have needed my father's help to escape prison, but that's probably because you're guilty as fuck.'

My mother stands up now. '*Please*, Charles, just sit down so we can sort this out before it gets out of control.'

I ignore her and start to walk towards the door. 'I'll see you back at Wilton Crescent,' I say as I leave. 'Enjoy the rest of your little gathering.'

'Charles,' my father's voice cuts through the darkness of the hallway, 'you've made a number of serious errors already regarding this business. Please don't add another to the list.'

I keep silent as I step through the front door and allow it to clatter shut behind me. I see Malcolm look up as I come into view and go to open the car door, but I turn on my heel and walk away from him and the house in the direction of the Thames.

I walk for about ten minutes down the road that snakes along the river towards Chelsea. When I reach the lower edge of Belgravia, I take a right turn down some steps that lead to the remnants of the old Grosvenor canal. There I sit and put my head in my hands, light from the moon reflecting on the surface of the water, flickering just out of the corner of my eye. I know I've been stupid. I know I've made mistakes. And, worst of all, I know everything my father has said tonight – about me being foolish, making mistakes, failing to know what to do – is completely correct. There will probably come a time when I will need the help of him and his unsavoury acquaintances. It sounds like he and my mother may have already figured out what really happened that night. And it won't be long before the police do too.

Chapter Twenty

RACHEL

Seven months to go

'Why were you crying by the photocopiers?'

The assistant head of the PR and marketing department at Streamline, Edward Rex, lounged back on his cream desk-chair, his expression showing not a jot of sympathy.

I sniffed, dabbing at my eyes with a tissue that really should be binned and replaced. 'I'm sorry. I've been having a bit of a tough time of late. Just … well, Christmas was a bit difficult.' His expression remained blank, although he moved his hand across his face to brush a flop of his red hair away from his eyes. When he didn't reply, I added, 'Just personal reasons.' I hoped he'd think it was boyfriend trouble or something. My dealings with Edward had been infrequent and brief up until this point, and I'd been embarrassed when he'd discovered me sobbing whilst printing off copies of a press release.

'I know this job probably isn't very riveting for you, Raquel, and I'm not going to lie to you, you're only here because Sophia was dead-set on appointing you. Why that is, I haven't yet found out. But – let me put this politely – you just don't seem like the Streamline type. You don't really make an effort' – he used this moment to look up and down at my grey skirt, second-hand white blouse and dark-grey cardigan – 'nor do you show much interest in beauty or make-up.'

This was unfair. I did use make-up – a little at least – and it was hard to show interest in lip balm or eye liner when all I was doing was stapling together meeting notes or throwing out old paperwork from office cupboards.

'I'm sorry,' I said. It was all I could manage.

'In a nutshell, Raquel, I think maybe this industry isn't for you. My wife's brother was much the same – had no aptitude for an office environment.'

Was he sacking me? Surely it couldn't be as easy as that, I thought. Not while Sophia was away. I took a deep breath and was about to try to gather my thoughts together when there was a light tap on the door.

'Oh, I'm so sorry to interrupt but I was looking for— Ah, there you are!'

I saw Edward's eyes widen and I turned round to see Meryl standing in the doorway, looking as stylish as ever in a spotless knee-length cream coat and holding onto a very expensive-looking handbag. 'So lovely to see you Rachel. I was actually just looking for you.' She was smiling pleasantly and looked as calm and collected as someone receiving guests in their own front room. She walked into the office without being invited and Edward stood up instantly. 'Meryl, I didn't realise you were paying us a visit today.'

Meryl smiled wider. 'Do you know, Edward, I really have been missing the office lately. I've always flirted with the idea of coming back to play a more day-to-day role in the running of the place. But, I suppose, I've probably got used to living a life of semi-leisure.'

She came over and took the seat next to mine, setting her handbag in her lap. Edward sat back down without a word. 'Do you know what my father said to me when I was twelve?' Meryl continued. 'I was growing up on Long Island and had probably got too used to the comfortable existence my family had provided me with. My father – he was such a wise man; made the best cider you'd ever drink – but anyway, he once said, Meryl, you're becoming complacent, you need to learn some *hard work*; a life of all play and no work never did anybody any good.' She nodded at Edward, while he, on the other hand, stared back at her, his mouth slightly open. 'So, anyway, my point is, I think the mind needs new challenges, new adventures. Do you know what I'm saying, Edward?'

A small pause passed before he realised a reply was expected. 'Oh ... um ... yes, I suppose so.'

She beamed. 'Good. I'm glad we're on the same page with this. Because, from what I've been hearing from Sophia, you've been limiting Rachel's work here to very dull tasks. You've practically made her into your paperclip monitor.'

His eyebrows rose at this. 'Well ... I ... er ... Sophia

never provided much guidance on what, er, what duties should be considered her…'

'Yes, she did,' Meryl said simply. 'I'm also surprised it's taken you this long to remember her name. *Rachel*. Not Raquel, as I heard you twice call her just now. You see, I've never been able to avoid the lure of eavesdropping. It's one of my weaknesses.'

Edward's jaw clenched. He looked like he was biting his tongue.

'Well, I'm going to take Rachel here out for lunch. We'll probably be gone a few hours. And when she returns, I trust you'll find her some more stimulating tasks to fill her time. After all, she's a bit old to be treated like your office intern. And of course, you have a bit of a history with interns, don't you, Edward?'

Edward made an uncomfortable swallowing sound and coughed. 'I … er … I'm sorry, what do you…?'

'We'd better be off,' Meryl said, 'I've made reservations for 1pm at Enoteca Turi. Lovely to see you, Edward.'

With that, she picked up her bag and rose out of her seat, then looked at me, making it clear I should do the same. I got up and, following her lead, walked out of the office, not giving Edward a second glance.

Enoteca Turi was an intimate Italian restaurant on the Pimlico Road. I'd never been anywhere so fancy, and the prices of the pasta almost made me swear. For Meryl, however, this was probably considered cheap and cheerful.

'Thank you for saving me from that,' I said, after the waiter had taken our order. 'He was laying into me a bit. It was silly really. I shouldn't have got so upset.'

I made a point of dabbing my eyes at this. Part of me suspected Meryl liked coming to the rescue of people – she did it so smoothly and with such a sense of knowing ease that it could hardly have been her first time.

'He's a tiresome little man, Edward. I can't imagine why Sophia has let him rumble on in that place for the past few years.'

The waiter brought Meryl her wine and me the Diet Coke I'd ordered. 'What you said about him having an interesting past with interns. Was that true?'

Her eyes sparkled a little at this. 'No, I just made it up on the spot. It certainly put the cat among the pigeons though.'

I laughed and took a sip of my drink. 'Well, hopefully he'll be a bit nicer to me in future.'

Meryl suddenly looked more serious. 'My dear, are you unhappy? Because you shouldn't be. You're an intelligent, competent individual. Anyone who can't see that is either blind or stupid or both.'

I smiled, a little sadly, and said, 'I just feel a bit lost, really. I didn't have a very good Christmas. It's just me and my dad, you see, so it's not exactly very lively. And coming back here and Edward being unpleasant to me... I'm very grateful for the job, don't get me wrong, it's just I'm... I don't know. Nothing feels sure or stable.'

Meryl nodded slowly, her expression suggesting she was contemplating my words carefully. She changed the conversation then, moving instead to talk about our upcoming book-club book and how much she hoped I'd be coming along. It was only when we'd cleared our plates and Meryl was sorting out the bill that she turned the topic back round to my depressing life.

'My dear, I have a proposition. If you wish to say no, think nothing of it; I will not be offended. I'm too tough and old to be easily offended. Anyway, for some time I've been thinking I could do with some help with some general life admin things. Take the load off me. It wouldn't be arduous work, just booking me in for hair appointments, my little dog Bunty's trips to the grooming salon, shopping, organising cars to collect me when I need them, or perhaps even driving yourself – I don't drive, you see, I could never work out the British road system. So, my proposal is this: how about you leave Streamline and come and work for me?'

A few seconds went by before I realised I was gaping at her. This was better than I ever could have hoped, ever could have dreamed. The thought of being so closely connected to Meryl, and in turn to the Allerton-Joneses, took my breath away.

'Really? You're offering me the job? I'm … not skilled in PA work. I've done retail and customer service, but I've never been a secretary or anything like that.' Even in my shocked state, I was mindful not to bite Meryl's hand off with eagerness. Keep it slow, play it cool was always my dad's method of selling cars when I was young, and I've found it to be a useful motto.

'I'm offering *you* the job. Honestly, I'd much prefer to

174

have you than one of those aspiring socialites with degrees, hoping to marry the first rich guy that comes across their path.'

I have a degree, I thought to myself, but I pushed the snag of annoyance to the back of my mind. What Meryl was offering was nothing short of golden.

'Also,' she continued, 'you can leave that little flat of yours. Come and stay with me at Eaton Square. I have a house far too big for a single old lady. Charlie has been telling me for years to allow a real-estate company to carve it up into apartments and make a killing, but I just can't bear the thought of the upheaval and, to be honest, money is overrated.'

Money is overrated. In any other situation, a phrase like this, spoken by a multimillionaire, would have made me bloody livid, but my mind was still spinning from this new bombshell: I was to leave Churchill Gardens. Move in with Meryl. To one of the most famous squares in London. Hadn't the Bellamys in *Upstairs Downstairs* lived at Eaton something-or-other? Faded memories of me watching old videos of the show on the sofa on rainy days with my mum swam into my mind. I could feel my heart pounding as I took in a slow breath. 'Are you sure?'

Meryl smiled kindly at me. 'Of course I'm sure. I wouldn't have offered if I wasn't. I'll have my lawyer draft up all the employment details, of course, to make sure I'm doing everything above board. I'll get him to sort all that out with you directly – National Insurance and all that; I avoid all paperwork where possible. In terms of salary, how does £40,000 a year sound? Of course, I won't be charging you rent or anything. We'll throw your accommodation in because, really my dear, it's you who is doing me a favour here. So, do you accept?'

Now, at last, I allowed my excitement to show through. Clasping her hands across the table, and letting a perfectly timed tear fall from my face, I said, 'Yes. Completely. Thank you so, so much.'

Meryl looked delighted. 'Excellent. Right, let me pay for the food and then we'll set off to the house. I can show you where you'll be living. I'll tell Sophia and Edward you won't be returning because you've had a better offer elsewhere.'

I nodded and sat quietly while Meryl paid for our meal. *A better offer.* She didn't know how much of an understatement that was.

Chapter Twenty-One

CHARLIE

Seven months to go

Things continued to get weirder at the start of the New Year. It set the tone for things to come, in some ways. When I say weird, I'm rather lumping together everything involving Rachel and Matthew and her proximity to our lives, although of course later on I would discover there were many strands to all of this. We were at Jerome's apartment when the next notable 'odd thing' involving Rachel occurred.

We'd been reading the Margaret Atwood novel for that first meeting in January and, to my surprise, Titus expressed an interest in joining. Although he'd always been very bookish himself, like me (until recently) he'd never expressed a wish to join in before, always seeming more content with baking cakes than participating in the discussion with us adults. But on this occasion, he arrived downstairs just as we were getting our coats on, asking if he could come with us.

'I've read the book,' he said. 'I'd really like to discuss it. And I haven't seen Meryl in ages.'

I saw Matthew looked slightly taken aback. 'Well ... I'm not sure. It isn't at Meryl's; it's over at Jerome's place.'

Titus rolled his eyes. 'But Meryl will be there, won't she? And Rachel.'

I looked up sharply at the mention of Rachel – too sharply, because I saw Matthew notice. I don't know if that was why he gave an automatic 'yes' to Titus, or if he just didn't want to get into a needless argument and end up being late. Whatever the reason, he said Titus was allowed to accompany us, and we all hopped in the X6 and set off towards Jerome's apartment.

The first disconcerting incident occurred just as we were driving up to Grosvenor Square. A car cut in front of us, causing me to break suddenly as we were turning the corner, drawing a muttered swear word from Matthew. I was about to tell him to calm down when the doors of the sleek black Mercedes in front of us opened and out stepped Meryl, followed by, rather astonishingly, Rachel. Her light-blonde hair was unmistakable, although her clothes seemed to have drastically improved since we'd last seen her. She'd never been badly dressed, but was always the safe-side of plain and unremarkable. Now, she looked ... well, sophisticated. Her hair was tied back and she was dressed in a jet-black trench coat and clasping a pristine cream handbag. It was starting to drizzle and as I watched she opened up a deep-maroon umbrella and used it to cover herself and Meryl.

Matthew shifted next to me, and I thought he was about to tell me to move on, but then the figures in front of us caught his attention. 'Is that Rachel?' he asked. 'She looks … well, different. And what's she doing with Meryl?'

I shrugged, 'How should I know?'

We watched them walk along the pavement, up the steps towards the apartment building, and then disappear from view. A hoot from behind us startled us out of our respective trances.

'Er, you going to move the car?' Titus said from the back seat.

I snapped into action, 'Yes, sorry.' I began to steer the car around the corner, my mind racing. What on earth was going on? Why had Rachel got out of that car with Meryl? And what was she wearing?

Inside Jerome's apartment, we found Rachel browsing the ultra-modern bookshelves (complete with under-shelf lighting strips), a large collection of Angela Carter stories held in her hands. Meryl was sitting near her, sipping a martini.

'Hello dear,' the latter said to me when she saw me approaching. 'How are you on this cold, blustery night?'

'Good, thanks,' I said, distracted by Rachel, who had closed the book and was smiling at me. 'Good evening,

Rachel,' I said, feeling it would be weird not to acknowledge her since she clearly expected a greeting.

Meryl then carried on talking. 'I don't think I've seen you since … well, Rachel here has decided to become my new personal assistant.' She said it with a wide, apparently overjoyed smile on her face.

'Personal … assistant?' I repeated, slowly.

'That's right,' Rachel said, also beaming. 'It all happened rather quickly, but it's been a good few weeks now. Almost a month, actually.'

I was partly furious at Meryl, my mother, even Jerome, for not making me aware of this sooner. Surely they all must have known? A weird development such as this? Because it was weird – extremely odd. Meryl didn't need a PA. She didn't really work anymore and spent most of her time flitting from one social occasion to the next. And if she did need some help, why wouldn't she interview someone with references and a track record of being good in that field, not some random stranger she met at a book club who used to stack shelves in a garden centre?

'But, I thought you worked at Streamline?' I said, momentarily forgetting my manners as I accepted a cocktail from Jerome without saying thank you.

'Well, I did until recently,' Rachel said. 'But Meryl offered me the chance to work for her.'

I turned to look back at Meryl. Her slightly mad smile had settled into a calmly reserved look of happiness and contentment. 'I have to say they were tragically under-utilising her,' she said, with a little shake of her head. 'So I offered her an alternative. It really doesn't do to have a smart, keen, young mind wasted behind a photocopier and endless pointless emails.'

I offered a vague nod at this, unsure how to respond. Eventually, and probably a tad belatedly, I decided to try to act pleased at the news. 'Well, I suppose once again you'll have a very easy walk to work,' I said. 'Must only be a fifteen-minute walk from Churchill Gardens to Eaton Square.'

'Oh, she's no longer in that tiny little flat,' Meryl said, looking scandalised. 'I couldn't have her living there. It just didn't feel right. Rachel's come to join me in my house while we find somewhere more suitable for her, closer to her place of work.'

Closer to her place of work? How could she get closer, unless she moved over to Belgravia itself – although that might be on the cards if Meryl had put her on a decent salary.

'It's so kind of you,' Rachel said, looking at Meryl with what she probably considered to be an expression of wistful respect. After all, Meryl was now her saviour twice-over, a benefactor beyond her wildest dreams, taking her from a council estate to Eaton Square with a quick flourish of her hand.

We had to go through the whole tale all over again when Matthew appeared by my side. Matthew was comparatively chuffed for Rachel, remarking how perfect he thought she was for the job.

'Why do you think she'd be perfect?' I asked him in a hushed tone later in the evening after our Atwood discussion, while the others were discussing politics.

Matthew looked confused at my question. '*Rachel*,' I clarified, impatiently. 'You said you thought she'd be "perfect" for the job of Meryl's PA.'

He shrugged. 'Well, I just thought she'd probably do a good job.'

'But without any experience? Without ever doing the job of a PA – or anything secretarial or organisational in her life? How can she be perfect?'

Matthew didn't seem interested in discussing the topic further. 'We don't know that. We don't really know anything about her past life before she came to London.'

How right he was.

The evening became steadily weirder still when Titus, who had enthusiastically taken part in the discussion on *The Testaments*, followed by Brexit, House of Lords reform, and alleged BBC political bias, politely asked Jerome if he could have a look at the extensive collection of paintings he had on the staircase leading to the upper level.

'Of course, dear boy. There are more on the landing upstairs, too. Go ahead and roam about.'

Titus eagerly accepted the invitation and left the lounge. I didn't notice Rachel slipping out too, but after five or ten minutes or so, I realised she had also left our throng by the fire in the lounge.

I'm not sure what it was that made me get up and go and explore as well – I had next to no interest in Jerome's depressingly gothic art collection, but I just had a strange, tingling sense that something was slightly off.

There was no sign of Titus in the corridor, the striking, very modern cream-coloured surroundings (the pale tones emphasised by the jet-black steps of the stairs) completely deserted. I climbed the stairs towards the landing and saw Titus, peering closely at one of the paintings on the landing. I was about to call out to him, to tell him it was time to be getting going, when I saw Rachel walk confidently from down the other end of the long landing gallery, remarking on the brush strokes of one of the paintings at the end. Titus listened to her and nodded. It was as if the two of them were out at an exhibition together, comparing thoughts on the work, like a couple of friends. I watched them, oddly mesmerised, and I had a strange sense of déjà vu – my mind leaping back to that first time Rachel went walkabouts at our house and was found upstairs, snooping around the main bedroom. As I watched, I saw Rachel lean in to study the painting that had seemingly transfixed Titus. She put a hand on his shoulder and brought her head so that it was almost touching Titus's and seemed to whisper something in his ear. And he smiled, then laughed.

I started to feel my balance go and I stumbled forward, grabbing hold of the side of the wall and knocking one of the framed paintings askew. Titus and Rachel both turned to see my baffled, and no doubt guilty, face looking back up at them.

'It's … time to go,' I said to Titus. I was slightly cheered by the fact that he didn't put up any protest at his and Rachel's time being cut short. Instead, he came down the stairs, his normal cheery self, and we all started saying our goodbyes and thanking Jerome for a splendid dinner.

'He didn't cook it himself,' Anita said, slightly sneeringly. 'If you want to thank somebody, his Vietnamese housekeeper is the one you should bring out of the cupboard and speak to.'

'She's not in the cupboard,' Jerome replied. 'And don't you think you've had a little bit too much wine, my dear?'

Anita said nothing in response, but clutched her glass protectively close to her, as if it might be snatched away at any moment.

On the drive home, I decided to bring up what I had seen on the stairs, aiming for a casual, making-conversation sort of tone.

'You and Rachel seemed to be enjoying Jerome's art collection.'

I heard Titus yawn, then say, 'Yeah, she seems to like the same sort of thing.'

'What painting was it you were both looking at? You seemed hypnotised.'

Titus considered for a moment, 'Oh, er, it was called *Justice and Divine Vengeance Pursuing Crime*.'

I nodded, as if I knew it well.

'By Pierre-Paul Prud'hon, I think.'

I drove on for a few seconds in silence, but the more I thought about this, the more it bothered me. Taking a deep breath, I just asked him outright. 'And what did she say to you about this bleak-sounding painting that meant she needed to whisper in your ear?'

I looked in the rearview mirror and saw Titus frown a

little, then shrug. 'She had just described what was happening in the painting, saying how powerfully she felt the main themes of the piece are conveyed. And she didn't whisper, she just spoke quietly; I think you're probably going deaf.' He smiled, playfully, but I was too distracted to acknowledge the teasing.

'What themes?' Matthew asked, acting the casually interested parent.

'Retribution and revenge,' Titus replied.

He said the words as if they were nothing. But they continued to haunt me all the way back to Chelsea.

Chapter Twenty-Two

RACHEL

Five months to go

I expected the Allerton-Joneses to be surprised at my new job and I was pleased with the way Meryl dealt with Charlie's obvious, snobbish disapproval.

Over the months that followed, as winter became spring, I threw myself into executing my role as best I could. I arranged appointments for Meryl, sorted out her social calendar, did the shopping, booked a mini-break away for her with her son, who was based in the States but flew to meet his mother in Paris every February. I'd worried at first that her housekeeper, Iona, would think her job was being taken from her, but she seemed thrilled to have fewer responsibilities. Meryl clearly enjoyed my company, taking me out to dinner at least once a week, but I never found her overbearing. I had a large room and bathroom all to myself in the house, on a floor above her bedroom. Meryl even had plans for me to eventually move into the house on Belgrave

Place that she was in the process of doing up. I would end up living in one of the new apartments there once the renovations were finished.

Me, in a luxury flat to myself in Central London, in one of the most desirable neighbourhoods in the country. It was something I'd never have dreamed of. I think, for years, I had been ruminating on how I wanted to change the past, rather than shape my future. Finding myself in this situation in London, working for Meryl, friends with famous actors like Jerome, and of course the Allerton-Joneses, made me realise how things can change. How the impossible can suddenly be made possible. I felt a little guilty for enjoying it all, considering why I had come here and what I was supposed to be doing. But I'd lived under a cloud for so long, it was impossible not to look up and enjoy it for a bit. To move on, at last. No, move on wouldn't be the right words. That suggests I was ready to let things go, to step off my chosen path. To move forward. That would be more appropriate. And a conversation I would have with Meryl that spring would show me just how far forward I was moving.

It was when we were going through her upcoming appointments for April that I found out her plan. We were sitting in her beautiful lounge; it was truly like something from *Upstairs Downstairs*, only with a more modern edge, and I had to force myself to stop staring at the décor around me. I had her diary open on my legs and was pencilling things in when I turned the page to the first week of May. 'Goodness, how this year is racing by,' she remarked, 'I hardly feel it's begun. Our New York holiday will be here before we know it.'

This was the first I'd heard of anything to do with New York. 'Oh, I didn't know you were going to the US. I'll mark in the dates, so we don't book anything over it.'

She produced her iPhone – into the calendar app of which I would later painstakingly copy everything from the written diary – and scrolled through her messages. I could see from the contact name at the top it was a message thread with Cassandra Allerton. 'Let me see… Saturday 9th to Wednesday 20th. Flying out Saturday morning and flying back home the Wednesday afternoon.'

I flicked forward in the diary to those dates and wrote at the top of them *New York*.

'You're so organised, my dear,' Meryl said, admiring how neatly I had everything laid out in the large leather-bound volume.

I laughed a little. 'I like everything to be laid out and in order. If you give me the details of anything you'd like arranged for when you return home, I'll get that done while you're away.'

Meryl looked puzzled. 'While *I'm* away? No, no, dear, while *we're* away.'

I stared back at her, blinking. 'You mean, you and the Allertons?'

Meryl smiled. 'Well, yes, Cassandra and Michael, and Charles and Matthew and Titus. And *you*.'

I continued to stare, this time with my mouth slightly open, only just comprehending what she was saying. 'What? You mean, you want me to come?'

Meryl laid her palms upwards in an *of course* motion. 'Oh, my dear, I'm not sure I'd manage the whole thing without you. You really are proving yourself to be indispensable.'

And with that, she put her phone away, gave me a kindly pat on the shoulder, and wandered off in the direction of the kitchen and her 11am green-juice smoothie, leaving me on the sofa with a sense of steadily rising excitement. It would be nice to have one last holiday, I thought. Before I go to prison for murder.

Chapter Twenty-Three

RACHEL

Two days after the murder

I sit in police custody, waiting. I'm still partly in shock at what I'm doing. But the other part is relieved it's all over now. That everything will, hopefully, be plain sailing from now on. It was fun while it all lasted, of course. Living with Meryl, mixing with people from a completely different world to the one I came from. But I always knew it wasn't going to last for ever. I think back to that time now not with regret, just contentment. I'm pleased I got to live a little myself before things had to end in this way. Because they always had to end in this way.

But as the hours, and now days, go by, I'm starting to wonder if everything is as clear cut as I've presumed. Is there, perhaps, something I've missed? Or have the other two talked? Talked too much? Tripped themselves up? Got their stories in a mix too far-fetched for the police not to suspect something strange is happening here? Because all this depends on one clear thing: Charlie and Titus must stick to the story. That's the only way this can all work. And for everyone to be happy.

My thoughts are interrupted by the arrival of Detective Inspector Susan Okonjo. She walks into my cell, leaving the door open, with another police officer, this one uniformed, standing behind her. 'Good afternoon, Rachel.'

Is it afternoon? I can hardly tell. I know more than one day has passed, but time is starting to get the better of me. When I don't reply, DI Okonjo carries on with whatever little speech she has planned.

'I've had a conversation with the CPS and it's time for you to be formally charged for the murder of Matthew Allerton-Jones. Do you understand what I'm saying?'

I nod.

'Good.' She turns to go, but stops before she's properly left the room. She turns her small, slim frame back round to face me, with a curious look on her face, like something's bothering her. 'I have to say, Rachel, when we brought you in, I thought this was going to be fairly simple. But it's not, is it?'

I stay silent.

'In fact, I've been putting off charging you because, well … something just feels a little odd.' She bites her lip, as if she's thinking about what she's going to say next. I get the feeling she's going off-script now. 'If I were to give you one more chance, one last attempt to unpick this whole thing, would you take it? We could have it out right now, you and me. You can tell me anything you want. Any details you're keeping back. Anyone you might be … protecting.'

She gets my attention with this. Slightly impresses me, even. But it's not going to work. She's wasting her time. So I tell her.

'I murdered Matthew Allerton-Jones. I went to the house to do it. It was the easiest thing in the world. If you're a real detective, it shouldn't be hard for you to work out why. You'll see I had a very good reason to. But I'm not doing your job for you. Charge me. Let's just get this over with. I'm not going to speak anymore.'

I see her eyes widen in surprise, but she doesn't say anything. Just watches me intently. Then she turns on her heel and walks out of the room, leaving me alone once more.

Chapter Twenty-Four

CHARLIE

Three months to go

The day before we were due to fly to New York, Matthew went AWOL again. I kept on trying his phone, worried that I couldn't find our passports and irritated he wasn't home helping me pack.

Even though I knew he was probably fine – stuck in traffic, out of signal range – I couldn't help but be reminded of October last year, when Matthew was absent just when I needed him. When Titus had been attacked. Although this wasn't as dramatic a moment, of course, if we didn't find the passports soon it looked like our part in the trip would have to be cancelled and my parents and Meryl would be jetting off without us. Then there was the strange instance at Christmas, when the car had broken down. All these signs were mounting up, and I probably, deep down, knew how stupid I was being then not to properly string them together. But up until that point, my marriage had been the most concrete, indestructible thing in my life. We'd been a proper partnership, a team, so unified and at one with each other, very different from, say, my parents' weirdly distant relationship.

He eventually arrived home later, apologetic and starving, saying he'd had to go on an impromptu trip to Surrey to see this ageing philosopher whose paper they were publishing in some dull-sounding left-wing polemic. I was less interested in where he'd been and more about where the passports could be, and, as expected, Matthew was able to lay his hands on them immediately in a drawer in the library that I'd forgotten even existed.

Matthew went to take a hot bath to de-stress after his hectic day and I took off my clothes and left them out for Jane to add to the other washing while we were away. I picked Matthew's up off the floor too, emptying his pockets of his wallet, some tissues ... and a train ticket. I almost missed it, caught between the tissues, and grabbed hold of it as it fluttered towards the bin. It was from Marylebone to High Wycombe. It made me pause. Why would Matthew need to go to High Wycombe? He'd said, minutes earlier, he'd been to Surrey, and blamed traffic for his lateness. Not trains. A deep, angry burn started to blush through me. Was he lying to me? He had to be, surely. But Matthew never lied. Not throughout our entire marriage had I caught him out in a lie, not even a small one. It felt incompatible with his character. Incompatible with my idea of *us*.

I was still holding the ticket when I heard him come out of the bathroom and walk back towards our room.

'What's this?' I asked, holding it out to him. In

retrospect, I'd like to say there was a definite flicker of something in his eyes, some look of being caught out. But in truth, I can't quite be sure if there was or if I imagined it, as he answered almost immediately and smiled his usual, gorgeous grin, taking a step towards me. 'A train ticket.'

'I know that,' I said, taking care not to sound angry, 'It's just, well, you said you went to Surrey today and the ticket is a return to High Wycombe.'

Matthew took off the towel around his waist and started to dry his hair. 'Oh, did I say Surrey? I meant High Wycombe.'

I frowned. 'That's … quite a mistake.'

He pulled a face. 'Is it?' he said. 'You make mistakes like that all the time. We're getting old. Cognitive decline, I'd wager.' He stood there, remarkably confident, his perfect naked body suddenly taking on an oddly alien, unknown appearance in my eyes, even though I knew it so well.

'It doesn't even start with the same letter,' I said. 'And you don't normally take the train. Surely you'd drive?'

He let out a sigh of exasperation. 'It's because I'm going to Surrey when we get back from New York,' he said, picking up some pyjama trousers and pulling them on. 'I made the arrangements earlier. That's what made me think of it. And I had a meeting in Marylebone this morning. High Wycombe is only thirty minutes from Marylebone station, and I was going with Ali, who lives in Marylebone, so it all made sense us getting the train from there.' He looked at me, still good humoured and smiling. 'All fine now?'

Eventually I nodded. 'Sorry. Yes, sorry. I was just

confused. The stress of not being able to find the passports…'

He nodded. 'It's OK, I understand. Now, turn off the light and come and join me in here.'

I smiled at him now, recognising the wicked slant his grin had taken on, but went to leave the room. 'I just need to check Titus is all good and packed, and bring up some things from downstairs. And you should dry your hair properly; you'll make the pillows damp.'

I left him in the room and went via the alternative bathroom, separate from our room, before I looked in on Titus. In the mirror my own face stared back at me. Still slightly flushed. Still pulsing a little with the small fire of anger that had ignited inside me.

When I got back to the bedroom, Matthew was in bed reading. Instead of reaching for my phone – Instagram being my normal alternative to Matthew's reading – I lay back into the covers, trying to calm my cluttered mind.

'You going straight to sleep? We don't have an early start; it's not even 10.30pm. You can sleep in in the morning.'

'Don't you just … sorry, nothing.' I rolled over, annoyed at myself for starting the sentence.

'Don't I just what?' I heard Matthew close his book and set it aside. 'Is this still about High Wycombe?'

'No, the holiday. I was just going to say that I still find it, well, odd, that we're going on holiday with Rachel.'

A sigh greeted this. 'Don't take this the wrong way, but … well, do you begrudge Rachel her, I don't know … her ascent?'

I pulled myself up on my elbows and looked at him. 'Her *ascent*? What does that mean?'

Matthew looked a little pained, as if unsure how to broach the subject. 'Well, she's rising in the world, isn't she? From council flat to Eaton Square.'

'Her Churchill Gardens flat was privately rented.'

Matthew tutted. 'You know what I mean. It must be quite a step up from her previous jobs – working in a garden centre or being a dogsbody in an office. Being Meryl's live-in assistant can hardly be a difficult job – she's so independent, I'm convinced she did the whole thing as a favour...'

'Which you have to admit is odd in itself,' I interrupted. 'And she's not just live-in; I believe Rachel has been given the option to live in Meryl's additional property on Belgrave Place, which is being done up just for her. I mean, is this just a way of giving her a house? She might as well just transfer thirty-three million into her bank account and be done with it.'

Matthew looked shocked. 'Why are you being so bitter about this? Are you jealous or something? And it's not a house; it's an apartment. And it wouldn't be worth thirty million.'

'I'm not saying I'm jealous. Of course I'm not fucking jealous...'

'Then it must be just snobbery,' Matthew said with a shrug, looking at me as if I'd let him down. 'How dare that little Yorkshire lass want a bit of what we've all got. Is that it?'

'Oh, spare me,' I snapped back. 'All I'm asking is for you

to agree with me that it's strange. She walked into a bookshop one day, bumped into us two and within a matter of months she's settled in the home of my godmother and might be set to take control of a household in one of the most desirable addresses in the world. Doesn't that make you pause, even if it's only to marvel at how well she's managed the whole thing?'

Matthew blinked back. '*Take control?* How well she's *managed* it? You're making her sound like a dormant terror cell, not a member of a book club.'

I stared at him defiantly for a few seconds, then sank back into the covers. 'I just find it odd.'

Silence fell between us for a bit, then Matthew lay back down next to me. 'Please don't say any of this when we're on holiday,' he said, his tone softer, as if trying to appeal to my more reasonable side. 'We're going to have a good time and I think she'd find a lot of this very hurtful.'

I didn't reply, just stared at the ceiling. After a while, I heard Matthew move over and turn the light out, plunging us into darkness. We didn't speak again until morning, and when we did, we avoided the topic of Rachel.

Chapter Twenty-Five

CHARLIE

Three days after the murder

The police arrive at Braddon Manor within less than forty-eight hours of us coming down here, three days after the murder. It is inevitable, of course, though part of me does feel like our calm little oasis is being shattered by outside forces.

I hear the crunch of gravel outside and put down a copy of a novel I've been reading then go over to the window. A smart Mercedes has pulled up outside the house and sure enough, Detective Inspector Okonjo and Detective Sergeant Stimson get out. They're always having a conversation and I hear the male voice say, 'Bloody hell, this place,' and then DI Okonjo says something in response I can't quite catch. 'Probably kept for tax reasons,' DS Stimson muses, and I pull back a bit as they walk past the library window and head for the front door. 'Would have been easier if they'd just stayed in bloody London,' he continues.

I get up and walk out of the library and into the hallway, opening the door to them just as DI Stimson rings it.

'Hello Mr Allerton-Jones,' DI Okonjo says, managing to hide any surprise at me opening the door so quickly. 'We hope you're holding up OK. As I said on the phone, we'd like to come in and give you an update.'

It's all in the detail, I think to myself, as I stand back and let them through. *Give me an update.* Question me further would be more accurate. 'You told us not to leave the country,' I say as I lead the way through into the lounge. I notice DS Stimson is peering around at the paintings on the walls with a mixture of disgust and fascination.

'Sorry?' DI Okonjo says.

Once we're in the living room, I motion for them to sit down. 'You asked us not to leave the UK, but you didn't say anything about not leaving London. I heard you speaking outside.'

DI Stimson has the grace to appear embarrassed.

'Like I said, we're here to give you an update.'

I nod. 'That's … very kind of you, thank you.' After my confident start, I'm now finding it difficult to gather words together, as if I'm not speaking in my native tongue. Before I can say anything else, however, the door opens and my mother walks into the room.

'Hello Mrs Allerton,' DI Okonjo says, getting in first before my mother can talk. 'We just need to have a chat with your son about the investigation and the next steps now we've had a confession to the crime.'

My mother nods in a business-like way. 'Yes, that

sounds very sensible,' she says and goes to sit down on one of the single-seater chairs.

'Actually, Mrs Allerton, we'd prefer to talk to your son alone, at present, if that would be OK?'

For a moment, I have a flashback to when I was fourteen and my mother accompanied me to a doctor's appointment. He'd gently suggested my mother step out of the room before asking me if I was sexually active and if I needed any STI advice. Twenty years later, I still sometimes feel like I'm turning to my parents for permission, guidance, advice. If they're around me, or present in the same building, they naturally feel like the default authority on everything.

'Oh, right, certainly,' my mother says, glancing at me for a second before retreating back through the door and closing it softly.

'Surprising,' DS Stimson says.

'What's surprising?' I ask, not liking the look on his face. It's cold and belligerent.

'Well, most people, when their husband, wife, or child is murdered, they keep, y'know, hassling us. On at our officers for updates all the time. They want to know where we're up to in the investigation. I just thought it surprising that, not only do you not bother us at all, but you then leave London and decamp to *this place*.' He gives the library a look of repulsion, as if we were sitting in a rat-infested cellar.

'The difference, Inspector – oh no, sorry, *Sergeant* – is that we know who the guilty party is, in this case. Rachel confessed at the scene. I'm sure I'd be ringing your number at every hour of the day and night if my husband had been killed by a mystery assailant still walking the streets of London, but in this instance that hardly seems necessary.'

The two detectives share a look. I begin to wonder if I've been shooting myself in the foot over these past few days. Maybe I've been trying too hard to fade into the background, to take the glare of the limelight off Titus and me and leave them to get on with charging Rachel. I try to compose my face into a pained and concerned expression.

'Look, I'm sorry, I don't mean to be rude. It's just … as you can imagine, there's no guidebook on how we should cope with this situation. It's all … it's all been traumatic.'

DI Okonjo nods. 'Of course it has. We do understand. I just have a few questions for you, then we'll leave you in peace for now.'

For now sounds ominous, but I nod.

'At the dinner, before Rachel arrived and the violent incident occurred, could you tell me what you, your husband, and Titus had been talking about?' I must look confused, as she then adds, 'It's all good background info. I'm just filling in some gaps that we didn't pick up in our first chat with you.'

'Well, I'm not really sure. It was … about Matthew's time in Scotland.'

'Matthew's time in Scotland,' she repeats. 'OK. What did he have to say about his visit home?'

I take a deep breath. 'How he was glad to be back in London, but he'd had a nice time visiting his childhood home, which is now lived in and managed by his cousin.'

DS Stimson opens up a notepad and writes something down.

'Mr Allerton-Jones, could you let us know at what point in the conversation Rachel entered the flat?'

I frown at her. 'Why is that relevant?'

'Just to get a full picture,' she says, almost casually.

At that moment, the door to the library opens and my father walks in. My mother probably alerted him to the police presence.

'I'm Michael Allerton,' he says as he comes over and stands behind the chair I'm seated in. 'I appreciate you're both doing your jobs, but before this conversation continues with my son I will have to insist we phone the family lawyer and ask him to be present.'

There's a silence for a few seconds, then DI Okonjo says slowly, 'Of course, that's all fine, but this isn't a formal recorded interview. Your son is just helping us get a full picture of what happened that day.'

I feel my father place a hand on my shoulder, his grip firm. He's warning me not to say any more.

'I would understand that more if you didn't have a suspect, Detective. But you do. One who handed herself in at the scene of the crime, I believe. Therefore I'm not entirely sure what you're doing here.'

DI Okonjo smiles, as if used to dealing with less enlightened members of the public, 'A crime like this is like a big canvas that needs painting, Mr Allerton. Of course, most of the painting has been done, but we just need the finishing coat – dotting the Is and crossing the Ts, if you forgive me for mixing my metaphors.'

'I appreciate that,' my father says, sitting down next to

me. 'But I still think it would be best if we waited for our family lawyer. I've already called him; he's on the way.'

DI Okonjo pulls a slight face, as if she's trying to hide her annoyance. 'Do you know, it is interesting, like DS Stimson said a moment ago, how unusual this is. Normally a widow or widower would be desperate to tell us as much as possible so as we can secure a safe conviction. This is … *unexpected*.'

I feel my irritation spike. 'Well, you know what, I'm getting rather fucked off by everyone implying I'm not grieving correctly. I'm sorry if I'm not a neat tick on your list of boxes to get through, but I think we'll do as my father suggests and wait for our lawyer to arrive.'

DI Okonjo definitely looks less impressed now, but simply says, 'As you wish,' and gives a brisk nod. 'Do you have an ETA? Should we come back another day?'

My father shakes his head. 'He'll be here in under twenty minutes. In the meantime, I'd like to speak to my son. This won't take long.'

Without waiting for a reply, he stands and walks towards the door. I glance at the detectives, who don't say anything, then I stand and head off in the same direction.

Outside in the hallway, my father leads me along the corridor and down the small run of steps into the kitchen. My mother is in there, waiting by the Aga. 'What's happening?' she asks as she sees us come in.

'We're waiting for Jacob,' my father says, then turns to me. 'Avoid saying no comment; only use it as a last resort. Try to keep things simple and stick to what you've already told them.'

I walk over to the fridge and take out some apple juice. Its cool sweetness instantly revitalises me, making me feel more alert and less as if I'm swimming through fog. 'It sounds like you're well-versed in lying to the police,' I say, flicking my eyes over to him.

Sensing dangerous territory, my mum starts talking about plans for dinner. My father holds my gaze for just long enough to communicate his displeasure, then turns away.

Jacob Wakefield arrives, as promised, in under twenty minutes. 'Lead the way,' he says in a brisk, business-like tone and my father, mother, and I walk back into the library. DS Stimson is examining one of the books on the far shelf, and jerks around like a child caught doing something they shouldn't.

'This is our family lawyer, Jacob Wakefield, OBE,' my father announces grandly, offering our new guest a seat.

'Thank you,' DI Okonjo says. 'As we said before, we'd like to talk to Charlie alone, though of course it's fine for his lawyer to be present.' She looks pointedly back at my father, meeting his stony stare with admirable ease. He eventually gives in and stalks back through the room and out the door, closely followed by my mother.

'So, have you had any more thoughts on why Rachel would have wanted to murder your husband?' DI Okonjo says, jumping straight back in as if we'd never had an interruption.

'Yes,' I say, simply. 'I think she wanted to fuck him. And he turned her down.'

I hear Jacob to my right take in a short breath through

his nose after I've said this, and the eyes of both the detectives widen. 'She wanted to start an extra-marital affair with Matthew?' The term 'extra-marital affair' sounds strange and archaic and at odds with her East London accent.

'Yes,' I reply.

'And she was unsuccessful in her attempts.'

I nod.

'And this has only just occurred to you?' DI Okonjo says, her eyes narrowing slightly.

'Yes,' I reply again.

'You see, when we asked you on the night itself, you said you didn't know why she'd want to…'

'I was in shock,' I say, feeling panic rising within me. 'My husband had just been *slaughtered* in front of me. I wasn't in the right state of mind to unpick her motives. But after having taken the time to think about it, I've come to the conclusion that it's quite possible she had a crush on … no, an obsession. With him.'

DS Stimson raises an eyebrow, 'But … why would she try to have sex with a gay man? Surely she knew Matthew wouldn't be attracted to her?'

My hands start to tremble and I rub them on my knees to try to calm myself.

'Detectives,' Jacob cuts in, 'my client isn't required to explain the desires of your suspect. A suspect who has handed herself in and confessed to the crime.'

'I understand,' DI Okonjo says. 'But the thing is, Rachel is refusing to discuss what happened or anything to do with the crime. In fact, she's barely said a word since we took her into custody.'

A strange, woozy mixture of relief and dread flows through me. I'm relieved Rachel hasn't given a wildly different version of events or been creating lies at length – lies I wouldn't be able to keep up with. But on the other hand, if she isn't talking at all, it's no wonder the police are digging.

'Are there any more questions for Charles, here?' Jacob says, shuffling a little, as if poised to leave.

'Yes,' DI Okonjo says, doing the opposite with her body, moving herself back in her chair, making herself comfortable. 'Could you explain what Rachel did or said prior to the murder of your husband that made you suspect she had romantic or sexual feelings towards him?'

After a few seconds of hurried thinking, I reply as firmly as I can, 'Yes. Our holiday to The Hamptons.'

DI Okonjo's eyes are piercing, her eyebrows slightly creased. 'And this was a holiday you invited her on?'

I shook my head. 'I didn't invite her. And by God I wish she'd never come.'

Chapter Twenty-Six

CHARLIE

Three months to go

'Stop looking at her,' Matthew said as he bent over my seat, looking for a book he'd added to my carry-on bag.

'What?' I said in response, certain I must have misheard him.

'You keep looking at her,' he said, lowering his voice to a whisper. '*Rachel*,' he mouthed.

'I assure you I'm not,' I hissed at him.

'You are, with a face like thunder.'

'Don't you think it odd,' I continued in a whisper, 'how she won't stop talking to Titus?'

Matthew looked over at them. Sure enough, they seemed to be deep in conversation. He straightened up just as one of the cabin crew squeezed round him.

'No, I think she's just being friendly,' Matthew replied.

'And Titus is being kind because she's new to all this and, like the nice boy he is, he wants to make her feel welcome.'

I assumed an unconvinced expression and Matthew rolled his eyes and went back to his seat.

My mood didn't improve much when we landed. As we walked out into the afternoon New York heat, I noticed Rachel slip on some stylish shades, no doubt bought by her employer, or by the sizable paycheque she was receiving for basically just organising a few hair appointments. 'Meryl's only seventy, only a little older than you,' I murmured to my mother as we waited in the airport for our luggage to be brought to us. Rachel and Meryl had nipped to the bathrooms, leaving Matthew talking to my father about tailoring; Titus was on one of the chairs engrossed in a novel, and my mother was deciding which magazines to discard. 'What has Meryl's age got to do with anything?' my mother asked, distracted, now reaching for her phone and turning it on.

'Why does she need someone to help her when she's on holiday? I mean, it's not as if we have to do anything for ourselves; we're taken everywhere and every bag or drink or meal is brought to us. Why does she need someone to do it for her?'

My mother frowned at me. 'That sounds a little insensitive, Charles. People need others at different points in their lives. Hasn't it occurred to you that Meryl might be lonely?' When I didn't reply she turned and looked around at the sun-drenched first-class arrival zone. 'Shouldn't you be Instagramming or something?' she said, as if suspicious at how little I'd been using my phone recently.

'I'm not in the mood,' I said, noticing Meryl and Rachel coming out from the bathrooms and over towards us. I quickly moved over to join Matthew and my father in their less than thrilling conversation about the decline of the businesses on Jermyn Street in recent years.

We were staying in a large house in the Water Mill area of The Hamptons – a property we'd booked a couple of years running now, since it suited everyone with its proximity to nearby restaurants, beaches, and shops whilst remaining pleasantly quiet and secluded. The building formed a square around the pool, with each side of the house functioning almost as a separate villa in itself. Matthew and I took one side, my parents the other, Meryl and Rachel had one of the smaller ends on the right, and Titus on the left. The main way back to the front of the house was an archway-shaped corridor that entered and ran through the villa Matthew and I were in.

The days that followed progressed fine, and in spite of my close eye on her, I didn't see anything particularly strange in Rachel's behaviour. She continued to talk to Titus, but no more than the rest of us – except me. She kept her distance from me – not that I was complaining. I much preferred not having to be polite to her or pretend to be interested in her stories about her past job as a photographer or views on whatever pretentious award-winning tome had been selected for the upcoming book club – a copy of which I had guiltily forgotten to pack.

On the fifth night – halfway into our stay – we went out to dinner at the Nick & Toni's restaurant in East Hampton. Rachel and Meryl decided to remain at home, allowing me and Matthew, Titus, and my parents time to breathe and be ourselves. Or perhaps that was just how I felt. While we were waiting for our antipasti, my mother mentioned how much she was enjoying Rachel's presence. 'Our world can be so insular,' she said, taking a sip of her wine. 'I feel we sometimes exist within an echo chamber and it's refreshing to listen to views and experiences from someone who's lived quite a different life.'

I saw my father's mouth grow thin and tense, a key indicator that he didn't agree. 'A little too left-leaning in a naïve sort of way,' he said.

'I'm left-leaning,' Matthew said, sounding mock-offended.

'But I don't think you're naïve,' my father said with a slight smile, 'whereas she has all the fervour of the *Daily Mirror* but no facts to back it up.'

'But that's my point,' my mother said. 'No matter how much we like to pretend otherwise, any left-leaning principles we might harbour are based on compassion and sympathy, not experience. Rachel has experience. It's so devastating she had to close her photography studio and gallery because the arts grants helping it were cut.'

'Maybe people just didn't want to see the artwork and photographs she was showcasing,' I said.

I saw Matthew turn to look at me and frown. 'You do realise a lot of the operas, plays, and ballets we go to see wouldn't exist if it wasn't for arts funding?'

I shrugged. 'I've never really thought about it.'

'No,' Matthew said, 'that doesn't surprise me.'

I wasn't keen on his tone, and I should have changed the

subject in order to avoid things getting awkward, but I couldn't help it. I wanted to twist the knife a little. 'Don't you think it's all a bit patronising, us adopting Rachel as if she's one of us? She's not a puppy. And anyway, she'll never fit in, not really. It's not our business to try and raise her up into a world she would never be able to get into on her own merit.'

I hadn't meant it to come out so savagely, and I saw the hurt bloom in Matthew's face. 'Not *one of us*? Can you hear yourself?'

My mother looked similarly unimpressed. 'Charlie, I hope you're not getting prejudiced prematurely. Your father was at least forty before he started blaming the poor for their own troubles.'

Before I could reply, Titus offered up a contribution.

'I like her,' he said, simply.

'I do too,' said Matthew. 'And I think only a snob would take against her presence.'

'I feel she understands me,' Titus continued, as if Matthew hadn't spoken.

I looked over at him. 'What does that mean? How can she *understand* you? She barely knows you.'

It was Titus's turn to shrug. 'I don't know. I just feel she … cares. When I'm talking to her, she really cares about my opinion on things.'

This was outrageous; the idea that Rachel could possibly care about Titus any more than we did was offensive to me. 'I think that's preposterous,' I said.

Matthew held up a hand. 'It's not preposterous. It's good that Titus gets on with her.'

I spluttered in exasperation. 'Why are we all talking about her as if she's now part of the family? She's only here while Meryl works through some late-life charity complex. Once she's got bored of her, Rachel will be back living amongst the hoodies in a council high-rise somewhere violent.'

Matthew put down his wine glass so hard I was impressed it didn't shatter. 'I think you're wasted on advertising; perhaps you should start blogging for the alt-right.'

My father let out a low chuckle.

'And if you think that's true,' my mother added, 'then you really don't know your godmother well at all.'

I couldn't think of an immediate response to this. Our food arrived seconds later and it was a good few minutes before conversation started up again.

It was later that night that things became very strange. We'd stayed out late, ordering more wine, with conversation flowing onto easier topics. At one point, Matthew had to nip off to take a work call, and when I went off to find the bathroom a few minutes later, I was irritated to find him leaning up against the wall near the restrooms, typing away on his phone. He looked startled when he saw me. 'Hi, sorry, I am coming back. I just needed to reply to a few emails.' Part of me wanted to ask more, but instead I just let myself into the bathroom and left him to it outside. Half an hour later, back at the table, I noticed Titus looking sleepy. I suggested we head back to the house. He objected to being the one who caused an end to the night, saying he wasn't a child anymore and we could no longer use him as an excuse for wanting to get to bed ourselves.

Once back at the house, we walked through the main entrance together then at the pool divided across the square into our separate living spaces. As I said goodnight to my parents, I noticed a light on to our left. Either Rachel or Meryl was awake, and if it was the former, I was keen to get to bed before she tried to come out and make conversation with us all.

It was very warm that night, and Matthew was fiddling with the air-con controls on the far wall. 'Just so long as it doesn't become fucking arctic,' I said as I took off my shirt and chinos and got under the covers. It was too hot for pyjamas and the cool, clean sheets of the bed felt heavenly against my skin. Matthew then joined me in bed and we ended up having sex for a bit, but I could tell he wasn't really into it and we both gave up and lay back to go to sleep without speaking. There was something distant about him – there had been for a while now – although I was struggling to put my finger on it. It was like he was in a boat, floating out to sea, and I was on the shore, trying to hold a conversation with him as he slowly glided away on the still surface of the water, further and further, until eventually neither of us could hear the other.

Despite feeling exhausted, sleep didn't come, although I could tell Matthew had drifted off straightaway. I got out of bed to walk around and considered taking a midnight swim to clear my head. Just as I was trying to locate my swim shorts, something made me stop. Matthew's phone was resting on the long desk-like table at the end of the room. It was on charge, connected to a lightning cable plugged in at the wall. Without allowing myself to think about what I was doing, I marched forward and picked up the phone. The screen lit up as I held it and I quickly toned down the brightness and turned on 'night mode' so that the harsh white-blue glare of the screen was replaced with an easier, warmer glow. I could see on the lock screen that he had three unread WhatsApp messages, but he'd changed the settings so it just said 'Notification (3)' rather than displaying them all as-written.

I looked over at him, apparently sound asleep on the bed. I didn't know his passcode; I'd only very rarely seen him using it, usually just opening it up when the device recognised his face or his thumbprint.

His thumbprint.

My heart pounding, I disconnected the device from its cable and carried it in my hands as if it were a precious stone, over towards my sleeping husband. I was tempted to just hold the screen in front of his face to see if it unlocked it then, but I worried that shining a light in the eyes of a sleeping person, no matter how low, was probably asking for trouble. Instead, I slipped back into bed and, very gently, moved my body up against him, as if we were snuggling down together affectionately. I sought out his arm and moved my hand along to take it. He allowed me to, responding in his sleep to my touch with slow, vague movements, his hand settling into mine as if pleased by the contact. I was starting to worry how I would isolate his thumb from our bunched-up palms in order to unlock the phone but then something happened that made the whole exercise pointless.

A shout – no, more like a scream – met our ears, coming from outside our room, over by the swimming pool. I jolted upright, Matthew doing the same, and in the midst of our sudden movements I felt the phone leave the grasp of my spare hand.

'What was that?' Matthew asked me.

Another shout sounded out, this time containing more words, two of them unmistakably being '*get out*'.

'I don't know,' I said, breathing heavily from the panic of almost getting caught. 'But it sounded like … Titus.'

He didn't need telling twice. He leaped out of bed, pausing only to pull on some tracksuit bottoms, then flung open the door and ran out onto the poolside. I did the same and followed, running after Matthew as he disappeared into Titus's room, a light now shining brightly from behind the curtains of the French windows.

The sight that met us inside was one even I couldn't have predicted. Titus was standing on the other side of the room. He was completely naked, his hands shielding his frontal nudity from view, his face the picture of confusion – perhaps even fear. And on the other side of the room, over near the far wall was…

'Rachel?' Matthew said, clearly baffled. 'What … what's going on?'

Rachel was dressed in a cream-white bikini, an outfit she'd sported a few times during our days spent by the pool. I looked from her and her outfit over to Titus and his vulnerable, naked body, backing away from her. 'What the fuck did you do to him?' I shouted at her.

Matthew walked towards Titus. 'Are you OK?' he said, bending over to pick up a pair of boxers from his discarded clothes on the floor. He tossed them over to the boy, who turned around as he pulled them on. His confusion and fear seemed to be giving way to embarrassment and anger now. 'I'm fine,' he said, almost roughly, 'I was just … it just made me jump, that's all.'

'What made you jump?' asked Matthew.

'And why's she in a bedroom with a naked child, dressed as if she's auditioning for fucking *Baywatch*?' I said.

'I'm not a child,' Titus snapped.

'I'm so sorry,' Rachel said. She looked as if she was about to cry. 'I … I got the wrong room.'

'*What?*' I shouted back, disbelieving.

'I'm sorry,' she said, and properly started to cry now.

'Charlie, please,' Matthew said, shooting me a warning look. He went over to Rachel and said in a kind voice, 'Can you just explain to us what happened?'

'Maybe we should be asking Titus that,' I said, rounding on him. 'Titus, what happened? Did she touch you? Where did she touch you?'

'Just my face…' Titus began to say, and I saw Rachel look over at him, as if mortified he'd offer up such a detail so readily.

'I thought I was moving a pillow across,' she said. 'I hadn't sussed out I'd gone into a different room. They all look identical.' She then buried her face in her hands and sobbed. 'I'm so sorry, Titus. I must have given you such a fright. It made me jump too, realising there was a person in what I thought was my bed.'

I made a noise of disbelief. 'Regularly go to bed in your swimsuit, do you?' I asked. My tone was probably a little too nasty, as Titus cut in, 'Dad, please, she said it was an accident.'

'I was going for a swim,' she sniffed. 'It was too hot; I couldn't sleep.'

'It's OK,' Matthew said gently, putting a hand on her shoulder. 'You're right; in the dark everything does all look rather similar.'

I was enraged that he was believing her preposterous story so quickly. This was something we should at least discuss together before we even entertained the idea that she'd just *accidentally* been scuttling around a teenage boy's bedroom half naked.

'It's my fault. I shouldn't have yelled,' Titus said, looking awkward now, bunching his slim, gangly frame as if he was cold. 'I just want to go to sleep. I'm sorry, Rachel.'

'Stop saying sorry,' I said. 'You don't have anything to be sorry about. It must have been frightening, finding someone crouching over you stroking your hair.'

'I wasn't stroking him,' Rachel said, getting up so she could look me in the eye, pleading, desperate, imploring me to believe her. 'Honestly, it was just a mistake.'

I stared back at her for a moment, not trusting myself to reply to her directly. Instead I turned back to Titus. 'Why were you standing naked on the other side of the room?'

Titus ran a hand through his very ruffled blonde hair. 'I'd taken my pyjamas off because it was too warm; the air-con isn't strong enough. When I woke up and saw someone in the room, I thought this was like, well, a home invasion or something. Like that film, *The Strangers*. So I leaped out of bed.'

'You see,' Rachel said, her red eyes still on me. 'It really is all a misunderstanding.'

To my shock, I heard Matthew chuckle. 'It really does sound like it. Come on, we should all let our horror-movie addict here go back to sleep. Maybe a few less of the home-invasion thrillers in future.' He said it jokingly to Titus, but the boy didn't smile. He just nodded. Matthew started to lead Rachel away, who was still sniffing and taking deep breaths.

I walked over to Titus and put an arm around his shoulder. 'Are you sure you're all right?'

He nodded, looking a bit dazed and sleepy. 'It just … made me jump, that's all. I thought I was having a nightmare.'

'That's completely understandable,' I said. 'Come on, back to bed.'

It reminded me a bit of when he was little, when I used to sit on the side of his bed and read him a story. I pulled back the duvet so he could get in, then said, 'Would you like me to get you anything?'

He pulled a face. 'Like what?'

'A hot drink?'

'It's, like, thirty degrees. And I'm not a baby.'

'I know, I know, I'm sorry. This … we … we all make mistakes, you know. Me and your dad. Because you don't have any older siblings, it means we haven't had a chance to perfect our parenting. This period you're going through … boy to man, that sort of thing…'

'Please don't,' he groaned, rolling his eyes.

'I'm just saying that it's probably going to take some trial and error and you may feel we're parenting too much or being too controlling; you're growing up so fast, and to us it's literally been the blink of an eye.'

He smiled. 'Any more parenting clichés? Or can I go to sleep?'

I smiled back. 'I'm just saying, have patience with us both. If it feels like we're still treating you like a kid, it's probably because we don't want to let those days go. And because it's all we've known for years.'

He nodded. 'I get it, don't worry.' He settled back into the sheets as if he were about to fall off to sleep straight away, then said, 'I think you're both great, by the way. I mean, some of the others at my school ask what it's like having two dads, as if it would somehow be strange. Especially the kids from countries where that wouldn't be OK. And I always say you're both perfect. Couldn't be better, really.'

Disconcertingly, I found myself feeling a little moved, and instead of saying anything in return I just reached for his hand and gave it a squeeze. After a few seconds, I got up and said, 'I'll let you sleep. Love you.'

'Love you too,' he said, then, as I was about to close the door, he spoke again. 'One more thing.'

I stepped back into the room, 'Yes?'

I heard Titus sit up a bit more in his bed. 'It was weird, you know. Rachel being in the room. I can't quite work out what was a dream and what wasn't but … I think she may have been standing here for quite a while before I realised she was real. It was … just weird.'

I didn't know what to say. Eventually I took a deep breath and said, 'Try to put it out of your mind. I'm sure she didn't mean any harm.'

A few moments of silence passed, then he said, 'OK,' and I heard him relax back down into the pillows. 'Goodnight.'

'Night,' I said softly, and closed the door, just as Matthew was approaching from around the side of the pool.

'Is he all right?' he asked, looking worried.

'I think so,' I said. I nodded towards our room, pointedly, and he got the message. Once we were inside with the door safely closed, I replied properly. 'He told me a bit more of what happened.'

Matthew looked worried. 'OK. So … what did he say?'

'He said Rachel was standing over him for quite some time.'

His face became puzzled. 'Then why did he scream and say it made him jump?'

'He thought he was dreaming at first, I think. Then when the figure in the room came over to his bed and started stroking his hair, he then woke up properly. It's enough to freak anyone out.'

Matthew nodded, slowly. He looked thoughtful, then said, 'I think I should go and check on him.' He went to move past me, but I held him still.

'Don't. He's going back to sleep. I really think it would

be best to just let him … I don't know, forget about it. Just for tonight. Then tomorrow we'll sort things out properly.'

This earned me a quizzical look. 'Meaning…?'

'Well, sending Rachel home for a start.'

He raised his eyebrows. 'I'm not sure we could do that, since she's not exactly our guest, is she?'

I thought about this. He was right of course, although her presence did depend on us tolerating her. 'Perhaps we could talk to Meryl,' I said, thinking out loud.

Matthew nodded. 'We can do that. Calmly.'

I frowned, offended. 'Don't say that. I'm not about to start shouting at her or anything.'

Matthew held his hands up. 'I know, I know, I just want to make sure we don't upset her. I think I should talk to her.'

'She's *my* godmother!'

Matthew sighed and walked away from me over to the table at the end of the room. I saw him stop and look around. 'Where's my phone?'

He didn't seem too worried at first, but then after checking under the desk and the armchair in the corner, I saw his movements become quicker. 'It was definitely here; I put it on charge before we went to bed.'

I felt anxiety start to spread through me. In the commotion, I'd just let go of the device and hadn't noticed where it had gone. It took us a good five minutes until eventually, after we'd stripped the bed, we found it tangled up in one of the duvet's folds.

'How on earth did it get in there?' he said, more to the

air than to me, although I was growing more and more concerned at how I didn't really have an answer.

'Maybe we knocked it off the table when we ran out of the room?' I said, realising how nonsensical it sounded after it left my mouth.

'That's not possible,' he said, staring at it in his hand as if it were about to start talking to him and explaining its sudden ability to fly.

'Then either this place is haunted, or your memory isn't as good as you think it is.'

He didn't seem happy to drop it, but to my relief he eventually got back into bed and we turned off the light.

Something was niggling at me and I didn't feel I could let the evening end without mentioning it. 'It is possible … that Rachel could be a paedophile. I know it's rarer in women, or at least I assume it is. But it's possible.'

I hadn't expected this to be greeted warmly from Matthew, and what he said next surprised me. 'It crossed my mind … but it doesn't really fit, does it? He's almost at the age of consent; it's not like he's a little child.'

'It's still illegal,' I said. 'Both here in the US, and back at home, even if he isn't exactly a virgin, as we know from his Kensington adventures – something you seemed way more worried about.'

'I know,' he said, letting out a sigh. 'I'm not excusing it. Let's just … talk about it in the morning.' He turned over onto his side, signalling the end of the discussion.

It took me a long time to fall asleep and, judging by the tossing and turning from Matthew, rest didn't come easy for him either.

Chapter Twenty-Seven

CHARLIE

Three days after the murder

I tell the detectives what happened that night in Long Island, keeping details as close as I can to the truth, whilst taking care to leave Titus out of the story. In his place, I put Matthew as the unclothed male in question, backing away from Rachel's midnight visitation.

'And how did Rachel know you wouldn't have been in the room with Matthew?' DI Okonjo asks, still writing in her notebook.

'I'd mentioned I was going for a run, earlier in the evening before dinner. I encouraged Matthew to join me but he said he wanted an early night.'

DI Okonjo doesn't look convinced. 'Still seems strange she'd take that risk, though. I mean, that's a pretty late run.'

I shrug. 'Well, she probably saw me leave. Waited for her chance.'

'Her chance to pounce.' DS Stimson nods, apparently

familiar with this kind of situation, which earns him a disapproving glance from his superior.

'Did your parents and Rachel's employer Meryl take against her after this … situation? I'm presuming you told them.'

A slow, icy trickle feels like it's making its way down my back. This was something I hadn't considered how to deal with. To be honest, I'd barely considered anything properly.

'No. We were going to the next day. Matthew and I … we talked about it, once Rachel had gone back to her room. But we decided not to say anything. Just to keep an eye on her. And to be fair on her, after that she didn't try anything again.'

DI Okonjo raises an eyebrow. 'We're going to speak to Meryl later,' she says. 'Get her take on the whole thing. She was understandably in shock when we first spoke to her, so it would be good to check over these details. See if anything new comes to her.'

I don't know if the detective sees the worry in my eyes, or if she's just waiting for a reaction, but she holds my gaze for what feels like a disproportionately long time. Then she says, 'We'll leave it there for now. But we may need to talk to Titus again at some point.'

The chill down my spine develops into an icy burn. I only manage a jerky nod, and, 'Right,' before I stand up a little too quickly and show the detectives out of the library.

'We appreciate this is a difficult time,' DI Okonjo says as she steps out of the front door. 'I hope you understand we just want to make sure the charge against Rachel is safe and there isn't anything … unusual going on here.'

'Unusual?' I ask, my voice sounding uncharacteristically high-pitched.

She doesn't reply to this directly, just nods and steps out the front door.

'Thank you for your time, Mr Allerton-Jones,' DS Stimson says, sounding a touch friendlier than he had when he first entered. Maybe the two of them have a good-cop/bad-cop thing going on that they haven't quite ironed out. Then I see DS Stimson look round the outside of the house once again as he walks down the steps, and shake his head with a smirk. We aren't people to them, I think. We're things. Props in their pantomime. Actors in their strange play, there to be moved about and manipulated.

'If they do need to speak to Titus again,' Jacob says as I close the door, 'just give me a call. And remember, you can ask to be present as the boy's appropriate adult. He doesn't need to do it alone.'

I nod. 'Thank you. I'm going to need to think about things for a bit. Do you want to speak to my father at all? I can go and find him.'

Jacob shakes his head. 'I'm actually running late for another appointment. Your father phoned me just in time before I set off.' He surveys me as if I were still a child, sitting on the window seat as my parents hosted dinner parties, occasionally trying to talk to the guests in my no-doubt irritatingly precocious way. 'Chin up, my dear boy,' Jacob says, laying a hand on my shoulder. 'And of course, it goes without saying, I am very, very sorry for your loss. I'm not sure I said that properly before. It breaks my heart to see your family experience something like this. But I'm sure you'll all come out the other side.'

I give him a thin smile. 'I do hope so.' I open the door again and Jacob leaves. 'Someone's delivered flowers,' he says, bending down to pick them up. 'Odd for them not to ring the doorbell.'

I take them from him. The bunch is made up mostly of roses, already arranged in a glass vase, and there is an envelope attached to them. I bid Jacob goodbye and close the door, setting the flowers down on one of the little tables in the hallway, leaving the envelope next to them. I'm about to go upstairs and check on Titus when my mother spots me from down near the entrance to the kitchen.

'Darling, what's happening? Have the police left?'

'Yes,' I say distractedly, not wanting to discuss what was said but knowing I probably should.

'Your father's in his study and wants to talk to you,' she replies, her worried eyes peering into mine. 'You really don't look that well,' she says. 'I think you should probably have a lie down.'

'I'm fine,' I reply, distantly. 'I just want to check on Titus.'

She looks even more pained at this. 'I really hope you know what you're doing,' she says, but lets me go without further protest.

I don't know what I'm doing. In fact, this past forty-eight-hour period has been a journey of painful self-discovery for me: that I'm terrible at tactics, planning, and thinking on my feet. I can feel the situation hurtling out of control and I take the stairs two at a time as I march upstairs.

Titus is in bed. It's alarming me how he seems to have taken to sleeping during the day since his father's death – although I have to remind myself it has still only been two days. I don't know how long shock and grief are supposed to last, but it's probably reasonable for a fifteen-year-old boy to still be reeling from the violent events of two nights previously. As I draw close, I discover he's not asleep, but reading a book on his side, the hardback cover pressed into the pillows. I sit down next to him and he closes the book, keeping his hand at the page he's up to, allowing me to see the title in full: Thomas Harris's *Hannibal Rising*. I find the bleakness of his reading choice – an unusually violent and genre-focused choice for a reader usually more concerned with the classics or literary fiction – so disquieting it almost makes me flinch. I decide, however, not to remark upon it. 'How are you?' I say quietly, as if the room itself were asleep and too loud a noise would cause frightening things to happen.

'I've been better,' Titus replies, pulling himself up in the bed so he's facing me properly.

'Do you need to talk?' I ask, laying a hand on his arm.

Titus shakes his head.

'The police were here just now. I thought they'd ask to speak to you, but they were just interested in me today. They'll probably return, though, once they've spoken to Meryl.'

He looks puzzled. 'Meryl?'

I take a deep breath. 'The situation involving Rachel, in

Long Island, when she came into your room at night … I told them about that. But I said it was your dad's bedroom – *our* bedroom – she came into, not yours. I said I was out for a run and she tried to … get with him. And he turned her away. I thought it would be a good way of making it seem like she was … I don't know … bitter towards him. But I forgot…' My voice shakes now, almost turning into a sob. 'I forgot that she might have told Meryl that it was your room, not Matthew's, she was caught in … so this may have just made things worse.'

I wipe my eyes and try to control my emotions, breathing slowly and clearly, my brain a mixture of panic at the situation and anger at myself for being so stupid – and for crying in front of Titus when I needed him to stay strong.

Titus surprises me with a small shrug. 'We'll just say Meryl's wrong. That Rachel was probably upset about the ordeal but said it was me in order to … I don't know … divert attention away from what really happened. In fact, are you sure Rachel would even tell Meryl anyway? Surely she'd have just been thankful nobody else heard the commotion and just, well, tried to forget about it?'

I'm impressed at how much more of a handle on the situation Titus seems to have compared to me. Even if I am keeping secrets from him. For his own protection, of course.

'Yes,' I say, nodding slowly to myself, 'you're right. You might need to say that to the police, if you're asked.

He nods. 'OK.'

I look at him, and he looks at me, and it's as if, in that moment, I can see a replay of the whole violent carnage of that evening played out in slow motion: the blood, the gasps of shock from Matthew, and then Rachel, standing there, telling us what to do.

'If you wanted all this to stop, right now, I wouldn't blame you,' I say, my voice low but thankfully steadier than it has been. 'If you didn't feel you can go through with this … with the lying, for the rest of your life, I would understand. I'm doing my very best for you, to make sure things don't change, to make sure me, you, my parents, all stay a united team. But if you think it will be too difficult, now is probably the time to say.'

He's still staring back at me, his face oddly blank. Then finally he says, 'I think we should carry on as we are.'

I give his hand a squeeze, then get up from the bed. 'I'll leave you to your book. But come and find me if you need anything.'

As I close the door, I see him settle back down into his strange reading choice, leaving me feeling even more uneasy than I had when I entered the room.

Back downstairs, I know I should go to see my father to update him on my talk with the detectives, but detour via the kitchen for a glass of water. I see on the table my mother's brought through the flowers I'd left in the hallway and left them on the kitchen table, the card now out of its envelope. I pick it up and glance through it. Then I see the name and freeze. It takes me only a few seconds to read the note, but I force myself to do it again, slower, taking in every single word, every fucking word. Then I pick up the vase and carry it roughly – vase, wrappings and all – and drop the whole thing in the sink, allowing the glass to smash. Grabbing a fire lighter from the windowsill, I begin flicking it at the flowers until the paper surrounding them catches alight. The roses themselves don't burn properly, but start to shrink and curl as the wrapping flares around them, the smashed glass encased within it now breaking loose into the sink. Then I hear a noise from behind me.

'What on earth are you doing?'

Chapter Twenty-Eight

RACHEL

Two months to go

I expected Matthew and Charlie to out me to everyone the next day after they discovered me in Titus's bedroom. But, to my surprise, nothing further was said about it. Or at least, nothing to me. I suspected Charlie may have mentioned something to his mother, because she gave me another of her strange looks over lunch the next day. I decided it would be best to keep my distance from all three of the Allerton-Joneses and instead keep my attention on making sure Meryl was happy and had everything she needed, along with getting through book after book by the poolside.

It was the week after we returned to London when things became difficult. Meryl was asking me about timings between her hair appointment and the book-club meeting in the evening. The two of us were expected at Carlyle Square at 7pm, and when I looked up at Meryl over the pages of her diary, I felt my lip tremble a little. 'I … I don't think I'll come,' I said, trying and failing to look and sound normal.

Meryl's kind green eyes rested on me. 'My dear,' she said, laying a hand on my arm, 'what on earth could be the matter?'

I let my knees collapse so that I was sitting on the sofa and Meryl sat down next to me. Her hand once again ended up patting my arm, and after a few seconds of swallowing hard to hold back my tears, I was finally able to speak. 'I don't think … I would be welcome.'

Meryl brought her hand back to her lap. 'I don't understand, my dear, why would you not be welcome?'

I dabbed at my eyes with the back of my hand. I was supposed to be keeping a cool head. A calm, clear game, that was my aim. But suddenly, I felt a real, burning need to confess something, anything, some aspect of what happened in New York, otherwise I felt like I would shatter into a thousand pieces. 'Something … something odd happened.'

'Odd, what do you mean, odd?' Meryl said, her brow creasing.

I couldn't hold her gaze for long, and instead focused on my hands, clasped around her diary in my lap. 'I … I walked into the wrong room, one night. I was by the pool reading and I fell asleep. All the rooms look the same from the outside around the pool area and … well, when I went back into what I thought were our quarters, I ended up in Titus's room. It was an accident, but when he noticed there was someone in his room he shouted. Not that I blame him; he must have been freaked to think a stranger was in his room. So Matthew and Charlie burst in, and because Titus was in bed ... unclothed ... and I was just in my bikini ... well, it looked...'

I looked to the side to see Meryl nod understandingly. 'It looked improper.' Meryl took a deep breath, then said, 'Listen to me, my dear. I'm going to let you into something that I ask you to keep to yourself. Both men are very protective of Titus. Understandably so; they are the boy's guardians. But it's all wrapped with the situation involving Matthew's sister, Collette, Titus's birth mother. She died of a drug overdose shortly after Titus's birth, same as the boy's father a month or two earlier over in Norway where they were staying. Tragic. Absolutely tragic. A total waste of life. So much potential, never realised. So all of that is tied up with their relationship with the boy. The pressure, the sense of responsibility to give the boy a stable, loving home – something he was denied when his parents died. Essentially, what I'm trying to say is, don't take it to heart. They've always been a tad over-protective. I'm sure they're just feeling embarrassed that they over-reacted.'

I nodded. 'I assumed it might be something like that. I just didn't know... I've been so worried that they think I was trying to rob them or like I'm some sort of deranged weirdo who scares people when they're sleeping...'

Meryl let out a little chuckle. 'I'm sure they don't think anything of the kind. But I understand if you don't want to come to the book club. In fact, you don't need to see them again for a long while if you don't want to.'

I smiled back to her. 'Thank you,' I said. 'I'll just skip

this meeting, then after that I'm sure things will get back to normal.'

Meryl nodded. 'Well, you can join me at the Ashtons's wedding anniversary party in July. They'll be there, but it will be a relaxed environment, and you can mingle and meet other nice, young people like yourself.'

It was my turn to laugh now. 'I fear I'm not that young anymore.'

'If you're not young, I don't know what I am,' Meryl said, smoothing out her cashmere cardigan. 'Right, let's order up a car and head to Claridge's. I haven't been there since Christmas, and we could do with a drink.'

Chapter Twenty-Nine

CHARLIE

Two months to go

Matthew made the decision not to tell anyone else about the odd situation involving Rachel in The Hamptons. He said he didn't think anything good would come of making a fuss, and that it was likely Rachel would distance herself from us anyway after her embarrassment. It turned out that he was right – at least for a time. The rest of the holiday passed without incident, and she didn't turn up to the following month's book-club meeting (Meryl cited a summer cold as the reason). I even allowed myself to believe we might be rid of her and she would, gradually, fade away out of our lives. Of course, I was wrong. And my life started to properly fall apart the night of Lord and Lady Ashton's golden wedding anniversary.

The Ashtons's manor in the Oxfordshire countryside was a major part of my childhood. With two hundred acres of grounds, not to mention all the many rooms and passageways throughout the house itself, it was a rich kingdom of exploration for an outdoorsy boy like myself. While Matthew spent most of his youth holed up in his bedroom at the top of his family's castle in the highlands with his face buried in the works of James Joyce, I spent many sun-dappled afternoons playing hide and seek at the Ashtons's manor, often accompanied by friends from school. When I was a teenager, I went through a phase of making out I didn't want to join my parents for long weekends with the Ashtons, claiming it was more exciting in Central London. This wasn't true. It's because I was experiencing my first major crush – that kind of intoxicating first love that hits you like a freight train and drags your hormonal brain through a thicket of emotions. And the object of that first crush was Rupert Ashton.

Ten years older than me, he had been twenty-three when my thirteen-year-old self first started to view him as a figure of desire. I'd gone through a phase of being a little shy of Rupert during the ages of eleven and twelve, not really understanding what it was about him that made me both eager to impress him and desperate to run away from him at the same time. I felt shy and awkward around him and his group of friends, and would try to keep out of his way whilst wishing I could be near him at every hour of every day. As I got older, I realised I was falling in love with him, and when I was sixteen I ended up telling him this on one long, warm midsummer night.

It had been a garden party that day, too – a smaller, intimate gathering to celebrate his younger sister's graduation (a double first from Oxford). I had wandered down towards the trees that lined the property, a bottle of wine in my hand that I'd pilfered from one of the tables, and I had a notion to get utterly drunk on it in a very grown-up, complicated way, using it to drown my sorrows and sexual frustrations. That was where I bumped into Rupert who, also alone with a bottle of wine, settled on a bench near the woodland, seemed to be doing the very thing I aspired to, except in a far more adult way. A few minutes into our conversation, he remarked that I seemed nervous and asked if there was anything wrong. That was when I confessed, telling him I'd loved him for years. He listened, smiled, took a sip of his wine, then put a hand on my knee. 'I really had no idea. And I'm sorry, but we're going to have to give this a couple of years before we do anything about it. But if you're happy to wait, I am too.'

I am too. Those words would stick in my mind for years to come – a promise of something coming later on, a little into the future, the thought that all may not be lost, all may not be over. And in that moment, all I could do was nod. Then Rupert continued, and my whole world lit up like gunpowder.

'Do you know, Charles Allerton, you've rather made my night. I was in a bit of a bad mood earlier. My sister and I had an awful row. But now you've cheered me up.'

He still had his hand on my knee and let it rise a few inches. It felt like his skin was mainlining electricity into my entire body. 'And for now,' he said, 'I'll leave you with this.'

In one deft movement, he took his large, athletic frame off the bench, bent over me, and brought his lips to mine. The kiss was both long and fleeting, momentous and light.

And then he was gone, away in the dying evening light back towards the house.

The year that followed could only be described as exquisite agony. I only saw Rupert three times, although each moment became seared into my memory. One was at the Ashtons's annual Michaelmas supper the following autumn. Once people had eaten and retreated to other rooms for drinks and chats out of sight, he pushed me up against the wall of the drawing room and kissed me with a passionate zeal that set my heart racing, his hands wandering around my body, making me breathless with my need for him. The Christmas that followed brought with it another turning point for me. That December had been unseasonably mild and after the usual polite dinner conversation, Rupert had suggested to me we take a walk outside to enjoy the evening air. I'd, of course, accepted, and he led the way around to the side of the house. We kissed passionately again, as we had a couple of months previously, and while doing so I felt Rupert guide my hand to his crotch. Then I became aware that he was putting pressure on my shoulder, as if trying to lower me down. I looked at him and he looked at me, a flame alight inside his eyes, and I allowed myself to be guided down. With hands trembling with anticipation, unable to fully believe what was happening, I undid his belt.

We then saw each other whenever we could over the following twelve months, and then finally became an official couple when I was eighteen. Our families were initially shocked at first and then, with remarkable speed, became generally fine with it. The whole thing felt simpler and easier than I had ever imagined. But relationships for couples at different stages in their lives can be difficult, and by the time I was twenty and in the midst of my degree at Oxford, Rupert was thirty and heading up a company founded to invest and encourage hybrid and electric-car development. His work was taking him all over the world. He had set up offices in California, Texas, and Paris, and even though my uni days were spent just a handful of miles from his countryside home, he was frequently at a distance of thousands more. When I was twenty-one, we separated properly. It was tearful, distressing, filled with that heart-wrenching sense of shock and loss that accompanies the end of many first relationships.

In the years that followed, we kept up an image of friendship so as to make things as easy as possible for our families, then as time healed the wounds and arguments were confined to the past, if not entirely forgotten, we properly became friends again – friends who had managed to shed the awkwardness of the end of our once very intimate acquaintance, and instead used the hundreds of hours we'd spent together as fuel for our friendship. All that time spent laughing, fucking, cuddling up together in front of old 80s action movies on the TV wasn't all for nothing. And things were fine. He came to my wedding. We caught up with each other's news at parties and events. Everything was OK. Grown-up. Platonic. That didn't stop Matthew from maintaining a slightly suspicious air whenever Rupert was around. Perhaps slightly intimidated by and aware of our shared past, Matthew often acted a little oddly when confronted with him, although this usually resulted in him making himself scarce rather than keeping a watchful eye on us. I don't think he ever feared adultery. I suspect he was more afraid of being compared to Rupert in terms of intelligence and charisma and success, and being found wanting.

And so, when we attended the Ashtons's golden wedding anniversary party on a golden July afternoon, it took Matthew just a few minutes into our journey to Oxford to ask, 'Will Rupert be there?'

The question triggered a pang of annoyance within me. 'Yes. I think his parents would be disappointed if their only son didn't turn up to their golden wedding anniversary.'

I heard Matthew sigh. 'I was only thinking he might have some business or something – some flying-car demonstration he had to be at in Seattle.'

This was a regular thing Matthew did – small digs, little ways of making fun of Rupert's achievements. 'Don't you think it's rather a good thing,' I said, my jaw tensing, 'that a young aristocrat and heir to millions, who could have just sat on his arse all his life, has decided to dedicate his time and energy to finding ways to stop the cars we drive from destroying the planet we live in?'

'I thought you didn't believe in climate change,' he muttered.

'I've never said that. I've said I don't approve of woke hysteria. Different thing,' I said, starting to get properly annoyed.

Another sigh from Matthew, this one sounding like a parent dealing with a difficult child. 'Of course, Rupert's job is very admirable. I didn't mean anything by it.'

'Good,' I said, 'because I don't see me taking up weird grudges towards your previous conquests.'

Matthew let out a splutter. '*Conquests?* I don't have *conquests.* Boyfriends would have been a better word, don't you think?'

'Would you like me to put my headphones on so you two can carry on in private?' Titus asked, his slightly amused face staring back at me from the rearview mirror.

I didn't respond to him, but gripped the steering wheel, my knuckles going white, and shot a look at Matthew. 'I don't think "boyfriends" would work – not exactly gender-neutral, is it?'

'What on earth is that supposed to mean?' he snapped back, but another quick glance his way was enough for me to notice the blush and the tremble of his hands as he shifted them in his lap.

A few beats of silence passed before I said, 'Nothing. Sorry. I'm just … just feeling a bit tired and grumpy. Ignore me.'

I didn't really know why I retreated, why I didn't have it out with him then and there, about my hurt at him not sharing his past experiences with women with me, about my suspicions that there was something going on with him that I didn't understand. Perhaps it was because Titus was in the car with us, or that I didn't want to arrive at the party and have to pretend to be all happy and polite after a potentially devastating row. Whatever it was, I carried on driving as smoothly as I could down the M40 and into Oxfordshire, and the rest of the journey slipped by mostly in silence.

We reached the Ashtons's house – official name Marwood Manor, although we only ever referred to it as 'The Ashtons's' – at just after 7pm and were greeted towards the end of the long driveway by a young man. I gave him the keys so he could drive the car round to whichever part of the extensive grounds was being used for parking, and we wandered through the open front door. Titus snuck away very quickly to talk to the Ashtons's granddaughter, Philippa, leaving me and Matthew to say hello to Lady Ashton out on the main patio. '*So* lovely to see you both,' she said, still looking remarkably young for her seventy years of age. 'I was just talking to your parents, saying what a handsome boy Titus is turning into. How is he doing at school? Working hard?'

'Very,' Matthew said. 'I think he's off talking to your granddaughter. Probably comparing exam syllabuses.'

Is that what we're calling it these days? I thought to myself, but smiled along with Matthew. Somewhere a bit further along in the conversation – it was after Lord Ashton had come to join us – I noticed her. Rachel was standing over near the rose bush, a glass of champagne in her hand. She was looking at her phone, then put it away and stared around. She looked bored. And awkward. As if she was regretting coming. *What the hell is she doing here?* I thought to myself, then remembered: Meryl must have brought her. Meryl and her strange insistence that the woman was a good, reliable companion, even though she'd known her all of five minutes. Even after what happened in New York. I found myself gripping my glass so hard, it was a marvel it didn't shatter.

Once the Ashtons had moved off to greet some new arrivals, I ushered Matthew over to a quiet section of the garden, slightly away from the nearest group of people. 'Rachel's here,' I said, nodding over to where she was, now walking towards the well-trimmed hedges towards the outdoor swimming-pool area.

'Well,' he said, 'I suppose we need to get used to her being wherever Meryl is.'

A sudden thought then struck me. 'Where's Titus?' I said quickly to Matthew.

He shrugged. 'Off talking to Pippa, I suppose. Why, you don't think he's *at risk* from her, do you?'

I frowned. I wasn't sure what I thought. But I definitely didn't like the idea of Rachel wandering around, unchecked and unoccupied, while Titus was out of sight. There was still something very strange about what had happened at the house in The Hamptons – something I didn't feel like we'd ever got to the bottom of.

'Oh, here we go,' I heard Matthew say. 'Your boyfriend's coming.'

I knew immediately who he meant, and turned to see Rupert Ashton walking along the lawn towards us.

'Don't call him that,' I whispered sharply to Matthew, then turned to him and smiled. 'Hey stranger, how are you?'

He beamed at me, that wide, ever-charming smile that had never lost its magic for me. Whilst Matthew could be described as 'nice looking' or even 'pretty' in one of those magazine-model sort of ways, Rupert was very much the definition of 'handsome'. More classic and traditionally masculine in looks, it was astonishing to think he was now approaching forty-six. He seemed to have stopped ageing a decade ago and only a few tell-tale grey hairs on his head suggested he'd reached forty.

'I'm very well,' he said, giving me a quick, strong embrace. He hugged Matthew too, enthusiastically slapping him on the back as if they were old rugby mates. I noticed Matthew stiffly reciprocating, his smile not meeting his eyes.

'Where's young Titus?' Rupert asked, looking around, as if the boy were hiding.

'Flirting with your niece, I think,' I said, and Rupert laughed. 'Your sister had better watch out or she'll have Titus for a son-in-law in a few years.'

'I'm going to get some more drinks,' Matthew said, clearly uncomfortable with the subject. 'Can I get you one, Rupert?'

Rupert waved one of his large hands. 'I'm fine, thank you.'

Matthew didn't wait for me to say anything; he just walked away towards the house, leaving me and Rupert standing in the shade by the trees. Rupert turned and motioned to a nearby bench. 'Care to sit?'

I nodded, and we settled ourselves down on the varnished wood, warm from the evening summer sun.

'Takes me back. You and me on a bench.' Rupert flashed me a wicked grin.

'Behave,' I said, but smiled too.

'He still doesn't like me, does he?'

I didn't need to ask who Rupert was talking about. 'Matthew doesn't *dislike* you.'

He let out a short laugh, showing he didn't believe me. 'But he doesn't approve of us remaining friends.'

I didn't really have an answer to this, because essentially he was right. I decided to move the conversation on. 'So, have you cured global warming with your electric cars yet?'

He nodded. 'Oh yeah, didn't you hear? The planet's now saved. I'm collecting my Nobel prize next week.' I noticed a mischievous glint in his eye that went beyond his playful words. 'No, it's just a question of backing the right developers and technology they've chosen. We've had some pretty exciting projects the San Diego offices are managing.'

I nodded. 'And are you still seeing … what's his name? The Canadian guy.' Rupert had told me he had started dating someone who used to work at a competing company – probably an attempt to advance both his sex life and business in one stroke. To my surprise he looked sad, and his gaze went a bit distant for a moment or two. We sat in silence for a bit – long enough for me to wonder if I'd upset him.

'No,' he said eventually. 'It didn't work. It never does with me, really, does it? Maybe I'm still pining for my first love.' He turned and looked at me after that and I felt a frisson of energy ripple over the back of my neck.

'I surely wasn't your first love?' I cast an anxious look towards the house, but there was no sign of Matthew returning with drinks. I was both intrigued as to where this was going with Rupert, but at the same time I wanted to avoid dangerous territory.

'Weren't you?' he asked, turning to me. 'And wasn't I yours?' He asked it as if it were a genuine question. As if he really expected an answer. I wasn't used to this. For years, we'd been able to socialise very happily without ever really digging into the past.

'I ... well, because you were older, and more experienced, I just presumed ... I don't know what I presumed. You seemed so close to your little group of friends. When I was fourteen I even saw you kissing Ernest Kellman around near the stables.'

His face looked pained at the mention of the name. 'I'd prefer not to talk about him, or any of that. I'm just saying that I think you underestimated what an important part of my life you've been. And I'm always here. If ever you need me.'

Now I felt irritated. 'Well, I'm flattered, but what use is that information to me now? I'm *married*; I have a son. I'm happy.'

He noticed the pause before the last word. The slight hesitation in my voice. He sighed, then took in a deep breath, as if building up to saying something. 'There are things I've been wanting to talk to you about. Things I've been wrestling with. But I don't know how much you know already. Or how much you've suspected...'

I twisted round to face him properly. 'What? What do you mean?'

Rupert avoided my gaze and looked at the floor. 'I ... I should have told you something. I've known it for a little while now. Something that happened...'

He broke off, his eyes now staring in the direction of the

house. I followed his gaze and saw Matthew strolling purposefully over the lawn. He wasn't carrying any drinks. In fact, as he came closer, I was alarmed at his appearance. His previously crisp, neat shirt was now crumpled and askew, partially untucked, and a button had come undone at the top, causing it to flap in the wind. The colour had drained from his face. He looked ill, as if he may faint at any moment.

Had he seen us together? Had he been watching, listening to me and Rupert? I dismissed the thought immediately. He couldn't have heard anything from so far away, and all he could have seen was us talking quite normally.

As he drew up, he barked four words in my direction. 'We need to go.'

It was an instruction, not a request. I felt both embarrassed and confused. 'What do you mean, "go"? We've only just arrived.'

He bent down and practically dragged me off the bench by my arm. 'Come on. It's really important we leave. Right now.'

Chapter Thirty

RACHEL

Less than a week to go

I looked at the guests as I passed them. Nobody made an effort to talk to me. Maybe they could sense how different I was, how I was from another world, another life, one that involved scavenging through the reduced section of the local Morrisons or trawling through company comparison websites to find train tickets at prices that didn't cause me to faint. Things these people had probably never done and probably never would.

Eventually, I ended up walking round to the south side of the garden, following a little path along a stone wall that snaked round and opened out on a little square. It was dotted with benches on each side, walled in by the perfectly manicured hedges. An ornately carved fountain tinkled away in the middle. It took me almost a full minute to realise I wasn't alone. In the corner of one of the benches, obscured by the fountain when I'd walked in, was a woman. She looked middle-aged – maybe fifteen or twenty years older than me – and not only had a glass of champagne but a whole bottle beside her. Her long, dark-blonde hair fell in waves out of its artfully-messy bun, with one strand knocking against her glass. I was about to turn away and go, embarrassed to see her eyes clock me, but she spoke, freezing me to the spot.

'Hello there,' she said. Although the words were simple and brief, her voice was low and drawn out in a slow, almost bored, way.

I smiled and walked around the fountain to go over to her. 'Hi,' I said, then added, 'I'm Rachel.' I regretted it as soon as I'd said it, worried I sounded too eager to please.

'Hello Rachel,' she said, her eyes squinting a little, as if she was having trouble focussing on me. Her words sounded the same as before, but were a little too slow and slurred into each other to sound anything other than drunk. 'Sit down, if you'd like,' she said, scooping up the bottle into her arms and cradling it, almost as one would an infant. 'How are you finding the *party*?' She emphasised the last word in a strange way, as though it was amusing to her one could refer to this gathering in such a way.

'It's … it's nice,' I said, unsure of what tone to strike. 'It's very grand.' Again, instant regret filled me as I said this. Once again, I was showing myself up to be the naïve outsider.

'Oh, sure, it's grand all right.' She didn't seem very impressed with this, and I was about to try and say something more interesting when she carried on. 'I find it hard to be here, I must say. Too many memories. I played around these gardens as a child, you see.'

'Oh,' I said, a little taken aback by this insight into this woman's past. 'And were these not, um, happy times?'

She made a sound of disbelief. 'Those days were fine, I suppose. This place was a bit like a second home at times. Me, my brother, and Rupert and Elena. Do you know Rupert and Elena?'

I remembered Meryl mentioning Rupert and, pleased I had something to add, I said, 'Oh yes, Lord and Lady Ashton's son. I don't know him, or Elena, but I … know of them.'

'Both unspeakably lovely people,' she said, hiccupping a little, 'even if Elena does have an unfortunate habit of going after other people's husbands. And Rupert hasn't been settled for a while now. He deserves a good life, Rupert. Probably the most decent person among us.'

I nodded along to this, as if I thoroughly agreed, and then something popped into my mind. 'Do you know the Allerton-Joneses? Matthew and Charlie?'

The woman sighed and nodded. 'Oh yes. Rupert and Charlie used to be a thing, once upon a time, but then Rupert wanted to go to the States, I think. Long-distance relationships can be so *tricky*, can't they?'

I replied to this with a 'Hmm', even though I'd never had one.

'So how do you know them, then?' she said, straightening up.

'I … er … I'm part of their book club.' I left a little pause, wondering if she was going to comment on this, but she didn't jump in so I continued, 'I actually work for their friend Meryl. I'm … sort of her live-in assistant.'

'An *assistant*? That's exciting. I would love to be organised enough to be someone's assistant, but I fear I'd have to hire one to be my own assistant just to survive at the job. Would spoil the fucking point of it.' She let out a short laugh at her own joke, then grabbed my hand, as if struck by a sudden thought. 'I know. How about I introduce you to some people? I know heaps of the guests here. I'll make you some *connections*.' She seemed excited by the idea. Part of me wanted to say yes, but the other part didn't fancy following this woman around like a little lost puppy.

As a compromise, I suggested we take a little wander around the quiet part of the garden, and she agreed with a little shrug, saying, 'Suit yourself. People are generally overrated, anyway.' We'd wandered away from the little fountain square to another area along the stone wall, and she spent a good ten minutes describing how there was a hidden garden here that was enclosed and never opened to the public – a sign of respect to Lord Ashton's first wife who died very young and apparently loved spending time there. On our way back round towards the house, the path opened out onto a large outdoor swimming pool, surrounded by little huts. She walked up to one, pushed open the French-window style doors and walked in. The inside was more comfortable and homelier than my old flat. There was even a chaise longue, which she parked herself on with her heaviest sigh yet, letting her empty glass fall to the floor. 'God, I'm exhausted,' she said.

Instead of awkwardly hovering, I chose to sit down in a

little single-seater armchair and tried to arrange my face into an expression that hopefully showed both empathy and pity. 'It's the heat,' I said. 'It makes me quite lethargic, too.'

'Oh, it's not that. It's more that I'm just tired of *bothering*, if you know what I mean. I try to be nice and smile and be friendly but it doesn't work. I enjoyed our little chat though, my dear. A nice little walk does one good.'

'Yes, me too,' I said.

'I haven't always been kind, you know. I was at a party once, years ago, when I was young. At this very house,' she flapped a hand towards the manor behind us. 'I spent the whole time swanning around as if I owned the place. Not caring who I offended or left out. I was rather careless, you know. Young people are quite often, I think. And so I wanted to be kind to you and try to make you feel welcome.'

There was something in her tone. The wistful note was back, and I got the feeling she was sharing something quite deep and personal. I almost felt embarrassed for listening.

'I did. Thank you for … for taking me under your wing.'

She made another little sound, half hiccup, half hollow laugh, then swung her legs over the chaise longue so she was lying down on her back. 'My brother Ernest and I used to play hide and seek around here. This was one of my favourite hiding spots. Then we'd fight and squabble endlessly.'

I started to feel a bit wobbly and I grasped hold of the sides of the chair. I could feel a rush of emotion rising up from somewhere deep within me. In a small voice I asked, 'Are you and your brother still close?'

She didn't reply for a few moments, and I wondered if she'd fallen asleep. But then she took a deep breath and said, 'Not so much now. We used to be. We both lived in the same apartment block for a while. He and his wife at the top, me some floors underneath. It was … it was nice.'

I nodded, unsure of where this was leading. I felt we were treading on heavy territory. 'Whereabouts did you live?'

'Charlwood Street,' she said, 'in Pimlico.'

This made me sit up a little, pleased to find a topic I at least had something to add to. 'Oh, I live in Pimlico. Or, *lived*, I should say, until I moved in with Meryl on Eaton Square.'

'And what do you think of it?'

I wasn't quite sure what she meant. 'Think of what?'

'The area. Eaton Square. *SW1*.' She said the postcode as if it were a disease.

'Erm … well … it's all very smart-looking.'

'It's a mirage. A charade. Stacks of money in concrete form, that's all. Rows of houses filled with people who haven't a clue about the horrors of this world. People who don't know what it's like to be on the outside, looking in. I was like that too, once. Many of the houses are empty now, with their owners using them to make their dubiously acquired cash that little bit more palatable.'

I felt myself become excited by her words. She was putting into words the feelings and suspicions I'd long had but hadn't been able to express. I tried to think of something clever to add to her comments, but before I could she leaned up on her elbows and said, 'Don't be taken in. Do what you need to do, and get out. That's what I say. Go and do something *real*. Be around *real* people. Don't waste your life on this insufferable bunch. They may all look pretty and friendly out there, but trust me, it's all a lie. Take my advice and run for the hills – and don't be afraid to burn the whole street down as you go.'

She was drunk and tired and probably unaware of what she was saying. But a fire was stirring within me. It was as if a match had been lit and pressed up against the kindling of all the rage and resentment and hot bloody fury I'd been feeling for so, so long. I got up and said, as calmly as I could, 'I'm going to go now. Thank you for being nice and showing me around. And … I'm sorry, but I didn't catch your name?'

While I was speaking, the woman had leant back down again and closed her eyes. 'Very welcome,' she said in a muffled voice, clearly already on her way to her alcohol-fuelled sleep. 'And my name … my name's Aphrodite. Mother loved the Greeks, you see, but my friends … they call me…'

But I never found out what her friends called her. Her words had started to slur together and she drifted off to sleep before she could finish her sentence. I watched her for a couple of seconds, then left. I had somewhere I needed to be.

Chapter Thirty-One

CHARLIE

Three days after the murder

My mother is standing at the kitchen doorway, carrying an old cardboard box, still staring at me. I need to think of something to say, so I settle for the blindingly obvious. 'I'm burning the flowers,' I reply.

'I can see that, but why?'

I can't help it. The tears I managed to just about hold in in front of Titus now flow from within me, causing me to gasp and sob. My mother doesn't see at first, and instead carries on talking to me. 'I've got something to show you…' Then she sees, and puts the box she's carrying down on the table and takes me into her arms, as if I were still eight years old.

'Darling, what's wrong?' she asks, then, probably realising that's a stupid question, says, 'Why have the flowers made you cry?'

Between my gasps and sobs I flick my hand at the table. 'The card,' I half whisper.

My mother extricates herself from our embrace and reaches out to pick the card up.

'Ah,' she says at last, 'I see.'

I rub my eyes, then look at her, puzzled. 'You do?'

She nods, then puts the card down. 'I do. It's from *her*.'

A few tears slip down my face as the name hits me all over again. The emphasis she puts on *her* tells me all I need to know.

'Oh, my dear,' she says, putting an arm on me. 'Go through into the library,' she says, gently, 'I'll bring you some tea.'

I do as I'm told, and take a seat on the settee facing the fireplace. I don't move. I don't do anything. I just sit there very still, the last of my tears still cold on my face. When my mother comes in with the tea, she sets it down and takes one of the seats to the side.

'You don't seem surprised,' I say in a quiet voice, not looking at her.

'No,' she says, with a sigh.

'You knew?' I look at her now, unable to keep the accusation from my voice.

'I found out a few days ago. The day before Matthew … before Matthew died. I didn't think you knew.' She nudges one of the cups of tea towards me. 'Drink some of that. It will help.'

I take some of the tea, but it's too hot to drink so I set it back down and look at my trembling hands in my lap.

'Do you want to talk about it?' my mother asks, her voice low and understanding.

'I think … I think I've had a bit too much talking for today already.' I lie back, letting the sofa take my weight and draw a slow breath in through my nose, then out through my mouth. Then something occurs to me. 'What was in that box you were carrying?'

My mother straightens up. 'Oh, goodness, yes, hold on.' She sets down her cup, gets up, and walks out of the room. Returning a few seconds later with the grey cardboard box in her arms, she sits back down in her chair and takes off the lid. I can't see its contents from my angle on the sofa, and she doesn't show me immediately.

'I would understand if you'd prefer not to go into this now, what with … everything. But I think this could be important.'

My interest is piqued. 'What is it?' I ask, leaning forward.

She takes a deep breath. 'I think I've worked out who Rachel really is. Or at least, I know where I've seen her before.'

Chapter Thirty-Two

CHARLIE

Less than a week to go

I stared around, at both him, then at Rupert, who looked just as puzzled as I felt.

'Is everything all right, Matthew?' he asked. 'Can I get you anything?'

'No,' Matthew said, so bluntly it sounded almost aggressive. 'We just need to leave. Where's Titus?'

I shook my head. 'I don't know. Somewhere around, I guess.' I gestured my free hand vaguely at our surroundings. The grounds were extensive and far-reaching, with a whole other garden area, like something from a children's fairy tale, stretching into the distance behind a stone wall that snaked around the property. If Titus had gone in there, I thought, it could take hours to find him, although it was more likely we'd find him chatting to Pippa round near the pool or helping himself to champagne.

'We need to look for him. Now.'

He started walking, dragging me along. I could see Rupert wasn't sure if he should follow or not. He chose to leave us to it, bidding me goodbye with a small nod as I struggled to stop myself tripping up.

'Let go of me,' I snapped at Matthew. 'You're being ridiculous. I don't understand why…'

We'd reached a cluster of people, standing around the swimming pool and I realised one of them was my mother. 'I wondered where both of you were,' she said, smiling at us. 'Your father's talking to that journalist you like in *The Times*. The one who comments on the media. If you like, we can go over and join—'

'Have you seen Titus?' Matthew cut across her, rather rudely in my opinion. My mother looked understandably taken aback.

'Er … no. Oh yes, hang on, he was talking to Pippa. I think they went off over towards the stables.'

Matthew didn't offer any sort of reply or explanation, just marched off in the direction of my mother's suggestion, one hand now glued to his phone as he tried to reach Titus on his mobile.

'What on earth is going on?' she asked me. 'What's wrong with him?'

I shook my head. 'I'm sorry, I … I think he might be unwell or something. I'll see you later.'

I left her looking perplexed and jogged to catch up with my husband, now walking around the little pool huts that were dotted around the swimming pool and towards the edge of the main garden where it merged into a field. When the stables came into sight, Matthew stopped dead so suddenly I crashed into him.

'What now?' I asked, feeling seriously annoyed.

He tilted his head, evidently listening. That was when I heard it too. Heavy breathing and gasps. Then a little laugh.

'I don't believe it,' he muttered, then continued to stride towards the first of the stables, walking around the back wall. I followed him round, resulting in us both being confronted by the same sight at the same time.

Titus and Rupert's niece, Pippa. The latter leaning up against the wall, the former leaning into her.

Pippa noticed us first and shrieked. 'Oh my gosh!' She started to bat at Titus's shoulder as he continued to thrust. Matthew didn't wait for him to realise; he moved forward and grabbed Titus, extricating the two of them.

'What the FUCK?' Titus shouted.

'What are you doing?' Matthew raged at him.

Titus was hurriedly trying to pull up his boxers, Pippa flattening down her dress and pulling on her shoes.

'What does it look like?' Titus yelled back.

'You are FIFTEEN!' Matthew snarled at him, looking angrier than I'd seen him in years. 'I can't deal with all this now. Is this what you've become? Shagging people behind the stables at wedding anniversaries? You are a CHILD.'

Titus's face was full of outrage and defiance. 'I'm tired of always being told what I can and can't do. I've done it your way my whole life and the one time I want to have a bit of fun you just—'

'FUN?' Matthew said, grabbing him by his lapels. 'This isn't *fun*; this is beneath you. This is reckless behaviour, the sort of thing your vile, drug-addled, nymphomaniac father would have done.' He shoved Titus away from him, and I saw the boy's face change from anger to upset. For a second, Matthew's reference to Titus's father confused me; I worried for a moment that he was talking about me. After all, I was no stranger to a liaison behind the stables myself back in my youth. But then it hit home. He was talking about Johnny Holden.

'Just leave me alone,' Titus said now, a sob rising in his voice. He turned to walk away from us, towards Pippa who was hovering on the edge of this strange scene, clearly unsure if she should wait to find out how it developed or seek shelter away from all the rage.

'Oh no you don't,' Matthew said. He grabbed Titus again, his arms firmly steering the boy around. 'We're going.'

To my surprise, Titus didn't put up much of a fight. Trying hard not to let his tears spill over, he rubbed at his eyes with the back of his hand and allowed himself to be led away. I opened my mouth to say something to Pippa, who was still staring at us, but couldn't think of anything to say. I just gave her a weak smile, then followed Matthew and Titus across the grass back towards the house.

We managed to get to the entrance hall before anyone stopped us.

'Charles? Matthew? Where are you going?'

I looked round to see my mother walking quickly to catch us before we left through the front door.

'I think … I'm afraid we're leaving. Matthew's not very well.' I gestured to him, but he was already down the steps to the driveway, ordering one of the young men at the entrance to bring the car round.

My mother peered at me, her eyes searching my face, trying to work out what was wrong. 'You look ... *stressed*. Has something happened?'

I looked back out to the steps and driveway outside. Titus and Matthew were now standing separate from each other, waiting for the car, Titus kicking moodily at the gravel.

My mother had seen them too. 'What's going on? Is Titus all right? He looks upset.'

I shook my head. 'He's fine. He's ... it's just all been a bit of a tense afternoon.'

She looked understandably confused by this. A crunching outside announced the arrival of our car on the driveway, followed by the doors opening.

'Charlie! Now!' Matthew called out.

'I'm sorry, I've got to go,' I said to my mother. 'It's just Matthew. He has a headache or something.' I turned away from her and began to walk down the steps.

'Should he be driving if he's feeling so ill?'

The voice wasn't my mother's. It was from someone else. I turned back and saw Rachel walking through the front door, glass of champagne in hand. There was something about her that instantly unsettled me. There always was, to some extent, but today it seemed amplified. Her eyes were bright, her face keen and inquisitive and I had a strange sense that she had more of a grasp of the situation than any of us standing here.

Deciding to ignore her, I turned back to my mother and said, 'I'm sorry. I'll call you later.'

I turned and walked down the steps and got into the already running car. Matthew didn't say anything as I closed the door and did up my seatbelt; he just reversed quickly to turn the car round then started driving off at a speed that felt excessive. In the rearview mirror I saw my mother go back inside the house. But a shape remained at the top step for a few moments longer. The outline of Rachel, the red sunset bathing the Ashtons's manor in an otherworldly glow behind her, watching us as we drove away.

The journey home was fraught and filled with bouts of Matthew and Titus shouting and snapping at each other. It only got into truly difficult territory when Matthew made another reference to Titus's biological father. Titus, who had maintained that it had been very wrong of Matthew to interrupt him when he was having sex with Pippa, said that he was a 'hypocrite' and was sure that both of us had done worse in our time. I saw Matthew's knuckles grow white as he gripped the steering wheel when he responded.

'I would just prefer it if you could control yourself when we go out as a family. We were at the Ashtons's wedding anniversary, not a student house party in some shithole flat.'

Titus scoffed, 'Now you sound like a snob.'

'I also noticed you weren't wearing a condom. *How* can

you be so stupid? You're supposed to be bright, intelligent, sensible. Do you know the risk you're taking?'

In the mirror I saw Titus go red. 'I seriously don't think Pippa has HIV or—'

'I'm not talking about fucking STIs, I'm talking about *pregnancy*. That's how mistakes happen. Potentially life-ruining mistakes. Young people behaving recklessly, shagging around without protection…'

'Mistakes like *me*, you mean?' Titus was shouting now, and I saw some tears fall from his eyes. 'You're saying just because I act like any other boy my age, I'm going to somehow turn into some no-good drug addict like my father? So you think it would have been better if I'd never been born?'

'For God's sake, I'm not saying that,' Matthew said and swerved the car erratically and had to act quickly to keep within his lane.

'Pull over at the hard shoulder when you're next able to,' I said firmly.

'What?' he said, glancing over at me as if he'd just remembered I was there.

'I mean it. You shouldn't drive when you're this angry.'

We made the swap a few minutes on, and continued our journey in silence, punctuated by the odd sniff from Titus, who had the pinched look of someone trying not to cry openly.

I'd been concerned how Matthew and I would finally find a time to talk alone, to unpick what exactly had made him so desperate to leave the party before the whole business with Titus had blown up. But the opportunity arrived quicker than I'd expected. As soon as we turned into Carlyle Square and shut the engine off, Titus got out and said he was going to bed and didn't want to talk. He stomped off up the stairs before we'd even closed the front door.

Matthew turned to look at me, the warm hallway light bathing his smooth, perfect skin. I felt a sudden need to go to him, to hug him, to tell him whatever was going on would sort itself out. But I didn't. Something stopped me. Maybe it was because I felt a shifting of everything among us. And now, I felt, I was going to discover something momentous.

'Let's go to the lounge,' he said quietly.

I followed and he turned on the table lamp as we went in. He went straight over to where we kept the drinks and poured himself a large whisky, knocked it back, then poured another. He didn't offer me one. He had started to pace, swaying almost, as if already drunk, apparently trying to muster something within him, some inner strength, tame some inner turmoil enough to say what he needed to say.

'Everything's fucked.'

He kept his eyes on the carpet as he said this, and took another sip of his drink. I sat down on the sofa.

'Please,' I said. 'Just tell me. What's going on?'

He didn't reply, just drank some more, and stared into the fireplace as if there were a blaze burning there rather than stone-cold coal.

'Has this got anything to do with Rachel?' I asked at last.

That got a reaction. He looked over to me, his eyes shining with tears. 'It has everything to do with Rachel.'

Chapter Thirty-Three

RACHEL

Less than a week to go

As Matthew went to leave the bathroom, I immediately seized him by the shoulders and pushed him back inside.

'Er … hey! What the…?' he protested loudly as I shut the door behind me.

'Be quiet,' I said, trying to keep my voice hard and firm.

'Rachel. What are you doing?'

Matthew made a move to get to the door, but I blocked his path. He smiled then, as if this was a game. I could see what was on his mind.

Without explanation, I walked purposefully over towards the beautiful, large bathtub at the other end of the room. The bathroom was about the same size as the bedroom I had back at Churchill Gardens, and instead of the tacky plastic baths I've used in every property I've ever lived in, with the exception of Meryl's, this one is separate from the wall and very deep. I stepped into the empty bath, right foot first, then left, then I sat down, stretching out my legs. They only just about reached the taps at the end.

'Relaxing things, baths. I don't have them often enough – always end up having a quick shower. In, out, then you're done. Baths are for the time-rich, really, aren't they? The people who can let their lives trail away while they float around in hot water and froth.'

He didn't say anything, just looked at me, as if he thought I was going insane, the smile now gone.

I took my hands off the edges of the tub and started to feel around the sides. 'Ah, that's a shame. No holes for bubbles. Not a jacuzzi, then. No, well, I suppose that would be considered a bit common for Lord and Lady Ashton. Although they've probably got a hot tub somewhere outside. Don't you think?'

I turned my head over to him with these last words. My heart was pounding within me and I could see, from the flush creeping up his face, his probably was too.

'Do you know, I've been feeling tired all day,' I said. 'Really exhausted. I could take a nap right here in the bath. It's lucky there isn't any water in it, of course,' I said, slowly and deliberately. 'I wouldn't want there to be … an accident.'

The silence that followed was like the kind you got after a bomb blast. Then I heard him stagger across the room. At first I thought he was coming for me, then I heard the toilet seat fling up and the sound of him retching, vomiting, then eventually, gasping as he slumped on the floor. Only then did I turn again to look at him. A shirt button had come undone, he had some sick on his chin, and his face was now a grey-white. He looked horrific. And I was glad of it.

We stared at each other for a while, neither of us speaking. Then he dragged himself to his feet, using the loo seat to steady himself, and slumped over to the sink and let the taps stream. He splashed water onto his face, into his mouth, spat it out, then took some long, desperate gulps.

'Just one sec,' I said to him, keeping it as causal as I could. I took out my phone, went to the camera roll and selected the photo I wanted. I then tapped 'share' and sent it to him as a WhatsApp. I heard the ping come from the pocket of his chinos, then the rustle of him fishing the phone out.

I waited for some reaction – rage, fear, threats, pleas for me to stay silent. But he didn't do any of this. Instead, he ran. Ran from the room and let the door slam shut behind him.

I gave it a minute, then got up, smoothed down my dress, and stepped carefully out of the bath. Everything seemed to glow brightly around me as I left the bathroom and re-joined the party. The world had come alive.

Chapter Thirty-Four

CHARLIE

Three days after the murder

My mother and I go into the library, her clasping the box she'd been holding. She places this onto the coffee table, kneels in front of it, and starts to rifle around. She takes a pile of several photos from inside and starts to lay them out on the polished wooden surface. 'These are the photographs we used in a display at your and Matthew's wedding. Lots of snaps of you both from your younger years.'

I go over and kneel down on the other side of the table. 'Yes, I remember them,' I say. 'They were lovely.' I lightly touched the matte-finish of one of them – a photo of me when I must have been fourteen or fifteen, having just won some rugby game, Archie and me holding our hands in the air. It feels like I'm looking at a different person. A different life.

'Well, I was sorting some things out and discovered these, and ended up having a look through them,' my mother continued. 'When I decided to put together the display, I needed to get a good range, and since the both of you have straddled the era of film and digital, it took some organisation to get shots from different points in your life. I asked Edith for a load of photos of Matthew and, well, you know how disorganised she was; she just gave me heaps of old photo albums and a load of SD cards. I think she didn't want to go through them all, since there'd be photos of Collette in there. She said she didn't mind pictures of Collette and Matthew being up at the wedding, but I can understand why she didn't want to go through them herself.'

I watch as she carries on laying out the shots. 'And you never gave them back before Edith died?' I ask.

'Oh, I did,' my mother says. 'All the albums and SD cards, but I had the contents of the SD cards printed, so I kept those. I spent ages looking through reams of holiday snaps and family gatherings – shots of the Jones family. Shots I think Collette took, or had taken by others, before she died. And … here.' She pulls out a photo. It shows a group of young people aged around nineteen or twenty. They're standing in the snow, surrounded by pine trees. 'They're all on holiday, somewhere cold,' Cassandra says. 'There's a hotel sign in one of the other shots. And look there. Right there. It's *her*.' I scan my eye across the people standing, smiling at the camera in the snow. I look along the faces and vaguely recognise some of them; they're Matthew's friends, mostly posh left-wingers who lament how terrible things are for the poor and the evils of carbon emissions whilst jetting off for a few weeks on the slopes.

The face in the middle is at first oddly familiar. Then the penny drops.

'Oh fuck, it's her,' I say, dropping back to sit down on the carpet properly. It is indeed her. It is Rachel. Staring back at me from a photo that must have been taken a good decade ago.

'It is indeed. With Matthew. I think they've been skiing.'

And now I know what this is. And where it is. And how it all fits into place. 'Yes, I see. I see that.'

My mother starts to gather up the rest of the photos as I continue to stare at Rachel's face. It feels like I'm holding a slice of Matthew's history. A time I've only properly imagined in my head, almost like a bizarre, surreal film.

'Don't you think it's strange?' my mother says, putting the lid on the box and staring at me. 'All this time, Matthew claimed not to know her. You both acted like you didn't know her.'

There's a note of suspicion in her voice now. As if she suspects Matthew told me everything before he died.

'Darling, we both know Rachel didn't kill Matthew. Your father is right; you'd better tell us what happened so we can deal with it before the police work all this out.'

I close my eyes for a second, that slightly hot, burning feeling of tiredness spreading through my face. Then I hear a noise, someone moving, then seconds later feel my mother's hand on my shoulder. 'Come on, tell me,' she says, 'sit up on the chair and tell me, properly, who Rachel is.'

A few beats of silence pass between us, then I hear

another voice – the resonant, deep voice of my father. 'Her real name is Rachel Holden.' I open my eyes, and my mother and I turn to look at the door where my father is standing. 'She's Titus's aunt.'

Chapter Thirty-Five

CHARLIE

Less than a week to go

I suppose, looking back now, there were many times when I could have interrupted and told Matthew that I knew everything he was telling me, that I knew about the whole situation with his sister. Her boyfriend. Titus. How he'd told me everything one cold autumn day in Kensington Gardens when we'd started to become a couple. But of course, he hadn't told me everything. Just the bare facts, with no real detail of what happened. Of what he did. So, sitting on the sofa in the dim light of the lounge, the evening darkening at the windows and turning into night, I didn't stop him or press him to get to the heart of the matter. I just listened, and allowed the truth to change our lives for ever. About how Collette had met Johnny Holden when she was at university as a one-night stand who'd turned into a relationship. How he supplied her and her friends with drugs. And how it quickly escalated from cannabis to MDMA and cocaine. Until eventually, Matthew and his mother intervened, sent her to a rehab clinic, and tried to convince her to leave Johnny for good. But, of course, that didn't quite work.

I sat, watching my husband standing there, tense and strung out, and got the sense we were arriving at a moment we'd always been destined to reach at some point. It was as if the world was changing before my very eyes. Things I'd regarded as certain, although unexplored, were exploding off into new avenues of unsaid truths and downright lies. An energy was burning through me – an energy that made me want to seize Matthew and shake the full story out of him and demand he tell me every last horrid detail. But I didn't do this. I had to let him tell it in his own way. Somehow I knew that would be the best thing to do. And judging by his body-language and flushed appearance, he was about to reveal something momentous.

'She tried to break up with Johnny,' Matthew said, his eyes distant, his mind back among the demons of his past. 'But as you can imagine, he didn't take the news well.'

Slight tremors became visible in his face in that moment. His cheek twitched; he blinked quickly and rubbed his eyes. I had the impression he was re-living something. An old memory he'd kept buried for years was being dragged to the surface. The past was coming back, ready to decimate the present, and there was nothing he could do to stop it.

'Johnny did something. Something I've … never really spoken to anyone about. Not properly. Apart from Collette.

She knew everything that happened. And I think it destroyed us both. Her through denial, and me from the sheer horror of it.'

Chapter Thirty-Six

RACHEL

Less than a week to go

I sat in my bedroom in Meryl's flat, my laptop open in front of me. I felt both excited and a little sad as I tapped away at the computer, opening up multiple tabs. I knew it would be one of the last nights I spent in a comfortable, gorgeous room. It would all change soon. But there were a few things I needed to find out first.

I knew showing my hand at the Ashtons's manor would speed things up. Remove the safety net I'd crafted for myself. But this lifestyle I'd managed to build was never meant to last for ever. In the years that followed, I would examine in granular detail those last couple of evenings of freedom as I went for evening walks around the quiet streets of Belgravia, or drifted through the private gardens of Eaton Square. Evenings when thoughts of giving up my main aim surfaced, like a dull, distant voice in my head telling me that what I was about to do was morally wrong.

That I should just carry on as I was. Living. Enjoying London life. There were times I even imagined an alternate future for myself, where I continued working for Meryl as her assistant, moving into the apartment on Belgrave Place when it was finished, having a flat all to myself of the kind I'd never have dreamed of before. Maybe Meryl would leave me something in her will when she died and I'd be able to keep the flat. I'd have been able to sell it for millions of pounds and buy a large estate in Yorkshire. Move back to start a new life as I journeyed through my middle age. But I'd dashed all hope of that as soon as I entered that bathroom in Marwood Manor and allowed Matthew Allerton-Jones to realise who I was. So whenever those thoughts of abandoning my plan surfaced, I let them float away, as if they were leaves on a stream.

The tabs I'd opened on my laptop were for a number of websites, some medical and some forums, giving clear instructions. They specified which knives would be best to use, which techniques would work with nearly all sharp blades, how to angle the knife, when to release the pressure. It was all there, easy to access at the tap of a few fingers on a keyboard. Like most things these days.

I didn't bother to use private browsing, not that that would delay the police much anyway. I had no interest in trying to put off the inevitable. When the computer forensics people searched my laptop, it would all be there, plain to see. If they wanted to know why, well, that would be a good test of their detective skills. They'd figure it out, in the end.

Once I had all the information I needed, I made my

decision. I would do it later this week. I'd give time for the shrapnel from my little bombshell to ricochet through the Allerton-Jones family for a few more days. Perhaps he'd tell his husband what he did. Or maybe he'd try to carry on as normal. Whatever he did, he knew I was there, nearby, less than a couple of miles away.

Waiting. Like a coiled spring.

Chapter Thirty-Seven

CHARLIE

Less than a week to go

I felt myself getting a little cold, wary of what he was about to tell me. Something new and clearly deeply uncomfortable for him to remember. Matthew took a moment to refill his glass, sipped and let the whisky swirl around his mouth. Then he set the glass down and said, 'Johnny Holden attacked me. I was staying the night at the castle alone. I was working on a PhD application and thought I'd appreciate the peace and quiet. Collette was in Durham and my mother was visiting a friend in Edinburgh. I'd been working late and went to bed at around one in the morning. At about 2am, I was woken by a thud, but didn't think much of it – just presumed it was a cat or something outside. It was when I heard a creak on the landing that I woke up properly. Four men walked into my room, dressed in black and wearing the masks of woodland creatures. A squirrel, a rabbit, a badger, and a fox.'

He winced, closing his eyes for a moment, as if pained by the images he was trying to describe. 'It's hard to put into words how paralysing fear can be. I thought I'd fallen into a nightmare, a literal, living nightmare. For a few seconds I couldn't move. Then I saw they were carrying rope. That was when I tried to run, but they grabbed me as I leapt out of bed and set about tying me up. They tied up my ankles and arms – not much, but enough so they could carry me easily even as I tried to kick free. Some material was put in my mouth and taped to my jaw. They took me down the old servants' stairs at the back of the house and out the kitchen door into the grounds. In the garden, by the fountain, they made me sit on one of the benches and then one of them brought out a knife. A thick, hunting knife. I can honestly tell you, in that moment, I thought I was going to die. I thought they were going to cut my throat and let me bleed to death on a bench in the garden, to be found by my mother or one of the gardeners.'

He stopped for a moment, then went over to the drinks table and poured himself some more whisky and took a sip. When he put the glass back down, I could see his hand was trembling.

'They used the knife to cut off my boxers. Slashing at the material, so I had scratches down my thighs. But aside from these few scrapes, they didn't hurt me with it. Instead, they humiliated me. Laughed at me. Made threats about what they were going to do to me. Jeered at me, as I sat naked and trembling, shining the torches they were carrying in my face then turning them off and on so I couldn't properly see. Then, when I thought they'd finally follow through on one of their sickening threats, one of them – the man with the fox mask – produced a bag ... like a freezer bag. One of them held a torch to it so I could see what it was. It was a bag of cocaine.

'Two of them held me down, while the fox and the badger covered the blade of the knife in the powder and then put it to my nose. Because my mouth was gagged, I had no choice but to breathe in. They held it there, the blade digging into me, as I tried not to hyperventilate, knowing the more harshly I breathed, the more cocaine I would take in. I'm not sure how much I ended up consuming, but they dipped the knife into the bag a number of times. It was the fox who kept making me take the stuff. And on one of the doses – the second or third, maybe – he said to me, 'Mess with your sister's life again, and we'll fuck you up worse than this.' Whether it was the drugs, or from trauma, or a cumulative effect as a whole, I felt my heart beating faster and faster and I began to feel extremely sick. I thought I was having a heart attack. The world had already been spinning, but at that point it felt like it had properly turned upside down. I couldn't tell what was happening any more. I may have had a small fit, or just blacked out, because I awoke to them lowering me into the fountain head-first, one of them shrieking in my ear; I'm not even sure what it was he was saying. It may have been just a long continuous moan to disorientate me. They kept pulling me in and out of the water, each scrape of the stone fountain against my flesh sending stinging pains all over my body. It may have lasted a few minutes or a few hours. I ended up passing out again. Perhaps they thought they'd killed me and fled. Maybe they just got bored. Or felt they'd completed what they set out to do. I could have easily drowned or died from the cold, left there half submerged and naked in the fountain for the rest of the night.'

I leaned forwards, astonished by his words and, strangely, compelled by them. I was gripped by this hidden chapter in my husband's life and how it had shaped him as a person, whilst all this time he kept it hidden from view. Like a bad dream you filed away and tried not to think about. Except this hadn't been a dream. This had been true brutal trauma. And I didn't know whether to hug him close and tell him nobody would ever hurt him like that again, or let my anger boil over and make it clear to him how betrayed I felt by him refusing to let me in on such a momentous part of his life.

When I opened my mouth, I paused a little, unsure of what to say. Then I asked the question at the forefront of my mind. 'How did Collette react when you told her what her boyfriend had done?'

A small tear fell silently from Matthew's right eye. 'I think that's the part that upsets me most, to this day.'

Chapter Thirty-Eight

CHARLIE

Less than a week to go

I struggled to see how Matthew's ordeal could have become any more upsetting than it was already. I was wrong, of course.

'Did Collette find you, after the attack?' I asked.

He shook his head. 'When I woke, I imagined it was her. That she'd come to rescue me. But it wasn't. It was just the teenage boy who worked with our head gardener on the estate. I'd gone through too much at that point to feel anything other than a dull relief. The lad – to my shame, I didn't know his name – seemed to think it was funny. The benches around the fountain were littered with vodka bottles, and one of the masks was floating in the fountain's water. The fox mask. I think the boy thought there'd been some sort of party. He may have even made reference to a stag do or something. I didn't correct him. I just nodded and tried to clamber out of the fountain, but struggled. He helped me out and offered me his jacket so I had something to wear on my walk back to the house. I'm not sure what it was about that – maybe just because it was a moment of kindness after experiencing so much horror – but it made me burst into tears. It probably terrified him.

'Although he was only about four years younger than me, it must have been a bizarre sight to witness – the man of the castle, found naked in the fountain of his own garden surrounded by vodka bottles and cocaine, crying like a child. But he didn't run; he just awkwardly told me things "weren't that bad" and we all had a wild night now and then. So he walked me back to the castle. He had to help me – I was trembling so much – and by the time we'd got up the stairs up to my room I think he realised something serious had happened, as he started to suggest phoning someone for me, perhaps even an ambulance. I begged him not to; I said I was fine and I didn't need any help. I just needed to go to bed, to sleep. Forget everything. But it wasn't over. There was a surprise waiting for me in my room. The boy opened the door for me and helped me in. I was shivering terribly by that point and he picked up a towel I'd left on the floor so I could put it round me. That was when he noticed the photographs. All over the bed. Must have been a hundred or more. Polaroids. They were scattered all around the duvet and pillows. I think he said something like "fucking hell" when he picked one of them up and offered it out to me.

'The first one I saw confused me. It was of a woman's naked breasts, a hand touching them. I asked the boy what it was doing there, but of course it was a pointless question.

I looked down at the rest of them and a few seconds later realised what they were. They were photos of Collette. In a lot of them, she was completely naked; some had her legs open. In many of them, she was accompanied by a young man. His face wasn't visible in most, but it was pretty obvious who it was. Johnny Holden. Some of them showed her sucking his cock, others were of him fucking her. She looked off her face, wasted, high, stoned. I was already in pure shock when I saw them, but this was the final straw. I crashed across the room into the en suite and was violently sick. I don't know whether the gardener's boy recognised Collette from the photos. He may never have seen her, since she visited so infrequently and the estate was so large. Or maybe he presumed I had some sick, incestuous porn thing going on with her. I don't know. But the vomiting made him even more keen to call someone, and again I begged him not to. In the end, he helped me into the bed, the photos brushed onto the floor, and filled a glass of water from the bathroom. I hope I said thank you at the time, but I think I fell asleep almost immediately. I slept through the whole day and into the evening, waking when it was getting dark around 7pm.

'My phone had been on my nightstand the whole time. When I woke, the battery was dead and I put it on charge. Tons of missed calls and messages came flooding in. They were from Colette. She said Johnny was furious, that he blamed me for getting her to leave him and give up the drugs. She was terrified of what he'd do to me. It was only moments after I'd showered and dressed that I heard the front door go. Part of me was terrified it was the gang of men back again for round two, but then I heard Collette's voice calling me. She was beside herself. She had got the train up, terrified of what she might find. I got quite upset when I saw her. She could tell immediately something had happened, even though I didn't really have any visible marks aside from a small cut under my nose from where they'd held the knife to me. We went down to the servants' area and sat in the kitchen like we'd done as children when we still had live-in staff. We were always getting in their way, but loved the warmth of the Aga and our cook, Mrs McDonald, often gave us gingerbread. Of course, on that horrible evening there was no freshly baked gingerbread. Just basic decaffeinated teabags, stale biscuits and Collette trying to get me to tell her what had happened.

'When she'd got it out of me, she cried and hugged me. Then I told her I wanted to call the police. That was when things turned tricky. She told me he'd got her fingerprints on bags of cocaine – a large shipment he was helping to distribute. He was starting to earn quite big money from it all, and she'd helped him pack some of it up and into bags. I asked her how could she have done such a thing, but she just shook her head, tears spilling from her eyes and said, "Oh dearest, if only you knew what love was like." I felt sick hearing her talk like that. Talk as if their love was some Romeo and Juliet star-crossed lovers' romance. I told her he was a psychopath; what he did to me was horrific. I thought I was going to die. She was upset by it, I could tell, but she said if I went to the police he had evidence that would land her in prison. Evidence that she'd assisted – even funded, with her own money – some of his criminal activities. She told me that if I could bear not reporting the incident, she really would go clean; never touch the stuff again. I asked if she would leave him for good too. Never touch him again. Never see him again. Never contact him again. She wouldn't assure me on that. She said things weren't that simple.

'That was when things turned bitter between us. I didn't want to talk to her after that. I told her she should go back to Durham. I wouldn't go to the police because I didn't want her to go to prison, but I couldn't be around her if she was still seeing him. I left her in tears in the kitchen. I feel awful about it now. And at the door, I said something worse. I told her he had images of him fucking her. They'd been left on my pillow. And I said, "I've still got them in case you want to keep them for your scrapbook." That was a reference to something she used to do as a kid – even into her teenage years.'

I nodded, 'I remember you telling me about it, when Titus used to do the same when he was younger.'

Matthew looked sad and distant after I said this. 'Perhaps he inherited her creative streak,' he said, his eyes shining. 'She didn't just do it for holidays, though. She'd fill these large, leather-bound books with photos of all sorts of things. Animals, pages from books, leaves. She'd always have a new project on the go. And somehow, me mentioning something so vulgar in the same breath as one of her childhood passions felt nasty. Ugly. Something broke between us that day. Things were never the same again, right up until she died.'

Matthew paused, and looked over at me. It was as if he

knew what I was thinking. Knew that I was going to ask the question that had been on my mind since he started talking. 'You never felt you could tell me?'

As I said it, his face crumpled into something broken, fractured, like a smashed mirror. For a second, I thought he was going to burst into tears. Then he pressed his fist to his mouth and took in a deep, shaky breath.

'There's more. A lot more. To be honest, all that stuff was just the beginning.'

Chapter Thirty-Nine

CHARLIE

Less than a week to go

Matthew settled himself down into the single-seater chair near the fireplace. He rubbed his face. Brushed his fringe away from his forehead. Then focused his eyes on the floor as he continued to talk.

'I wanted to believe Collette would keep her word about no longer taking the stuff. I really did. And for a while, it looked like she was managing to do it. Then it became clear she was still seeing him. Still spending time with Johnny, even though she knew what he'd done to me. I began to have panic attacks. Would wake up at night, convinced the men in masks had returned and they'd castrated me or raped me with the hunting knife, or bound me up again in ropes. I began popping pills – opioids, on prescription – convinced I could still feel the bruises from their rough treatment of me. I was terrified Collette might bring him to the highlands and I'd have to see him face-to-face. I started to avoid her, even though this clearly hurt her. I was tempted to have it out with her, tell her she'd betrayed me, her brother, by continuing with that psychopath. But I didn't. I couldn't talk about it all. It was at Christmas when she came up to me and asked – in fact pleaded – for me to join her and our mutual friends, David and Sylvia Gibson, along with some of their cousins, on a skiing trip in Norway. They'd hired a few cabins and she said she was worried about me and it would probably help. I didn't have to ski; she just said a change of scene and being around people would help both of us. She was worried about me, sitting in the castle with my thoughts. Eventually I gave in. She was going for a couple of weeks at the start of January before her university semester began.

'The first few days were actually really good. Like, more than I could have ever thought possible. It did wonders for my spirits, and the change of scene really did have a rejuvenating effect. I'd always got on well with the Gibsons and it was really nice to spend time with them again. Their cousins were really nice too. All of it was going surprisingly well. Until one night, when we were having dinner in the main hotel building, Collette disappeared off for about half an hour. When she came back she had snow in her hair; she'd evidently been outside. Later I would discover she'd been outside to let someone into her cabin. Someone who'd just arrived. In Norway.'

As Matthew paused I felt myself tensing, realising where this was heading. Of course, I'd always known the vague circumstances around the death of Titus's father, but never had Matthew told me them in such clear detail, with such deliberate attempt to get the whole story across to me, the full picture. And I had a really horrible feeling of foreboding that I couldn't shake off. A strong part of me even wanted to run out of the room, out of the house, away from his strained, slightly trembling voice. Away from what secrets it could reveal. But I didn't.

I carried on listening – a decision that would change our lives for ever.

———

Matthew had to take a quick break at that point. He'd been talking for a while and hadn't gone to pee since we'd got home from Oxford. While he went to the bathroom, and no doubt checked Titus was still safe in his room with his music playing, I went into the kitchen and grabbed some leftover pizza and pushed it into my mouth. I was suddenly starving. When Matthew came back he glanced at the pizza in my hands, and I instinctively offered it out. He shook his head and went back into the lounge. I followed, sat down, and allowed him to continue.

'The holiday became something of a nightmare from then onwards. Collette stopped joining in as much with our activities. She mostly just spent time with Johnny in her cabin. When I realised he was there, I very nearly flew back home, but even that seemed impossible. I was sick outside in the snow; I struggled to get out of bed in the mornings. The closest I got to him was when Sylvia insisted we all had a photo together with our ski things. A whole bunch of other people had joined us in the week – university friends of Sylvia and a few guys David knew from home, who in turn brought their girlfriends. Somehow, the increase in numbers helped me feel a bit better. Anyway, we were having a photo done near one of the slopes – Sylvia had asked one of the staff to take it – and just as we were gathering round, I heard a voice I couldn't forget. It was his voice. Johnny's. He and Collette had joined us without me noticing. I'm not even sure what he'd said – something about him being fucking frozen. But it instantly took me back to that night. The black-clothed figure in the fox mask, pressing the cocaine-covered knife against my nose. And then I briefly saw Collette's face. Her eyes. She was off her face. High as a kite. And something in me snapped. I left the group and went back to my cabin and packed up all my things. David came and found me just after I'd called reception to ask for a car to take me to the airport. He was confused why I was going. Did Collette know I was leaving? Was I feeling unwell? He kept asking all these things, but all I could do was shake my head and say I had to go home. And I did. I flew back to Scotland that afternoon.

'My mother was concerned when she saw me getting out of the car without Collette. I'd felt relief wash over me when I boarded the plane and managed to hold myself together so I didn't end up the mad one sobbing in first class. But once I'd stepped inside the castle, I fell into my mother's arms and sobbed. I told her he was there. Johnny Holden was there. And I thought Collette was using again. To my shame, I abandoned both my mother and my sister after that. My mother kept questioning me. Wringing her hands about how she couldn't get on a plane but how she wanted to go and find Collette herself. I didn't help her. I left Scotland, went to London for a few months, and tried to bury myself in PhD research. It was March when I discovered Collette hadn't returned from Norway. I was astounded by this news. It had been over a month, nearly two, since I'd flown back to the UK, leaving her there. My mother phoned to tell me Collette was pregnant. She was out there in Norway expecting her first child. Her first child with *him*. So we went out there by cruise ship. It took two weeks. Collette was dismissive and rude to us both, even though we'd travelled all that way. Johnny was belligerent and sneering towards my mother and when I started to get angry he said to me, "Calm down, love, don't want you crying like a girl, do we?" I knew of course what he was referring to and it had its desired effect. It made me want to leave immediately. But in the end, Collette practically threw us out.

'We missed the birth, months later – something that still pains my mother. She had a horrendous bout of flu, and wasn't able to leave her bed – not that Collette gave us much warning. My mother pleaded for me to fly out and be with her, give her some support, so I did my best to push my fears of Johnny to the back of my mind and flew back out on what was now a familiar journey. They weren't coping. Worse than not coping. They were a mess. It became obvious within minutes of being in their company that they were using something. I wasn't sure what, but both were lying there like zombies on the beds, sofas, while the baby – Titus – was crying in a horrible plastic cot. I shook Collette, trying to wake her. She just murmured something like, "The birth was horrible" then went back to sleep. Johnny was dead to the world, asleep on the sofa in his pants like some teenager recovering from a hangover. Then I noticed the plate next to him. And the needles. And the bent spoon.

'I should have taken the baby and run away with him or something – just left them both to their vile habits – but I didn't know how they'd sorted it with passports and hospital visits. I was completely out of my comfort zone, out of my area of expertise. Collette and I had a bit of a shrieking match when she woke up properly. She took up the screaming Titus in her arms and said it was normal for mothers to go a bit off the rails in the first few weeks. I told her intravenous drugs was a bit further than off the rails. She said that stuff was just Johnny's; she hadn't touched it. I asked what she had touched, whether she was breast feeding, whether the drugs could be getting into her child's mouth. She told me to fuck off and more or less kicked me out of the flat. I went for a walk around the woodland. Had dinner up at the main hotel building. Booked into a room there and slept for a few hours. Took a shower. In the late afternoon, I wandered back down to their cabin. It was twilight and I could see their lights were on, including the hanging ambient lighting of the veranda. As I walked up the steps, it became clear someone was in the hot tub. It was Johnny. He was asleep, or smacked out of his head, once again, his chin lolling in the water. Then, as I got to the top of the steps, I saw what was nestled in his arms. Nearly underwater. It was the baby. It was Titus. He had sat down in the hot tub, high off his head, with a baby in his arms. He was dangerous. A sick psychopath.'

Matthew paused, his eyes wide at me. And at long last, something fell into place. That horribly cold sense of dread that had been growing within me was rising. My eyes met his. And then I knew what he had done. Knew where this was heading. Had I always suspected this to be the case? Had I known, deep down, that there was something troubling about the death of Titus's father? Maybe. But that wasn't what was burning within me, threatening to break out, to lash out, to make me tear down the house with rage. It was the fact he was only telling me now. That he'd let us build a life together, involved me so closely in the life of his adopted son, with this lie buried so deep into the fabric of our existence. In that moment, I wanted to scream. But I said nothing. I just waited, and before long, he took a deep breath and continued.

'I walked over to the hot tub and immediately lifted Titus out of the water. Thank God I arrived when I did as his head could have been submerged any second. Johnny had had him wrapped in a towel, which was soaked through with water. I picked up Johnny's discarded clothes on the floor and used them to dry the baby off, then I went inside, jiggling him in my arms, trying to stop him crying. Collette was asleep on the sofa. She stirred a bit when I came in and mumbled to shut the baby up. She may have thought I was Johnny. She had a massive joint in her right hand, which was resting up against the sofa. Considering they were living in a wooden cabin, the idea of them messing around with lit joints and flames terrified me. I took the joint from her fingers and crushed it out onto a plate on the coffee table. I put Titus down in his cot and he stopped crying after a minute or two. Then I went back out to the lounge. Collette had gone back to sleep and Johnny was still in the hot tub outside. Time sort of slows down for me from that point onwards. But I know quite clearly my thought processes as I watched what was happening. As I walked closer, I could see that Johnny's limp, pale body was sliding off the ledge inside the tub. And he was slipping deeper into the water. I expected him to take a gasp as the waterline went past his mouth. I expected an instinctive attempt to cling onto life to kick in. But it didn't. Then it crept past his nose as his head dropped forwards, submerging the rest of his face into the warm water. No thrashing. No wild attempts to save himself. He just slid under. And didn't come back up.'

It was time for me to speak now. For if I didn't, I feared I would scream. 'You didn't do anything to save him?' I said the sentence quietly, but my clenched teeth betrayed my trembling emotion. Matthew noticed and he looked devastated by the question.

'No. But … please … can't you understand? Can't you see why? He was *destroying* Collette's life. He put me and my mother in an impossible situation. We would have been forced to involve the police, lawyers, potentially land her in prison. Social services. Custody battles. And not to mention what he…' he stumbled, his voice quivering in a half sob, 'what he did to *me*. I still dream of that night. A bolt of panic runs through me whenever I see a children's animal mask. Have you ever wondered why sometimes I jerk awake in the early hours and struggle to get back to sleep? I'm *haunted* by it. Haunted by what he and his masked maniacs did to me.'

'Then why didn't you tell me?' I stopped myself from shouting, but I rose out of my seat and stood, in the centre of the lounge, unsure if I wanted to fly at him in rage or leave the room in protest, unable to cope with the depths of his secrets, the amount that had been unsaid between us. 'You told me you weren't there. You've always said... You've ... *lied* to me all this time.'

'Oh, come on, what good would it have done? That's not something anyone wants to know. That their husband is guilty of, what ... manslaughter? Maybe not even that. And besides, I prevented a death. The only reason Titus is alive upstairs now is because of me. Can't you celebrate that? Can't you cherish that one brilliant part of what happened?'

I was close to shouting at him that it was not enough, not enough to excuse the years of deception, but then something else struck me. I paused, then collapsed back down onto the sofa, my head in my hands, my fingers rubbing into my eyes. I allowed a few more seconds to tick on as I tried to make my heart slow down. Then I said, as calmly as I could, 'I still don't understand what the fuck this has to do with Rachel.'

Chapter Forty

RACHEL

Less than a week to go

In the nights leading up to the murder, I allowed myself to dwell on the past. Allowed myself to dwell on memories I normally tried to keep locked up. Doing so both stoked me up to press forward, and reminded me why it all mattered. As if I needed reminding.

Travelling over to Norway to find my brother was one of the most difficult, most stressful times in my life. Through talking to some of Collette Jones's university friends, and Johnny's business acquaintances, I'd discovered Matthew Jones had flown out to try and convince his sister to break up with my brother and come home. He was staying in a room in the main building of the posh hotel complex. Of course, I couldn't afford anything of the kind, what with my mounting credit-card debts and the less-than-secure state of my income. So I booked myself into a hostel on the outskirts of the forest, a half hour walk from the ski resort. It was a dreadful place – mix-gendered dormitories filled with penniless students going backpacking and various other unsavoury-looking characters. I was terrified. But I had to carry on, for the sake of my brother.

The first shock was to find out he was now a father, meaning I, of course, was now an aunt. I had no idea Collette was pregnant; they'd been out in Norway for so long at this point, and I think she stopped him from letting his family know. I hammered on the door for ages before it was opened by a sleepy-looking Johnny. His hair had grown from the close-shaved look he had when he was in England. It reminded me of when he was younger, his scruffy blond hair adding to his cheerful, sunny personality. I saw Collette wandering into view behind him in a dressing gown, clutching something making a mewing, coughing sound.

'Oh my God, Johnny,' I gasped, my hands rising to my mouth in shock. 'What have you done?'

That meeting didn't go well. He was either drunk or stoned and accusing me of 'stalking him like a fucking nutcase'. Things got heated pretty quickly the next day when I went back and told him it would break Mum's heart when she found out he'd had a child without telling her and that he needed to come home and we could work out what to do all together. He'd stood up, standing shakily in the hot tub he was sitting in, towering above me, told me I was being selfish and just wanted us to be a 'happy little family' which was, according to him, 'a fucking fantasy I needed to let go of'. He then called me a bitch and told me to fuck off. I knew it must be the alcohol or drugs talking, but I still looked back up at him in shock. That was when it caught my eye. The mark on his right arm. Little circular wounds, merging together into one blot. Needle marks. So he had started on heroin. And short of calling the cops and trying to land my own brother in a Norwegian jail, there wasn't anything I could do to stop it.

I only saw Matthew three times when I was there. Well, four times actually. But I wouldn't discover the third until a long time after. The first was when I saw him strolling towards the cabin on the first day I arrived, the second when I had journeyed into the main building of the hotel, desperate for a proper meal. I'd been buying snacks at a nearby petrol station, but on the third night couldn't bear it any longer. I went into the luxurious, warm main entrance of the hotel, and was about to be shown to a table in the restaurant when I saw the occupant of the one next to me. 'Oh please,' I said very quietly to the waiter, 'perhaps … a table near the back, by the windows?'

'Of course,' the waiter said, giving me a kind smile. Before I was led over to the other side of the restaurant, I glanced at the young man. He was pretty-boy handsome, and everything from his cream cable-knit jumper to his manicured nails shouted money and comfort. He was rubbing his eyes with his hands, and when he set them down on the table I saw his face. Stressed, tired, a man – no, a boy – out of his depth. I've often wondered, looking back, how things might have turned out differently if I'd gone to sit at that table and explained to him we were both there for the same reason. Offered to join forces in persuading our siblings to come home. But I didn't. I went and ate a horrendously expensive meal I couldn't really afford on the other side of the restaurant, and kept my head down for the rest of the evening.

The next day I went for a long walk around the grounds of the hotel, and into the forest that bled into its grounds. Even though I was in the process of giving up my studio and photography business and looking for other employment, I still carried my camera around with me to take occasional pictures. There was something about it that soothed me.

That was the day Johnny died. I flew back to England in the late afternoon. I would never forgive myself for not trying to visit him again. The body was returned to us in the UK – Collette wasn't married to him, and I don't know who they considered his next of kin, nor how the Norwegians worked the whole thing out, but eventually we were allowed to hold the funeral at home in Bradford. Collette came on her own. She sat at the back, sobbing quietly. None of us spoke to her.

The months and years that followed were almost unbearably difficult as my mother's cancer took hold, her grief over her son's death knocking down any fighting spirit she may have had. Her strict Catholic upbringing caused her to refuse to believe she had an illegitimate grandson out there in the world.

Years would go by before I would scroll through my old hard drive, about to be discarded, and stumble upon my photos from 2005. When I would realise what I had actually photographed, that day in the woods. How I had shot a clear view of Johnny and Collette's cabin. The figure in the hot tub on the deck. And the man standing over him. The man in a cream cable-knit jumper.

Chapter Forty-One

CHARLIE

Less than a week to go

Matthew continued to tell me his horrible story as I sat on the sofa with balled-up fists. How Rachel had joined him, the Gibsons, and their friends. How he hadn't really spoken to her, how she'd blended into the group of university friends the Gibsons had brought. He barely remembered seeing her. Now, he realised that she must have gone over there with a similar aim to his: to check on her sibling, make sure they weren't relapsing into old habits, and hope for their safe return home. After he'd said all this, it was enough for me to put two and two together.

'This is why she's been trying to get close to Titus. This is why she's been so weird. So keen to worm her way into our family, into our lives. And you, with your weird encouragement of her. So fucking naïve. And Christ, she struck gold, didn't she, living off Meryl's money over on Eaton Place.'

'Eaton Square,' he corrected.

'I don't give a fuck!' I was shouting now. 'How long have you known? How much danger has Titus been in while you've been keeping all your secrets close to your chest?'

'I only found out today. She confronted me. That's why we had to leave the party so quickly. I couldn't be anywhere near her. I can't be anywhere near her. That's why I'm telling you all this ... because of what she might do.'

I ran a stressful hand through my hair. 'What can she do? What did she say to you?'

Matthew looked very close to tears now, and as he reached a slightly shaking hand for his drink on the mantelpiece, I saw some tears slip from his eyes. 'She has a photograph. A photograph of me. Standing on the veranda. And Johnny's sitting in the hot tub. And I'm standing there, holding Titus. Watching him.'

I pinched the bridge of my nose, trying to take in oxygen slowly. 'And what is she going to do with this photograph? Try to go to the police? Blackmail us?'

I looked up at him shaking his head. 'I don't know. I was too sick to say anything. I just knew I had to get away from her.'

'And she's worked out the truth, has she?'

I saw a flicker of something in his face. He looked down, then back up to me, but there was an odd lack of focus in his gaze. 'Yes,' he said. 'She thinks I could have saved him.'

I got up. I'd had enough. I couldn't have taken any more

even if I'd wanted to. I was both exhausted yet so pumped with adrenalin I felt I could run a mile.

'Where are you going?'

'Out.'

He followed me to the hallway as I stepped into my shoes. 'Please. Can we talk about this?' He was properly crying now. And part of me wanted to comfort him. Wanted to gather him into my arms. Allow him to cry into my shoulder. But another part of me was on fire with a much darker, less forgiving emotion. It's how I always feel if I'm betrayed, deceived, left out of a loop. And this was one big fucking loop he'd left me out of. I took one last glance at the flushed, tear-stained face of my husband. Then I stepped out of the house, letting the door slam behind me.

I walked out onto the main road and along its steady curve up to Sloane Square. I didn't have any real destination in mind. No real direction. I just knew I had to walk. I only came to a stop once I reached Eaton Square. I didn't know Meryl's house number off by heart, but I slowed when I got to the part of the long, neat street where I thought she lived. Rachel was in one of these houses right now, assuming they'd already returned from the party. I could knock on the doors until I found her. Demand to know her side of the story. But I knew this was foolish. So I turned away and carried on walking. I passed garden squares. Houses with darkened windows. Busy late-night bars, loud with drunken merriment. Armed police officers outside embassies. I passed my mother's house on Wilton Crescent. I didn't think, I didn't dwell, I purposefully shut everything out as best I could, letting my feet take me away through the warm night. When I was in the midst of my stride, I thought I'd be able to walk far beyond Westminster, through the East End and out into Essex, perhaps even as far as Braddon, where I could shelter, alone in the large house, leaving my problems in London behind me. But in truth, I barely got much beyond my own postcode before I looped back round onto The Mall. I wandered in the direction of home, past Victoria, taking a brief detour onto Eccleston Square to pass my first adult home, fresh out of university. It felt like a lifetime ago now, like I was passing the former home of another person I vaguely knew, rather than myself.

With every step, one word circled my brain, pecking at me like a hostile bird: truth. Why was I so obsessed with it? Why did it matter so much? Why couldn't I let sleeping dogs lie? Matthew's deception had surely been to protect both me and Titus from a truth neither of us could do anything about. And, in the grand scheme of things, what he'd done hadn't been *murder*. Not really. The man probably deserved to die. Matthew wasn't beyond redemption or forgiveness, surely?

An image flickered in my mind. Dim and undefined at first, then suddenly it flared, bright and searing. The look on Matthew's face when I'd asked about Rachel.

And she's worked out the truth, has she?

There was something there. Something about that particular moment that sent shivers crawling over me.

I was outside a Sainsbury's on Elizabeth Street when it finally clicked. It was as if my world had exploded and a weight had been lifted off my shoulders at the same time. Because everything now made sense. And I knew absolutely why Matthew felt he could never tell me everything.

I arrived back at Carlyle Square at about twelve-thirty in the morning. The downstairs was all dark, but I could see as I got to the landing that the lights were on in both Titus's bedroom and mine. Ours. Matthew was sitting on the bed. He'd evidently been crying hard; I could see the red blotches under his eyes even in the dim light of the bedside lamp. There was something about his stillness that pricked the raging, burning anger inside me all over again. I'd calmed myself down as I'd approached the house, practised slow and steady breathing on the long walk back down the King's Road. And I tried now to make sure I retained this sense of calm as I closed the door gently behind me.

'I thought you might have gone to spend the night at Wilton Crescent,' he said, looking at the floor. 'What with your mother staying at the Ashtons's.'

I took off my blazer, folded it over, and hung it on the back of the chair near the window. I kept my moves slow and steady, though still felt the tremble of my hands as the material left my grasp.

'I thought about it,' I said, 'but in the end I just went for a walk. I went over to Eccleston Square. Just for a look around. But then I just came home.'

He glanced my way at this, confused. 'Your old place?'

I nodded.

'Why? I thought someone else now lives there.'

'I don't know why. Maybe I just wanted to go back to how things were before.'

A few beats of silence echoed crushingly between us. Then he said, 'Before you met me?'

I let the silence go on some seconds more. I chose not to acknowledge his question. After a few more seconds, he started to say how sorry he was, but I'd had enough. 'Please just stop,' I said, simply.

He looked at me as if I'd slapped him. I don't think I'd ever spoken to him so coldly before in my life. It's weird but, looking back, I think it might have been that moment, that tiny moment in the midst of this terrible time, that broke something vital within us. Like when an athlete tears an important ligament or breaks a tiny important bone, and although they can carry on walking and running or jumping or swimming, nothing is ever the same again. The pain continues to hamper, to hinder, to stop them hitting the heights that had come so naturally before.

When the silence became unbearable, I finally spoke. 'I've worked it out. I know what you did.'

Chapter Forty-Two

CHARLIE

Three days after the murder

My father walks into the library and sits down in one of the chairs. He nods at the seats opposite him, clearly suggesting my mother and I should get off the floor and sit down properly. We do as we're told. 'So you've told us the truth, at last,' he says, in a level tone.

I look at him and say cautiously, 'You knew?'

'I wouldn't be very good at my job if I didn't have good research resources,' my father replies, calmly. 'I found out today.'

'Charles, you kept this to yourself?' my mother says, turning to look at me. She looks a little lost, then a frown starts to line her brow. 'Has Rachel been stalking you, all this time? Planning this? But why would she want to kill Matthew?'

I don't know how much my father knows already, but

something within me knows it would be futile to dodge their questions any longer. I take a deep breath and, keeping my gaze on the coffee table in front of me, I tell them. I tell them what Matthew told me, just over a week ago, when we returned from the Ashtons's party. I tell them how Johnny Holden orchestrated an attack on Matthew and ruined Collette's life. How she gave birth to Titus in Norway, and how the eventual death of Johnny resulted in Matthew becoming a murderer. My parents listen in silence. Then my mother speaks.

'You've known this all this time and you didn't say anything?'

I look up at her and try to show in my eyes how difficult, how painful, this all is for me. 'I had to keep Matthew's secret. Telling anyone else would have put them – you – in an impossible situation.'

She lets out a tired, disappointed sigh. 'Yes, but when he was killed, this would have been a perfect thing to tell the police,' she says. 'It makes her motive clear.'

I hold out my hands, imploringly. 'How would I have explained not going to the police myself when I knew Matthew had murdered – or at least had a part to play in the death of – Rachel's brother? I stayed silent for days. I didn't go to the police and tell them anything when I found out, and besides, making it sound like it was to do with Rachel's crush on Matthew takes the attention away from Titus and makes it look like Rachel's just simply a psychotic jealous scorned lover.'

I look over to my father, hoping he will at least show he

understands the predicament I'm in. He fixes me with a hard stare, then speaks in his low, firm voice. 'You've been so incredibly stupid, Charles. The police will find this out. As we speak they'll be scouring Rachel's background and they'll make the connection, if they don't get it out of her first.'

Suddenly, my mother holds up her hand and says, 'Stop, Michael. This is all going to be OK. It will all work out the same in the end. They'll uncover the reasons, Rachel will go to prison for murder, and Charlie and Titus will be safe. Even if she decided to backtrack on her confession, this is still a pretty damning motive. As long as Titus holds his nerve.'

As she says this, I see my father looking between us both, looking even more grave and concerned than he did moments before. 'Part of me thinks it would be best if we didn't talk about this, but your mother has told me what Titus said to her the night before Matthew's murder. And I agree with your mother that Titus needs to be protected. He's got a great future ahead of him, I'm sure. It would be a tragedy if the police find out the real truth about this.'

I stay silent for a while after my father has said this. Then I stand up. I don't plan on leaving. I've done enough walking away from my troubles. I just go to the window, look out at the dying light of the late afternoon, then return to sit back down and face my parents. 'I'll be forever grateful that you're both ready to rally round a boy who isn't even your biological grandson. It means a lot to me. That you've both been there for him throughout his life.

And through all this. But I really have to ask: why are you so sure Titus killed Matthew?'

My mother and father stare back at me in amazement. 'But … I thought we all understood that that's … what happened, surely?' Cassandra says. Then her face changes. And she looks at me with a mixture of pity and horror.

Chapter Forty-Three

CHARLIE

The week of the murder

The morning after our night of hell, I woke to find Titus standing over me. I was on the sofa in the lounge, having been unable to spend the night next to Matthew after our discussion. I'd bypassed our guest bedroom and instead opted for the lounge – something to do with putting sufficient distance between us. Titus was fully dressed in a white Ralph Lauren shirt and light-blue shorts.

'What are you doing down here?' he asked, his expression unreadable. 'Did you and Dad argue? I heard the front door go a couple of times.'

I pulled myself up so I was leaning on the arm of the sofa, the material slightly rough against my bare arms. I hadn't wanted to return back upstairs to the same room as Matthew to get my pyjamas, so I'd shed my evening clothes and slept in my underwear, using a cashmere throw as a makeshift duvet. 'Yeah, we did,' I replied.

'About me?'

I looked back up at his face, seeing the hardness, the resolute toughness that had become more frequent over this past year.

'Sort of,' I said, being deliberately vague. If only he knew to what extent the whole thing was about him, and how he'd nearly died one cold night in Norway, he wouldn't look so unbreakable. 'Are you going out?' I asked, looking again at his attire.

'Yeah,' he said, brushing his fringe out of his face. 'I'm going over to Melanie's in Kensington for the day. Maybe the night too.'

This was something I hadn't expected. 'What? Melanie…? You mean … the eighteen year old?'

He nodded, and I could see in his eyes the slightest glint of satisfaction. He knew this news would disconcert me. Catch me off-guard.

'Yeah. Although she's nearly nineteen now.'

I noticed now the leather Mulberry travel holdall by his feet. 'You're … going to her place … to stay?'

He sighed in an over-the-top exasperated way. 'Calm down. Only for a night or two. I'm not leaving home.'

'But,' I spluttered, 'after yesterday? You and Pippa? And now you're going to see Melanie?'

He shrugged, a tiny grin edging at the corners of his mouth. 'Yeah, well, Pippa and I aren't exactly an item. So I'm still a free agent where that stuff's concerned.'

I looked at him in astonishment. Then I thought, should

it astonish me? I'd been in love with Rupert for most of my teens, but I certainly hadn't remained celibate throughout the intervening years before we'd become a proper item. But this was different. This was Titus. He was supposed to be young, innocent, a child, not some confident London Lothario sewing his wild oats left, right and centre. I thought about telling Matthew, bringing him down here, having it out with Titus, both of us a united front. And then, an instant after having this thought, I found I just didn't care. Fine. Let him do what he wanted. Let him try to shock us. If Titus's aim was to cause a stir and freak us out, he wasn't going to get it.

I let myself thud back onto the sofa and lay back down. 'OK. Whatever,' I said. 'Text us your plans when you know them.'

I could tell by the way he stayed there motionless that I'd surprised him.

'So … you're fine with me going to Melanie's?'

I shrugged my shoulders and pulled the cashmere over me as if I was going to go back to sleep. 'Sure. Just use a condom this time, OK?' I closed my eyes and turned away from him.

Still he didn't move. Then, after what felt like an age, he finally said, 'I don't know what's going on here but it's driving me up the fucking wall.' Then I heard him grab his bag and stomp out of the lounge. The slam of the front door followed quickly after.

I got up off the sofa and, fishing my phone out of my trousers from the floor, walked slowly upstairs, unsure if I was going to find my husband in bed asleep or ready to start up the conversation we'd been having the night before. In actual fact, neither was the case. The bed was empty and made, although not quite as neatly as how Jane did it. I showered whilst my phone was on charge and came back to see a string of messages from Matthew. Three were sent around midnight last night when I was out on my long walk, and the fourth was sent at 6.40am this morning. It read:

We both need some thinking time. I've gone up to Scotland to stay in the castle for a few days. I left a message for Titus but if he asks tell him he can call me. I love you.

I put the phone down without replying.

The night before had ended with Matthew confessing everything to me. The true story about what had happened to Johnny Holden that night on the veranda in Norway. How Matthew had been … modest about the level of his involvement in his death.

After I told him I knew he had murdered Johnny, Matthew sort of collapsed. I watched, not going over to the bed to comfort him. Just watched calmly, waiting for him to pick himself up and stop shaking enough to talk. His worst nightmares were becoming real before his eyes and I couldn't bring myself to display the compassion he so desperately wanted in that moment. I did, however, avoid shouting and raging. I stayed calm. I asked him to explain.

Although, of course, there wasn't really much to explain after I'd worked it out. Just for him to correct a small detail: that he hadn't stood by to watch as Johnny had sunk slowly under the water and drowned of his own accord. Instead, he'd helped Johnny on his way, laying a hand on his shoulder to tip him off the ledge into the hot tub and under the water's surface.

He carried on making his excuses, going round and round, saying the same thing over and over again about how it was his only choice, he just wanted to save his sister, it was a moment of madness but he acted out of love. 'Was it though?' I eventually cut in. He blinked at me, confused by the question. 'Was it entirely out of love?' I clarified. 'Or was it something else?'

'What do you mean?' he said, although Matthew wasn't stupid. I think he'd worked out the point I was making.

'Well, you said yourself how much of an effect Johnny's attack had on you. How his awful treatment of you that night in the grounds of the castle had haunted you. So I'm asking: are you sure you killed Johnny because of the danger posed to your sister? Or for another reason? Like ... revenge.'

He kept his eyes on me. Staring wide. Pleading. 'I just wanted to save my sister.'

Another lie. I knew it as soon as I heard it. Whether it was because he couldn't admit it to himself or because he couldn't bear telling it to me, I don't know. But after that moment, I didn't want to hear any more.

'Well then, that was a fairly pointless reason, wasn't it?' I said, flatly. 'Because she died less than a month later. You know, if Johnny Holden had still been alive, and they'd been together when she took that industrial dose of heroin, maybe he'd have been able to save her.' I knew my words were cruel, but I said them anyway. They didn't bring me satisfaction as such; they were more anaesthetic to my pain and anger and a steadily churning nausea that had started to rise within me once more.

Ignoring Matthew's pleas to stay, I went to the bed, picked up a pillow and told him we'd speak in the morning. I was done.

Of course, we didn't end up speaking in the morning. We wouldn't end up speaking until the day he died.

Chapter Forty-Four

CHARLIE

The week of the murder

The heat wave that had engulfed the south of England from mid-June to late July burnt itself out as we entered August. Suddenly the skies were grey, the temperature was colder, and autumn was definitely on the horizon. Golden leaves littered the pavements of Chelsea; they'd fallen prematurely due to the searing heat, and now, coupled with the colder weather, gave the impression of October rather than late summer.

Matthew stayed away from the house for five days. Part of me wondered if he'd ever return at all.

I couldn't face going into the office, so told them I was unwell and stayed in the house, unsure what to do with my time. Things reached an apex when Jane started hoovering around me, so I tried to do something productive – from reading to exercise – but conflicting senses of both tiredness and buzzing restlessness consumed me.

On Tuesday morning, when I was answering a few work emails on my iPad at the breakfast bar in the kitchen, I heard the thud of the front door and then a bag being dropped onto the carpet. My heart instantly started to pound, expecting Matthew to stroll into the kitchen, but it wasn't Matthew. It was Titus.

The realisation was both one of relief and disappointment. I wasn't even sure what footing I was on with the boy at the moment after our borderline row on Sunday morning. He'd sent me a message the day before that just read *Still alive*, but nothing more.

'You've decided to move back home, have you?' I said, meaning it to sound only semi-serious.

'I hadn't moved out,' Titus said, coolly. He wandered over to the fridge and drank some orange juice from the container, then filled up a glass.

'So how was the shag-athon?'

Titus narrowed his eyes as he surveyed me across the kitchen countertop. 'That's a bit … I don't know, inappropriate.'

I shrugged a little. 'Well, if you're going to act inappropriately, womanising all round London before you're of age to do so, I don't think I'll bother sugar-coating my language.'

He set the glass down with a thud. 'Where's Dad?'

'Scotland,' I replied, starting to type out nonsensical rubbish in an email just to make a point of showing my attention was elsewhere.

I saw Titus watching me still and after a few more seconds I paused and turned off the device. 'Things are just a bit … a bit, well … your dad needed some space for a few days. Things will be back to normal soon, I promise.'

A flicker of sadness entered his eyes, and I saw a glimpse then of the kind, loving, sensitive boy that had been gradually growing harder to see over the past few months. I moved round the kitchen island and put a hand on his shoulder. 'Are you OK?'

His jaw jutted out a little and his lips tightened as if he were trying not to cry. He then sniffed and gave a curt nod. 'Yeah, fine.' He took a step back from me and said, 'I'm going to go upstairs and take a shower. Pippa's coming round.'

That made me freeze. 'What?'

He adopted the same slightly belligerent, matter-of-fact tone he'd had on Sunday morning when he told me he was off to stay at Melanie's Kensington flat. 'Yeah, she's in town with some friends on a trip to Harrods and said she'd pop by. She might bring a friend with her.'

My mouth opened and shut like a fish as I tried to think of a response to this. 'She … she just thought she'd pop by, did she?'

This earned a shrug from Titus. 'Yeah. Don't worry, we'll keep to my room.'

I gaped at him, 'But … you've *literally* just got back from Melanie's. And whatever you were doing there for two whole days, I'll bet it wasn't just tea and crumpets. And now you've got Pippa just *dropping by*, maybe with a *friend* in tow?'

The tumbler landed on the floor with a smash, spraying the hard tiled ground with tiny glass fragments. It hadn't been aimed to hit my head, but the shock shook me so thoroughly it felt like Titus had pulled a gun on me. 'Just back the fuck off, OK?' he shouted at me. 'Just because you two now live practically like priests or brothers doesn't mean I need to with my friends.'

His words astonished me. 'What did you say?'

'You know what I mean. You guys don't fuck any more. Haven't for ages.'

I could feel the blood rising to my face, and a nest of panic and anxiety that was already close to the surface was now flooding through me. 'That is none of your ... and how the hell would you know about our sex lives?'

'We live under the same roof! It's not a huge house. My room is next to yours.'

Images flashed through me. Me laying a hand on Matthew and him moving away. The time I tried to follow him into the shower and him stepping out of it. The weeks and weeks going past without him properly touching me. Us briefly attempting sex in New York but opting for sleep instead before we'd got very far. Me trying to keep up the pretence that there wasn't something wrong, some change that was growing between us. And now here was our teenage son, proving that my efforts to keep up an everything's-fine façade had been in vain.

I thought about telling him we do it quietly or when he's out, but the thought of even speaking about the subject made my stomach turn. And, of course, it would have been lies. All lies. And lies were something I hated. But before I'd thought up a dignified response, he'd walked off, stomping up the stairs, then slamming the bathroom door. I heard the hum as the boiler kicked into action.

It took me a while to locate a dustpan and brush – not usually my domain – and I'd just finished sweeping up the last splinters of glass when I heard movement on the stairs. Titus stood by the door to the kitchen, dressed in a crisp new shirt and chinos, though he hadn't yet put any shoes or socks on.

'I've come to say sorry,' he said. He put it in a brisk, business-like way, as if it were a task on his to-do list he didn't really want to complete, but knew he probably should.

I sighed as I poured the glass into the bin and set the cleaning implements aside. 'It's fine. I'm sorry I made you angry.'

Even though I wasn't properly looking at him, I could hear Titus's breathing. There was something else he wanted to say. 'I shouldn't have said those things … about you and Dad and … well … I don't think you're like priests.'

Against my better judgement, this made me laugh. 'I'm pleased to hear it. I didn't realise our … problems were so noticeable.'

We were both silent for a few moments, then I spoke again, this time addressing something that had just struck me. 'When you say … well … you implied that you can hear things. From our room. Can you hear things clearly?'

It was Titus's turn to blush now. 'A bit. But it's fine. Melanie hears her Mum and step-father at it all the time.'

I shook my head. 'I didn't mean that. I meant … can you hear us talk?'

An odd expression passed across his face. 'Are you accusing me of eavesdropping?'

Keen to avoid setting him off again, I waved my hand to reassure him. 'No, no, not at all. I just ... I was worried ... did you hear our discussion on Saturday night ... in the early hours?'

I was desperately trying to think back to that night, the dreamlike quality to those small hours when I'd come back from my pounding of the streets, gone upstairs and told Matthew I'd worked out what he'd done. Figured out his lies. Had Titus still had his music on? Or had I, in the sheer terrible impact of the moment, forgotten about him entirely?

'Why?' Titus asked, still looking at me strangely. 'Were you talking about me?'

Now that was the question. Because, in one way, Titus was exactly who we were talking about. The way he'd survived almost certain death. How he had been saved. And how someone else hadn't.

I opened my mouth, took a deep breath, and said, 'If you heard anything, you can tell me.'

Our eyes met and for a moment I thought I saw something within them – a tightening, a sharpening, something hard and resolute, walled-up and impenetrable. Or maybe I just imagined it. When you're looking back, it's hard not to let what would happen later influence your view of events. In truth, maybe there'd been nothing in Titus's eyes to betray any hidden knowledge. In fact, before he'd even had a chance to reply to me, the doorbell had sounded and he'd walked off to answer it.

I watched from the kitchen as Pippa Ashton, mercifully

on her own, stepped into the hallway, clocking my presence in an instant then quickly looking away. She looked as if she'd just stepped off a fashion shoot for Burberry, and paused only to hang up her coat.

I pottered about the kitchen for a while, trying not to imagine what was going on upstairs. Part of me felt like I should make my presence known – perhaps choose this moment to execute a Marie Kondo-style excavation of all clothes, shoes, and books in the house, and clatter around noisily with cardboard boxes destined for charity donations in the hope the noise would put Titus and Pippa off. But, of course, I didn't do this. In fact, all hopes of me going upstairs were dashed when I started my ascent towards the main bedroom to change into my gym attire and I heard a rhythmic thudding and moaning coming from the direction of Titus's bedroom. I turned on my heel automatically and sat in the kitchen eating reheated lasagne feeling conflicted, cross, and confused. I needed Matthew to deal with this situation. He was my touchstone where Titus was concerned. The man of discipline and decisive action. I opened my phone to take a look at Instagram and saw my follower count had stalled; people were messaging to ask where I'd gone, lots of people debating whether I'd 'just given up' or if 'something bad had happened'.

I was about to type back a bit of a terse response to a few of them when I heard a commotion happening upstairs, a loud banging, like a door being slammed, then someone shouting, 'Just leave me the fuck alone!'

It was Titus. He was shouting and then the sound of crying reached my ears as a dishevelled Pippa ran down the stairs and started to pull on her coat – back to front to begin with – and cursing at herself when the arms wouldn't fit.

'Shit, SHIT!' she shouted, flapping the thing.

'Pippa, are you all right?' I asked, going into the hallway to help her. 'What's wrong?'

'She's leaving.' Titus's voice sounded from the landing, echoing impressively, like some god speaking from above.

Pippa threw one terrified look my way and then flew out of the front door, leaving it crashing behind her.

'Did you upset her or something?' I said, turning to Titus. 'She looked really rattled.' I started to march up the stairs when I didn't get a response. 'So what happened then? Did she find out about your other woman?'

I arrived at his doorway in time to see him pulling on some trainers and a hoodie. 'I'm going out!' he barked at me through his tears.

I rubbed at my face, taking in a deep breath, trying not to let this new drama be the thing that caused me to snap. 'Please, just sit down and tell me what's wrong.' He ignored me, shoving my shoulder out the way as he exited the room and ran down the stairs. The front door crashed closed again after him, leaving me wondering what the Maxwell-Foxes next door must be thinking of us.

I considered going after Titus, or getting the car out and crawling the streets of London looking for him. But I didn't. I went back to the kitchen and sat, silently, my thoughts running around in my head. Morning turned into afternoon, and still I sat. When it reached 2pm, I ate a strawberry yoghurt, tried watching some television, then eventually phoned Titus. To my surprise, he picked up. 'Hello?' he said. His voice sounded groggy, as if he'd been asleep.

'Titus, please tell me where you are. What happened earlier? Are you all right?'

Perhaps I shouldn't have pressed three demands for answers upon him, because my questions were greeted with silence.

'Titus, please. I know things are difficult and I wish I could give you more answers but … can you just tell me where you are? Then we can talk a bit and you can explain what upset you.' When silence greeted this once more, a sudden thought hit me. 'You haven't gone to find your dad, have you?'

He let out a mocking laugh. 'Christ. I'm not in Scotland. I'm at Granny's. She's out though.' There it was again, that strange slurred quality. Had he been drinking?

'Stay there. I'm coming for you.'

'No, don't. What the fuck is the point? Just … leave me alone…'

'Just stay where you are.'

The call went dead. He'd hung up. Cursing myself for not handling it better, I grabbed my car keys, exited the house and threw myself into the BMW and started the engine. A hold-up due to a broken-down bus outside Peter Jones caused me to start hyperventilating. Why I was panicking so much, I didn't know, but something in Titus's tone had troubled me beyond anything the day had thrown up so far. Something so bleak, bitter, furious. It was like he was transforming into a force I had never thought I'd have to reckon with – something unpredictable, filled with rage, the polar opposite to the Titus I had known and cared for and loved like my own son for most of his life. Just as the traffic started to move, my phone rang. 'Titus?' I shouted into it without registering the caller ID.

'No, it's me,' said the voice of my mother, calmly. 'But Titus is here.'

I let out a sigh of relief. 'Oh, you're home. That's … that's good. Sorry to shout, it's been … well, things are a bit tricky right now.'

'As I can imagine,' my mother said. 'But at least that's one thing off your mind. Titus is safe here at Wilton Crescent and you don't need to worry about him.'

'I was. Worried, that is. Really worried. He sounded drunk on the phone. I was worried he was doing something stupid or reckless…'

My mother let out a slightly exasperated sigh. 'Darling, he's almost a young man. He isn't ten years old. The drink will wear off and he'll soon calm down.'

'So he's drunk, is he?' I said, the volume of my voice rising again. 'At fifteen years old in the middle of the afternoon. And where did he get it from, anyway?'

'And you were never drunk at fifteen, were you?' she said, slightly archly. 'Charles, can you just give the boy some breathing room, just for today? He'll stay the night here and I'll drive him over to Chelsea tomorrow morning. How does that sound?'

I nodded, even though she couldn't see me. 'Fine,' I said.

'OK. I'm sorry for getting worked up. It's just … everything's been a bit strange…'

'Ever since you left the Ashtons's on Saturday?' she asked. She didn't sound too inquisitive, but I couldn't face an interrogation from her about that now.

'Yes,' I said. 'And a bit before… I can't really explain it now.'

A large Range Rover hooted behind me; I'd failed to move on a green light. I touched the accelerator and, in a split second, made the decision to continue driving deeper into Belgravia rather than turning back for home. Something odd was happening here and I wanted to have it out with my mother and Titus without delay.

'We can talk about all this another time,' my mother continued. 'Although, darling, perhaps don't reach out to the Ashtons today, or even any time soon. I think it will be for the best.'

I digested this sentence for a bit before answering. 'What do you mean?' I said. 'Reach out? That's a strange way to put it. Reach out about what?' The image of Pippa running down the stairs, her tear-stained face looking at me with fear etched upon it, floated to the surface of my mind. Not quite believing I was now having to ask this question of my own mother, I once again uttered the words that had been most on my mind all day. 'What's going on?'

I heard my mother's slow intake of breath. She held it for a few seconds, then exhaled slowly, buying herself time. 'Just … give me this time with Titus.'

'Does this have something to do with Rachel?'

She ignored this question. 'We're going to talk some

things through. Then I'll bring him home. And then you and I will go out for a little chat.'

The steady poisonous flow of anxiety was seeping through my body. That horrible, paranoid feeling you get when the walls are closing around you. *They all know something*, I thought to myself. Titus, Matthew, the Ashtons, even my mother. After everything I'd been through with Matthew, all the secrets that had been brought to the surface, there was still a vital ingredient I wasn't quite seeing.

'Charles, darling? Are you still there?'

I took a left without indicating, causing a hoot of outrage from another driver. 'I'm coming to yours now,' I said.

'No, Charles, really…'

I cut the call. I'd see her in less than a minute, anyway.

I managed to dial down my reckless driving as I came out onto the stately surroundings of Belgrave Square – too many Met police vans around for *Fast and Furious* antics – and before long I was slowing down as I arrived outside the pleasingly curved stretch of houses on Wilton Crescent. The door to my mother's house opened before I'd even parked. She had her arms folded and although she didn't look angry, exactly, she was evidently troubled in her controlled, fuss-free sort of way.

'Charles, please do as I ask and go back home.'

I stared at her. 'How can you ask me that when Titus is inside, smashed out of his mind?'

'He is not smashed out of his mind,' she said, cutting me off. 'He is a little upset at the moment, a tad worse for wear, but he'll be fine before long and I request you give him the chance to be upset without becoming a meddlesome parent and making things worse. Even with the best of intentions.'

Rage ignited the worry within me. 'Meddlesome parent?' I snapped. 'Is that what you think I am? At least I'm there for him, living under the same roof. At least I haven't swanned off to Belgravia and splashed out on some Regency palace all for myself.'

I knew as soon as I'd finished that I had gone too far. Hurt flashed across my mother's face, followed by a tightening that I had come to associate with her infrequent bursts of anger. She stepped onto the pavement so she was closer to me and said, 'Charles, please pay me the compliment of presuming I know what I'm doing. Go home, go to work, just keep yourself occupied until I've had time to get things sorted. And stop shouting in the street, or you'll disturb everyone at the High Commission of Singapore.' She nodded to the house on her left. Then she turned on her heel and walked back inside and closed the front door.

I stood motionless on the pavement for almost a full minute, then got back into the car. Every movement felt like a mountain of effort, as if my body had taken on rigor mortis. With fingers that felt numb and brittle, I switched on the engine and slowly turned out onto the road towards Piccadilly. If I'd known that the worst of that day was yet to come, I may not have even managed that.

Chapter Forty-Five

CHARLIE

The day before the murder

The final part of that cold, unseasonably autumnal day in August would become one of the worst times in my life. Not the worst day of my life. That would follow on soon after.

It began with me driving to The Ritz to get drunk. This was something I used to do during my later teens and early twenties; if life got too bothersome, I'd reach for the brandy or vodka, or if I was really desperate, whatever beer there was to hand. I had my car parked for me, settled myself in a corner of the Rizzoli Bar, and was sinking into a pit of rumination when my phone buzzed with an email. It was to my personal account, not my work account, otherwise I wouldn't have paid it any notice. And the preview on the notification made my stomach lurch.

FROM: Rupert Ashton, SUBJECT: Something important

I unlocked the phone at once and accessed the message, almost knocking over my glass of brandy in my haste.

I read Rupert's words through once. Then again. It was a long email, and it took me a long time to allow the words to fully sink in. Then, afterwards, things started to get … well, to get dark.

Dearest Charlie,

This is a very difficult email to write. In fact, it may well be one of the hardest things I've had to do. These past couple of years have tested me. I've truly started to appreciate what the words 'stress' and 'anxiety' actually mean after a lifetime of using the terms casually and without thought.

So. Where to begin? I should start where this whole situation began for me, and that was at the Old Bailey two years ago during the trial of Ernest Kellman, James Knight, and Peter Catton. I had spent the afternoon giving evidence about our time at Oxford. I won't go into the details of that, as I'm sure you're very familiar with the case and my connection to those involved. That in itself has caused me many a sleepless night, wondering if I should have realised something sooner, acted sooner, told someone of my suspicions. But I was weak. I ignored signs. I buried my head in the sand. And I promised myself I would never do that again. Which is one of the reasons why I can't stay quiet any longer and why I'm writing you this email. My mother would advise me to keep out of business that doesn't concern me, but because of our shared history, I feel this business does concern me. We're all tied up in this. We're all culpable. Except you. You're the most innocent one out of all of us.

So, to come to the point: your husband and my sister, Elena, are having an affair. And I am so sorry to have to tell you this. On my day of giving evidence in court, I dropped in on her at her Knightsbridge flat. I had been very nervous about my court appearance and didn't want to return to the Chester Square house alone. Elena was there, and so was Matthew. They were having sex in the dining room; I could see them as soon as I walked down the hallway. There was music playing – Vivaldi's 'Cessate, omai cessate' – and they hadn't heard me come in. I was about to leave the house immediately, since it's rather awkward finding one's sister having sex with her husband, but of course the man wasn't her husband. When I saw Matthew's face, I can't describe to you the shock – although I fancy it must be a mere atom of the shock you must be feeling now, reading this. That is, of course, presuming you don't know? In some ways, I've always thought ignorance is bliss. I know you, Charlie. I know you're far from stupid. Even if you are not aware of what has been happening between Matthew and Elena, I expect you have been suspicious. Certain signs must have set off warning bells. I tried to tell you all this when I saw you at the weekend, but I didn't get a chance.

I wish I could make the blow easier by telling you it was just the one time, one moment of madness for which Matthew must have suffered hours of guilt. But it wasn't just the one time. It's been going on for a while now, and, well, it's happening now.

Matthew is at Ashton Manor as we speak. I saw his car parked in one of the more secluded areas, where we keep the motors we don't often use. I only went via the house to pick up some suits I left there at the weekend. I don't know where you think he currently is, but it's likely he's lied to you.

Honesty was always at the heart of our relationship. It didn't fall apart due to dishonesty, but instead because we could only ever be honest with each other. That may well be the better way to be, but it didn't mitigate the pain of losing you. I've always liked Matthew and have always been happy that you've been happy. But I know how much you value the truth and the clarity it brings to a situation, and if I carried on keeping this secret, I fear it would stain the friendship we've managed to sustain over these years.

You probably get the sense that I'm tiptoeing around saying something here, so I'll just come out and say it: I love you, Charlie. I always have and always will. I suspect difficult times may lie ahead for you, and I wanted to make it clear that whatever support you need, whether that be friendly advice, a shoulder to cry on, someone to whisk you away or simply help you forget about the pains of the day, I am here for you. I'd better stop there, because I fear this letter is teetering dangerously on the verge of becoming poetry – or worse, song lyrics. But I mean what I say. Please consider it. Whatever you need, I am here.

With much love, always,

Rupert.

I suppose one could say this moment was that important tipping point. The moment when a course of action is decided that will affect the lives of many for years to come. Was it at that point I decided to do what I did? I can't be quite sure. When did I know I was capable of it? Was it when I got that email, basically giving me both a motive and a happy ever after? Although of course, if that were the case, wouldn't it have been easier to divorce Matthew and walk off into the sunset with Rupert without the threat of prison hanging over me?

Of course, it isn't that clear cut.

A perfect storm had to be created in order to get me to that point, and I was already being battered around by it while sitting in The Ritz, getting drunk on expensive glass after glass. But no, I didn't pre-plan it, not in scrupulous detail or with any degree of criminal ingenuity. I just sat there and imagined it. Imagined all the ways I could hurt Matthew the way he had hurt me. It wasn't that the love I had felt for him over the years had vanished; if anything that fuelled the violence of my imagination. After all, they say love and hate are closely related. And, by God, they are.

It was Archie I ended up calling. There are some moments when you realise your best mate from school knows you better than anyone – even those you're supposed to love. I slurred my words down the line, telling him that it was all over with Matthew. He drove down to The Ritz and was there within half an hour, not that time meant much to me by that point. He helped me stagger out of the bar, bundled me into his car, and drove me off to his house in Park Crescent.

I woke up in a state of dizzy disorientation the next morning in one of his guest rooms amidst the cool, new-feeling sheets, and wearing a pair of Ralph Lauren Polo Sport tracksuit bottoms that weren't mine. My brain was filled with hangover fog, and with a mounting sense of horror I remembered the revelations of the previous day. Rupert's email, the rise in anger and hatred towards Matthew. My sense of hurt and betrayal was still raw within me, as if I'd just discovered a physical gaping wound on my body.

I padded across the landing, barefoot and feeling a little chilly. I heard some noise coming from downstairs and before I could get to the final step I heard Archie's voice.

'That you, Charles?' he called out.

I went down into the hallway and found Archie sitting in the kitchen. 'How are you?' he said, looking uncertainly at me over the rim of his coffee. Without waiting for a response, he got up and poured me a cup from the machine. I took it from his outstretched hand and sat down at the table.

'I'm … not sure.' I took a sip of the warm, dark liquid, not properly tasting it.

'Well, considering how out of it you were last night, I'd say that's not as bad as things could be.' He was still watching me intently, as if I might start shouting or crying.

'You should look at your phone,' he said, and got up and walked over to the kitchen counter.

'My phone?' I replied, puzzled.

'Your clothes are being washed. You were sick on them. I

put your phone on charge down here.' He went to the end of the kitchen countertop and unplugged my iPhone. 'Of course, I wouldn't normally read your messages, but I couldn't help notice one that popped up on the screen this morning.'

With an unreadable expression, he passed me the phone, the movement causing the screen to light up. And I saw what he meant instantly.

I'm coming home. Should be there by 7pm. We could have food in and talk about things? I could pick up some Ottolenghi? I love you.

Matthew was coming home.

Suddenly, the little safe-haven of Archie's house felt under threat. The real world was going to come spilling in.

'I don't want to see him,' I said.

'So what are you going to do? Ignore the problem?'

I noticed the breakfast pastries and fruit on the table and helped myself to a pear. I cut it up, thinking about my answer, trying to do a temperature test of my own feelings. You see, to some it may sound insane to say it, but even at that point I knew exactly what I needed to do. What I *wanted* to do was go back upstairs to Archie's guest bedroom and spend the day pretending I didn't have a husband, or an adopted teenage son who was acting out, or a mother who wasn't being honest with me. But that was different to what I *needed* to do. And that, to me, was obvious.

I was intelligent enough to know that most people wouldn't be able to make such a mental leap. I also knew that it would be a mistake to tell Archie about my plan. Like so many others, he wouldn't have appreciated the clear beauty in justice for betrayal. Corrective action for lies that have been told. I remember once Matthew looking through a copy of the *Sunday Telegraph* and remarking on a piece about a woman who had killed her cheating husband by driving off a cliff in a murder-suicide gone wrong. He died. She survived. And so did his lover, their mutual friend who was in the back of the car and able to tell the police about the argument that had unfolded and how the woman behind the wheel deliberately accelerated towards the cliff edge in an attempt to kill them all. Matthew had said that the woman who killed her husband can't have truly loved him, otherwise she wouldn't be able to inflict the risk of life-changing injuries or, as it turned out, death upon him. He could be so naïve sometimes. So I told him it was *because* she loved him so much that she was completely capable of doing so. Love was the vital ingredient. And when combined with betrayal, the resulting reaction can have the power of a nuclear bomb.

'I won't ignore him,' I said, finally meeting Archie's gaze.

'What are you going to do?' he asked. His voice was still calm and free from fear or accusation. But there would be many times in the future when I would wonder if he knew then how all this would turn out. Because what he said next suggested he always had a good measure of me. And the type of person I was, or would one day become.

'I would urge you, Charles, to pause before deciding to do anything substantial.'

I frowned at him. 'Substantial?'

Archie held my gaze, then spoke slowly, as if choosing his words with great care. 'I think we both know that you don't react well to being betrayed. You don't take kindly to being made a fool of. I wouldn't want you, or your anger, to drive you to do something … irreversible.'

We continued to look at each other, neither of us speaking for a long time.

Then he said, 'Charlie, I think we both know what I'm referring to.'

I knew. Though I'd forgotten how well he knew *me*. How much I had let him see of me in the past, and how much that must be worrying him now. Archie was the only person I'd ever really spoken to about the thoughts I had when I was young. The thoughts I'd always had, if I'm honest. One night when we were both sixteen, he'd come over to spend the night in St George's Square. I used to find the holidays without him rather tough. He was the best friend a guy could have at Eaton and we'd find every excuse to be in each other's company when we weren't at school – to the point where, when people heard that I was gay, they presumed Archie was my lover. This wasn't true. There was nothing sexual at all about our close friendship, but there was a deep foundation of love that had never gone away. And because of this, that night in my bedroom when we were sixteen while my Dad was out at his club, no doubt blackmailing some government minister into creating another legal loophole to his benefit, I spoke to Archie candidly about my deepest secret. About how often my mind would turn to violent thoughts. A yearning for violence. For retribution to be meted out to those who wronged me.

'When do you think about these things?' he'd asked, turning to face me.

'Every day,' I replied. 'When someone upsets me, when a teacher mocks me, when it's clear someone I fancy doesn't fancy me, when someone pushes past me rudely in the street…' I remember his eyes looking into mine as we lay together on my bed, a horror movie VHS playing in the background.

'Tell me some of the things you think about,' he said. He kept his tone calm and measured, but I could tell his interest had been piqued.

'Just … hurting them. Kicking their teeth in. Stabbing them in the heart. Watching them bleed.' His eyes widened just a jot at this but, credit to him, he didn't even flinch.

'Is this … a sex thing?' Archie had asked, frowning a little. The suggestion of this hadn't angered me – it just sort of baffled me.

'No, not at all.'

I could tell this slightly puzzled him. I think if it had been a 'sex thing' he'd have at least been able to chalk it up to sadism or a weird kink. But without that context, he wasn't going to understand fully. I knew then and there that whilst I wouldn't receive any judgement or criticism from Archie on the subject, I wasn't going to get any answers. It was clear that he would never really appreciate the sense of completion, the sense of satisfying inevitability of imagining hurting people, and using this as a kind of weapon against others every day of my life. Although his next words had given me some inkling of a deeper disapproval: 'Perhaps ... don't talk to anyone else about it though. Wouldn't want them getting the wrong idea about you.'

He gave me a small smile, but there was something else in his eyes that I couldn't quite put my finger on. Disappointment, perhaps? Or concern, maybe? I looked at his face for a few more seconds but there were no other clues, no other ticks of repulsion or fear, so I pulled my eyes away from him and turned back to the film we had been watching.

Now, two decades on from that conversation, its reverberations still echoed between us. A teenage boy's confession to his best friend, coming back to haunt two grown adults at the brink of middle-age. Occasionally, throughout the years, Archie had touched on this conversation. I think it had been his way of cautioning me against my own nature. Steering me onto the right path. My mind flicked back for a second to the lunch we'd had earlier in the year, when he'd referenced my assault on Jasper King at school. One of his little warnings, perhaps, to keep me on my guard. Remind me of what is right and what is wrong.

I thought of all the things I could say to him in that moment. Reassure him. Tell him I wouldn't do anything terrible. Anything 'irreversible'. But I couldn't bear to go near the subject. Instead, I just told him I was going to pick

Titus up from my mother's, then go home and have a think about things.'

Archie raised an eyebrow. 'Things?'

'The future. Between me and Matthew.'

Archie took his time selecting an apple from the bowl of fruit in front of him, in the end opting for a deep red Gala. There was something slightly less tense in his face, as if my words had reassured him a little. He cut his apple slowly and said, not looking at me, 'And Rupert?'

The name, spoken aloud, sent a shiver down my back.

'Rupert?'

Archie allowed his eyes to meet mine now. 'Well, he does have a part to play in all this, doesn't he? A big part.'

I didn't say anything and, after a moment, Archie continued, 'From the sounds of the email – and if you don't remember, you pushed your phone upon me and demanded I read it – it appears that you have a choice laid out in front of you.'

I frowned. 'What choice is that?'

Archie chewed thoughtfully, then swallowed and said, 'Stay married to Matthew. Try to find a route through all of this shit. Or walk off into a fairy-tale sunset with the Prince Charming of your dreams?'

He was right. But, of course, it was never a future I could contemplate. I firmly expected to go to prison for what I was about to do. I was vaguely aware of the possibility that my father, through his labyrinthine connections in law and government, might be able to save me from incarceration through some clever defence in court, but all of that was just background noise. Just a distraction from the clear course of action: make Matthew understand his betrayal in the clearest and most severe way possible.

'Just a word of caution,' Archie said, 'fairy-tale endings rarely work as neatly in real life.'

I nodded. 'I know. And don't worry. I'm under no illusion that this will end well.'

Chapter Forty-Six

CHARLIE

Three days after the murder

My mother stares at me. She opens her mouth to speak, closes it again, then finally says, 'I never would have thought it possible … that you could kill Matthew.'

'You never thought I would be capable?' I ask.

She shakes her head. 'Never of something like that.'

Had Matthew been surprised, too? When he realised what I was doing, a split second before the knife slid into him. Had he been shocked that his husband was – always had been – capable of murder? I guess I'll never know.

But perhaps that was what he'd been trying to say as he'd struggled and gasped, trying to cling on to life.

After.

That's what I thought he'd said. Maybe he'd been about to say 'After all this time…'? After all this time, how could I do such a thing to someone I loved? This question carries me off into my own thoughts for some moments, then, when I return to the here and now, I give voice to a more pressing, practical one. 'Why were you so quick to think Titus had killed Matthew?'

My mother and father exchange a glance, then she says something that takes me by surprise. 'Because he told me he wanted to. When he came over to my house, the day you thought he was missing. He was very upset. Somehow he'd found out Matthew was cheating on you. He wouldn't tell me who it was or how he'd found out. He was so distraught at the idea that Matthew *could* cheat on you. It appalled him. He's always seen you two as the epitome of a stable home. He said he hated him. Wanted him dead. I told him not to tell you, that I would think of a way to let you know. And then, two days later, when I got your call to say Matthew had been stabbed … and the slip-up you made when you said to me, "Rachel has confessed, she's taking the … she's confessed to the crime," it all became clear to me that she wasn't the guilty party.'

She starts to cry, and dabs at her eyes. My father leans forward and says, 'So all this time, we were puzzling why Rachel would want to kill Matthew, when you knew all along, and at the same time we were trying to protect our grandson from being arrested – when in fact we should have been looking at our son.'

I look my father in the eye. He's always been fairly unreadable, but there's something in his eyes now that I think I can make out. Something different, that I truly haven't seen before. It's like he's impressed. Like he's viewing me in a completely different light. There's an intensity in the air, as if the atmosphere has become so heightened by their realisation, you could almost taste the tension. It's like something is on fire in the room, as if the smoke of the burning flowers Elena had sent has travelled up from the kitchen and started to singe the wallpaper.

At last, I nod and say, 'That's about the long and the short of it.'

Chapter Forty-Seven

CHARLIE

The day of the murder

Archie drove me over to The Ritz to get my car after we'd had breakfast. He'd lent me some clothes to wear and, due to him being a good inch or two shorter than me, I could feel the cool breeze of the late-morning air around my ankles as I stepped out of his ridiculous Spyder car and into The Ritz to sort out the parking charge. I vaguely wondered if I'd still be over the limit, although my drunken blackout had been relatively early in the evening and I felt perfectly in control as I said goodbye to Archie with a hug and a promise to call him if I needed somewhere to retreat to if things got tough in the days ahead.

When I arrived at Wilton Crescent, I was informed by my mother that Titus had slept in late and had been quiet and subdued when she had spoken to him briefly that morning. She said he'd been quite upset the night before and that I should keep an eye on him. One of the big things

I would regret, in the weeks and months, maybe even years, to come was that I didn't pay more attention to Titus on that day. In fact, I barely registered him as he slipped into the seat next to me in the car and grunted his acknowledgement when I told him Matthew was coming home. I was too caught up in thinking about the knife I would use. And the look I might see in my husband's eyes as I slipped it into his heart.

In the end, after an hour's deliberation back home, I decided on a heavy, weighty carving knife as the tool for the job. It fitted in my hand like a glove and its sharp edge glinted in the warm light of the setting sun. I laid the table for dinner as I listened to Titus wander about upstairs. I'd said he could stay the night at Melanie's flat and he'd looked suspicious at my apparent ease at the suggestion, then elated. We hadn't discussed his outburst the previous day. To be honest, I barely remembered it. I was so caught up in anticipation for when Matthew got home, the whole episode just seemed trivial and irrelevant.

Things became tricky when Titus arrived in the kitchen and said he wasn't going out after all. Melanie had another boy at her apartment, apparently. It seemed both of them were sleeping around. No wonder my disapproval of Titus having multiple girls on the go seemed prudish to him. 'Well … perhaps you could see if another friend is free?' I said, tentatively.

He sighed. 'I get it, you probably want to have a fight with Dad without me listening. Don't worry, I won't get in your way. I don't want to talk to him. I'll just have some food and leave you to it.'

This wasn't ideal. I knew it, and yet I still carried on. The idea of Titus being present in the house should have stopped me. I would come to understand that seconds after Matthew's death. But before, I don't think I was capable of thinking rationally.

Matthew looked nervous when he walked in, as if expecting gunfire to erupt from the landing above. I just called out, 'In the kitchen,' and let him walk the short distance alone, no doubt wondering what mood he'd find me in.

'I've got the food,' he said, by way of a greeting. He placed the Ottolenghi bag on the neatly laid table. 'Where's Titus?' he asked, looking around, noticing the table was set for three. 'You said in your text he'd be out.'

'He's upstairs. His plans fell through. His friend couldn't see him tonight after all. He said he'll come and eat. Then we'll talk.'

The look of a frightened rabbit facing down an oncoming lorry flashed across his face, but he didn't argue.

We dished up the food in silence and before long Titus wandered into the kitchen and sat down, ignoring Matthew's presence.

'I'm sorry I had to go away,' he said, going over and awkwardly trying to hug the boy, who remained stiff and unresponsive, sitting straight-backed in his chair. 'But I'm home now. Things will get back to normal, I promise.'

This didn't elicit a response, so Matthew sat back down and started to eat slowly, his eyes darting between me and Titus.

I felt a cold gust of air flow around the table. If I'd been in a more present state of mind, I'd have registered it properly and investigated where it came from and realised that Matthew had, in his trepidation on entering his once peaceful, happy family home, left the front door open, his travel bag stopping it from closing properly.

'I thought you were going to be at a friend's,' Matthew said to Titus, probably trying to get onto a nice, easy topic.

'I was supposed to be at Melanie's,' Titus said, looking at his food rather than at Matthew.

'Ah,' Matthew said, clearly less impressed with this. 'Is she busy or something?'

'Probably getting fucked by Nathaniel. He's in the year above me. He gets laid a lot. Always manages to work out which girls are easy. And Melanie's definitely easy.' He said this with a half laugh, half sneer. Again, if I'd been properly alert, I too would have been disconcerted by his language, but it felt as if I were observing the whole scene playing out under water. It was all strangely distorted and murky, like shapes and sounds, instead of people and words.

'Titus, I know you must be upset with me, and I don't blame you, but there's no excuse for language like that. And I especially don't want to hear you talking about women that way.'

Titus did his half laugh again. 'But it's true. She's got quite a few of us on the go. That's why I'm fucking Pippa. And I doubt I'm Pippa's only conquest, judging by how well she sucked me off the first time. But I dare say sluttiness runs in the family…'

'That is enough!' Matthew shouted at him, rising from his seat. Titus leapt up too, white with anger, and slammed his chair back into the table, causing the plates to clatter. He stormed out of the living room and ran up the stairs, leaving Matthew and me sitting in the now oddly silent room.

That was, of course, the moment I should have realised Titus knew about Matthew and Elena. And that Pippa must have been the one who told him. But I wasn't in the right state to make the connection. Instead, I was having an odd flashback to when I had, for a period, played the clarinet at school. The night I had my first recital at one of their end-of-year concerts, I was both excited and nervous to perform. The thought of performing in front of others properly for the first time brought with it a buzz, a sense of risk and danger – mild of course, but intoxicating. I remembered as I waited in the empty room away from the performance area, my hand had trembled as I poured myself a glass of water. But, minutes later, when I came to pick up my clarinet from the table and go through the door out to the waiting audience, my outstretched hand closed around the instrument without a tremor. It was completely steady. Everything was going to go according to plan. I just knew it. And it was like that right now. With Matthew's hypocrisy swirling around me like wisps of smoke – his indignant, self-righteous anger at his son's behaviour while trying to hide his own – I had no difficulty in picking up the knife from the table. The knife that wasn't needed for the meal, but nobody had noticed. Matthew noticed it, of course, as I took hold of it with my perfectly steady hand. And as I walked around the table, calmly and quietly, towards him, with it held tightly in my grasp.

I think it was the surprise of the whole thing that stopped him properly fighting back. That was quite a gift, where forensics was concerned. It meant there was no blood splatter to incriminate me, no scratches on my face, skin cells crammed under his fingernails. He was sitting still in shock as I leant down towards him, held his shoulder with one hand and pushed the knife between his ribs. I felt the tip of it snag and crunch through something as I pushed it deeper. He started to panic, once he'd registered what was happening, but I'd managed the insertion well and he wasn't able to do much more than fumble, clutching limply at the knife within him as the blood soaked his light-blue shirt and he struggled to say what he so desperately wanted to say.

I never found out how much Titus had witnessed. Or why he'd come back to the kitchen. I just remember turning round and finding him standing at the doorway, his mouth slightly open, his face even paler than it had been before. I saw him sway a little, and suddenly I was able to act like a responsible parent again. I pulled his chair back out from under the table and sat him down. I poured him a glass of water. He took a meek, quiet sip from it then set it down on the table. There was a strange companionability to the silence, as if we were both sheltering from a storm that was going on all around us. And in the quiet and stillness, I found I too could no longer stand.

I don't know how long we sat there at the table, but it can't have been longer than a minute or two. I didn't hear Rachel come in. I only registered her presence once she was in the room with us. Taking in the scene. Her eyes open in

... amazement? Horror? She looked at the two of us sitting there, then just said, 'The door was open.'

She then walked over to Matthew's body. I saw her touch his neck with her finger. Then she pulled the knife out of his chest. It's odd, but for some reason I imagined him gasping for breath as soon as the knife was out, as if it were the only thing stopping him from taking in oxygen, like something trapped in his throat. But he remained still as she stepped away, the bloodied knife in her hand. She looked down at it for a few moments, then said, 'I'm going to call the police now. Stay quiet while I talk to them. Whatever I say, whatever you hear, don't interrupt me.'

We didn't agree or disagree. We just stared at her. She seemed to be controlling her breathing, trying not to take in too much air too quickly, as if she was fighting not to become emotional. In spite of her efforts, I noticed a tear falling down the side of her face as she sat down in the unused seat at the table and took out her phone. And in spite of my odd, hypnotised state, I couldn't help but ask, 'Are you OK?'

A strange thing to say, I know. It would have been normal to ask her what she was doing, why she wasn't screaming, running from the house, or demanding an explanation. But I think we've already clarified that I'm not that normal. Nothing about this situation was very normal.

She didn't reply to my question. Instead, she stayed sitting at the table, with the knife on her lap, the blood staining her light-blue jeans, and took out her phone.

'Police please. A violent incident. I've killed someone.' She waited for a second, apparently listening to the person on the other end of the line. After the pause she gave them our address, went silent once again, then continued. 'No, he's not breathing; he's dead. I stabbed him. Please send the police. There's no need for any armed response or anything like that, I'm not going to hurt anyone else. I have the murder weapon, but I'll put it down on the table when they arrive. I won't resist being arrested or anything like that. I'm ending the call now.'

If I wasn't already sitting, I might have fainted. As my vision started to cloud and distort, I became vaguely aware of Titus getting up from his chair and walking out of the room. Part of me wanted to call after him, tell him not to leave the house, but I wasn't able to and, as it turned out, I didn't need to. I heard the creak of the stairs as he walked up them slowly, presumably towards his bedroom.

Once the police had arrived, I would find him there later, before we were led away to the police station for questioning, an officer behind me, making it clear we needed to leave.

'Rachel's confessed,' I told him, his tear-filled eyes staring back at me.

Then he asked the question that had been burning through me over the past half hour. The question that probably helped plant the seed of doubt into the police's investigation.

'But … *why*?'

Chapter Forty-Eight

CHARLIE

Seven months after the murder

It's an unseasonably hot day in April and I'm driving from London to Oxford. I even have the window down – something that would have seemed like madness the week previously – and I enjoy the light breeze on my face as I move slowly along in the traffic towards the Oxfordshire countryside. I drum my fingers on the steering wheel, listening to an unknown rock track, then switch up the vibe, tapping on my iPhone with one finger, selecting some sweeping piano music which bathes me in its lush, romantic tone and I feel my mood lift. I am, for the first time in a long while, happy.

I drive the car smoothly up to the Ashtons's manor. I sold the BMW late last year, swapping it for a lower, smaller Porsche. I felt I needed a change. Best leave the past in the past. The house on Carlyle Square has also been sold; I set the ball rolling as soon as I could. I was curious to find how little attachment to it I had after what happened. I just knew that was a section of my life that had come to an end. Titus had no wish to stay there either. After living between my mother's Wilton Crescent property and the manor in Essex, Titus and I had temporarily moved into a hotel. We needed some space away from my parents, even if they thought it was silly when we could have stayed in either of their properties. But there was something about the impersonal anonymity of hotel life that suited us both in that strange hinterland between Rachel being charged and the trial. Those autumn months where both of us seemed to be sleepwalking through our lives. I think my mother would have liked Titus to move in with her, but the boy was adamant he wanted to stay with me. I don't know whether she was afraid for his safety, remaining in the care of a murderer, or if she just wanted to keep an eye on him. Whichever it was, she'd finally relented, pleased at least that we'd picked The Hari, a hotel within walking distance of her house.

Last week, however, we'd let our rooms go and had moved – permanently for now – into Marwood Manor. Lord and Lady Ashton had recently decided the place was getting too big for both of them to be rattling round in at their age, and had moved into the still sizable, 1980s-built annex to the north of one of the surrounding fields. They assured us they wouldn't bother us every day and that Rupert, Titus, and I would more or less have the run of the manor to ourselves.

The question of Elena is a thorny one and something that has been solved only temporarily. On the lucky side, she decided to take a job working for the Republican party in the US. She'll be out of our hair most of the time, leaving her daughter in the UK to live with her father in his Clerkenwell apartment. It suited their fractured family dynamic just fine. Especially since she and Titus still seemed to be equally keen on spending time with each other.

I arrive at Marwood at about 3pm to find Titus and Rupert playing tennis in one of the courts round the back of the house.

'Who's winning?' I call out as I watch them from the side.

'We've rather lost count,' shouts a breathless Rupert as he only just catches a ball fired from Titus from the left.

After their tennis match, Rupert and I walk back to the house whilst Titus practises his serve. 'A letter came for you today,' he says. 'I didn't open it, but I think … I think you should read it immediately.'

I look at him, puzzled. 'Why?'

'Because I think it's come from HMP Graze Field.'

The name doesn't click for a second. Then one word enters my mind with a combination of a jolt and a shiver. 'Rachel.'

He nods, then walks over to a wooden tray on a side table near the front door and hands me the envelope. I open it, read for a few seconds, then look back at him and nod. 'It's from her.'

Graze Field Prison is an imposing, seventeenth-century manor house, now repurposed to hold female convicts and young offenders. It looks like something out of a horror movie as I approach it in the car and follow the signs to the car park round to the side near some fields. The prison entrance, then the process of signing in and being searched to get inside, is a lot more mundane and routine than I expected, although by the time I'm seated with everybody, the trepidation of what I might find on the other side is starting to get to me. I see Rachel immediately when we're sent through into a large room resembling a school hall. It's not that she looks particularly different from the other women in here; it's her body language that sets her apart. She looks as cool and alert as if she were a manager of a company about to interview a prospective new member of the team.

'Hi,' I say, trying to keep my voice as calm as she looks. I'm not sure I succeed, as it comes out as more of a low bark.

'Hello Charlie,' she says, and gives me a thin smile. I notice now how her physical appearance has markedly changed since I last saw her at the trial. Although she always had a slim frame, she's lost a notable amount of weight. Her jaw and neckline are now pronounced and sharp, giving her a more unforgiving, maybe even crueller, look than before. 'Thank you for coming.'

I take my seat, feeling awkward and a little nauseous. I find it hard to meet her eyes; she keeps hers trained on me, like a sniper fixing on a mark. 'Well, like you said in your letter, I didn't really have much of a choice.'

'That's right.' She gives a short, business-like nod, as if satisfied I understand her message. I get the feeling she's enjoying having the upper hand here. 'Since we don't have long, and I think we'll both agree that we'd be better not to make meetings like this too frequent, I just thought it might be good for both of us to go through a few things before we start off properly.'

I frown at her. 'Start what off properly?'

She smiles. 'The rest of our lives, of course.'

The smile unnerves me. Makes me wary about what she's about to say.

'So,' she says, shifting her chair closer to the table. 'Now the dust has settled, I wanted to explain everything. I thought it was ... well, your right. Right to know.'

'Why you did what you did?' I ask.

She lowers her voice to barely a whisper. 'Why I gifted you your freedom.'

I don't like the way she words this, and I feel my insides tighten as I finally allow my eyes to meet hers.

'This is all going to sound a bit harsh about your dead husband, I'm afraid, but since the last time I saw you together you'd just plunged a knife into his heart, I don't think you'll find this too upsetting. But if you need a break at any point, do say.'

It's a weird thing to say, reminiscent of the police interviews I'd gone through in the months after Matthew's death. I don't reply, just wait for her to carry on. She clearly has a little speech planned and, in spite of my discomfort, I'm keen to hear it.

'I wanted your husband dead for years. Really, really

375

wanted it. Desperately. I imagined all the ways one could possibly kill someone. You could probably call them fantasies. They helped me get to sleep at night. Anyway, you've probably worked out by now that Matthew killed my brother, Johnny.'

I nod.

'I thought you might have. Did he tell you? Or did you piece it together yourself?'

'He told me,' I reply.

She nods. 'I thought his conscience might crack. Was it, by any chance, on the day of the Ashtons's anniversary party?'

'Yes.'

She nods again. 'Men really are so predictable, aren't they?' She rolls her eyes to the ceiling. 'And they have a habit of underestimating women. Matthew underestimated me. What I would do. What I would endure. But I don't think you did.'

'No, I didn't,' I say. 'I knew there was something … wrong about you. Something Matthew, in his constant effort to be nice to people and make friends, couldn't quite see.'

Rachel looks at me, her face thoughtful, and I wonder if there's perhaps a touch of respect in the gaze. But then she says, 'He was just so keen to get to know me, wasn't he? That took me by surprise at first, but when his WhatsApp messages started getting more and more flirty – well, I worked out he swung both ways. He was after something else from me other than book chat. That's another thing men all have in common: they think with their dicks. You weren't much better, really … so frightened that I was trying to seduce him or I had some perverted obsession with your adopted son. It always just comes down to sex, doesn't it? Didn't think to look elsewhere, did you?'

Her tone has become quiet, low, dangerous. I stay silent, uncomfortable in the knowledge that her assessment of me and Matthew has been, at least so far, depressingly accurate.

'First, let me clear up why you killed him,' she says, sounding a bit more business-like again. 'It was because of his affair with the Ashtons's daughter, wasn't it?'

I give her a short nod.

'And did you find that out on the night of the party?'

'No,' I say. 'A bit later.'

A look of surprise flashes through her face. 'Oh, well, I had presumed he would have told you everything all at once. Especially after ... oh gosh, you don't know, do you?'

'Know what?'

She grins, relishing being the bearer of news. 'Know that he was shagging her *at the party*. I caught them. They were in the bathroom, him and Elena. I'd followed them, of course, and could make out the shape of them through a crack where the door doesn't meet the hinges. I waited until they'd finished before I confronted him. But, well, it's all a little bit tacky, isn't it? And a bit ironic, really, since I'm fairly sure the reason why my brother was allowed to die was because you lot viewed him as tacky. Working class. A low-life. Not one of the club. Went to a comp in Bradford, not a private school in Berkshire. A salesperson and small-scale entrepreneur rather than a high-flying company director or fashion designer or politician.'

This irritates me, as she probably knew it would. 'He was a drug dealer.'

She shakes her head. 'No, I'm sorry, but that's wrong. He was a drug *user*. He was unwell.'

I let out a noise of disbelief. 'He chose to take that stuff. He knew the risks. He knew the law. He knew what it would mean as soon as he started smoking and sniffing and injecting.'

She continues to shake her head, slower now, as if staring at a hopeless child. 'Such hypocrisy. I would bet anything in the world – not that I have much left to bet – that you would indulge in a line of cocaine after a night at a glitzy awards dinner. Or perhaps the odd pill on a night out?'

I'm furious at my own body for betraying me; the rage building within me causes my face to burn hot, the back of my neck prickling.

'I think to most people it would be blatantly obvious what you and your lot do. You shift the goalposts for the less privileged. The goalposts that dictate what's right and wrong, what's success and failure, what's deserved and undeserved.'

'I haven't done anything of the kind,' I say through clenched teeth.

'Then why wasn't my brother allowed to live?'

'Because,' I say, louder than I intend, then lower my voice again, 'because he was a layabout, drug-dealing vermin who destroyed the life of his girlfriend and the family that surrounded her.'

More shaking of her head. 'You've got it the wrong way round.'

This makes me pause. 'What?' I say, looking at her knowing, infuriatingly self-assured expression. She sighs.

'It wasn't Johnny who introduced Collette to drugs. It was the other way around.'

There's a shifting of the ground beneath me. A sense of déjà vu is corrupting my sense of reality, as if I'm being thrown back to a time in the past. Matthew standing next to the fireplace in our lounge. Telling me everything. Everything in his own words. *His* words. Things fitting into place for me. And now here it is happening again. Different truths, different stories. And always me, the one in the dark, the one from whom the secrets are kept.

'You've been lied to,' Rachel says, simply.

I shake my head. 'No ... no that's not ... Collette wasn't into drugs before she met Johnny...'

Rachel shrugs. 'I can't prove it, of course, but from what Johnny told me, she already had established connections with dealers before she started her degree at Durham. Johnny just had the misfortune to shag her one night out the back of a club during her first term. Like your husband, he had a bit of trouble keeping his dick in his pants. But when he met Collette, he changed. He was always a kind, caring boy. Always looked out for me and Mum and Dad. Worked multiple jobs in shops and factories to bring in money. But when he started seeing Collette, his kindness and sense of duty went into overdrive. Everything he did was part of this huge effort to please her. And, thanks to her slipping an MDMA pill onto his tongue that night in the alley behind a club, he developed a taste for the same substances that she'd become acquainted with at whatever posh school she'd attended.'

I can't cope with this. This is all wrong. It can't be true; it just can't be. I've seen photos of Johnny Holden. He looked awful – drug-addict thin, tattoos, not the kind of guy you'd want to meet on an empty street at night.

As if she can read my thoughts, Rachel carries on, 'I think your crowd just presumed he was the more natural criminal. Couldn't possibly be dearest, darling Collette, could it? With her Dior coats and Mulberry handbags and a cut-glass English accent even though she was Scottish. But honestly, can't you see there's a problem if you never thought to question all of this? Never thought that maybe there was a clear attempt to paint her as the victim, him as the poison, the parasite, the thing they needed to get rid of.'

I shake my head, slowly. 'I … don't know… I never thought…'

'No, well, you wouldn't, would you.' Her lips twist as if in revulsion at me. 'You really are all the same.'

'But Matthew said … he said he was attacked. By Johnny. He said Johnny and a group of other young men turned up in the night and terrorised him. They did terrible things. Threatened to castrate him, kill him, forced him to take cocaine… It was … it sounded monstrous. And it was because he had been trying to get Colette to give up the drugs, distance herself from Johnny, do rehab or whatever was necessary to keep herself away from that sort of lifestyle.'

Rachel raises an eyebrow. 'Johnny? Terrorise someone? I

can promise you, no matter how many drugs he took, I can never imagine him *ever* doing something like that.'

I am struggling to fit this together in my head. 'So you're saying … Matthew was making it up?' Even as I say this, I realise I can't accept it, not when his description of the event had been so chillingly detailed. Rachel's view of her brother must be a delusion, warped by her years re-living rose-tinted family memories before everything went wrong.

She looks back at me as if I'm stupid. 'He's already proved to be a liar at heart, hasn't he? Did you even know he fancied women? In fact, did you even know him at all?'

This question hangs in the air between us for a few moments. I don't answer it, and I don't think she expects me to. Then she carries on, 'Even if he was attacked, I could very much imagine other people not wanting him interfering in his sister's life. I imagine she was very useful to a number of dealers – putting them in touch with other rich, young people like her. Maybe she was a bit loose with her tongue, blamed her brother too loudly for her attempts to detox.'

She may be right about some things, but she's wrong about this. I am sure of it. I'd seen the horror of those memories come to life in Matthew's eyes. Rachel must be blinded by her guilt, her sadness, her love for her deceased brother. Although I suppose, perhaps, she could suspect that of me. Blinded by guilt. Blinded by love.

I bring my hands to my face and rub my eyes. I'm suddenly feeling very tired. I thought all this was put to bed. I thought I was free from this turmoil.

'So maybe now you can understand why I wanted your

husband dead. But in case you haven't fully realised how deep my hatred goes, I'll give you some context. I was happy before Collette came along. I'd opened my own photography studio and gallery space in Bradford. I'd made a life for myself. But then Johnny needed to borrow money. He said he'd been stupid and borrowed some money from dodgy types. I gave it to him, of course. I couldn't bear the idea of him being beaten up by thugs for the sake of a hundred quid. But then he needed more. And more. His behaviour became alarming. Once I'd got a handle of what was going on – the drugs, the drinking, and who was the cause – I went to Collette's flat. Spoke to her properly. Begged her to leave him. She told me to fuck off. Accused me of being a meddling bitch. Told me they were in love. Well, that love didn't exactly go very well for them, did it. Nor me.

'I sold my gallery space to pay for Johnny's rehab, along with a good chunk of my parents' savings. It didn't work. He absconded. And, of course, ended up jetting off to Norway with her. He told me where he was going, at least, which wasn't always the case, giving me the chance to follow him over there. I tried to confront him a few times, but he acted like I was being whingey and stopping his fun. He told me I was an embarrassment in front of his new friends. But I saw the way they looked at him, with his strong Yorkshire accent amidst their plummy Oxbridge vowels. Him boasting about getting his first batch of fitness clients for his personal trainer business while the others smirked behind their hands at him. He was embarrassing himself enough without my help. Not that I excuse their snobbery. I firmly believe they'd have been the same towards him even if he'd been more reserved, less hyper. He hadn't gone to Eton; he hadn't grown up in a townhouse in Chelsea or amidst the rolling hills of a country estate. He was an outsider. They'd have made him feel it regardless.'

I shake my head. 'You don't know that. Not for sure.'

She rolls her eyes at me. 'Still defending the clan, are we?'

I breathe out slowly, trying to control my emotion. 'Stop grouping people together like that. It's identity politics, pure and simple. And I detest identity politics.'

'Well, you would, wouldn't you? Maybe because you've had advantages handed to you from birth that others can only dream of. But yeah, do correct me if I'm wrong. I do love being lectured to about privilege by a male millionaire with aristocratic ancestors.'

'It may have escaped your notice,' I say, through gritted teeth, 'but I have, all of my life, been in relationships with men. And it wasn't so long ago when my so-called privileged elitist community would have ostracised me if I had chosen to carry on being true to myself and not been a good little boy and married a woman to keep up the perception of respectability. So don't you dare think my position in this rich-people fantasy you're so keen on believing in has always been so safe. I lived with the chance of being an outcast every single day of my youth. I'm just lucky to have been born when I was and not a few decades before. But of course, none of that suits the narrative that you're so desperate to craft, so do feel free to ignore it.'

Her eyes flash and she places her hands flat on the table.

Her voice takes on an ice-like whisper. 'May I give you some advice? Stop pissing off the woman serving your jail sentence. You are playing with fire.'

The words hit home. I hate myself for it, but I close my mouth, biting back the retort I so want to fling at her.

A pinched, angry expression has settled on her face now, and it remains as she opens her mouth to speak, then stops, clearly finding the sentence she's trying to get out too difficult to say aloud.

'I did something … unforgivable,' she said, brushing away a tear from the corner of her eye. '*We* did something unforgivable. Me, Mum, and Dad. We let Titus go. After Johnny died, we let him be taken in by Collette's brother, a man who I had never properly met, and Collette went home with them. At the time, it was too painful for us to even recognise the baby's existence. Mum's Catholicism, mixed with her grief, warped her into something close to madness. Then followed cancer and chemotherapy. It's no wonder she couldn't face reality. Dad was of the opinion that the child would have a better life growing up with a rich family. And to be honest, I don't think he had the strength left to fight or even be involved in the care of a young child. When I think back, there are so many things I regret, but I think my actions around then weren't made by the same person I am now. Watching my mother die before my very eyes, dying herself just after her own son had passed away, knowing she was leaving behind her a father and a daughter fucked up by grief … that sort of thing changes you. Pulls you inside out. It's easy to look back now and say how, if I had that time again, I would have fought for us to be a part of the life of our nephew and grandson, our last connection to Johnny. But it sends you mad, that sort of thinking. If you dwell on it for too long. Maybe it did.'

For a moment, I wonder if she's finished talking. The angry expression has now been replaced with a far-off look. I get the feeling I could get up and walk away and she wouldn't see me. Then, at last, she speaks. 'I suppose he told you how I knew what he'd done. How I'd photographed him. It was an accident, actually. I was very lucky to have been gifted an exceptionally good camera, by 2005 standards, by my partner at the time. He was keen for me to get back into photography. So while I was in Norway, I took photographs in the forest surrounding the hotel accommodation. And thanks to its then pioneering full-frame sensor and 12.8 megapixels, I could make a very close extraction from the digital image in Photoshop and blow it up to fill the screen. I probably don't need to tell you what it showed me.'

Her eyes fix on mine meaningfully. I nod. 'Matthew,' I say, my voice croaky from not speaking for so long.

She nods back. 'Matthew. Standing there. Holding Titus in his arms. Watching my brother in the hot tub. You can see he's asleep in the photo. And Matthew does nothing. Doesn't try to wake him. Doesn't try to save him, to lift him out of the pool. Johnny was smaller than Matthew. The drugs had made him thin and wiry. It would have been nothing for Matthew to save his life. But he didn't. He had the chance and he left him there to die alone.'

'How do you know Johnny wasn't already dead? Maybe

Matthew simply saved Titus from drowning in the arms of an overdosed corpse.'

She doesn't look impressed with this. 'Because in spite of the heroin and cocaine in his bloodstream, my brother managed to inhale quite a bit of water before his heart stopped. Corpses do not try to breathe under water.'

She pauses for a moment, as if to let this sink in. I take advantage of the pause to ask another question. 'Why didn't you just go to the police? Or track down Matthew then and there?'

She sighs. 'Because my mother died. Literally the next day, after I found the photo. And it took it all out of me. For a time, at least. But in the years that followed, an obsession started to grow. I kept an eye on any news I could find about him, which wasn't much. Just his work and graduation. The internet was a much smaller place, back then. Before we put every single little thing online, as people do today. It seems strange, but I was a lot more fixated on hating him and wishing him dead than I was on checking my own nephew was OK. But I knew Titus was living a happy life. I found a photo a few years later of him on the Eaton Square school website playing a tambourine. He looked happy. I only stopped obsessing because I fell in love. A guy I'd been friends with for years. The guy who'd given me the camera, actually. Kevin, his name was. He was insistent that I let the past go. He said it was unhealthy me obsessing about the Joneses, although he never knew about what I'd seen in the photograph. He just thought I hated them because of Collette's influence on Johnny and their snobbish attitudes towards him. He said he'd support me if

I wanted to try to re-enter Titus's life, but he thought my burning hatred towards them needed to either be cleared up or let go. So I let it go. In theory. I moved on with my life the best I could, although it never quite worked out between him and me. It felt weird, us being intimate like a couple, since I'd regarded him as a platonic friend since I was, like, seven. We pretended there weren't any problems for years, until he eventually said he wanted children with me. I knew then that things needed to end. So we parted and left the flat we were renting together.

'Even though I'd started up my photography commissions again over the years, I couldn't support myself on them alone, not without Kevin's income. So I got a job at a garden centre. And it was when I was working there that, on a fucking miserable day, I came across your Instagram account. It was on my "recommended" feed. A charming photo of two men and a boy standing around a cake they'd just baked. I can't even describe to you the effect the photo had on me. After all those years of burying that side of my life and trying to move forward, to be confronted with it again … well, it was like someone had started choking me. And everything sort of imploded from that moment onwards.

'It became absolutely clear that I needed to find Matthew and make him pay for what he did to my brother. I suppose I was depressed, not in my right mind, but I genuinely welcomed the purpose it gave me. It was as if I'd been sleepwalking through my life in black and white and suddenly someone had turned it into Technicolor. It was astonishing. I'd wanted Matthew Jones dead for so long that to finally give myself permission to go after what I'd wanted was like one of those moments religious people talk about – an epiphany. So when I saw him lying there, saw you'd got there first before me, it felt like the most natural thing in the world to confess to the crime. Because it was what I had come to the house to do. I don't consider myself a Christian or anything, but sitting there, with the knife, waiting for the police to arrive, I felt calmer and more content than I had ever felt before. I felt close to God, or what people call God. I don't have a name for it myself, but you can call it what you like – the creator, the universe, destiny. It's probably too much for you to understand. But it's genuinely how I felt.'

I stare back at her. I'm both terrified and impressed. Impressed at her description of the experience and her ability to articulate it, and terrified by how closely it resembled my own. The sensations, the sudden calm that had enveloped me after the bloodletting was – she was right – an experience to which one couldn't help but attach religious significance. It was divine, in the true sense of the word, with vengeance and justice coming together to stabilise an imbalance in the world. It was something greater than anything the day-to-day human life encountered, and therefore required such language to even come close to describing it. Those who claim there is no beauty in violence really have no clue.

'The irony is,' she says, after a few moments of silence, 'that I planned to do it exactly the same way as you did. I'd even studied which area of the torso to drive the knife into – an internet history detail which was very useful to the police during the process of charging me. So to find the job already complete, with you sitting there at the table, I must admit I was kind of grateful. I was grateful you'd done what I'd wanted to do for so long. Which made it easy to do what I did next. I knew Titus loved you as a father – someone who had been there throughout his life, unlike me. And I needed to do something to avenge my brother's death. So confessing to it in court and coming here kept that sense of purpose going; it meant I could pay Johnny back for not spotting the signs of his decline sooner, not succeeding in steering him towards a safer path. Not being a good enough sister, daughter, or aunt. Who knows, maybe after ten years here I'll feel differently. But for now, you and Titus are free to live your lives.'

We are running out of time, and I get the sense from her tone that we're coming to the end of our conversation. Just one thing sets off a small warning bell in my mind and makes me look back at her with mounting concern. 'For now?' I repeat back.

Rachel considers this for a few seconds, then says, 'Be careful of Titus. It's a lot for him to handle on his own. That secret. It has the power to become … explosive. One day, he may need your encouragement to stay silent. If I were you, I wouldn't get complacent. Or take his silence for granted. Just … be careful.'

Whatever I had expected Rachel to say, this was not it and it throws me off balance. 'I … what? I don't think Titus is going to say anything…'

'Just look after him the best you can,' Rachel cut across me. 'For me. That's all I ask. Do that, and all will be fine.

And hopefully, I'll never have to use this.' From her sleeve, which she's kept bunched around her right hand the whole time, she allows me to see something small and silver with a flashing red LED on its side. A digital recorder.

'Why … how have you…?' I look around at the prison staff either side. Neither of them seems to have noticed anything.

'Oh, you can get anything in here, so long as you know the right people. It would have been a bit harder in the first prison I was in, before the trial. A lot hotter on the rules. But this place has rather lax security in comparison, and in the end it's all just a question of making connections. Honestly, Charlie, for a man of the world, you really are very naïve.'

The call to end the visitation session sounds around us and Rachel starts to get up. 'Although, you're not really a man of *the* world, are you? Just *your* little world.'

I don't know what to say to this, so I remain silent.

'Well, best of luck with your new life,' she says, with a small smile. 'All going well, I'll see you in about fifteen years.'

Chapter Forty-Nine

CHARLIE

Seven months after the murder

The drive back from the prison seems a lot greyer and colder than it had done two weeks previously when I was driving from London to Oxford. My conversation with Rachel continues to echo through my ears. The things she said about Matthew. And Titus. The future, which had felt so bright and idyllic, suddenly seems uneasy and unsure. As if once-still ground is now breaking apart beneath me. It has taken me months to achieve a sense of equilibrium, any kind of stability. And now it has been disrupted.

But of course, all this is just in my head. Nothing has changed. Nothing is different. Rachel's words don't have to affect me if I don't want them to. I could decide just to ignore her warnings. Her suggestion that my position isn't as safe as I'd like it to be could just be her trying to unsettle me. Things will be just fine, I try to tell myself as I park the car outside the manor and go inside.

I go into the library, pour myself a brandy, and take a sip. I'm about to send a text to Rupert to ask where he is when I hear noises coming from the passageway that leads down to the indoor swimming pool. It sounds like whooping and shouting, as if an entertaining game were being played inside an echoey cave. Sure enough, Rupert, Titus, and Pippa are engaged in some sort of ball-throwing contest, with Rupert apparently taking on two against one. He gives me a big sweeping wave with one of his large hands as I come in, earning himself an inflatable ball in the face for his drop in focus.

I sit by the side of the pool on one of the loungers and watch them for a bit, then unlock my phone and start mindlessly scrolling. The habit to open Instagram still kicks in occasionally, and I find myself falling into its clutches once more, the photos unfurling before me, senseless and bland. Until my hand brushes against the icon leading to my profile. And picture upon picture of me and Matthew fills my screen in a cruel, beautiful grid. I've been so sure, for so long, that what I did was right. Was just. Was necessary. But now, after speaking to Rachel, I find a niggling feeling threatening to take hold. Doubt. The feeling is doubt. And it terrifies me.

I leave the poolside and go into the changing area and march straight into the showers, letting the cold jet of the water soak me. I take deep breaths, trying to stop the panic, the burning anxiety taking me over.

'What are you doing?'

I turn around and see Titus at the doorway, his trunks dripping, his hair, darker from the water, hanging slightly across his face. He looks concerned at my behaviour. We've become spies, really. Each of us watching the other, waiting for someone to crack first under the strain. I think I've been pretending it isn't true. Pushing myself to believe everything's fine. It really isn't.

'I just … felt hot,' I say, stepping out of the shower, my shirt sticking to me as I move. 'So I took a shower…'

'In your clothes?' he asks, raising an eyebrow. 'Why don't you just get your swim things and come in the pool?'

I laugh, playing for time, but it comes out false, and Titus knows it. He knows I'm faking. Instead of answering his question I go and sit down on the long bench in the centre of the room. I hope he will come and sit next to me without invitation, but he doesn't. He just stays there, standing still, looking at me. Eventually he speaks.

'I need to talk to you about something.'

I look up at him properly. His words don't comfort me; they do the complete opposite. But I reply in the way all dads should reply. 'You can talk to me about anything.'

He nods, as if he expected this response. A pause passes between us, then he says he wants to start seeing Pippa properly. Like, boyfriend and girlfriend. 'I realise this will probably upset you, after what her mother did, but I love Pippa and we want to be together. I won't talk to her mum, and you won't need to either. But I like her too much to worry about that now.'

This is not what I was expecting, and I'm so relieved that I laugh – properly this time – feeling the tension start to flow out of me, my shoulders starting to relax.

'What's funny?' Titus asks, looking a little irritated, and I reply, still smiling, 'Nothing. That's all fine. Pippa's a lovely girl. I just … thought you wanted to talk about something else.'

Titus gives me a weird look, then walks over to the far wall and takes a towel from the folded pile in the corner. I hear him tug off his wet trunks and toss them to the side, then start to dry himself. When he comes back into view, his hair is out of his eyes, the towel tied around his waist, his expression blank and unreadable. 'I will *never* want to talk about that,' he says at last.

His response sends a jolt through me. 'Of course,' I say, standing up, putting a hand on his shoulder. 'I understand. I just … want you to be OK.'

Titus looks me in the eye and nods. 'It's done. Finished. We don't need to talk about it.'

He walks to the other benches over to the side where his clothes are folded in a pile and turns his back to me, but I can't let the conversation end like this. 'I agree,' I say, slightly hurriedly. 'So long as you're OK?'

He stops, then turns around and gives me a small nod. 'I'm fine, and don't worry, I'm not going to tell Rupert, or Pippa, or anyone for that matter.' It's now that I notice a weird look in Titus's eyes. I just nod at him, unsure what to say. There's a hardness in his expression that's disturbing me. I'm about to leave, to give him the privacy to dress alone, but he speaks before I reach the door.

'Actually, while we're on the subject, it would be helpful, when Pippa comes over to stay, that she sleeps in my room. With me. Instead of a guest room.' He pulls on his jeans, tightening his belt with a loud snap.

I'm thrown by his words. 'Well, er … I don't really think that would be appropriate. You're both still fifteen…' I trail off, and Titus's expression turns cold.

'We're nearly sixteen. And I want it that way.' He's now doing up his shirt buttons, calmly and carefully, without a single tremor in his fingers. 'I'm sure you could make it OK with Rupert. And also, we'd like to go on a holiday later in the spring, once we turn sixteen. Just the two of us. And we'd need some spending money, of course. That would be OK, right?' He stares back at me, a defiant glint in his eyes. 'I mean, I think it would make me feel a lot better if all those things could happen. If you see what I mean.'

The panic is back, flooding through me, returning with such a rushing force that the momentary relief I felt seconds before now feels as if it were a cruel trick. As the boy I've spent the last ten years of my life with looks back at me with a slight smile playing on his lips, I feel my ability to talk leave me. Eventually I nod, and manage to whisper, 'Of course.'

Titus grins. 'Thanks Dad. I knew you'd understand.' And then he goes back out to the pool to join Rupert, leaving me sitting on the changing-room benches. Trying to stop myself shaking.

Epilogue

ELENA

Three years after the murder

The main lobby of the St Regis hotel, Washington DC, was surprisingly quiet the day I got the call. I'd been meeting up with a prominent website owner to discuss him contributing to the re-election campaign I was co-managing – a quietly spoken, smooth sort of man of around fifty. Even though there was nothing remarkable about his dress or appearance, he seemed to exude charisma and power.

'I thought you'd have wanted to meet me with the rest of the team,' he said, sitting down and accepting a glass of wine. 'Not that I'm complaining. It's not often I get to have a drink one-to-one with a British aristocrat.'

I laughed and batted away his comment as though it was unnecessary flattery, like such things didn't really matter. I've learned that's what people expect, and it usually works. They let their guard down a bit after that.

'Malcom, you've met the actual President twice already. I'm sure that's a lot more impressive.'

He leant forwards at that point and I caught the scent of his aftershave. Like a cool, crisp autumn evening. 'Elena, I'm not into *appearing* impressive. I've done that my whole life. I just want to keep the right guy in The White House for as long as possible. And making a sizable donation should send a loud enough message.'

I raised an eyebrow. 'I think your move into journalism and think-pieces might be doing that already.'

He let out a short, sharp laugh, 'Well, that's another reason why I'm really pushing the content side of the platform. Longform journalism shouldn't be confined to the papers and news sites. We get millions of eyeballs every day. Let's start educating those eyeballs.'

Here we go, I thought. He's about to mention her. Any second now.

'Which brings me around to your daughter,' he said, 'and what a fine writer she is too.'

I'd become aware of my daughter's contributions to FreeTalk, Malcom Driver's social-media platform-turned-right-of-centre-blogging-site, shortly before he reached out to us to make a donation. Pippa had started writing some gossipy girl-about-town newspaper column during her first year at Oxford and had been poached by FreeTalk to write for them with a stronger emphasis on her political stances. Her series of articles and essays were published under the headline 'Pippa Ashton: The Way I See It'. Why anyone should care about the way my nineteen-year-old daughter sees the big issues of our times was a mystery to me.

Although, that said, I couldn't deny the fact that her writing commanded attention, helped along by the deliberately over-the-top headings, like *Are Universities Becoming a Threat to Democracy?* and *Why Loopy Vegans Need to Shut the F*** Up About Fox Hunting*, and, in a three-thousand-word 'long read' which ended up going viral, *Why I'm No Longer Talking to Poor People About Privilege*. All of these caused me some anguish – not necessarily because I disagreed with the points she raised, but because of the way they were presented, as if their sole purpose was to offend people and cause outrage. That wasn't a nuanced debate in my book. That was, to coin a phrase I'd once heard Elliot Gould say in a Steven Soderbergh movie, 'graffiti with punctuation'. But if Malcom Driver was impressed by my daughter, so much the better for the campaign, I thought, as I smiled at him over my glass. I was about to try to move the conversation on, but he remained stuck on Pippa.

'And I hear she's getting married, isn't she? To some dashing young man – the one her Instagram is covered in. Titus, isn't it? It looks like he likes a bit of a party, but they seem a charming couple. Although she'll be quite a young bride at nineteen. That's young these days, right?' His face stayed perfectly neutral as he said it, but I could tell he was interested to hear my thoughts on this. And I had a lot of thoughts. Like, why the hell Pippa was being so stupid about marrying that bland, empty-headed boy. Like, how she should wait until she was at least some way into her twenties before entering into something as serious as marriage. Not to mention my unease about her temporarily living under the same roof as Charles Allerton, a man who will hate me for eternity.

'Hello…? Elena, are you OK?' Malcom was looking at me, his head turned a little.

'Sorry,' I said, realising my thoughts had carried me off momentarily, 'I'm … yes … Pippa is certainly making her mark on the world.' My phone then buzzed in my pocket – on silent, but the vibration was loud enough to make Malcom raise his eyebrows. I cursed inwardly, but Malcom nodded at my phone, saying, 'Please, do answer. I'm in no rush here.'

I glanced at the screen. Trip was calling. I felt my heart sink a little. Trip was a twenty-eight-year-old bartender I'd been seeing for the past nine months. Two months ago I moved him into my house in Kalorama. It was just easier having him at home, there when I wanted him, and he was normally happy to tuck himself away on his laptop in another room when I didn't. He desperately wanted to be a screenwriter, hammering out *House of Cards*-style political thrillers, even though the closest he'd ever come to that world was pouring drinks for the odd senator. I was about to cancel the call when I noticed he'd texted a few times. Two words stood out quite clearly from all the rest as if propelled from the screen. *Rachel Holden.*

'I'm sorry, I'm … I'm going to have to…'

'Please, go ahead,' Malcom nodded, making it clear it wasn't a problem.

I accepted the call. 'Ah, there you are, I was about to hang up,' Trip said, sounding slightly excitable. 'Did you see my texts? I thought I should—'

'What is this about?' I cut him off. 'Tell me quickly.'

'Well, it's a bit odd. It's about this package that arrived for you. It's strange because when I opened it I saw—'

'You *opened* a package addressed to me?' I repeated, my moment of outrage momentarily causing me to forget I just wanted him to get to the point quickly.

'Yes, but … well, I thought it was for me, because there was a load of other stuff delivered today that was and…'

'Just tell me what it is, Trip,' I said, irritation building.

'It's a letter,' he said. 'And a CD.'

'A CD?'

'Yeah,' he said, sounding slightly nervous. 'I haven't played it. But … well … I did read the letter. It's weird. Like, I remember you telling me about this Rachel woman who killed your … friend. Well, from what the letter says… Fuck, it's weird. I think you should just come and read it for yourself. Or I can photograph it and send it to you, but I think you're going to want the CD so…'

'Don't play it. Don't do anything with it. Just leave it.' I cut the call.

The bar and hotel lobby surrounding me suddenly seemed blurred and glistening, like my depth of field had been altered, as if looking through a camera lens. I had the strangest feeling of the world shifting just a notch out of balance, sliding everything the wrong way.

I needed to make a decision. I knew what I should do. I should stay and try to get Malcom to commit to a rough figure of funds before I left him. But at the same time, I knew I wouldn't be anywhere close to my best charming self.

I walked slowly back to where he was sitting, trying to decide how to play this before I reached him. But it turned out I didn't need to. Malcom looked up from his phone when I arrived saying he actually had a work emergency he had to deal with and he would send me his offer by email. He assured me it would be substantial. I thanked him, then got my driver outside to take me straight home, all the time my brain whirring over and over.

In the house, Trip launched into his apologies instantly.

'I don't want to hear it,' I said, holding up a hand to stop him talking.

He looked sheepish and chastened. He was in his 'loungewear', which was basically pyjamas, and for a moment I felt like I was his mother and he my teenage son, being reprimanded for doing something naughty at school. I told him to tell me where the package was and he pointed to the grey marble kitchen countertop. I walked over, picked it up, then told him to leave me alone.

The letter was written on what looked like cheap A4 printer paper. I got the feeling that the author's handwriting wasn't normally neat, but extra effort had been put in to make it readable. And there was something else present too. The letters had been carved onto the paper with a lot of pressure, causing the page to be thoroughly indented on the back. Was that a sign of how studiously it had been written? Determination, perhaps? Or maybe fury?

I scanned it quickly, then sat down in one of the chairs in the living room and forced myself to read it through calmly again, taking my time over every word.

Dear Elena,

How odd it is for me to be writing to you, considering we never properly met. I think you might have nodded and smiled to me at your parents' anniversary party. But all that was years ago now. Back when you and Matthew were shagging.

Sorry, I realise that's quite blunt, but there's no point me being polite. I realise you've probably hated me for years for killing the man you loved. Or maybe you didn't love him. Maybe it was just sex, or a distraction from whatever else you used to fill your time with. I don't care, really. But trust me, you're better off without him.

It's odd to think how connected we are – now more than ever, with your daughter and my nephew about to walk up the aisle. You see, the problem is, I'm not really sure they're the best match. They're so young. And does she really want to marry a boy who's becoming known for hosting loud, debauched boat-parties? Or does she expect him to lay off the drink, drugs, and orgies when the wedding ring is firmly on his finger? If she does, I think she's in need of some motherly advice from you, sharpish.

So that's why I'm writing. I'm not happy with the way my nephew's life is going. And I doubt you're happy about your daughter marrying him. That's why I'm writing to you now, after all this time. You see, what you think happened didn't really happen. It's too long to write in this letter, but I've included a disc containing a recording I made a few months after my trial. It's a conversation between me and Charles Allerton. As you'll discover, the whole thing's a bit of a bombshell. And I trust you'll use it well.

Kind regards,

Rachel Holden.

After my second reading, I paused on that final sentence. *I trust you'll use it well.* What did she mean? I got up and walked over to the sound-system and put the disc into the slot. I listened to the whole thing, sitting there alone in the living room, my pulse quickening, my head spinning. Then, after it was finished, I sat for a few minutes more, doing nothing.

Once I felt capable of standing, I got up and headed towards the stairs, ignoring the questions from Trip as I went. As soon as I was seated at my desk in the study, I opened my laptop, navigated to the British Airways website and booked a flight to Heathrow. Then I unlocked my phone, scrolled down to a contact I'd hardly ever used and typed out a short message.

Hi Charlie. I'm on my way back to England. I think it's time we had a chat.

Acknowledgments

This book was written in 2019 when the world was still normal and edited in 2020 when the world changed so completely, so perhaps more than ever it's important I give thanks to those who helped keep the process on course and provided support and encouragement when things seemed disconcerting and the future uncertain. I would like to thank my wonderful agent Joanna Swainson and the whole team at Hardman & Swainson for their support throughout the writing of this book. Huge thanks to Bethan Morgan, Charlotte Ledger, Melanie Price, and everyone at One More Chapter and HarperCollins for their enthusiasm for this book and for being such a warm and welcoming home for my writing.

Endless thanks to my parents, sisters Molly and Amy, granny, and uncle for their continued support and for helping to make sure the very difficult year of 2020 was still filled with joy. Thanks to all my friends who have been so wonderful, with special thanks to Rebecca Bedding,

Thomas Bedding, Meg Wallace, Corinne Gurr, Emma Ruttley, George Doel, Lucy Clayton, Alice Johnston, Frankie Lowe, Rachael Bull, Timothy Blore, Martha Greengrass, Olivia Judd, Chloe Lay, and Pippa Rugman. In the book world – from authors to booksellers and many others – I'd like to thank Cally Taylor, Bea Carvalho, Kate Skipper, Kate McHale, Phoebe Morgan, Rowan Coleman, Sophie Hannah, and Charlotte Duckworth.

A massive thank you to all my colleagues at Waterstones and everyone in the Ecommerce team. I hope our Glasshouse Street Nando's trips can one day happen again.

Thanks to Steve Bowyer and Tom Mitchell for their generous advice on the police procedure elements in *The Dinner Guest*.

And last but definitely not least, I'd like to thank all the booksellers who have helped my books reach the hands of readers over these past two years. Their job is so important to the fabric of our reading landscape, and I'd like to give special mentions to the booksellers of Waterstones branches in Southampton, Brentwood, King's Road Chelsea, Romford, and Chelmsford.

ONE MORE CHAPTER

YOUR NUMBER ONE STOP

FOR PAGETURNING BOOKS

One More Chapter is an
award-winning global
division of HarperCollins.

Sign up to our newsletter to get our
latest eBook deals and stay up to date
with our weekly Book Club!
<u>Subscribe here.</u>

Meet the team at
<u>www.onemorechapter.com</u>

Follow us!
 <u>@OneMoreChapter_</u>
 <u>@OneMoreChapter</u>
 <u>@onemorechapterhc</u>

Do you write unputdownable fiction?
We love to hear from new voices.
Find out how to submit your novel at
<u>www.onemorechapter.com/submissions</u>